CONSIDER THE RAVENS

CRESSIDA DOWNING

NO EXIT PRESS

First published in the UK in 2026 by No Exit Press,
an imprint of Bedford Square Publishers Ltd,
London, UK

noexit.co.uk
@noexitpress

A CIP catalogue record for this book is available from the British Library.

ISBN
978-1-83501-472-1 (Paperback)
978-1-83501-473-8 (eBook)

2 4 6 8 10 9 7 5 3 1

Typeset in 11.25 on 13.75pt Garamond MT Pro
by Avocet Typeset, Bideford, Devon, EX39 2BP
Printed and bound in Great Britain by
CPI Group (UK) Ltd, Croydon CR0 4YY

The manufacturer's authorised representative in the EU for product safety is Easy Access System Europe, Mustamäe tee 50,
10621 Tallinn, Estonia
gpsr.requests@easproject.com

CONSIDER
THE
RAVENS

For my incredible daughter Lyra (who insists on being first, always), my amazing son Kyle (who would be a fantastic raven pet owner), and my lovely husband John (who has promised he may even read this one day). Without you, it might have been written sooner, but life would not have been nearly as much fun. Love you all and thank you so much for your unique brand of support.

Consider the ravens: for they neither sow nor reap; which neither have storehouse nor barn; and God feedeth them: how much more are ye better than the fowls?

Luke 12: 24

Prologue

The raven flew into the tithe barn. It was a cold morning and the air was completely still. But there was something wrong about the space. A man hung from the rafters and a stool lay on the floor.

The bird hopped up to the stool, turning his head to the side. It didn't hold his attention for long. He turned to the man. He knew him. The body smelt fresh but wasn't moving. The rope holding him to the beams was roughly tied around his neck, digging into his flesh. The raven flew up to him and landed on his shoulder, starting the body swaying gently in the morning air.

There was nothing shining about the man. Not his eyes, they were a dull blue now; not his clothes, worn and patched. The raven pecked speculatively at his hands but there were no rings.

'Pol! Come now, where are you?'

The raven's head turned at the voice he knew so well. There was nothing here for him, nothing to eat and nothing to collect.

'Pol!'

As he flew back through the barn door, behind him the man was still swaying silently in the barn.

Chapter One

St Lucy's Day, 1494

Linnet was so cold her legs had become mercifully numb. That didn't help with the slipping and sliding over the wet sands and the mud, but at least the stinging, freezing pain was gone. She stopped again to try and find her way. The path had seemed simple from the shore, but that was over an hour ago, and she cursed herself, not for the first time, for her impatience to get on the island. She should have got a guide. She would only have had to wait another night, but then the thought of Guy coming after her flooded her with fear again, and she knew she couldn't have waited.

She looked over the seas that were creeping ever closer, the water rushing up and away, like a playful creature. The sky had got darker since she started, not only the lack of daylight on this, one of the shortest days of the year, but with slate storm clouds and a grey sprinkle of snow showers. Holy Island lay in front of her like a delicate curl of land, and felt further away than when she left the shore. She was close enough to see the brooding shape of the Priory overshadowing the village houses. 'Unlovely and unloved,' her father used to say about it, she remembered now. She'd seen many cathedrals and priories, and they could soar, floating above a city or a town, but here the Priory squatted, heavy on the thin island, absurdly large for its place.

She put her head down, she would get as far as that small dark boulder ahead of her, and then try and work out the safest route again. The white stones the landlady at Beale had told her to look out for were almost impossible to see in the gloom. She was almost all the way to the boulder when it moved, startling her enough that she lost her footing and sat down heavily on the mud. It was a seal, staring at her with frank curiosity with its dark, soulful eyes, before slipping away silently into the suddenly deep sea behind it.

She sent up a quick prayer of thanks to St Gertrude as she realised this would have been the path she took and she would have drowned in a matter of minutes. She had always invoked St Gertrude ever since she'd seen a shrine to her with the little mice carvings, and of course she was a saint who could conquer the sea and the storms. Saint Lucy would do nothing for her today, even though it was her saint's day. Precious little light around but wait – a flash of white stone showed her another way and she scrambled to her feet and, walking like a drunk with the wind and the snow flurries around her, made it safely onto the beach where she began shaking and couldn't stop.

It took a while for her to hear the man speaking to her, but when she looked up, it was Tom. Tom the fisherman she remembered from her childhood visits to the island.

'What are you doing here?' he was asking, looking concerned, but with no glimmer of recognition.

'Tom,' she said. 'I'm Linnet, you remember? From years ago?' Just saying her real name after all these years felt like a blessing.

And then he did remember and a smile spread across his face. He helped her to her feet and started talking and remembering. She interrupted to ask after his mother and he stopped talking again, and shook his head and said 'last year'.

And she felt her heart sink a little at the thought of a woman who had been so kind to her, fallen into dust.

'I'd better take you to the Prior,' he said and started leading the way up to the Priory, the buildings disappearing into the gloom as night fell, and she followed, meekly enough for now, her mind racing as to what she was going to say. They went past the big door to the Priory Church, firmly closed, and he took her through a gate at the side into the inner courtyard, and past a bustling kitchen to the Prior's parlour.

He knocked but it was empty, the singing coming from the Priory Church telling her why.

'You can wait in here with the fire to warm you until he's back. I'll go and tell him who you are, it's Prior Richard, he's heard of John-the-Lies of course so he'll know.'

And with that, Tom had left her there, looking around this elegant room which felt so far away from the cold, wet, dark walk she'd just done. As she warmed through, the needles of cold came rushing back into her legs and hands, and she put her bag down and began to stomp her feet a little to get the pain to go faster. Her little finger gave that special extra ache from the time Guy broke it, a pain she clung on to now to remind her why she had fled. Walking around the room she could see letters left on the Prior's desk. She glanced carefully at the door before looking down to read what she could of the first one.

It was from the Bishop of Durham who was scolding the Prior for not having dismissed one of the monks sooner. His drunkenness was bringing shame to the island, the Bishop had written, and something about the unsteadiness of his hand. Was this dismissed monk a scribe? If so, she may have found herself a way to stay here for a little while at least. At worst, she would have a night here before she had to make more plans. The waters had rushed over the path she'd taken as soon as she'd reached the beach, there was nowhere for her to go until the tides changed.

Voices outside gave her just enough time to move away from the desk and the letter and she composed herself to be looking down demurely as the Prior came into the room. Tom was talking to him, and they were followed by a shorter man who glared at her with frank suspicion.

She tried to discreetly brush off the worst of the mud from her cloak, but realised it would make no difference. Her hair was still plastered to her face, swept into rough tendrils by the wind and the snow flurries, and she looked, she knew, slovenly.

The Prior held up a hand to stop Tom speaking and spoke directly to Linnet.

'Tom says you're the daughter of John-the-Lies? What are you doing here, woman, and what do you want us to do with you?'

His words were brisk but his tone wasn't harsh and she pinched her hands together behind her back to give her the vigour she needed.

'My father said he would be coming to Holy Island and I lost my lodgings and had to move on, so I thought to come here and wait for him. I won't be a burden though, I can work for you while I wait.'

She wouldn't tell him where her father had gone, nor the suspicions she had about what he was doing there, or the danger he might be in.

He frowned at her and gestured for her to go on.

'I can scribe if you've a need of it, and I'm a limner and can make inks.'

Tom leaned forward. 'Her father taught her the inks and the scribing, Prior, she were ever so good at it even as a little girl, she—'

But the Prior silenced him again and beckoned Linnet forward to the desk, sweeping the letters and papers away until he found a scrap of parchment.

'Write the Pater Noster on there then, show me what you can do.'

Thankful for the few minutes she'd had to warm her hands, Linnet found her pens and her little travelling pot of oak gall ink, and muttering the familiar words, began to scribe them, then stopped.

'I can show you more, Prior, do you have a hand you'd like me to copy?'

His face sharpened with interest then and he pulled a few pages from a prayer book towards her and said, 'Copy that.'

She looked at the hand, cramped, wavering, the dispatched monk's hand she was sure, and then did her best to mimic it but also smooth it out, making the marks and the flourishes seem purposeful, more graceful and intended. She was so intent it made her jump when the Prior spoke again.

'Yes, you can stay here, at least to finish this prayer book, and then we'll see. Speak to Ann in the kitchen, she'll tell you where you can sleep.'

'And will I get paid?'

The smaller man pushed forward then. 'When the Prior is doing you kindness in having you stay here? How dare you—'

But the Prior stopped him. 'That is Brother Oswyn, our bursar. We will pay you for a fair copy when it is done and I'll decide what that price should be.'

She nodded. Honour was satisfied. He knew she was skilled and she knew she would not work for nothing but board.

She felt like she held her breath for the next few hours as she was taken from the parlour to the kitchens, shown the privies near the stables, met a prickly woman, Ann, unimpressed with her or the task she'd been given, and finally shown to a small cell above the kitchens with some bales arranged so that she could sleep on them and a poor blanket to cover herself with.

She'd made it. For a while at least, she would be safe.

Chapter Two

St Agnes Eve, 1495

The light was going but that wasn't what drew Linnet's attention from her work. The voices outside the Scriptorium were not quite arguing but there was something strained, and one of them belonged to someone she didn't recognise.

She flexed her hands to get the blood moving in them again, got up and went to the doorway, careful to stay in the shadows. The Scriptorium was at the end of the Chapter House, overlooking the inner courtyard where the Prior was walking slowly past with a visitor. The man, a monk, was stocky and dark-haired, with pale skin. His robes looked freshly washed, pressed smooth, although not as clean at the bottom. His arms were folded, hands resting on his rounded stomach. Something about the wiry black hairs on his white knuckles made Linnet flinch a little and she drew further back.

She could see a novice monk following them, but not one she recognised. He looked old for a novice, a large man, head down, at a respectful distance, having to slow himself from his usual stride to stay at their pace.

'—of course and we're delighted to help you, Father Nicholas. Our Priory is open to you for anything you need.'

'It's not about delight, Prior. I am here to see that you are working according to the Rule, and to the Bishop's requirements.'

Father Nicholas must be an Inspector. His voice was high-pitched but deliberate and slow. Linnet had visited monasteries under inspection before. If the Inspector couldn't find any fault, he would have to invent something, to show he was doing his job. Most holy houses had plenty of faults though.

'Yes, yes, I'm sure you'll find we are in order. Take care in the Priory Church, the new floor is being laid and it's uneven.'

The Prior didn't sound his usual calm self, but a little uneasy.

'How much is the floor costing?'

'It was paid for by the Bishop in his kindness, he—'

'The last Bishop.'

The Inspector stopped, glancing around him as if already looking for errors he could note down. Catching sight of the mud on the bottom of his robes, a stark contrast to the rest of their cleanliness, he turned back to the Prior.

'Who is the boy who takes visitors over the way to the island? He made us wait another hour although the way looked clear, and then I am minded he took us a long route, and my horse stumbled several times.'

Linnet tried not to let a laugh escape her. It would have been Daniel or one of his three brothers. Only their mother could tell them apart. Large and freckled and slow to speak or move, their eyes were quick with malice, and Tom told her they only took the shortest route if they were assured of a good payment. The more they disliked the look of you, the muddier you got.

'Oh, the boys from the inn at Beale, they have walked the route for years now and I'm sure he will have been keen to keep you out of harm's way.'

She caught a glimpse of a slight smile on the Prior's face and wondered if he too noticed how the rudest visitors were the dirtiest to arrive on the island. The Beale boys had a grudging respect for the Prior, she knew, and he for them. The way onto the island was treacherous and it was hard to be sure when it would be safe, and when covered in water. The fishermen knew the times but couldn't explain how they knew how it changed, and at times, they got it wrong, to their cost. She hadn't dared to venture back off the island since her arrival over a month ago, memories of that night still fresh enough to chill her through.

The men kept walking down the passageway towards the guest quarters and Linnet lost sight of them in the gathering gloom. It was now cold as well as dark. The Scriptorium was a small room, taking up the end space of the Chapter House, set within the calefactory, a place for the monks to warm themselves between their tasks. That had a fire most of the time but the thick wall didn't let much heat through. The Scriptorium also had a fireplace but with just Linnet working in it, there was no fire. She shivered as she drew her cloak around her. It was more holes than cloak, but still soft and warm, in parts at least. One of the best things she'd stolen.

She turned back to her work to put away her quills and ink when something large swooped at her. Startled, she jumped backwards and knocked the ink over.

'Damn, damn, damn!' At least it was the oak gall ink which she had plenty of. She mopped it with her dark cloak which wouldn't show the stains.

'You marn't say that. Not here with the Fathers.'

She jumped again. 'Isabelle, you're as sly as that bird of yours. Creeping up like that!'

The dark-haired child and the sleek black raven looked at her in unison, heads both tilted as she cleared up the mess they'd made.

'You wan' get that cloak mended. Tom'll do it for you.'

It was like having a nagging conscience made flesh, the child always lurking and telling her what she should and shouldn't do. Isabelle didn't seem to belong to anyone on the island, although the women in the kitchen at the Priory would feed her if she turned up at meal times. She was dirty and wild, but had a strong sense of order, even if she didn't think it applied to her. Her pet raven, Pol, was equally stubborn and strong-willed.

Linnet hadn't spent much time around children, or ever wanted them, not even when she was first with Guy. When she was a child herself, her father had taken her along with him as he took the obituary rolls from monasteries to priories to cathedrals. She was petted by the young monks, given sweetmeats by the older ones, and fussed over by the cooks and the laundry women. In between those floods of attention, they would walk for miles and sleep under hedges. Her father was saving the horse money and the inn money for a rainy day, although they always seemed to have plenty of rain as they travelled. She wondered if he still did that. He must be more than fifty now, too old for those long walks surely, if he were alive of course.

She had no idea why Isabelle kept following her around but she didn't like it. The child drew too much attention, always asking questions and bringing that raven with her. She was too tired to shoo her away tonight, though. Neither of them would have anything to eat if they didn't hurry. They left the Scriptorium, the little girl skipping slightly, while Linnet picked her way between the loose stones, and the raven hopped from low wall to hedge to rock before flying away into the dark.

They passed the Refectory where the monks were waiting for their food. The Prior and the Inspector and the other man were coming back from the guest lodging where the

Inspector would be staying, just next to the Prior's parlour. Linnet wondered who would do the reading while they ate. She thought Oswyn, the bursar, was most likely, he would enjoy showing off his Latin for an important guest.

The kitchen was busier than usual, Ann sweating as she stirred and chopped and shouted. She had set up lamb cakes for St Agnes Eve, ready for the young girls on the island, Linnet too old at twenty-five, and Isabelle too young, to take part in the traditional ritual, eating the cake and sprinkling the corn on the field to see the face of your beloved. The cakes had been pushed to one side for this unexpected visitor and Linnet could see Ann was not pleased.

Linnet and Isabelle slipped into the back of the room, staying out of the way. The talk was all about the Father and his inspection. There hadn't been an inspection for many years now so some thought he was bound to find much to complain about. Another faction stoutly defended the Prior saying he was a clever man and would know what to say and do to keep the report favourable.

Linnet began making a list in her head as she sat there; she could think of at least five ways the Priory was breaking the Rule. Who knew what the new Bishop wanted anyway – he might have new strictures that the Prior didn't even know about. She knew religion was merely a veil over their motives for many of the powerful men of the Church.

The bustle began to die down as the monks' food was taken out. Linnet ate quickly, even the leftover food was better when there were visitors. The soup had more vegetables and even some scraps of meat in it for once. She slipped out as Isabelle was begging for a bit of pastry.

She bumped straight into the bursar, Brother Oswyn. He couldn't have done the reading as he still had his cloak on. He took her by the arm, laughing.

'What are you running from, Linnet? Have you been up to no good?'

She took a quick step back, shrugging off his hands. His breath was hot on her face, but sweet-smelling. He stepped in closer again, almost whispering. 'I know your secret, Linnet, and I bet the Prior would like to know it too. A little Dutch mouse told me something tonight that I think he'd be interested in.'

Linnet forced her face to go blank and looked at Oswyn as if he'd not said anything at all. The noise of the kitchen behind them carried through the night air. Linnet wondered how long he'd been waiting for the moment to pounce, looking to feed off her fear. She'd been on the island for more than a few weeks and he'd not said a word until now, contenting himself with scowling at her if she passed him.

Well, damn him. The sound of the curse echoed in her head as loud as if she'd shouted it at him. She wasn't going to give him the satisfaction though. Anyway, the only reply she could make would be 'Which secret?'

Instead, she hit back. 'Have you seen the new Inspector yet? He'll be wanting to look at your figures, I'm sure.'

Oswyn frowned, distracted by news he wasn't aware of. He had been on the mainland today and come back later than these visitors, that much was clear. She glanced at his cloak, fully splashed with tide mud and again supressed a grin.

'Where's he from?'

'Durham, I think. He was talking about the new Bishop.'

'Ah, Bishop Foxe, of course.' He was back on firmer ground now, about to tell Linnet how he'd met him, given him good advice, been his best friend for many years, something like that. He'd go back to baiting her later.

As he drew a breath, he was distracted by a movement behind her.

'Child! Are you hiding in here? Be gone with you!' Oswyn shooed Isabelle away like a pest, and Linnet took her chance to escape.

The young novices were running around, fetching candles, wine, good bedding for the visiting Father. Despite her fears about Oswyn, Linnet enjoyed the sense of urgency. The monks were far fewer in numbers than they had been when she was a child visiting. She thought there had been about thirty then, double what it was now. This priory felt like it had been forgotten by Durham and the rest of the country. Even the Christmas celebrations had felt muted. She'd ignored them, going only to the church services she saw Ann going to, hiding in the Scriptorium the rest of the time, trying not to garner any attention, working hard on the prayer book.

Ann was marching out through the gate to the nearby field, carrying a torch and the cakes, with a gaggle of the young island girls around her giggling with excitement. Her face was a mixture of grim satisfaction and lines of disappointment. They would chant '*St Agnes is a friend to me, I give this gift to help me see, who my helpmeet shall be*' as they threw seed over their shoulders. Someone, the liveliest and loudest, probably Molly the innkeeper's daughter, would squeal that she'd seen a wraith, and they would all run off in a frenzy of excitement. Linnet wondered what Ann had seen in the grain when she was young, surely not the sot she was married to now, who she largely ignored, and who had only managed to give her one living child.

She saw Tom standing in the courtyard. She had been going to ask him about mending her cloak even before Isabelle suggested it.

He smiled at her, then shook his head as he saw her cloak.

'Linnet, what do you do with your clothes? For a scribe who spends her time inside, how do you get those holes and tears?'

Linnet shrugged; she had no idea either. Sometimes she'd sit down to illustrate a page, and hours later, hands frozen, she'd look down and her clothes would be sporting new marks and rips as if the animals she'd drawn had been playing with her. She was a grown woman with the clothes of a ragged child.

Tom lowered his voice. 'Isabelle told me the Inspector is here.'

Visitors were good for gaming so Tom would be hoping for some sport with the Inspector's retinue, although Linnet didn't think the novice monk looked likely and he seemed to be the only person who had come with him. The monks would be staying away from the inn for now too. Tom's blue eyes were bright with dicing fever regardless. He made a good living as a fisherman, but his time on the water didn't compare to the chance to win and win again, and he would lose as if his money was swimming away from him. He'd not been like that when he was young, she wondered if his mother's death had started his fondness for the dice.

'Can you mend my cloak then?'

He muttered a bit about how she was only friendly when she wanted something from him, but they both knew that wasn't true. They would talk most evenings – sitting by the sea or in the tavern.

She left him the cloak. If she'd been cold before, she was slowly freezing to her bones now. She wondered if the Prior and the Inspector were still talking or if they'd gone to sleep. If they had, the Prior's parlour might have the end of a fire she could warm herself by. The Chapter House was brightly lit and warm but she couldn't risk going in there, of course.

She listened, just outside, but there was only a low crackling. Cautiously she slipped inside. No men, a glowing fire, and some peace and warmth at last. She spun slowly in front of the steady heat, like a chicken on a spit, but just as she was feeling some warmth returning to her, she heard voices coming.

She froze. She had no business being here. Looking around, she crouched down behind the big chest. Stupid. Why had she risked her place here for a moment by the fire? And now, hiding like a disobedient child. This was just what Oswyn would want. He'd never fully accepted why the Prior had let her stay, and she could feel his eyes on her at all times, looking for a mistake to cut her loose.

The Prior, the Inspector and the novice came in, talking louder than before and with more cordiality. Father Nicholas had been well fed, but the Prior had obviously taken care that the food wasn't too rich.

'I've asked Brother Oswyn to join us. He was busy today but he should be along soon.'

'I'll only need to see his accounts, if he has them ready?'

The sharp tone was still there in the Inspector's voice, only slightly softened by the spiced wine he was sipping. Linnet could smell the nutmeg and the sour heat underneath it, the wine in the Priory was not of the best quality.

'He's very conscientious, Father, they'll be in good order.'

'And what monies do you have coming in? I know the farms to the north have been harried by the Scots and are being tardy with their rent.'

'Yes, we have had some requests for more time which we are assessing. Fenham Farm has paid this year but not its arrears. We are also producing prayer books and the like for some local gentry.'

'Do you have a scriptorium here? Which of your monks are scribes and which limners?'

Linnet kept listening but there was silence for a minute, only the fire crackling and the chairs creaking a little as the monks settled themselves after their meal.

Prior Richard seemed happy; he was paying her a pittance but it was all hers. Would the Inspector think her presence here unholy? She wondered what Oswyn might say to him, something that might make him insist she left? She was already holding her breath, folded into as small a space as she could manage, hands gripping the rough wooden edge of the chest next to her.

'We have – a woman,' the Prior faltered a little.

Again, a moment's silence.

'A woman? Well, Bishop Foxe is not against the idea of cheap labour when you can find it.' But he didn't sound pleased.

She could hear the novice shifting his feet but he didn't speak up.

The Prior breathed an audible sigh of relief as he continued. 'She is the grown daughter of John-the-Lies – have you met him? No? He's one of the Obituary Roll-Bearers. He's known to carry inks and extra parchment with him, always got a good story to tell, although who knows how true they are. He knows all the history of the holy houses and is quick-witted. As she travelled with him, his daughter picked up her skills. Anyway, she came here to wait for him. She can scribe, make inks and illuminate, we can use her skill.'

He was confident now, back on his favourite subject. 'There's some leftover parchment from when they tried to have a scriptorium here before. One of the farmers is saving his male calves for me, and the tanner can make more parchment, not the highest quality but good enough for purpose. We could produce more if we had more learned monks. We have some books here too, so don't need to wait for the quires for copying.'

Borrowing quires was troublesome for some religious houses, Linnet knew. They got the best books to copy if they had the ear of the bishops. She'd seen no sign that the Prior was well connected. Perhaps he could use this time with the Inspector to become favoured by Bishop Foxe.

'What about this woman, why did she not become a nun if she is skilled in scribing?'

Linnet struggled not to snort. That had never been her wish, although when she and Guy were in disguise, she'd dressed as one. If danger threatened again, a nunnery might be a good place to hide. Lost in thoughts of herself as a nun, she missed the rest of what they were saying.

Oswyn came in and the Prior introduced him. From where Linnet was hiding, she could only hear the men, not see them. Father Nicholas was coughing now, with Oswyn banging him helpfully on the back. Perhaps the wine had gone down the wrong way.

Once they were settled, the talk turned back to the accounts.

'Of course, you must come and see my books tomorrow, Father Nicholas, and you—'

'I'm Brother Cassian.' That must be the novice. A rough local voice, from a man well into his middle years.

The Inspector grunted in assent.

'My door is always open to you, knock for me.' Oswyn's voice had its customary and oily charm. Again the Inspector didn't answer.

The Prior took him out towards his lodgings, telling Oswyn to show Brother Cassian to the dormitory, and Linnet could finally make her escape, out into the inner courtyard and across it to her room above the larders.

Chapter Three

It was raining. Starting with the slow rain in the air that caught at clothes and hair and settling in to a solid sheet of water coming down unceasingly.

Linnet stood outside the kitchen and looked out across the church and the graveyard. Everything was grey, the Priory's warm stones washed out by the grey light, the grey water, the grey sky. The land around was still, the only sound the streaming rain, and dimly through it, the people hurrying and cursing at their labours.

The Inspector strode through the inner courtyard without minding the weather at all, as if he was protected from it somehow, although his hair was plastered wet to his scalp. The Prior followed, eyes narrowed and thoughtful from beneath his cowl. The novice was looking around at the Priory with keen blue eyes.

Isabelle and Pol were almost dancing in the rain, with the bird flapping around her head as she span, not noticing the monks until they nearly ran into them. The Inspector stopped for a moment as if to assess their presence, then marched on, through a large puddle, splashing the child from head to foot.

Linnet smiled. It wasn't kind but the dripping child's barely contained fury and the bird's indignant hopping brightened the grey day.

The Prior stopped to ruffle Isabelle's wet hair and say something to her, before catching up with the Inspector. The child ran off mollified, the raven swooping behind her.

All the monks trooped through, going to Prime, their second morning prayers. Their usual chatter was subdued by the Inspector's presence. Today he would watch them at their offices and rites, and tomorrow he would start on his report. Brother Marcus was a half-step behind Oswyn as usual, close enough to breathe in the air the other was breathing out. Oswyn walked a little faster, trying to put more space between them, but as his legs were half the length, Marcus only had to stretch a little to be as close. And just a pace behind the two of them, the childlike skipping of Brother Maykin, too fresh-faced for anyone to call his given name of Matthew, shoving and whispering with the other younger monks, despite their attempts to be solemn.

After the first morning bustle, the courtyard fell quiet again, with the rain the only noise, falling on the stones with a dedicated solidity, a sworn devotion of wetness.

Linnet roused herself. She'd been standing idle for nearly half an hour, just watching the rain and the people. Watching the rain and the people from under the courtyard eave, as if she were a lady of leisure. It was also foolish to be out here, not hidden away in the Scriptorium.

In the silence, the fear about Oswyn's words from last night came rushing back. What had he found out about her? What did he mean by 'a Dutch mouse'? She knew he'd been at the Durham Priory as a novice, but he'd left years before she and her father had been in the area. The monks were always moving, from priory to abbey to cathedral. Migrating crows her father used to call them.

She thought about her father and the last time she'd seen him. It must have been about five years ago. His face, a mask of indifference, her own red with shouting. Did she regret running off like that? No, not even with what had happened since. She couldn't have stayed any longer and she hadn't wanted to travel with him. He said he was off to scribe for one of the makers of bibles overseas, but she knew there was more to it, something hidden from her. He wanted to marry her off, have her safely looked after, he'd said. She had asked him safe from what but he'd refused to answer. Even if they'd not argued, once she was no longer a sweet child on his travels, for the nuns and servants to fuss over, she'd have been a burden and he didn't take kindly to burdens.

He didn't take kindly to much, although none of his friends would have known it, always laughing and joking and telling tales. It was Linnet who saw his sour side, the silences that lasted for hours. As a small child, she thought he'd a set number of words and he'd use them up with the monks, leaving nothing for her. Older, she realised his words were currency and he hoarded them, flashing them around as bait to catch greater prizes, not to be wasted on a useless girl as they walked and rode between his fishing grounds.

There was the roll they carried, sometimes two rolls, for the monks to write their remembrances on, then there were the secrets, the stories and the gossip and the news, which could be dangerous, taken from town to town. He had meetings with men who never gave their names, who didn't look at her or pay her any mind, low talking and then tasks given. Letters of introduction written, documents made that she doubted were real.

The monks were in the Priory Church now, singing their prayers. Linnet could hear them from the Scriptorium, the familiar words and patterns washing over her like the rain. She ground up more oak galls for ink, sharpening quills from goose feathers, scraping the vellum smooth for use. When her mind was taken up with worry, she couldn't write, but there was always other work to do. The oak gall ink scent rose up to soothe her, the spicy notes so familiar.

People thought of scribes sitting on their high stools loftily writing but they didn't see all the preparations and the labour – and backache – that took up so much of the time.

Linnet stood up and went back out to the courtyard to stretch. As a child, all the walking she did with her father had kept her supple but now her days were spent in the Scriptorium with the books. Ann in the kitchen thought of her as idle, which she supposed she was in her eyes. She didn't lift heavy pots or scour them, or constantly have her hands in water, even on the coldest days. None of the island women had much time for Linnet, she wasn't pretty or young, or interesting to them, not a good source of gossip or chatter. She'd never had close friends. Only Tom now.

The monks were filing out of the Priory for their tasks. They seemed smoothed out and set apart after their singing. Even the ones who quarrelled most, pinching each other during mealtimes and fighting for the best tasks, came out looking almost saintly. She envied them those moments of certainty and peace.

As she watched, that smooth surface began to crack and fall off as they became themselves again. Godfreyd pushed arrogantly past Brother Benedict, a short, round-bellied monk who was always following him around. Godfreyd had somewhere important to go to, at least he thought so, probably the Infirmary. He was a strange Infirmarian, he so hated touching people she'd noticed, but was very aware of his senior position in the Priory.

Oswyn was bustling and trying to catch up with the Prior and the Inspector. She could hear him starting to talk about 'when I met the Bishop'. The Inspector looked impatient and kept turning his face away. They went off to the Prior's parlour. Brother Marcus looked after them wistfully, wanting to join them. He had his eye on Oswyn's role, she knew. And of course, Brother Maykin, showing off to the other novices as he chattered on about St Vincent, the topic of the day's sermon. She heard him say the saint's body had been protected by ravens – she wondered if Isabelle knew that.

If Oswyn was busy trying to impress the Inspector, she hoped he would be distracted from her and her past. He would probably prefer to keep taunting her for longer anyway. She'd seen him the same with others, a sly insinuation here, mockery there. She thought he grew fat on people's secrets. Was he really a threat?

She'd stood around long enough today. She went back to the prayer book and wrote methodically for several hours. Sometimes it really did feel like work.

At one point she could hear voices outside. She looked out of the small window in her room and could see the Prior and Oswyn were arguing with each other, but in low tones, trying not to be heard. The Prior was leaning back against the damp wall, ignoring the cold that would be seeping through. Oswyn was trying to tell him something – she heard 'if someone were not who you thought' – but the Prior brushed him away, eager to get back to the Inspector.

Was Oswyn about to tell the Prior about her? Thanks to the Inspector, it would have to wait. She could do nothing without knowing what he was going to say, so she would have to keep quiet. Back to her book.

Another disturbance brought her out in the late afternoon. She could hear squawking and yelling and something being thrown. Looking out, she saw Oswyn chasing Isabelle out of his room. The raven was fluttering around aggressively, swooping at him while the child dodged his hands.

'And don't creep in here again, you rat!' Oswyn yelled at her, raising his voice above the loud croaking from the bird, who seemed to be taunting him, swooping just out of his reach.

He was rarely seen to lose his temper, unlike the Prior who would often be seen shouting, and Linnet wondered what Isabelle had been doing. The noise and commotion had brought out the Prior and the Inspector. The Inspector looked askance at the girl and the bird again. Linnet could see he was asking the Prior about Pol. Whatever the Prior said didn't seem to satisfy him, as he shuddered and crossed himself.

Maybe the Inspector was afraid of ravens. Linnet knew some of the islanders spat when Isabelle and Pol went past. Ravens were supposed to bring death.

Oswyn saw the men talking and hurried over, eager to smooth away any impression of disorder and keen to take his moment.

'I trust all is well with the inspection so far? The Prior has asked I show you my books tomorrow.'

The Prior looked irritated at Oswyn's interruption but nodded.

'And perhaps we can talk about Durham? And the Bishop? I hear he is making great changes there?'

The Inspector also seemed unwilling to talk, nodding equally abruptly. The Prior nodded towards the novice, who had followed them out. 'Brother Oswyn, take Brother Cassian to Father Thomas, he can help him with the garden until we need him again.' And with that, the men went back into the Prior's parlour and with a firm bang of the wooden door, that was that.

Oswyn looked after them thoughtfully and then turned towards Cassian. Their voices carried clearly over to Linnet as she stood there in the shadows.

'Bit old to be a novice, aren't you?' he asked.

The novice flushed slightly, but stood his ground. 'Aye, well God called me so I dinna complain to him he were late.'

Linnet wondered why he had become a novice now. Most men of his age had a trade, a family. He was her father's age, she thought.

'And you're travelling with Father Nicholas? Did you not have a monastery to stay at and learn your lessons?'

'The Bishop wanted him to have another monk with him, and couldna spare a full Brother.'

'And we've to look after you while the Inspector does his duties? I've not got time to hold your hand while you do your lessons.'

'Well no one was asking you to, I'm able to do my own learning.'

The flush on Cassian's face had deepened and he was standing close to Oswyn.

'Don't speak to me in that tone, Brother!' Oswyn's tone was sharp, but he took a careful step back. 'Now follow Brother Maykin away to the gardens, you'll find Father Thomas there and he can have you do some weeding.' He grabbed the young monk who was passing and pointed them both to the far corner of the outer courtyard where the gate led to the ground the monks tended.

Cassian didn't move at once, staring at Oswyn with narrowed eyes, before he turned away and headed off.

Neither monk had seen Linnet, watching from the shadows.

The black cat slunk past Linnet's ankles. He was damp and smelled of outdoors, rain and smouldering fires. The Prior and Oswyn might think they were in charge of the Priory but the cat had other ideas. Linnet had been tempted to give the cat a name, Tibet or Mite maybe, but she'd stopped herself. Names made you attached to things, and she needed to keep a little removed, on watch to keep herself safe.

The light had gone and Linnet was straining to see the words. She set her work aside and went to find food but it was too late, another evening when she'd missed the meal the kitchen provided for the Priory servants. She would have to ask Ann for any scraps that were left over.

Isabelle was sitting in a corner of the kitchen, laying out herbs and plants and stones covered in lichen around her, singing and counting on her fingers. Pol kept moving the herbs and hopping across her patterns until she lost patience and shooed him out.

'What are you doing with those, Isabelle?'

The child didn't answer, brushing Linnet's question aside. She gave up trying to talk to her and finished her bread. It was stale, the hard end of a loaf, nothing to soak and soften it in. Ann showing again what she thought of her.

It was still raining. No one was lingering outside and no one was chatting. Linnet didn't want to go to bed yet, she felt restless and irritated. Maybe she should think about moving on. If the Prior here could accept a female scribe, there would be other places she could work. Or she could make inks and sell them at market as she'd done before. Or she could thieve enough to keep herself fed. She'd not got caught yet. She took pride in the fact she never thieved for profit, only for food, or those special items – the ones she felt deserved to be looked after properly – the ones neglected by others that she knew she would cherish.

There was a sudden hubbub of noise as a rowdy group of men fell into the kitchen. They were covered in stone dust, the new masons here to finish the floor. The usual babble of languages, only one or two were Englishmen, the rest from all over. There was a constant flow of workers keeping the Priory running, no wonder the Prior was so concerned with the accounts. The different accents reminded Linnet about the

'Dutch mouse'. Was one of the masons Dutch? She listened carefully but the noise was too great to hear any individual voices clearly. When she got the chance, she would have to find a way to speak to them and see what she could find out.

Despite the rain, Linnet left, there was little space in the kitchen now. She held her skirts up as best she could but encrusted mud was dragging them down. Her small room was damp and often the mud would stay for weeks, crusting but too wet to brush off. Maybe she should think about becoming a nun after all, with someone else to keep her clothes clean and fresh. She envied the monks who never had to think about such things.

She'd read the Rule of St Benedict and thought that back in time, the monks had done their own washing and cleaning and cooking. Maybe that was before the gentry started sending their sons into orders.

Outside she saw Oswyn heading towards the Priory Church to light candles for Compline. He came over to her at once. She readied herself for more baiting.

'When were you at Durham, Linnet? I know you and your father spent some time there.'

She shrugged. 'On and off when I was a child. We moved a lot.'

'Your father certainly likes to travel. When did he tell you he'd be coming to the island?'

She flinched. 'He said something a little while ago.'

'I'm not so sure he did, did he, Linnet?'

He was right of course. She thought fast. 'But what did you want to know about Durham?'

'I'm not sure you're old enough, what is your age?'

'I'm twenty-five.' She wasn't entirely sure. Her mother had died when she was small and her father hadn't cared enough to tell her.

'Pity,' he said, distracted as she had hoped. 'Too young to remember.'

She chanced a question.

'What were you talking about with the Prior this afternoon? I heard you from the Scriptorium.'

He looked at her sharply, did he realise she was also a watcher and a secret-gatherer? 'We were talking about Bishop Foxe, a very important man. He has the ear of the King, you know. He wants everything catalogued and valued so he can account for the church's property.'

She knew he couldn't really know the Bishop but she was interested in what he was saying anyway. The King had been on the throne for ten years or so, but some still thought of him as a new king. No one was quick to make a lot of noise about a king these days, in case they were accused of treason a few short months later, when the tide had turned and the laws had changed. The big families up here, in the north, they had felt the sting of this. Henry Percy had been imprisoned by Henry VII, but released quickly afterwards and was now often seen in his court. The Nevilles talked loudly about how Henry had a right of succession before the Battle of Bosworth, but everyone knew that swords and fighting men had spoken, rather than family trees and the right of kings.

She'd heard talk of one of the princes coming back to claim his throne, but she wasn't sure what truth there was in that. The talk in Bishop's Lynn had been that they'd never been seen since their time in the Tower of London, and she felt sure that two small boys would have been no trouble for men of power to hide away, only to be seen as bones after that, if at all.

'What business is it of the King's what the church has?'

'Everything is the business of the King.'

He lost interest in her again, turning to talk to Brother Marcus who had appeared behind him. Marcus had been here since the turn of the year, just after her arrival. He had moved from another monastery and come in ready to be the bursar, as his old Abbot had sworn he would be. That was a promise that the Prior had no trouble breaking. He might not like Oswyn – Linnet didn't think any of the monks did – but he saw no reason to replace him. Marcus had taken the news calmly, but persisted in behaving as if he were Oswyn's senior apprentice, always trying to talk him through a new method of working, or with an idea for the books. Oswyn flattered him from time to time, but more often dismissed him.

She went back out into the rain and kept walking.

Lost in thought, she found herself at the water's edge down at the fishermen's beach below the Priory buildings. The fog had rolled in and she could see almost nothing around her. Any moonlight was obscured by the clouds, the world around her a dark haze of rain falling and waves rushing in and out. Wearily she trudged back up the small slope to her room, dim candlelight shining through the Priory Church windows over the fields showing her the way.

Chapter Four

She needed egg whites and stale vinegar to set her inks, and she was in luck. Ann was making nun's kisses, those little custardy tarts that the Prior loved so much. Linnet could see the jug of egg whites at her side, but she didn't want to ask while Ann was busy beating the custard.

As she stood nearby, waiting for the right time, Brother Oswyn came in, full of his own importance, waving his ledger book at Ann.

'What's this cinnamon, Ann? Have you used all that was brought last time the pedlar was here? I can't see the need for this and long pepper both.'

Startled from her baking, Ann stared at Oswyn with almost open insolence. She'd no time for any of the monks bar the Prior.

'Brother Oswyn, cinnamon and long pepper are not the same. You'd be sure to notice if these nun's kisses had long pepper in them – and the Prior wouldn't be pleased, or his guests.'

Before Ann could stop him, Oswyn dipped a fat finger in her custard and tasted it. The kitchen fell into a shocked silence.

'I taste no spices in this, but it is fine, I'm sure you could cook as well without the expense. I've a mind to tell the Prior we've no need of spices when the pedlar comes next.'

Ann's chin and her sagging neck were scarlet and blotched, like an angry chicken, Linnet couldn't help thinking, as she slapped Oswyn's hand away from her bowl.

'It tastes good, as you say, because it has the cinnamon in it! Without it, it would be naught but a posset and fit for no decent table. I'll be talking to the Prior mysel – he'll be hearing from me. If my kitchen canna have spices, you'll be the one cooking as I'll be gone, do ya ken? And ev'n the bairns here wouldn't be putting their dirty fingers in my pudding, I'll not be having it.'

Oswyn took a swift step back as the angry woman advanced on him, which took him backing into Linnet, standing so far unobserved by the wall. She felt his weight on her foot as he stumbled backwards and then suddenly he was inches from her face.

'And you, what are you doing in here? Are you not in the Scriptorium? The Prior doesn't pay you to gossip in here with, with…' He stuttered a little and she could see he was rethinking whatever words he had been about to use about Ann and the others in the kitchen.

'I'm here to ask for egg whites for the ink.' She was answering him but also talking to Ann whose fury seemed to have ebbed a little. She'd get the vinegar another time, better to be off.

Ann nodded silently and handed over the jug. 'I'll be wanting that jug back this afternoon, mind,' she said before turning her back on the pair of them. Ann's tempers were legendary. Linnet wondered how long this one would last. She could hear Ann muttering loudly about Oswyn as she left the room, how he messed up her kitchen by coming in wet after his early morning swims, and what a stupid idea it was to swim in any case, especially now, in the dark and cold of winter.

Linnet had seen him coming back from those swims, and

seen him sidle into the kitchen to steal freshly baked bread before the proper time, too hungry and cold from the water to wait. She couldn't imagine going into that dark, muddy water from choice.

Outside the kitchen, she tried to leave without catching any more of Oswyn's attention but she couldn't move fast enough, keeping the jug steady in her hands. He pinched at her arm and she had to twist to stop the jug falling.

'I've not forgotten your secret, Linnet. You're not here waiting for your father, are you? I happen to know John-the-Lies isn't in England, is he?'

Linnet fought to keep her face still and the jug upright. Her father had never spoken to her of which side he backed in the Cousins' War, and she had never known which king the men who tasked him with spying were working for. Had Henry's reign meant he needed to stay away, or was he working for him? And the real question was, what did Oswyn know about it and what would it mean for her? Before she could think what to answer, someone interrupted.

'Do you have the ledger there, Brother Oswyn? I must see this today for my report.'

It was the Inspector. Linnet watched as Oswyn changed himself once again, one minute haranguing Ann, the next retreating and blustering and threatening her, and now –what was his air now?

'Yes, yes, I'll bring it to you, you'll find all in order. I am, of course, at your service to help with any questions you may have.'

Obsequious, certainly. That was the Oswyn she often saw with the Prior and any guests of importance, but something else too. Something with a different balance of power, something watchful, something reminding her of Pol and his cruel eyes when he spied a prey.

'Have you been long at Durham, Inspector? Did the Bishop bring him with you or were you there already?'

'We met when he was conducting affairs of state in France, so I came to Durham with him. He's chosen me to be his Inspector, to see to it that all the daughter houses are fully compliant with the Rules and the monies are in order. The monies being what I am asking you to show me, of course.'

It was a pompous little speech, which came with a flash of insincere teeth in a half-smile. Linnet was sure he'd made it before at other monasteries and priories, a shutting down of any other talk so that the other would know the seriousness of his purpose.

'Quite so, Inspector.' The tone was mild but Oswyn's eyes had sharpened still further. He gave the Inspector a long and frank searching look, quite out of place for his position. It wasn't a pleasant look.

To Linnet's surprise, the Inspector took a step backwards, and hurried away, throwing a hand up in thanks as he went, nothing more to say.

Linnet took that as her moment to leave too, carefully carrying her egg whites while her mind flitted about wondering what Oswyn could know about her father, and how dangerous that knowledge might be.

Back in her Scriptorium, she strained the egg whites into a wooden bowl through a thin piece of cloth, and whisked them hard with a small tied bunch of thin twigs she kept for this. Ann had an excellent whisk she coveted but she didn't dare ask for that too. Her own would do.

Once she had the thick clouds of the egg whites done to her liking, she covered the bowl with a cloth. She would use the drainings tomorrow to make her colour inks secure. She began pounding the dried honeysuckle seeds she had in her stores, she would start by making a vivid leaf-green. She still had a bit of the rusted iron powder she could add to it too.

The Prior came in suddenly as she was looking through her receipts for her inks to remember how much iron rust she would need.

'Linnet, I've had Ann in my parlour talking my ear off about Brother Oswyn. Something about his fingers in the custard? Can you tell me what you saw?'

He looked annoyed and more than a little confused. Linnet couldn't suppress a smile.

'I think Brother Oswyn wanted to know that Ann wasn't using spices recklessly, he had his ledger with him.'

The Prior sighed, and she didn't envy him, caught between the fussiness of the Bursar and the fury of the Cook. He loved his food and Ann's skill with herbs and spices. If it came to a choice, Linnet would say the Cook would stay. She'd noticed he got on best with the villagers who worked for the Priory, much better than the monks. She wondered what his family had been like, he didn't seem as polished as some of the noblemen's sons who were now in orders.

His eyes caught on what she was doing.

'What colour ink are you making there?'

'A deep green, good for leaves.'

'And what plant are you using?'

She explained it in obscure terms, she was not one to give away her receipts, not even to the Prior.

'What do you mix in first, the powders or the liquids?'

'It's different for the different inks, and sometimes I have to make the powders finer or blend it when it's warm.'

Their talk came to a halt while he stared hard at her bowls and powders for a long while, before frowning and leaving the room again.

She worked on the seeds until it was too dark to see, covering it all with a cloth to start again the next day.

Chapter Five

She woke hard, sweating yet still somehow cold, reaching for her familiar cloak but of course it wasn't there. Gasping she sat up, trying to clear the nightmare and calm herself.

The Priory at night was never truly quiet. She'd slept through Nocturnes and the monks were walking back quickly to the dormitory to catch up on a few hours of precious sleep before Lauds. She looked out of her window to watch. Her room overlooked the inner courtyard opposite the dormitory and the monks sometimes walked that way back from the Priory Church rather than take the inner staircase, which was damp, pokey and had treacherous holes in it. The rain had finally stopped. She could see candles and hear a low murmur – had they forgotten about the Inspector and the Rule of Silence? She counted them back, dark shapes with the odd flickering light, Godfreyd the tallest, following the others with his easy stride.

She pulled the rough blankets back over herself, disturbing the black cat who often crept into her room. He resettled once she'd lain down again, leaning heavily against her. She ran her hands gently over him, the soft fur contrasting with the coarse wool as her breathing returned to normal. Tibet, she whispered softly and rebelliously to herself.

What had woken her? In the dark, Oswyn's threat loomed harder and sharper. What was she going to do? She had a feeling it had something to do with the secret scrolls her father used to carry, not always from monastery to monastery, but to men in inns and men on the road. Men with their faces covered whatever the weather. She remembered him poring over family trees, wills and landownership documents, much talk of who was related to whom and what that could mean. Or could Oswyn have heard something about the work she and Guy had been doing? Guy came back into her mind as if he were standing in a dark corner of the room. She could remember when she first saw him, drunk and angry in that inn in Cambridge. What had drawn her to him? The good paper careless in his pocket that she'd taken before he'd seen her, that was one thing, he'd never known she'd stolen it. But then he'd seen her and thrown all his attention and gaze on her, talking up a storm and so interested in her and who she was. She'd lost herself for a while. And then the forgeries, the illicit indulgences, the work for Warham. Could Oswyn know about that? No, that wasn't possible. No one would be talking.

Warham's men wouldn't gossip like fishwives. They'd come in the night with knives. They'd act, not talk. She shuddered as she remembered the body of the young scribe in Ely market. His throat an open shout of red, the townspeople sure it was a drunken squabble gone wrong, but she knew he'd been working for Warham, he'd told everyone. Not something Warham would have wanted. Would those men come here? Did they still care about what she and Guy had done now that Warham was in London? Or was Guy the bigger threat? She forced herself to be calmer. The causeway was drowned as it often was at night. They couldn't come now. They couldn't know she was here. She was sure she had hidden any trace of her journey. Oswyn was probably just toying with her to see what he could find out. The Inspector would keep them all busy for now anyway.

She was falling asleep, with the cat purring and warming her, when something else woke her again. Two voices, quarrelling. Rising and falling, angry but trying to keep quiet.

She got up and crept down and out into the courtyard, the stones cold on her feet through her thin hose, as she tried to work out where it was coming from. She liked walking around the Priory at night, there were often secrets to find and sometimes small things to take, and no one to see her, most times anyway. But now, there were two monks outside the Chapter House, one was definitely Oswyn. She got close enough, still hiding in the shadows, to hear some of what they were saying.

'You've no right to come looking through my papers, none at all! I'll be talking to the Inspector about you, and recommending he deal harshly with you.'

'Dunna talk cack, man, you've nowt to tell him. 'Tis him that's reporting on you all, not t'other way about. And—'

The other monk's voice got lower here and Linnet couldn't hear it without getting closer, which she dare not do. She could dimly see him in the moonlight, leaning over Oswyn. Was he holding his habit by the neck too? The older monk seemed to shrink back as the novice (she was sure it was the novice, it seemed the shape of him), shook him off contemptuously and strode off.

Quickly, she returned to her room before she could be seen. By the time she woke again, it was hours later. The cat had gone and the day was long started. A bright, cold day washed clean by the rain of the day before. She threw water on her face to shake off her night fears. She had work to do.

She liked working on the great works but the tiny prayer books and commonplace books helped her better her skill. A mistake on a large letter for a bible that stood on an altar could be turned into a beautiful curl of text, or a sparkle of gilt. There was no room for error in the little books. Her text was even, looping sweetly across the page as she counted spaces and margins in her head, the Latin words echoing in the sparse room. When it was just her in the room, it felt spacious – ready for a cluster of monks to be sat there scribing. It was clean in the middle of the room with four plank desks and stools, but dusty and neglected in the dark corners around the edges, piles of discarded papers and some crumbling stone.

'Brother Oswyn is drown'd.'

Startled yet again by that child. Isabelle was out of breath, she'd run in, full of a story to tell.

'That's a terrible thing to say about one of the Brothers.' Linnet assumed Isabelle was playing a game of some sort. She was impatient to be rid of her again, she had a lot to write today and it would take her precious time to get her rhythm back.

Isabelle tugged on her sleeve. 'He is so drown'd. Tom is with him on the beach. The Prior's going down there now.' Her stubborn little face was setting into a familiar defiant scowl but Linnet could also see fear in her eyes. She'd probably seen a lot of death in her short life, a small child during the last bout of plague the island had suffered, and the usual sickness and accidents that culled the islanders.

They left the Scriptorium and Isabelle led the way, full of the importance of knowing the news. They came down from the slight hill of the Priory onto the fishermen's beach where the boats were pulled up when they came back from the catch. A curve of stony land that looked up to the Heugh on one side, which overlooked the Priory, and the rocky outcrop on the other end, hiding the lime kilns that the monks used to use from time to time. The beach was largely empty now apart from a small crowd of men on the shore.

Oswyn was lying on the ground. He was clad in his white undershirt, his habit neatly folded a few yards away on a rock. He could have been resting from his daily swim, but he was so still.

Linnet couldn't quite understand what she was looking at. She found herself seeing the scene in little flashes, like drawings around the edge of the page. The calm sea with the sun sparkling off it. The dead man's hand lying on the cold stones, white – almost blue – so clean against the dirty ground. The sandals of the monks standing over him, shifting as they talked and gestured and prayed. Brother Maykin's voice rose above the others, she could hear him telling all around him that he had told Oswyn not to go swimming as he did, that the older monk hadn't listened to him but had thanked him kindly for his concern. Lies floating up already as the dead lay there, unable to speak up. Oswyn had never spoken kindly to anyone, finding Maykin an annoyance if anything.

She was shocked at his death, but also, she realised, with a stab of guilt, so relieved. He wouldn't be telling her secret now, whatever one he had got hold of. She sent up a quick prayer to St Gertrude, asking her saint to forgive her for her wickedness, and to keep her safe from this dangerous sea.

'Tom said he weren't to swim,' said Isabelle. 'No one should be swimming. The sea's too cruel he says.'

Tom heard his name and came over to them.

'Take the girl away from here,' he urged Linnet.

'She brought me here,' she replied stupidly.

'Told you he was drown'd,' Isabelle muttered crossly. Linnet's disbelief had not been lost on her.

'What happened to him?' she asked Tom now, her head buzzing with questions.

He shook his head slightly, turning away from her hard

gaze. If he had anything to say, he wasn't going to say it to her now.

The Prior was organising some of the men to carry Oswyn up to the Priory when he caught sight of Linnet and Isabelle. He hurried over.

'Linnet, and you, little one, we are not talking about Brother Oswyn to the Inspector – do you understand? He's at private prayer at the moment so he won't have seen this.'

Linnet thought about where the guest room was, it didn't have a window that looked out of the Priory, just into the passageway, so he wouldn't see anything while he prayed.

They both nodded instinctively then Linnet asked, 'But why?'

He sighed. 'I don't think there's a Rule against swimming but if there is, I don't want the Inspector to add it to his report. I'm having Oswyn taken to the Infirmary and we'll say he's sick for the next few days.'

It made sense. Oswyn's odd daily swimming habit could only attract attention, especially now he'd drowned.

'But, Prior Richard, what about his account books? Didn't the Inspector need to see those?'

The Prior looked shrewdly at Linnet for a moment.

'You can go and get them ready for him. He'll need them set out in my room.'

They left the beach. Linnet looked at Isabelle wondering if she should try and comfort her in some way but the child wasn't crying. She looked so much smaller without her raven with her, just a child, nothing different about her. The thought conjured the bird, and he swooped in, coming to land a few feet away from her. Isabelle gave a small cry of delight and Pol echoed her, bobbing his head up and down and puffing up the ruff of feathers at his neck before solemnly following her as she skipped away, hopping sedately in her wake.

Linnet hurried to Oswyn's cell to get his books. He had his own private room, set aside from the dormitory with its cubby holes for each monk. Only the Bursar and the Prior had their own places to sleep and she'd never seen into the Prior's sleeping place. Oswyn's room was clean and tidy, a plain bed and a few neatly folded clothes on a stool, an old wooden chest, nothing out of place apart from several candle stubs on the floor. He'd hoarded the best blankets, she noticed, wondering if she could borrow one or two while the Priory was in disarray. Not that she intended to give them back.

She opened the chest at the bottom of the bed. More good woollen blankets, he was making sure he would not be cold whatever the weather, and a dozen candles. And his account books. Like most bursars, he kept two sets of accounts. One was just the figures, the other was the household book that he would put all the information in daily for him to calculate later. She hesitated. Which would the Prior want her to bring? She opened both books. She could tell they had been bought in for him to write in, poor quality paper and plainly bound, she'd seen their like for sale before. The account book was clear, neat Latin in a careful hand. The household book was more carelessly kept. She noticed the bottoms of several pages were ripped and torn, with text scribbled anyway. Well then. Only the account book.

But on an impulse, she took also the household book for herself, to look at later. Perhaps the Prior would need the figures Oswyn hadn't copied over. She could easily make it look as if it were his hand.

She felt deep unease being in his cell, as if at any moment the door would open and he'd be upbraiding her for being there. She told herself off. He was dead. He couldn't shout at her.

Defiantly, she decided on the dark brown blanket from the

chest, shaking it to fold it properly. A small cloth bag flew out of the folds. Curious, she opened it up but there were merely tiny screws of paper, covered in ink but no words, just scribbles again. She folded it back into the blanket, gathered up the books and, for good measure, added the good candles and candle stubs to the top of her pile.

No one would notice her carrying a blanket, women's work to be doing that. She refused to feel bad about the candles. Oswyn couldn't use them anymore. A little voice echoed in her head 'once a thief always a thief, Linnet' but she shook it off. She may as well make the most of this moment.

'What are you doing?' It was Marcus, he was always on the lookout for anything and maybe he was already having a look around the room he would hope to be moving into. She'd forgotten about him. She stepped back, dropped her head to make herself shorter than him, shrinking into herself a little, and muttered her reply. The Prior, the books, to the study.

She risked a quick glance at his face, but saw no speck of grief. She supposed he would have an easy path to the position of bursar now. At least he would think so. She wondered if Oswyn had enjoyed his daily swim partly because Marcus would never have joined him for that.

'Well carry on then.' As she thought, the blanket and candles hadn't attracted his notice at all.

The account book left in the Prior's room, and the blanket and candles, the household book and the curious little bag of paper twists all safely hidden in her own room, she took a moment to sit outside in the graveyard of the squat village church opposite the Priory. The high building cast its shadow over the stones, but she sat where there was a hint of warmth in the winter sun.

She shut her eyes, thinking again of the body on the shore. The white of the clothes and the man's skin surrounded by the black of the monks clustered on the shore, and the clear green of the water washing up on the stones.

'Linnet, are you sleeping?'

She felt his breath on her face before she opened her eyes. Hot but not unpleasant. She looked at Godfreyd bending over her. He was so tall that he must spend all his time bending within the cramped rooms of the Priory. She wondered idly if his back hurt him. She doubted it. He was well made, like the forms of wooden statues she'd seen in some of the cathedrals, all in proportion, strong arms, even features.

Money shaped bodies as well as houses, she knew. Even illness seemed to glance off them more lightly, leaving fewer scars and blemishes.

'I heard you saw Oswyn on the beach.'

She looked around for the Inspector cautiously, then nodded.

'The Prior's brought him to me in the Infirmary. I've got him covered up so that no one would know, you know…'

'That he's dead?'

Godfreyd flinched slightly then nodded. 'We're saying he has the bloody flux, no one wants to be around that. I know we have to keep him there for the Inspector but there's only so long I can keep up the pretence. He'll start to smell bad soon.'

The monk's well-made nostrils flared with disgust.

'They'll think it's the flux making him smell so bad,' Linnet pointed out.

He didn't look convinced.

'Anyway, what happened? What did you see on the beach?'

'I just saw him lying there, already drowned.'

Linnet felt the scrutiny of the man's gaze and shifted a little. But she'd done nothing – this was not her death. This was purely Oswyn with his mania for his daily swim in the freezing waters across the harbour, always talking about how his healthy body informed his healthy mind, quoting something in Latin and displaying his shivering and not so healthy-looking body on his way back to the dormitory before Lauds, dripping on the clean floors while the servants rolled their eyes.

She'd seen him in the water a few times, head up and full of his own importance, while the curious seals watched him from a safe distance, mockingly, she liked to think. He used to swim from the beach where the fishermen gathered, round the Heugh, and come out at Cuddy's Isle, never stopping to pray there as some did, but merely passing it.

As she thought on it, she remembered the argument she'd seen last night, Cassian threatening the Bursar, leaning over him. She went to say something but bit it back; none of her business to talk to Godfreyd about it.

Godfreyd was mulling on something. He'd lost his usual sleek, arrogant look.

'He was definitely dead when you saw him, Linnet?' he asked insistently.

'I didn't see him breathing if that's what you're meaning.' It came out sharper than she meant. She needed to remember to keep civil, even with the monks she didn't like. She was free to be herself here on the island, but only a meek, quiet version of herself.

Godfreyd didn't usually spend time talking to her. The only times in the past were when he wanted a recipe copied into his leech book 'and quickly, woman'. She hadn't realised he even knew her name. Now as he stood there, he ran his eyes up and down her, getting the measure of her and finding her wanting. She flushed under his close attention, colour coming to her usually sallow cheeks. She didn't get looked at these days, she was judged to be nothing special, which only worked to suit her. She'd hated it when she was just grown, all the glances and the sly pats and touches. Plaiting her long dark hair back severely and wearing only the drabbest clothes had helped make her more invisible, habits she had kept up. It hadn't stopped the odd grab at her in the dark corridors, from a monk or a novice in the shadows, someone feeling safe enough to threaten her without fear of consequence, but it felt routine, no real interest in her but a marking of territory, a reminder not to become complacent in this place where she was an outsider.

She'd heard Godfreyd was the eldest son of his family, not the one normally given to God, but that there'd been some reason they wanted to get rid of him. He'd arrived at the monastery with a carriage full of goods and even a servant, although the man had returned with the carriage. Ann gossiped that he had his own good linen to sleep on, nothing that the other monks could manage.

Linnet knew that some smaller monasteries and priories didn't have servants, but on this small island, the Priory relied on the villagers for most of the hard work that kept it going. In turn, the villagers clearly had pride in 'their' Priory, even if they grumbled about the monks and their ways. It was the focus of the island, most of the houses clustered at its skirts, and the inn just outside the Priory gates. The farms spread out further away, but the farmers' wives were often in the courtyards, visiting Ann with meat or cheese, or collecting their loaves from the Priory bakehouse.

The Prior spent a lot of time with the fishermen, talking to them about their catch and getting them to row him to Inner Farne, or Seahouses. She sometimes saw him looking at them, as they sat and knotted nets, with something almost like envy, and wondered if he came from a seafaring family. Godfreyd though, he kept himself apart from all the villagers, speaking to them only if he had to, speaking to the younger monks and the novices as if he were in charge of them, which made it all the stranger that he was talking to her now.

He was the Infirmarian but it was odd he preferred to stand back and let others do the leeches and the cleaning and so on. Unlike other infirmarians she'd known, he never added his own remedies or corrections to his leech book and just copied remedies entire. She stifled a laugh as she realised a patient who was already dead was probably his perfect patient. Oh God, was she laughing about Oswyn already when he'd not even been dead hours?

She caught a flash of movement behind Godfreyd – Isabelle again, running now. She got up to leave and he reluctantly stood aside. What had he actually been trying to ask her?

She spent the rest of the morning working on the prayer book, losing herself in the curves of the ink on the page. Lady Margaret had asked for it to be 'plain and useful'. She'd not met the woman but she knew a Lady's idea of plain would be ornate nonetheless. She'd heard from Oswyn that Lady Margaret was not a great lady, although her husband, Lord Edmund D'Aganet, was part of the Percy family, if a distant part. She was a young wife he'd married after he was widowed last year, and not from a high family. Doubtless she would spend his money on whatever caught her fancy, and for now it was a prayer book.

Putting down her quill, she laid her desk plank flat, picked up her pricker and began to mark out a cat, curled up sleeping in the capital letter of the prayers for serenity. She gave it something of the look of Tibet. As she was planning the colours, looking at her inks to see what she had, the blues of Oswyn's body flashed back into her mind again. She shuddered. He'd looked so very cold. On impulse, she decided to go and see his body in the Infirmary. She couldn't understand what had happened and she needed to know as much as she could, it was the only way she might remain safe.

She could go into some of the rooms of the Priory, but not all. The Scriptorium obviously, although the older monks called it the stores room, from when it used to house barrels that weren't in use. It had been cleared out a few years ago but still wasn't really the best room to use for scribing. The best rooms had large openings in the wall and took in all the daylight. Her Scriptorium only got light for a few short hours in the middle of the day during the winter, although summer would give her more time to scribe and illuminate, if she was still there then.

She had never entered the Refectory, nor the Chapter House, but the Infirmary was always needing someone to carry herbs in, or ointments out, or have words added to the leech book, so it wouldn't cause anyone to notice if she went and had a look now. Women weren't generally allowed into any of the inner rooms of the Priory, but somehow Linnet was tolerated. Ann had taken advantage of this and Linnet was not averse to borrowing tinctures or herbs for her when asked. Ann made her own remedies which the island women came to her for, and coveted Godfreyd's wide range of tonics, left from an older monk who had cared about curing his brothers. Ann and Linnet both knew that he was careless enough not to notice if the odd bottle or vial went missing from amongst the massed ones on the dusty shelves.

The Infirmary was dark, a single candle lit by the door in the stone room which lay in the corner of the outer wall, just behind the guest room the Inspector was staying in. The shutters were closed 'to keep the vapours from spreading' Godfreyd always said. He wasn't in there. A dead body didn't really require a lot of attention after all.

Oswyn was swaddled on the bed with herbs burning in saucers near him, as if helping him breathe. The smoke from them caught at her throat a little. She crept closer. She thought he would seem smaller in death. All that hot air gone, all his self-importance gone. Somehow though, he seemed longer, more substantial. He'd been short and puffed up but now he was solid, a lump of flesh. She gingerly unwrapped his hands; was she going to hold one while she said a prayer? What had come over her? This was a man she didn't like – hadn't liked – and who would have been able to destroy her, if he had the right one of her secrets. But something drew her to his corpse.

'Are you the scribe woman?'

The voice from the doorway was the novice. She jumped slightly, a voice in her head reminding her: not dead, not dead, not dead.

She turned. 'Yes?'

'What ails the Brother?'

What had the Prior decided was wrong with him? Flux. 'The Infirmarian says flux, or something similar.'

He took a careful step back but she couldn't see his face, just his outline against the light from the outside.

'You'd better wash well before ye sees the Inspector. He wants notes taking. Who is the Brother?'

'Brother Oswyn. Why doesn't the Inspector use you to write his notes?'

Linnet had spoken without thinking but the novice replied anyway.

'My scribing ain't up to much yet. He says I'm to practise my lessons more before I can write for him.'

He left, crossing himself and muttering a quick prayer for the sick monk.

Linnet realised she'd been holding the dead man's hand tightly and let go abruptly. The cold from him had seeped into her. As she let go, one of his fingernails caught her. Startled, she looked more closely at his hands. They were cut and bloodied and his nails were torn. He must have been scrabbling at the rocks and trying to get out of the sea. But if he were near the rocks, he could have climbed out surely? That part of the beach was shallow, the fishermen had to push their boats a way out unless the tide was right up. He normally started his swim there, so strange to drown right at the beginning when he was at his strongest and warmest. She noticed his face had a cut across it too – on his cheek – the sides of the cut open and fleshless. Was this really a drowning?

She needed to ask Tom about how a man drowned. The fishermen didn't like talking about the sea's dangers, even mentioning the words was seen as bad luck. But Tom might answer some of her questions.

With her prayer interrupted, the impulse seemed foolish. She'd spent her life in priories and cathedrals but her conversations with God were strictly limited, and always through her saint, like others she knew. Speaking to God directly was for men of the Church.

Her hands scrubbed clean, and ready with a fresh quill and her best oak gall ink, she knocked on the Prior's parlour where the Inspector had settled himself and his papers. If he wanted to make use of her skills did that mean he wouldn't put her in his report? He might. She would keep her head down and say as little as possible.

The fire was roaring. The Inspector had made himself comfortable in the Prior's rooms, chair pulled up to the warmth, desk near him with papers spread across it. He didn't look up as she came in, just waved her to the corner impatiently. She looked around wondering what he wanted her to do. Nothing struck her so she just stood there, feeling foolish – but warm and foolish.

It was the first time she'd had a chance to look at him in the light. He was a broad man, pale with dark hair. He sat awkwardly in the chair, as if at any moment he would get up and pace about. He was looking at the papers but didn't have a quill in his hand so was tapping them absently as he read silently.

'Can you take dictee?' he asked finally.

She nodded and sat down at the other small table with her quill ready. He began to speak quickly and she scribbled fast to keep up. He was doing his dictee in English; she wondered if he would change it into Latin for the Bishop later.

The words flowed through her and she wrote without listening to the sense of what he was saying. Finally he stood up abruptly and left the parlour, telling her to wait there.

She flexed her wrist as she waited, then looked back at the words. Nothing stood out as an immediate danger for the Prior. The Inspector had noticed some of the monks were wearing the wrong habits, but that wouldn't cause too many problems, very few houses had pristine linen for all the Brothers.

Since his arrival, the prayers had been observed for most offices (they never seemed to sing Vespers) so, as far as he knew, the Brothers were pious and observant. It was lucky he'd not been here before she'd come, when the scribe monk had been caught once again drunk and half naked in the village square, his misfortune leading to her fortune. Perhaps they would get a good report. Perhaps Durham would send more monks here again but she didn't think so. The Cathedral needed all the monks they had to manage the pilgrims who swarmed around the city every day. The Holy Island Priory was no longer important. A pilgrim might come once a season but no more than that.

Her legs were stiff and numb now, so she got up to stretch and went to the doorway to look for the Inspector but there was no sign of him. Perhaps she should go back to scribing her prayer book. Or would he get angry to come back and find her gone?

As she hesitated, the Prior came into his parlour.

'Ah, Linnet, the Inspector has gone to pray and will not be needing you for the rest of the day. He says to put his papers in order.'

She began stacking the papers on the table, careful to spread out the ones where the ink was still wet. As she moved them, she saw Oswyn's account book underneath, and stopped.

The Prior looked over and saw what she was looking at. He sighed. 'He was foolish not to fear the sea.'

Linnet feared it. Not least when it came in fast over the sands. She'd not got caught so far, although that first night she'd come onto the island, she knew she'd been but a step away from drowning. The Beale boys were most people's safest way on and off the island, or the boy who lived and worked in the Priory stables. There were pale stones placed to help see the route, but finding them amongst the rocks and the seaweed was no easy task. She wondered too if the islanders would move them sometimes, keep their hand in to show what they knew and invite danger to those who wouldn't pay for their safe guidance.

'Where did Isabelle go?'

Linnet shrugged. 'I've not seen her since we came away from the beach.'

'Well if you see her, send her to me.'

She nodded and left, eager to get back to her prayer book. Why did the Prior want to see Isabelle? Maybe to scare her further into keeping the secret of Oswyn's death.

As she came out, she heard groaning from the guest room above. Unable to resist her curiosity, she crept up the short flight of stairs above the Prior's parlour quietly and glanced through the knotholes in the door frame. The Inspector was kneeling on the floor, beating his bare chest with a thorn branch, praying loudly as it caught his flesh. Little beads of dark blood were forming in thin lines on his pasty, white skin. She could smell the sweat off him as he moved, mingling with the iron tang of blood in the air. Shuddering, she backed away, bumping into Cassian.

'Are ye spying on the Inspector?' His voice was angry but quiet, careful not to disturb his master.

'No, no I was just – I came from scribing for him and didn't know if he wanted me to wait longer.'

'He'll send me to fetch you if he does. I don't hold with women writing, t'ain't right.'

Linnet felt the sting of the insult but kept her face still. 'Why's that then?'

'Men do that. Women keep house.'

No new notions here. Just the usual she'd heard many times before.

'But he asked me, not you,' she couldn't resist biting back.

'It's only while I'm learning. I'll be right with my letters soon and he can use me for all he needs.'

'Did you want me to help you?' The offer slipped out before she thought better of it. Something about the man had sparked her pity, trying to learn something new at his age.

'You? I dinna think so, lass!' He was laughing at her now, his anger gone as quickly as it had come, and he walked away, back to Father Thomas and the gardens.

Chapter Six

Linnet worked hard and finished her cat illustration. She was pleased with the way the shape fitted the letter, the arch of the cat's thin back being the curve of the C. In the late afternoon, she walked up to the Heugh, the little cliff behind the Priory, just to stand there and look out.

With her back to the land, she could see the ruins of St Cuthbert-By-The-Sea, a forlorn heap of stones sitting on Cuddy's Isle. The first place the saint had withdrawn to – to have his peace away from the monks. She remembered scrambling over to it at low tide as a child, left to her own devices while her father drank and chatted. It had been falling down then but she thought the roof had been intact.

Looking around and further out to sea, she saw the lights at Bamburgh Castle, down the coast, but couldn't see Inner Farne in the gathering gloom. Those islands sat too low to be easily seen, except when the two monks who lived there lit a beacon to signal to the Priory.

The dark was coming in, spreading out cold fingers across the sky. She shivered as the cold swept in with it. She really needed her cloak back.

The Priory sparkled beneath her, the candlelight glowing through the fine glass windows of its church. In the outer courtyard, the usual busy evening was beginning. She could see the monks, released from their day's study or work, flowing out to walk around the yard, and talk and gossip.

Voices rose in the still air up to where she was sitting on the stones. She could see the story of Oswyn's drowning being handed from group to group. The Brothers crossed themselves, looked sombre, then rushed off to tell someone new, always looking over one shoulder for the Inspector and Cassian, and reminding each other that those two weren't to know about the drowning. Brother Maykin, always in the centre of each group, gesturing and nodding with a put-upon gravitas.

The Heugh was a favourite place for Linnet. She could watch the busyness beneath her but sit in solitude. The Priory, so towering and imposing from everywhere else on the island, sat neatly below her now, tucked away from the crag and the cliff edge.

There was a small stone ruin on the top, protecting her from the wind off the sea, giving her just enough shelter to bear the cold a little longer. The island was covered in these ruins, some from earlier monks she supposed, some abandoned farmhouses.

As she watched, she saw a small figure rush across the outer courtyard – Isabelle. But where was she going? Her raven wasn't with her and she didn't stop at the kitchens, but ran into the inner courtyard and then straight into the Priory Church through the south transept.

She wasn't allowed into the Priory Church any more than Linnet, any more than any woman of the village, but the monks were out now so she was unlikely to get caught. Most priories kept women out of their churches and chapels, the local men being allowed in but only up to the rood screen. Durham Cathedral allowed women in – or they would have lost too much from pilgrims she thought – but only up to the black stone line in the floor. Linnet had heard the story of the young pregnant daughter of a Scottish king, lying and blaming St Cuthbert for the baby, and being struck down into hell at her words. Her father had repented his anger, and she had been found, some miles away from the castle, bleeding and without the bairn. The saint had shown his mercy, Linnet had been told, but women were barred from his tomb and his churches. She wondered sometimes what had led the girl to lie, what had led her to fear telling the truth more than blaming a saint, what her father was repenting for – but none of that remained in the story that was told now.

Why was Isabelle going in there now, though? Linnet had barely even seen her at the village church, she was not a pious child despite her insistence on rebuking Linnet for cursing.

Linnet shrugged. She was not in charge of her and she wouldn't bother herself with it. The Inspector would be gone soon, they could bury Oswyn, and the Priory would settle back into its pattern.

She started back down the field, the way almost too dark now to see, so she stumbled slightly, a white flash from a disturbed rabbit running away. The field had strange stones that were hard to see under the grasses. Some said the old priory had been here, not where it was now. Some talked about the bodies that were buried there from St Cuthbert's time, the reason an old whitened bone or two might come to light when the field was dug up. She decided she'd find Tom and ask about her cloak and see if he would talk about how a man drowned.

She tried the tavern near the market square. The room was smoky and full of people drinking and shouting and she had to push against what felt like a wall of noise and sweat to reach him. He was in the back, ale in front of him and dice on the table, but he was alone.

'No one playing tonight, Tom?'

'No, I've not been in long.' He took a pull on his ale and looked around, speculatively, judging his chances of a game tonight. He turned back to her, so they couldn't have been good.

'Why are you in here?' His question wasn't an accusation.

'I was looking for you, Tom. I'm getting cold without my cloak.'

'Ah, it'll be done soon, pet. How is the maid – after, you know, this morning?'

They both glanced around but no one was listening to them.

'I've not seen her since, although I think she was sneaking into the Priory Church.'

'She needs talking to, I've never seen her looking so shaken.'

Linnet sighed. By that he meant Linnet needed to talk to her. Tom would have tried, she knew. He had been so kind to her when she was a child visiting the island with her father, taking time to play with her and show her how his boat worked and the knots he made in his nets. His mother had been alive then, a tiny woman, who had seemed so old to her when she was a child, probably the age Tom was now. She never said much, her few words in a tongue Linnet didn't know, but she smiled a lot, and always had a barn cake or something to give her.

'Have you seen anyone else drown, you know…'

Tom looked at her steadily. 'Why are you asking me? Of course I have, but out at sea most often. Anyway, you saw the man, he was a fool to swim around here. We'd all told him but he wasn't a man who liked to hear anyone else's voice apart from his own.' His words were calm and steady but his voice not. She noticed his leg moving jerkily under the table and his glance now roving around the room. She hadn't seen him like this before, he almost always seemed untroubled by the monks and village squabbles, but tonight he was clearly disturbed for some reason.

Why was she asking about Oswyn? She didn't know. All she could think was that the body on the beach felt wrong to her. It seemed to be one thing but she felt it was another.

'Can ah sit mysell down here with ye, man?' It was Cassian. Had he overheard them? She didn't think so.

Tom moved up amicably. 'Did you want a game?'

Cassian laughed. 'Nay – better not. Ah dinna think the Inspector would take kindly to that.' But his fingers played with Tom's dice, flicking the small wooden cubes over with the air of a man who knew them well.

Linnet had got up to leave but Tom gave a tiny nod so she sat back down.

'So what were ye before a brother?'

'Carpenter.'

She glanced at his hands, cuts and scars covering them, some old and white now, some fresh. Why was he here now, was he spying for the Inspector to see who was there, who might be gambling or drinking, like the last scribe sent off the island?

Cassian turned his attention to Linnet.

'And how was it ye are here then? Scribing and all.'

'I was to meet my father here, the Prior knows of him, and they had started a prayer book for young Lady Margaret from the Percy family, you know, when the scribing monk was sent to another house.' And her hand and drawing were better than his and she didn't drink like he did, she thought, but didn't add. She'd had to cover up many of his mistakes in those first few pages, a shake here, the words with the wrong letters, and even draw over his plaintive hungover scrawl, a flourish of flowers now, not a wail about vomit and how 'ale has killed us'.

If the Prior hadn't needed the prayer book worked on, she would have maybe sold them inks, or worked for Ann in the kitchen, relying on scraps and charity.

'Are you not supposed to be abed now? Ready for prayers later?'

Cassian sighed. 'I'm not accustomed to having to get up afore the second sleep. I wake a course but I would take the time to chat to me wife, or lie and enjoy the warmth. And now I canna sleep with the other brothers so well. In Durham we've our own cells, not like here. I canna take the snoring.'

Linnet was used to being awake, many were, but only those who had candles to spare could do anything useful in that middle of the night time when the first weariness of the day was slaked. The second sleep was always deeper, warmer somehow.

Tom laughed. 'I've heard Brother Marcus is right noisy, and Brother Maykin talks in his sleep—' He cut himself off suddenly.

Cassian leaned in. 'What else have ye heard?'

There was a short pause as Tom looked down, avoiding Cassian's gaze. 'Nothing.'

Linnet realised Cassian was here to glean secrets. He was new to trying though. She could have told him. Get Tom an ale, make him talk about gaming, slip in the questions when he was thinking of other things.

'Do the Brothers come in for an ale, for a game?'

'Seems to me,' Tom said slowly, 'you'll not be making many friends coming in and asking after ye fellow Brothers like that.'

'Ye calling me a talebearer?' Cassian's voice rose sharply and he got up, spilling some of Tom's drink.

Tom also got up and tried to calm the man, but Cassian was red in the face and his hands were clenching. Linnet wondered if some of the cuts on his hands were from fighting, not his carpentry tools. He overcame his anger with a visible effort, swallowed hard, making to leave.

'Na, man, sit yourself down again,' Tom said mildly, and to Linnet's surprise, Cassian smiled suddenly, and did sit down.

'Ah'm sorry, man, this temper of mine hasna got any sweeter since I put a habit on. It's nae easy to be a man of God, I tell you.'

Tom laughed. 'It's nothing I could do. What took you that way?'

Cassian shrugged, keeping the conversation easy and light. 'Had enough of being a carpenter. But that were afore I tried to get my head into the books. If I'd know it were that hard…'

Linnet could see the flash of something else under his cheerful expression, there was another reason he wasn't saying, she was sure. The two men kept talking, drinking and striking up a friendship as they did as they realised they were near enough the same age. Linnet left them to it.

Linnet went back into the Priory through the small gate into the outer courtyard past the stables and the ruined kiln shed. The main gate to the inner courtyard was always locked at night. There was a shape in the corner, a man, stumbling and drunk, looking for a quiet place to piss, she supposed. Seeing her, he swung around, still pissing.

She took a quick step back to avoid the splash and was hurrying past when he grabbed her sleeve.

'It's Mary innit? I know you, Guy's girl. He said you might be here.'

Chapter Seven

The shock of hearing that name made her freeze. He was breathing beer into her face while looking searchingly at her, squinting a little in the dark. One of the masons here to make the floor, she realised.

'I'm not Mary.' She shook him off and began running towards the Priory.

'Ah, I'd know you for sure, it's Mary, yes,' he shouted after her, then turned back into his corner.

Breathing fast, Linnet clung on to the rough stones of the Priory wall. Should she leave the island? Not now, the tide was in, but tomorrow. If she didn't take much with her no one would come looking. The Prior would be angry she'd not finished the prayer book but he'd find someone else to do it. Her cloak though…? She couldn't travel without it – she'd freeze. And travel? Where could she go? This island had seemed so safe and so far away but now she wasn't sure. She had almost no money left from her trip here either, and the Prior was not going to pay her, with the work not finished.

She knew the man, Jack. He'd come out drinking with Guy and the others a few times, both in Ely and in York. How had he recognised her? What did he mean when he said Guy said she might be here? She felt her thoughts whirling around her head.

*

She'd first met Guy in a tavern, shortly after he had been rusticated from the university. He was loudly declaiming how unfair this was, how his tutor had it in for him, how he was too clever for them, and calling for more ale. She didn't listen to what he was saying, she was thinking about taking the things he had scattered about him, carelessly. She tested his attention the first time by coming up and clearing some of the mess on the table, sweeping away walnut shells and chicken bones from the food the men had eaten. As she thought, they didn't pause in their talk or drinking.

The second time she came up to the table, she took more mess, but also a fine stack of papers, only slightly marked in one corner by spilt ale, which she had quickly put away in her skirts. But she must have paused too long because suddenly Guy had her wrist in his hand. She froze, was this the moment she finally got caught?

'I know what you're up to, girl, coming back to the table like that.' He was smiling at her, confident and showing off to the crowd. He pulled at her wrist until she was sitting next to him, half on his lap. His friends roared their approval while she kept thinking fast, what could she say?

'What's your name?'

'Mary.'

It was the first that came to mind. Had she any idea it would be hers for nearly five years or so, she would have chosen something prettier, she sometimes thought.

'So tell me, Mary, which of us fine men have caught your eye then, that you would keep coming back to the table and pretending to clear?'

She laughed in relief, and said, 'Why you of course!' It wasn't entirely a lie, he was a handsome man, dark hair, good clothes, and he was lively.

After a few days when he told her he was going to scribe to earn himself a living, now that his parents had cut him off and the university had thrown him out, she was happy to help him, sharing her inks, showing him how to cut pens for the best hand. It was a slow realisation that it was her doing the scribing and the work, and him spending the money, but even so, at the start she was happy to do it. He flattered her about her hand, showed interest in her ink receipts, took her advice on how to get work for them. That flattery was only ever when they were alone. In company he took the compliments for her work with a smile, giving all the impression that she was his maid, his girl, his helper, and nothing more.

She didn't care, she was living the life her father said she never could, earning a living by her pen. She sometimes thought of sending him a letter to tell him about her happiness, but was unsure where to send it, or even what name he might have been using.

It took less than two years for the shine to wear off, and for her to see Guy for what he was. He always had to have the finest clothes, even if they didn't have enough money for lodgings or even food sometimes. He lied to their customers about how fast they could do the work, leaving her to scribe faster and more carelessly than she wanted to. And his fine words, they had been the honey to trap her and were worth nothing. He didn't waste those on her any more, not now she was doing his work for him. Even so, she was stuck with him, she felt, for where else would she go?

Jack, she remembered now, was a mason who often came by their home. She'd never liked him, especially, not after that night at the tavern. He'd been sitting close to her. She could smell the sweat that had dried on him earlier in the day, warming now by the fire. He kept looking at her as if to try and find her place, unsure as to whether she was Guy's girl or just his maid.

Sitting back a bit, Mary tried to breathe lightly, not wanting to take in the sour smell any more than she had to. She almost missed the quick exchange of signs between Jack and Guy. A slight gesture from Jack towards her, a shrug from Guy, a giving smile although that touch of steel underneath was there. And then Jack's hand was in her lap and feeling up her skirts as he pulled her closer. Sweaty, warm, thick fingers pinching at her thighs and further up.

'Go on then, give us a kiss, Mary!'

Without stopping to think, she pulled his hand away and in front of her face, blocking him, and biting down on it.

'Ow! You bitch!'

Jack's reaction stopped the other talk as the men turned around to look.

Guy laughed. 'That's Mary for you, she's a wild cat at times!' She wasn't sure if he was pleased she'd fought back, or angry that she was showing him up.

Everyone else laughed, including Jack, although he was shaking his hand lightly, trying to take the sting out of it.

She was brought back to herself by a noise, a small whimpering noise carrying across the quiet courtyard.

No one was around so she pushed open the big heavy wooden door into the Priory Church and saw Isabelle. The child was curled up on the cold floor on the north aisle, next to the rough edges where the new tiles were being laid. She wasn't asleep – her eyes were open and staring up at the stone roof. Linnet could see her in the light from the moon coming through the big windows.

'What in God's name are you doing here, child?' She couldn't leave her here.

Isabelle sat up but kept looking up at the ceiling at the gilt stars painted there against the dark blue.

'I killed Brother Oswyn.'

Her voice shook a little. She spoke with a mixture of pride, horror and fear.

For a moment, Linnet almost believed her. The child spoke with such conviction. Then she started to cry and the spell was broken.

'What nonsense are you talking, Isabelle? Come sit next to me here and tell me what's happening.'

Slowly the child unfolded herself and crept over to Linnet's side. They sat on a hard wooden pew and she began to talk. It was a jumble of Father Oswyn this, Pol that, something about witches and then finally, sobbing, she admitted she'd told him to 'drown hisself' and then he had.

'Start again, Isabelle, I don't understand what you're saying.'

'Pol was in the Father's room and he got angry with him and with me. Pol had taken some of his papers, I think. He said Pol was my – my family.'

Family? She thought for a minute. 'Familiar?'

'Yes and that I was a witch and a witch's brat and I should stay out of his things and I said if I'm a witch then I curse you and you can go drown and, and—' She broke off into sobs again.

'Oh, Isabelle. He just drowned. You didn't curse him.' She hoped she was sounding comforting. Should she hold the child? Sometimes she felt she'd missed some part of adult life, having no children despite her time with Guy, and not knowing a household. She knew Ann regarded her as a useless woman, somehow getting away without that burden of house and child. Still, she had to try. She made a cautious move towards her but Isabelle looked up and bristled slightly. No holding then.

'But why did he drown hisself this time when he swam safe all the other times? There weren't a storm or anything?'

It was a good question, one Linnet realised she had also been wondering about. She was surprised, now she thought about it, that neither Tom nor the Prior had mentioned this.

Anyway, it was late and they needed to leave the nave before the monks came in for their next psalms.

'Come on, Isabelle, where do you sleep? Time to go back there, I think, and where's your pet?'

Isabelle got to her feet, indignant. 'He's not a pet – he's a raven. He's hisself and no one else's. We understand us is all.'

Like a familiar, Linnet thought wryly. She steered the child out of the western doorway not a minute too soon, and Isabelle ran off to the kitchen where she often slept in a corner.

The monks were nearby with their candles and chanting. Linnet could see Cassian amongst them, following close behind the Inspector. She noticed the other monks were leaving space around him, they already knew he would be watching them for his master.

Linnet was too late to leave the church now, she should have gone when Isabelle went, so she stepped back into a darker corner, away from the candles. The few monks went behind the rood screen to start their prayers. The Priory Church was only lit with what they needed for prayers as Oswyn kept a close eye on the numbers used. Or someone else would be doing that now, she supposed.

Once the singing and the chanting were over, the monks filed back to the stairway and the dormitory. She had never rid herself of the habit of stealing in where she shouldn't be. It had served her well as a child and since. Stiff and cold, Linnet shifted, waiting for the moment when she could get to her bed, but as she was watching, she noticed two of the monks holding back. One must be Godfreyd, the only monk tall enough to stand out amongst the others in the flickering candlelight. He was blowing them out one by one. The other, round-bellied and smaller, Benedict, she thought, was helping him with the candles. But he held onto one of them, and once all the other monks were gone, he and Godfreyd went up another stair to the choir and the triforium up above. She watched the candlelight flickering but couldn't see what they were doing. And suddenly the light went out.

Before she could stop herself, she ran across the floor of the church and began creeping up the same stairs. In the dark, the steps were uneven but solid and she kept her hand on the wall, edging up slowly, wary of what she would find. She had gone up a dozen or more steps when she heard noises in the alcove just above her. She froze, alert to the sounds but couldn't make out any words, just breathing and rustling.

A sudden cry made her jump, and realise the danger she was in, and she turned and went as fast down the stairs as she could, none the wiser about what Godfreyd and Benedict were doing up there, although she had an idea, and it didn't surprise her.

She went back to her cell above one of the cellarer's rooms, and Jack's presence came flooding back into her mind. Should she run? Or could she persuade him he was wrong. She'd not changed her appearance but then she didn't look anything special. A dark plait, brown eyes, slight, tall but not if she bent her shoulders, then no one noticed that.

She was angry now. Why should she run again? How long would she have to run for?

She couldn't sleep, thinking about Guy and their life together again. They'd not lived together anywhere for long, moving on once they had exhausted his credit at a lodging house, flitting before the landlords got suspicious. She had been so good at taking all her things, wiping a place clean of her presence in minutes, leaving nothing to say where they were going. She thought her childhood of travelling had perhaps taught her not to feel too easy anywhere. The road felt natural, and settling in a new place, more like home than a home would have been.

Guy had had a comfortable childhood, he liked good lodgings with good pallets and chairs, and was often tempted to try and take them with him when they left. She would patiently explain yet again that it would be easier to travel light and the next town would also have a bed and a chair. She didn't bother pointing out that he would be chased for theft if he took furniture, a far more serious crime than skipping a week's lodging fees.

So where had they been when they knew Jack? Ely first, down in the eastern corner. They were in a small room in a house by the river, swans regularly bursting through the vegetable patch she'd tried to keep, nibbling at the young plants before they could take hold. Then they'd met again in York later, when they'd fled the east, Jack there to work on the cathedral, she remembered.

The real question was, did he know about Warham and his men? She'd been so careful when they came up with the scheme but had Guy? Wary when sober, but a stream of hints and boasts when drunk, and he was sure to have got drunk with Jack. She reassured herself though, Jack might know something about how she'd left Guy but surely he had no connection to Warham or his men. She curled up around Tibet who had come in while she was thinking, and fell back asleep.

Her dreams were dark and full of water.

Chapter Eight

She went to find Isabelle, to see if the child was happier than the day before. She was sitting sullenly outside the scullery door, idly tossing a stone from hand to hand as Pol watched over her. The shadows under her dark eyes showed she'd not slept well either, probably still fretting despite Linnet's attempts to cheer her.

'Come on.' Without waiting to see if she followed her, Linnet went in to see Ann who was busy kneading dough.

'Can Isabelle sift the flour for weevils for you this morning?'

Ann nodded, distracted, and gestured towards the barrel, 'but get her clean first,' she added with a quick glance at Isabelle's filthy hands and nails.

It was arranged. Linnet helped her bring the barrel out into the sunshine where she could see the black mites more clearly. Isabelle protested loudly as she was scrubbed with cold water and a sliver of Ann's ordinary soap but submitted nonetheless.

She watched as the child sifted and gently shook the flour, showing a grim satisfaction when she found the creatures. Pol was nearby, ready to swoop whenever Isabelle threw one out his way.

When he caught one in mid-air, the child burst into delighted giggles and Linnet realised again that she really was a child, not just an annoyance, and she wondered who was looking out for her.

The raven could move with great care for such a large bird. When she'd first seen him following Isabelle, she'd thought for a brief, horrifying moment he was after hurting her, before she'd seen him settle on her shoulder, claws light on her, huge against the child's small frame, but balancing carefully and crooning in her ear.

The Prior walked past, smiling as he watched what the girl and the bird were doing, then, his face darkening on seeing Linnet, snapping at her, 'You should be getting on with the prayer book, Linnet, not sitting here playing with the girl.'

He turned back and whispered something to Isabelle. She looked intent and then nodded, the flour sifting now just a task to be done before some work for the Prior.

What did he want the little girl for? He'd been spending more and more time with her lately, barely interested when first Linnet arrived on the island, but always talking to her now. A thin trickle of unease moved down her spine as she thought of it. She dismissed it as she went to the Scriptorium. There was too much to think about.

Hours later she was stiff and her head hurt from too much time peering at the text she was copying. The light was fading so she lit one of the candle stubs she'd taken from Oswyn's room. It gave her another hour of careful scribing before it finally flickered and went out. She knew that a proper scriptorium had strict rules against using candles but this was far from a proper scriptorium. Anyway, she was more careful than most monks and there was no way she would set fire to hours of work by recklessly flinging her hands around or leaving it lit when she left the room.

In the last gentle cream glow, she remembered the bag of paper scraps she'd taken from Oswyn's room. She'd brought them with her in her kirtle to have a closer look at when she had the time. Now she smoothed them out on the writing desk. Each was a small piece of paper. There was writing on them but nothing she could decipher, not complete letters. They didn't look like practice notes though – the script flowed too much for that. She put them away again, no clearer.

Hungry, she headed to the kitchen. She could see the Prior talking to Isabelle again in the inner courtyard, just outside his parlour. She was giving him a handful of items, like an offering. Linnet was too far away to see what the items were. The Prior patted the child on the head and she skipped off towards the kitchen too.

'What were you giving the Prior, Isabelle?' she asked as she caught up with her.

'It's our secret,' the child replied with great importance and wouldn't be drawn any further.

They ate in silence at the back of the busy room again, Linnet keeping an eye out for the masons who were sometimes fed with the other workers, squeezing in around the edges of the busy room as Ann and her servants chopped and basted and rushed about.

This had to be how Oswyn had discovered one of her secrets. One of the masons talking perhaps – they travelled a lot so had much to say, she knew. Was it Jack? No – Oswyn wouldn't have just taunted her if he'd known she was hiding from Guy, he would have told the Prior straight away. And Jack had only known who she was after Oswyn drowned. That wasn't it.

As if thinking about him had conjured him, Jack appeared at the table. Sober now but still leaning too close and too loud.

'It is Mary, I knew it was!' He clapped the table triumphantly and began to sit down. Linnet shrank back and arranged her face in the most perplexed expression she could manage.

'I'm sorry, I'm not Mary. I'm Linnet.'

Isabelle looked up, her mouth still full of bread but always happy to correct someone, anyone. 'She is Linnet. She scribes here. She's not Mary. There are four Marys on the isle and she ain't one of them. She's not from the isle, mind.'

Jack smiled and turned to the child. 'Where is she from then, your Linnet?' He was treating this as a huge jest, Linnet realised, not accepting her denial.

The girl sat up straight, ready to give Jack all the particulars. Was there anything Isabelle knew that could put Linnet in danger? She didn't think so. She'd been so careful on the isle, only telling what would fit her story. Was a child going to unravel all that now?

'She's a roll-bearer's daughter, you know John-the-Lies?'

Like most of the island people, Isabelle assumed that all mainland folk knew each other.

Jack smiled but looked puzzled. Linnet thanked herself yet again that she'd never talked about her father when with Guy. Isabelle took his confusion for ignorance.

'A roll-bearer takes the rolls. From one priory to the next. And the monks and that, they write on the roll to say how sorry they are that someone important died, and they put prayers on, and sometimes pictures—'

'Yes, child, I know what a roll-bearer is.'

Isabelle shrugged. 'Anyways, she came here to wait to meet him, and she can scribe so the Prior is making her do prayer books while she waits.'

Linnet nodded as Jack turned back to her. 'I'm sorry, I don't know you.'

Deliberately she shrank back a little further and looked down and mumbled as she spoke. As Mary, she'd been used to looking men in the eye, taking her space in the room and holding her ground. And look where that had got her.

He muttered something and got up, not before another sharp look at her. The scribing was a connection of course but not so rare as to be a sure link. Anyway, no one had ever seen Mary scribe, Guy taking all the credit for her hard work. She was known only as an ink-maker. Isabelle came over to sit next to her, full of questions, but Linnet stopped her with a glance.

They finished eating in silence and went out together. Pol hopped over to Isabelle as if he'd been waiting for her outside the kitchens.

'Why do you call him Pol?' Linnet asked. 'You say he's a male bird?'

Isabelle shrugged. ''Tis his name. I don't know why.'

Almost everyone at the Priory knew his name too, from Isabelle calling him day and night. The bird looked at Linnet with his bright black eyes, head cocked. She shuddered slightly – she'd seen him hunt and kill a baby rabbit once and not forgotten it. The flash of the bright black feathers with their purple and blue tones swooping down on the terrified creature, the quick shake of the rabbit's neck and then the gorging on the blood and the innards like a fat nobleman with grease smeared over his face, lording it over his peasants.

The girl and the bird left together, on another mission, heading out of the Priory gates onto the island, full of secrets, the girl singing and the bird croaking and purring back at her. No wonder they thought she was a witch – or a witch's brat.

Linnet went in search of Tom again. She liked spending time with him, more so during the day. At night it was another story when he was feverish with the need to play the dice and spend his money. He would be brisk and dismissive, looking right through her.

The monks were coming out of the Refectory, going to the Chapter House for the last reading of the Rule before the

Great Silence. It wasn't the Great Silence here on the island, the Prior normally encouraged them to talk and learn together in the Chapter House. She wondered if they were quieter now the Inspector was here. Linnet tried to think of a monastic house where they had been truly silent and couldn't. The monks didn't count the sign language they all used either, she thought they were hardly keeping the Rule of Silence if they simply substituted hands for voices. She'd learnt that language early, fascinated by the quick movements of the men's hands and how they could make a tiny gesture mean a whole word.

The Inspector lagged behind, deep in conversation with the Prior, on their way to the Prior's chamber. Godfreyd went past the Chapter House to the Infirmary talking loudly about examining Oswyn. Linnet considered slipping in again to have another look at him but decided not to. It was risky, and besides, he'd be smelling quite bad by now.

Tom was sitting by the harbour when she found him, throwing stones into the water. She felt suddenly awkward about talking to him. Ann had made a mean comment that morning, about her setting herself at him. She'd never thought of him as a lover. He was a fair bit older, and anyway, she counted him as her friend, and she'd known him when she was a child. Ann seemed to like people in boxes, paired up neatly, doing their work as set down by scripture and habit, not strangers like Linnet, somehow existing on her own and doing something special.

'After your cloak are you?' he asked, not looking up.

'Is it finished?'

'It will be soon, I'm nearly done.'

'I was going to talk to you about Brother Oswyn, whether you thought anyone disliked him, I mean *really* disliked him.'

He looked up, sharply, but she just looked back at him, innocently.

'He just drowned. I told you already.'

'Yes, but he got a lot of people annoyed, I think. Don't you think so?'

'Mebbe.'

He wasn't giving anything away.

'What about Brother Godfreyd?' she asked, determined to find out more.

'What about him?'

He'd turned his back to her and was throwing stones again.

'I thought maybe he didn't like Oswyn?' she persisted.

'Ah, you know those monks, none of them get on all the time, they're cooped up together like a flock of hens and they start pecking when they're peevish.'

'Yes but—'

'I heard two quarrel the night before Oswyn drowned, and it weren't Godfreyd. I was out near the stables, thinking I'd left my net there to dry out maybe, and right after Vigils, when they should have been abed, two monks hissing at each other like geese.'

'Did you see who they were?'

'No, no.'

She was sure he was lying but she didn't know why. Why would he leave his net drying by the stables? He wouldn't, he'd leave it on the beach with the other fishermen's nets. So what was he doing by the stables? She thought about asking that, but decided on a different question.

'If you didn't see who then how did you know it wasn't Godfreyd?'

'Weren't neither of them tall, lass, you know how he stands out from the rest of them.'

As he said that, she remembered the quarrel she'd seen and heard that night, Oswyn and the novice. But was that later? Or had Tom been watching too, also in the shadows?

'Did you ever want to leave the island, Tom?'

'No, I had my mother to look after until last year, and the fishing is good. Where would I go anyways?'

'But no wife, Tom?'

His face looked haunted suddenly, darker, but he laughed as he got up. 'Never found a woman who didn't ask too many questions, did I?'

She reddened, worried he might think she was interested in him that way. No matter, she followed him to the inn where he was quickly surrounded by the masons, Jack amongst them, and a wild game of dice started. She noticed he was gambling hard and his laughter was forced. She'd never seen him lose so fast, but he kept going, putting more and more coin on the table in an attempt to win it back, until at last it was all gone.

The masons clapped him on the back as he left, promising another game tomorrow, and settled in to more drinking.

Jack glanced over at her and she slipped out. Best not to attract his attention if she could help it.

'Watch yesself!'

She'd been so busy looking behind her that she'd walked straight into the parish priest, Sir Cyrus. He was staggering about, clearly soused, a quiet man, except at the pulpit or the inn.

'You want to watch yesself – the company you keep,' he continued, stabbing one sweaty finger at her but missing. 'That Tom is a sinner. That witch's brat is a sinner. You'll be sharing a table with them in hell.'

'What makes you say that?'

'Something not right about that Tom, always crying and praying in my church.'

She'd seen Tom head into the church often of an evening. Was he asking for forgiveness for his dice? When she first came back to the island, she thought he was happy but the longer she'd seen him, the less that seemed true.

'And – and that brat!' His face was purple with indignation and beer. ''Tis not godly to be prancing about with ill-omened birds. She should have died with her mother, that one.'

'What happened to Isabelle's mother?' Linnet asked. She realised she had no idea where the child actually came from.

The priest waved his hands around. 'The sickness, the one that took all the families down the way. They found a heap of bodies in that hovel she lived in and that changeling – about two at the time – sitting in the corner, not a worry about her, playing with a raven chick.'

The image formed, unbidden, in Linnet's mind. Flies probably, the stench of death, and Isabelle, her back to the chaos around her, focusing on Pol as if her life depended on it.

The priest was muttering prayers and curses, all mixed up, as he stumbled back to his house.

Struck by what he'd said, Linnet looked in at the church, but it was dark and silent, just a rat or two scurrying about.

The next day was still and clear, almost spring-like if not for the cold in the air. Tired from another night of bad dreams, Linnet walked slowly to the Scriptorium, faces swimming around her as if she were underwater.

The fishermen went out early but Tom and the Prior were off to Inner Farne. The Prior would go there to pray in peace every now and then. Peace for him but a long round trip for Tom and the other fisherman, rowing against all the crashing waves and the strong current.

Isabelle was off with her secrets again, talking to herself and Pol, apron gathered as she collected a herb here, a weed there. She thought she saw her playing amongst the old kiln stones in the room next to the stables, clambering up and then jumping off.

The Inspector was in the parlour with Oswyn's account book, making notes and sometimes calling loudly for wine or bread and cheese. Marcus was there too, talking at the Inspector to show off his thoughts on the accounts. The Inspector didn't seem to be listening to him.

Linnet spent the morning cutting parchment to size for the last few pages of the prayer book, carefully picking through the sheets to find the pages with the fewest holes and scars. Her good knife she'd had for years now, stolen from a market stall before she met Guy. She hummed to herself as she sliced through the tough skins, marking the lines first with prick holes to make it easier to cut. The village tanner was nearly ready with the next skins for her to look over.

She had to stop a few times to sharpen her knife. She wouldn't use it on bread and cheese like most did, keeping it clean and sharp for her work, and tearing her food by hand instead.

'I see you're still at your manuscripts here.'

The Inspector's slightly reedy voice made her jump. He walked into the Scriptorium like it was his own for him to wander around as he pleased which made her bristle.

'Have you seen printed books yet?'

'Yes, I've seen several.' They might be on the far side of the country but they weren't cut off from everything.

'What did you think?' He seemed truly interested in her opinion.

'They look very clean, Father. Very crisp to the eye.' She also thought they looked cheap. She couldn't see them lasting. The gentry wanted things made just for them after all, not something anyone could have. How was a printed book to be special? You couldn't order it differently as you could when copying quires, you couldn't add in a flourish here or there – although she'd seen some of the printed books left spaces to fill in a coat of arms or a painted initial letter.

'Not as pretty as some of the writing you do. Costs plenty though, I expect.'

He was leaning over the prayer book now, looking at the gilt and the images she'd spent hours on.

'Some inks are more costly than others,' she admitted.

'How did you know how to make them? Who taught you?'

'The monks we met, me and my father.' She wouldn't tell him about the copy of Theophilus's *On Divers Arts* that she had stolen. It was a poor thing, it had been in a fire and half the pages were missing, and she wasn't sure the scribe who copied it had it right. She had used the recipes for ink though, and written her own adaptations on it. She was sure the Abbey she had stolen it from hadn't missed it – the scribes there were lazy and never looked to make anything more than oak gall ink. It was one of her most precious possessions, that and her knife.

'Have you seen the Holy Island Gospel in Durham?' he asked.

Was this a trick question? It was held in a special shrine by the monks, she certainly shouldn't have seen it. She looked blankly at him.

'The blues,' he was musing now, as if she weren't there, 'the divine blues.'

'That would be the lapis lazuli,' she explained, 'from the East. The Prior is hoping to get some for the work we'll be doing here.'

He looked around suddenly as if hearing her for the first time. 'I think I saw a note for that in Oswyn's book. Come look at it with me.'

She followed him into the parlour where he rifled through the accounts until he found the right page. Brother Marcus was near, watching closely as they looked. A note, right at the bottom of a page, carelessly scribbled in, not Oswyn's usual hand, Linnet noticed, but he wasn't always neat.

'Yes,' she said, 'the Prior will have ordered it off one of the pedlars, I've not seen it yet though.'

She would love to work with it. The Virgin Mary's cloak perhaps, or a divine sky for the sparkling gilt stars.

The Inspector abruptly lost interest in her and the lapis and turned his back on her to get back into the books. She slipped from the room, back to the Scriptorium.

She had indeed seen the *Holy Island Gospel* once. There was little in Durham Cathedral she'd not stolen a look at while they lived there. Not a big book but so richly filled with images and words. She'd looked through it by candlelight, after the pilgrims had gone and when the monks were all asleep. It had been brought out late to show a visiting bishop and left safe in the room off the shrine to be put away with full ceremony the next day, locked away in the book safe.

She shouldn't have been in the room or anywhere near the shrine, which was well past the black line on the floor of the cathedral telling women to stop there. A child though, she could slip through shadows and she had learnt how to jiggle locks and get into rooms that had been left carelessly shut.

Even then, books had entranced her. She remembered running her hand over the bumps and curls of the letters, curious about the gloss marked out beneath the words. Her Latin was slight, but the gloss, the words underneath, even though they were supposed to be English, didn't mean much more to her. Her favourite pages were the drawings of pillars surrounding lists of words. They reminded her of the pillars in Durham Cathedral, and here at the Priory, with their sharp lines cut at angles, making patterns.

Linnet had never slept much, and it served her well. As a child she could wander freely at night without anyone asking what she was doing, or giving her little tasks. She could also get into forbidden places and take things without anyone seeing.

She'd never felt bad about what she thieved. She had a rule (although she suspected all thieves thought they had a rule). She only took from those who had plenty and those who she felt had wronged her or others in some way. Or, of course, if she really really wanted it.

Her good cloak was from a travelling pilgrim's wife, rude and cruel to the child who was with them. Linnet had taken great satisfaction in watching her having to wait for hours for her husband to come out from seeing the saint's tomb. The wife had put it carefully on a pew to save her place for later and blamed everyone around her for thieving it. Not Linnet though, who had unpicked the fine stitching decoration and hidden it away until that pilgrim, that wife and that cloak were all forgotten, swept away in the tide of more pilgrims, more wives, and more thefts.

Chapter Nine

Tom was scrubbing his boat viciously when Linnet found him the next morning.

'Fucking bird shit,' he muttered furiously, 'fucking Prior brought a duck back with him.'

Linnet tried not to laugh. The Prior had a soft heart for injured animals, and never turned his quick temper on them. The black cat that lived in the Priory who disdainfully avoided almost everyone else, followed him around like a dog. She'd known priors and abbots with dogs and birds for hunting, but this Prior hadn't shown any interest in going on a hunt while she'd been here. Not that the island lent itself to such, maybe he did when on his travels.

'What does he want with a duck?'

'It had a damaged wing. One of those cuddy ducks and it came and sat in the boat and wouldn't get out. He's taken it to his parlour.'

'What does he do over there – apart from rescuing ducks?'

'He talks to the two that are out there – Brother Aldus is getting pretty old now – and then he goes ferreting about in the old chests and that. I don't know and I don't care.'

With that he turned his back and she gave up trying to talk to him. Tom was like the weather. He could talk for hours, about nothing much in particular, or he could be short and sharp, like most of the island's men. Talking was not something they could easily do, unless it was in the tavern.

It had been different when she visited as a child, he had had all the patience in the world to listen to her questions and show her things. Mostly they'd been on the island for a few days but they'd stayed for nearly two months one time, the Prior at the time wanting to put a truly magnificent prayer on the obituary rolls. She remembered her father scoffing at that. 'Man never even met the one who died,' he'd said dismissively, but the Priory had put them up for all that time, and he'd gone off for many a quick trip to the local towns and the castle, up to God-knows what, leaving Linnet behind to amuse herself.

Tom had spent afternoons with her when he'd come from the fishing, telling her about his catch, telling her stories about the island and Cuthbert and the monks and what they had been up to. She wondered now at his patience, and his kindness for the girl she had been. She saw some of it with how he spoke to Isabelle.

On her way into the Scriptorium, she peered across the way into the Prior's parlour through the open door – curious about the duck. She could see it right against the back wall, near the fire. She came in a bit further to get a better look at it. It gazed warily back at her, huddled up on the floor, pretending as hard as it could that it wasn't there.

'That be a cuddy duck. St Cuthbert's special birds they were.'

'Isabelle, you need a bell on you!' The child had made her jump again. 'I know it's a cuddy duck, the Prior's brought it back from Inner Farne just now.'

They looked at the duck which had shut its eyes and tucked its head away. If it couldn't see them, it couldn't be seen. Pol hopped up towards it, curious at what had taken Isabelle's attention, but didn't do more than peck very carefully at its tail feathers, which the duck ignored.

'What are you doing in here anyway?'

'I'm bringing special things for the Prior. We have a secret.'

Again, that lingering sense of unease flickered over Linnet. She'd come across monks who liked secrets with little girls before. The only time she'd seen her father angry on her behalf had been when he found her in a monk's cell. The monk had been explaining that some sins weren't sins and he'd show her, when her father burst in and punched him hard in the face.

At the time she'd not known why and was terrified they'd get into trouble, but the monk had appeared at the Refectory that evening, blaming his bruising on a fall and avoiding her eye and her father's. From then on, there was a new rule. Never go to a monk's cell, even if they say you must.

Feeling a sense of duty now, she put her hand on Isabelle's shoulder. 'Is he making you do anything you don't like? You can tell me, you know.'

The girl shrugged off her hand indignantly. 'I always does what I like. And what's it got to do with you anyway?' She turned away and put down her little bundle of things for the Prior. 'Anyway – what's you doing here?'

'I came to see the duck.'

They looked at each other for a minute and then at the duck – still hiding its head stubbornly – and suddenly they were laughing as they left the room.

As they slipped out of the parlour and into the inner courtyard, they walked almost straight into a meeting of all the monks. Godfreyd was standing next to the Prior looking solemn and pompous. The Inspector was nodding along to something the Prior was saying.

The Prior raised his hands for the small murmurs to die away.

'I am sorry to announce, my Brothers, the death of Brother Oswyn. He has been suffering from the flux for these past few days, and despite Brother Godfreyd's skills, the Lord has taken him for his own.'

The monks bowed their heads in prayer, some attempting a look of surprise or sudden sadness. Godfreyd must have had enough of the body in his Infirmary and persuaded the Prior it was time for Oswyn's sad demise. Maykin had his head up, nudging those around him, with an almost satisfied air.

The Inspector stepped forward and addressed the silent monks.

'Who amongst us would be ready to meet our Maker? Who needs to examine his soul? Can you swear you would be gathered to the Lord in good faith if he took you tomorrow? I am saddened by what I see amongst you, Brothers. You are idle in your work and idle in your prayers.' He was thundering now.

The Prior's head was bowed, but Linnet could see his mouth twitching.

'As you know,' the Inspector continued, 'I am writing the report for the Bishop, but you are all writing a report, every day, your body sets the ink on the record of your soul. I am but a poor servant here to see you truly follow the right way to the Lord, but you, you know what you have done.' His voice broke suddenly on the last word and he fell silent.

The Prior looked around his startled monks. He himself rarely gave this kind of sermon. 'As the Inspector said, it's a good time to think about our own souls. Let the rest of the day be set aside for private prayers. Brother Godfreyd will task a few of you with getting the body ready for burial tomorrow but you might think on this further.'

The monks were left to scatter in their groups or singly. Brother Benedict was praying loudly for Oswyn's soul, but his show of piety was lost on the Prior who was paying no attention. Brother Maykin's voice could be heard above the rest. 'Of course I know all that Brother Oswyn knew. They'll call on me for the details of it all, all his works. The things he told me are… well…' Linnet could see him pull a quick face that looked just like Oswyn and the novices near him stifled laughter.

'Father, about the books…' It was Brother Marcus.

'I'll let you know in good time, Brother.' The Prior dismissed him with a wave, and Marcus looked down to the ground. Linnet could see, as clearly as if he spoke, the frustration in him. If not Marcus, who would be bursar now? She knew he thought he would make a better bursar than Oswyn had, but she had seen his hand, and it was scrappy, showy but written without care. She wondered if he took better care with the numbers.

Pol flew down from the top of the dormitory where he had been looking at the gathering and joined Isabelle as she skipped off – probably towards food.

The Prior caught sight of Linnet and beckoned her over.

'I want you to record Oswyn's death in the annals. He died of flux – you understand?'

She nodded, wondering if she would have been told to record him as drowned if the Inspector hadn't been here.

'And ask Ann to bring some bread to my room, it can be stale, perhaps in a little milk.'

'For the duck?' she blurted out.

He looked at her, smiling. 'Yes, for the duck. You've met my new guest then?'

She nodded, realising as she did so that she'd admitted going into his parlour. 'I saw Isabelle going in,' she offered in explanation, although of course if Isabelle were doing some service for the Prior, she had the right to be there and Linnet did not.

'If her wing doesn't mend, I'll give her to the kitchen,' he said.

She doubted that would happen. He would find a way to keep the duck with him if she didn't recover, she was sure of it.

The Prior took the bread from her for the duck without a word, waving her away, busy talking to Brother Marcus. She came out of the Priory and walked down to the harbour where she sat on the harbour wall to eat the bit she'd kept for herself in the thin sun, Tom coming to sit next to her.

'Seen the duck then?' he asked.

She nodded, mouth full of bread.

'Ah well, I suppose the Prior could do worse things than rescuing the odd bird.'

Linnet swallowed her bread. 'There are worse than him in the Church, that's for certain.'

'Meet many on your travels before here then?'

He seemed truly interested in her time before the island. She felt the warmth of the sun and Tom's friendship and her belly full of the bread she'd eaten, and relaxed a little.

'I've seen churchmen lie and steal and all sorts.' She paused, wondering what else to say.

'We've got Sir Cyrus,' he pointed out. 'We know right enough that men of God have their sins too.'

Linnet always thought it was strange that any parish priest could call themselves 'Sir', like the gentry, especially the likes of Cyrus, as far from a nobleman as she could imagine.

'And Oswyn. I know it's ungodly but I am not sorry he drowned.'

Tom took a long look at her and she stared back. She had said it now and she was going to stand by it.

'No,' he said at last, 'I can see you're not sorry. Did he harm you?'

She laughed a little, but then took time to think about it. 'He might have been going to, he said he'd found out my secrets.'

Tom raised one eyebrow. 'Secrets? You, Linnet? Why, we all call you the open book down amongst the fishermen! Surely you don't keep none from us.'

She made a face at his jest. Since she'd been on the island, she'd not said much to anyone, it was true, not even Tom. Mostly their talks were of the day, the island people, what the monks were doing. Sometimes he talked about the fish he'd caught, sometimes she talked about the manuscript work, both interested but ignorant of each other's skills.

He pressed her. 'What did he know about?'

She hesitated, then the words came out in a rush, the relief of talking about it for the first time. 'I made indulgences.' Tom looked confused so she explained further. 'Rich men have them, a piece of paper promising them a quicker way into heaven if they pay good money for their sins, less hours in purgatory.'

Guy was talking, describing how beautiful he could make an indulgence, boasting of the quality of their inks and the neatness of his hand. It wasn't his hand though, it was hers. He always did the talking, but she did the scribing and the illustrations. She wondered how much longer she would be content to let him take the praise for her work. After two years, she was no longer taken in by him as she had been to start with.

'Mary here does some of the illustrations, and she makes the ink, taught by monks!' Guy pulled her forward like a dog he'd taught to do tricks, and she curtsied and smiled. She took a curious look at this churchman, Warham, who had sought them out. Most of their scribing work was for rich families, not the Church. She'd asked around and knew he only had two livings, both small villages near Cambridge, but his clothes were richer than that would suggest.

Warham held up an indulgence for Mary and Guy to look at. She skimmed it quickly.

> To Our Beloved in Christ… the infirmities of human frailty, fearing that by the delights of this world you are being swallowed up unawares as by the waves of a great sea… at the point of death you may feel a full remission and grace…

It went on for a full page of script, but she could see how it was phrased, the sins, the penance, the rewards. She thought of a border of little wavelets to pick up the ideas in the words.

Warham agreed to Guy's terms. They would make him indulgences for three men of his parish who were ready to pay for their sins. And the money raised would go to his parishes of Cottenham and Barley.

After he'd left, Guy turned to her with excitement. 'He came to see us here, in Ely, Mary. He could have gone to any of the holy houses or university colleges in Cambridge, but he came to us. He must have heard of our work, we'll be able to put our prices higher if it's known we're working for a high-placed churchman.'

'He's got two livings only,' she protested, 'not such a high-placed man. And he said he'd pay your price only if no one heard that we were working for him and if we never made indulgences for anyone else. Why do you think that is? And what of that other scribe, the one that spoke freely of working for him? I don't think he died in a brawl, he was not the fighting kind.'

She had felt Warham's ambition though, burning off him like a hidden flame. This was a man who would be high-placed in no time, she knew.

Guy brushed away her concerns. 'You always look on the bad side. Look at the prices he's paying. Can't you be happy at what's happening?'

'But why isn't he using a Pardoner – like the other churchmen do?'

The Pardoners had great bundles of indulgences, ready to fill in the petitioner's name and the price paid.

'You know why, he doesn't want any of that money going to a Pardoner, or back to Rome. The Pope has enough, what does he care about a small church here?'

So she said no more, and they delivered the indulgences to Warham. Despite Guy's hopes, they heard no more from him for months, but then he was there, at their rooms in Ely again, this time with two servants flanking him.

'Your work was fine, I'd like you to make some more indulgences for me. This time for the parish of St Mary's-By-The-Sea, Cambridge, and leave the petitioner's name off. I will get one of my servants to write it in later.'

Guy was delighted and soon lost in what grade of parchment, what prices they would charge, what illumination and what quality of ink. She wrote down the particulars and kept quiet, until Warham left.

'We're on our way, Mary. He will tell his friends now, and we'll have so much work to do we'll be able to move to better rooms and—'

She stopped him. 'Don't you see, Guy? St Mary's-By-The-Sea, Cambridge?'

'What of it?'

'There's no sea in Cambridge. He is having us make forgeries. He'll sell these indulgences in other places and take all the money for himself.'

'I worked it out, Tom, you see. He needed money, Warham,

I mean. He had two livings but I could tell he wanted to be more than a country cleric, he was hungering after power and influence and he had none. His family were nobody special. I asked around, he had no one to talk for him at court, but he was well-respected all the same.

'He could talk a problem through, and some of the Cambridge college masters would call for him for advice and scripture learnings. I think he knew if he could get the money together to go to London, to seem like he were someone, then he could advance.'

'And these papers you made for him? They would do that?'

'Yes, an indulgence is for a rich sinner. But Warham was keeping some of the money for himself, I'm sure of it. It was safer for him to do ones for the false churches, no one would come looking for the money for those.'

She paused then, thinking of the time he'd come back when Guy was out. She'd said he wasn't there but Warham said he knew it was her hand who did the scribing, her who knew how to follow a hand previously written out, and he'd given her something else to do. Not to tell Guy.

'A family tree, a lineage,' she told Tom. 'His brother had married into the St Ledger family, and he wanted me to draw him up a new one. Only this time it was his mother who was a St Ledger, to show he was a nobleman and worthy of the King's attention, if it were asked.'

She'd done it – of course she had – but she had been fearful of what it would mean. She realised she'd been talking for a while, remembering those days, and Tom was looking at her, nodding slowly as he worked out what she'd done. He didn't look disturbed by it though, and she wondered who else had confessed their sins to him, lulled by his steady gaze and calm air.

She'd not mentioned Guy though, it embarrassed her to think of how she'd been smitten with him, and then hurt by him.

The dread of the men coming for her swept over her again and she realised she was being foolish. Why had she talked about it? Warham had said that he would know if she spoke of this ever, that he would find her and he would make sure she was imprisoned for forgery. Not what she'd done for him, but some other charges he would fabricate. She'd got her own protection against that but she didn't want to put it to the test. He was a powerful man now, often down in London she'd heard, with the ear of the King and now Master of the Rolls. He'd never said anything about the other scribe, but the men with him had mentioned it, laughing and winking at her, so she knew the lesson she was being asked to learn.

Her biggest fear was Guy though. She knew he thought she'd stolen from him, and he wasn't one to forget or forgive. She was sure he must still be in the prison in York, but when might he get out?

Here on the stone wall, in the warmth of the sun and Tom's interest, she'd eased her conscience for a while, but for what? Now she'd said more than she meant to.

Tom realised she was saying no more, so went back to his food. One of the reasons they were friends was that he knew when to leave her to her silences.

They *were* friends, she knew, and it was possibly the first time she'd had a friend. Guy had been a lover, then an irritation and a danger; her father never treated her kindly, not even when she was a grown woman, and she'd been too wary to get close to others when she'd been Mary. Since running the last time, she'd been too busy hiding, staying out of sight.

'So where were you before here?' he asked. 'Was it like

this?' He waved at the sea and the sky, the view from their perch on the wall.

She thought about Ely where they'd spent the most time. The town huddled at the foot of the cathedral as it soared above the Fens, the wide marshes, the small paths and roads and the knot of houses and hovels.

'No,' she said at last, 'nothing like here. It was inland, away from the sea, although there was plenty of water about, but the fishermen only caught eels.'

Tom nodded seriously. 'Good money in eels. So which is better, here or there?'

This time she didn't have to think at all. 'Here!' She just hoped she would be able to stay.

Back in the Scriptorium, she got down the heavy annals, undisturbed since the last entry when Brother Alfred had been sent away, and carefully entered Oswyn's death 'by flux'.

Chapter Ten

She heard a commotion outside the kitchen. Jack and the other masons were standing around Tom who had his hands up as he tried to talk his way out of trouble. Their voices had carried across the inner courtyard into her Scriptorium and roused her from her writing.

'Come now, man, you owe us the coin you lost to us.' The masons were pressing in on him, weighing their stone-hammers from hand to hand.

'Of course, of course, I gave my word, it's solid, you can ask anyone around here.' But Tom was shifting from foot to foot as he spoke and she could tell he was desperate to be away.

'Tonight then? At the inn?' It was Jack who spoke.

'What's this then?'

Brother Cassian strode into the middle of the men, used to taking the centre of a space, and something of that authority remained, even though he was only a novice.

Jack looked him up and down, contemptuous of a man in a habit. 'Nothing to concern you – Brother.'

But the other masons were walking away. The monks paid their wages, they didn't want any trouble with them.

Linnet had seen men undone by their debts before. Tom could have been undone by the masons arriving, with their wages from their last job hanging heavy on them. They had looked like ripe fruit for the plucking but it had turned sour.

She went to go after him but thought again. There was Tom by the harbour wall, thoughtful and kind Tom, and then there was gaming Tom.

Cassian turned to Linnet. 'He's like me brother was. He's beholden to the gaming, is he? Perhaps I can pray with him, turn him to the light?'

Linnet didn't say anything to that. What could she say. She looked at Cassian more closely now. He didn't move like the Brothers, used to their habits and their sandals, she could see him now, shifting his shoulders as if the rough material was itching him. It would be, she knew, unless you were lucky enough to have money like Godfreyd, and the choice of softer cloth. She wondered again what had led him to become a monk, but she wouldn't ask. There were better ways to find things out.

As she walked back to the Scriptorium, Cassian followed her. She hoped he wasn't going to question her now, but he didn't seem to have a purpose, just drifted in after her. He took out his worn copy of the Rule and sat down at one of the other chairs. She could see his mouth moving and his finger moving slowly across the page as he struggled to make out the words. Eventually he threw the book down in a fit of temper, and stood up.

She picked up the book and gave it back to him. 'It gets easier you know. The more you work at it. You must have taken time to become a carpenter, it didn't happen a day to the next, did it?'

For a moment she thought he was going to hit her. His face had darkened and she could see his hands tense, but he turned and left instead, hissing, 'There's nothing a woman like you can teach me.'

*

The noise from the tavern was greater than usual that night, and Linnet could hear loud shouts from across the square. She went in to see if she could talk to Tom but he was sat with the masons.

'More ale for my good friends here!' he shouted, waving his tankard at Beth who was serving.

'I'll see your money first, Tom,' she said, giving him a straight look.

In reply he just scattered coins at her, turned away and roared with laughter at something one of the masons said.

Jack looked up and caught Linnet's eye and made a coarse gesture, which had her blushing. She left the inn, wishing she could be Mary again and gesture back, not the quiet Linnet who kept her head down and her tongue clean.

The Prior's parlour was lit up with many candles, the good ones. The Inspector and the Prior were talking loudly, the desk piled high with manuscripts and books. Seeing her passing, the Prior called her in.

'Linnet, we need you to order these.' He gestured at the piles of old accounts, some of which had mildew on the bindings. How far back was the Inspector going?

She fetched her pen from the Scriptorium to make marks as she worked and sorted. Marcus was working on one of the books, splattering ink as he wrote. He had his arm bent around the book, hiding it from Linnet's view, hoarding the numbers. From time to time, he would look up to see what she was doing and sigh and shake his head, but she ignored him. If the Prior thought Marcus could do it all, he wouldn't have called her in.

As she worked, the men forgot she was there and resumed their conversation.

'The Bishop is looking for more revenue?'

'Yes, the King is a man who watches the pennies, wherever they fall in his kingdom. The Bishop is one of his most trusted advisers so he is wanting to prove how strict he can be with his houses.'

'But the King himself won't concern himself with the likes of us, surely?'

'The Bishop tells me that the King reads all the documents that pass across his desk. He's not a man who likes to rely on others to know what is happening. He checks it all himself.'

Linnet could see the Prior stroking his upper lip as he thought.

'I have hopes, Father Nicholas. I have big hopes for this Holy Island.' He leaned forward, the better to capture the Inspector's attention.

Linnet kept her head down and listened quietly.

'This is the heart of St Cuthbert, our Priory here – is it not? I know some say the saint's bones should return here, not stay at Durham, but of course that is not what I think.'

The Prior gestured politely to the Inspector, and through him to Durham. The Inspector acknowledged the courtesy with a wave of his hand.

'But we could become a centre of learning, of scribing, a centre for books. We only produce a few poor chapter books and prayer books now but we could start a full scriptorium, dedicated to St Cuthbert. A pilgrim could come on from Durham, walking across the dangerous sands to the place where the saint drew his comfort, to the Inner Farne to see where he passed his last days and lay their hands on his resting place?

'We've still got the pilgrim's door into the Priory, and that resting house at Beale – we could open it up again. I think it slept fifty pilgrims a time before.'

So this was his purpose, a holy place to rival Durham, a way for him to become a great prior, his name recorded in all the books they produced. But was it dangerous of him to tell the Inspector this? Would he feel the Prior was setting up the Priory to challenge Durham?

'You'd need more than a woman scribe for that though, wouldn't you?' The Inspector sounded doubtful and the two men turned to look at her. Not forgotten after all. She kept her head down, smarting a little from 'poor chapter and prayer books'. Her work was better quality than that drunken scribe had been making before she arrived.

'Linnet could train some of the younger monks. Brother Luke is learning how to stitch quires together. He could learn a good hand too, don't you think, Linnet? And maybe Brother Maykin?'

She nodded. Luke did have a steady hand and he could read and write well. It was the first she'd heard of a plan to train him though. Maykin, however, they'd have a hard job keeping him still enough to write for any time.

The Prior began to talk about the cattle and the tanner and the prices of skins but the Inspector interrupted him.

'Well the Bishop would look favourably on a profitable scriptorium, I'm sure.' He looked tired and stood up to leave. 'Enough for tonight though, don't you think? The real business is this report. The rest can wait.'

The Prior nodded courteously but Linnet caught his irritation as he looked down. He'd wanted to talk more about his great hopes and was offended by the Inspector's lack of interest. Seeing Linnet watching him, he snapped at her to leave too.

'Get gone, Linnet, you've no need to be here any longer.'

She wasn't tired so she went to the stables, the masons were sleeping in the outhouse next to them. Maybe she could find Jack and persuade him she really wasn't Mary. Or would it be more dangerous to pay him attention? She wanted to find the

Dutch mason if there was one too, to hear what he might have told Oswyn. She paused in the doorway, unsure what to do.

She could hear low voices in the stalls and crept in, curious, her back against the rough wood, feeling the splinters prickling through her clothes, her feet in damp straw that she tried not to rustle.

'Did anyone see you coming here?'

That was Godfreyd.

'No, everyone's abed.'

Wait. That was Tom. Why was he meeting Godfreyd? She peered round the edge of the stall. They were standing close. She couldn't see their faces, just their shapes in the dim moonlight. Godfreyd was taller than Tom, and broader. Tom touched Godfreyd's cheek but Godfreyd pushed his hand away.

'Not now. I wanted to talk to you about Oswyn, were you there when they pulled his body out?'

'Yes. He swam every day. We all thought him mad for it but every day, there he was, walking out of the sea again as if he'd been paddling in the shallows.'

'Did anyone question it? That he drowned?' Godfreyd's voice was urgent, scared maybe.

'No, no one else swam. Why are you asking about it?' It was clear Tom was uneasy talking about it.

'He hated me, Tom, he really hated me, but I can't believe he's gone.'

'He did like folks' secrets that's for sure. Did he know about—'

'No. Not this. Just what I was sent away for.'

Godfreyd turned away and Linnet caught sight of his face, now ugly with grim satisfaction.

'I'm glad he's dead, I'm glad he's rotting in the Infirmary.'

Tom sighed. 'Come now, Godfreyd. The man was a prick

for sure, but no one deserves to drown.' But she could hear something else in his voice, something he wasn't saying.

'I wouldn't go talking about it anyway,' he went on. 'You weren't the only one who hated him. Linnet is glad he's dead too, and—'

But Godfreyd spoke over the other names he was saying. 'Linnet? The scribe woman?'

'She said he was threatening her with telling her secrets.'

Godfreyd's face must have said something because Tom laughed at the idea.

'No, she wouldn't have killed him. I saw her face when his body was on the shore and she were as astounded as anyone else.'

Linnet was frozen with fear and rage. How could Tom tell Godfreyd what she'd said? She was angry with herself too, a fool for thinking she could start talking. They were talking too quietly now so she didn't hear what else was being said, although she thought she heard 'Warham', jumping only as a loud croak interrupted them. Could he be talking about the indulgences too? How dare he!

Meanwhile, Pol had flown into the stable and Linnet took advantage of the noise to creep away again, back to her room, her mind busy with what she'd seen and heard. As she left, she thought she saw another figure, also hiding in the shadows, but when it didn't move, she wondered if she were mistaken.

It wasn't the first time she'd seen men touch each other, but she'd not known Tom was that way. Godfreyd was different. She must have been right about him and Benedict then. Who on earth thought punishment for lusting after men was best served by sending him to a monastery? No one who had ever been to a monastery, that was for sure.

If Godfreyd had wanted Oswyn dead, had he helped that happen? Perhaps they'd quarrelled. The cut on Oswyn's face could have come from being struck by a ring. Godfreyd wore one, his family's seal that he'd managed to keep despite becoming a monk. Who else did Tom mean – who hated him? Would Godfreyd have told Tom if he had killed Oswyn? They were talking to each other about everything it seemed, no secrets there.

Anger kept her warm as she returned to her room. She didn't care about Godfreyd, she'd not liked him and she'd known there was something wrong about him. But Tom? Her friend Tom was a sinner and a sinner with a man she despised. Even worse, he would casually use her secrets, throwing her words about as if they were nothing to him.

Chapter Eleven

She'd not been long asleep when the noise woke her, and everyone else in the Priory she was sure. It was a crashing noise, louder than the sea all around, and then a horrible high-pitched keening and screaming.

She could hear commotion around her as people ran down to the stables, where the noise was now added to by the horses who were frantic and thrashing about. The stable boy was trying to calm them but that screaming kept riling them.

Linnet was in her shift and the cold was burning through her as she moved quickly through the crowd of horrified onlookers outside the old kiln house, next to the stables. Somehow she found herself inside just as the Prior held up a candle to see what was happening.

The terrible whiteness of a face, frozen in horror, still breathing, but surrounded by the fallen stones from the old kiln, crushing the air out of his body as he tried to struggle free. All could see it was to no avail. Blood was already seeping out amongst the dust and dirt on the floor.

She could see his eyes flitting about from shadow to shadow as he tried to say something. She thought she heard him say, 'But I didn't know, I didn't know. He didn't share a thing with me,' but by then the monks were all crowding in, shouting in horror and trying to pull the stones off him. The

Prior, the Inspector and Cassian were at the front, but despite everyone's efforts, the air had been crushed from him and the light left his eyes as his head lolled down at an uncomfortable angle, a trickle of blood from his mouth joining the dust on the floor.

The Prior held up his hand in the flickering candlelight and said simply, 'Stop,' and the monks who had been so frantically pulling and pushing at the rubble of stones became still.

Linnet could hear their heavy breathing as they stood in the shocking silence, and the faint whimpering of someone beginning to cry, was that Luke? She looked around at the faces all touched with horror and disbelief. How had this happened?

The Inspector was first to break the silence, pushing back his cowl and turning to the Prior. 'Why was this dangerous pile of stones left here? And what was your monk doing out of his bed at this hour?'

The Prior flinched. 'It was a kiln, and we had plans to remake it in time, but I… I think we had forgot it.'

Linnet suddenly thought of Isabelle, her game of playing amongst these stones – and her heart skipped but then she saw her, at the Prior's side, face agape at the body in front of her, hand creeping up to take the Prior's who squeezed it without looking at her.

The Prior looked around. 'Does anyone know why Brother Maykin was here? At this hour? What he might have been doing?'

A confused jumble of voices rose up but none seemed to have an answer. A jape of some sort seemed to be the only thought that they had. Maykin was widely known for his silly ideas, and perhaps he was planning something here to be played in the morning.

'Let this be a lesson to you, Brothers,' the Inspector said

with an air of finality. 'No need to be out of your beds or planning tricks, no need—'

'Enough for now, man, let's come back in the light and take poor Brother Maykin to his rest and we can save the sermons for his funeral.' The Prior's words contained a thin edge of fury and the monks began to file out of the small space, going back to bed, although who would sleep now.

The Inspector did not look best pleased to have been stopped in this way, but he nodded and left too. Soon only Linnet was left, with the body of the young monk disappearing into the dark now with the candles gone. Although fear was beginning to wake in her, she was frozen to the spot, still wondering. Why had he been here? What did those half-heard words of his mean?

The little moonlight lingering in the doorway showed her the scuffed floor, the tumble of the stones, and the monk's hand dropped down and still. She saw something still gripped in his hand and steeled herself to unpeel his fingers, one by one, until the scrap of paper came loose.

And then the horror rose in her again and she fled, back to the safety of her cell with the images of the death playing and replaying in her mind as she tried in vain to sleep.

Chapter Twelve

She must have slept because she woke with a mixture of fear and rage, rage at Tom. It had hardened with the night and stayed with her during the day as she made sharp marks on the parchment. She felt distressed and betrayed. She knew it was her own fault for talking to Tom. Why had she trusted him? She'd been an ignorant child when she knew him before. She didn't know who he was now.

The Priory was sullen, a spark gone out of it as the monks went about their duties. Maykin's body had been dragged clean of the stones as soon as it was light, and placed into a winding sheet. As Oswyn's body had not yet been buried, the decision was taken to put both bodies in the same grave, and hold the ceremony for them both. All other duties were stopped for this to happen right away, the Inspector eager to have it done and the Prior seeing no reason to wait any longer.

Poor Maykin, Linnet thought, always claiming to be so close to Oswyn and now pressed up against him for all eternity.

After most of the light was gone, she went to the kitchen for food, and Tom was there. His open, friendly face made her want to slap him.

'Come sit with me, Linnet?' he asked.

She shook her head and pushed past him, going to sit with Isabelle in the far corner, turning her back to him.

When they were done eating, she tried to get past him without him seeing, but he stopped her, puzzled by her manner. Seeing she wasn't going to talk to him, he turned to Isabelle instead.

'Come see what I caught today – it's an ink-fish.'

Isabelle's attention was caught and she followed him out. Unwillingly, Linnet followed. She liked seeing the strange things he found in his net, but she wasn't forgiving him.

The moonlight was good enough to pick out their way to the shore, and he had kept it in the prow of his boat, in a pool of water, surrounded by wet sacks, so it was still alive. One of the creature's eyes stared balefully at them, with an edge of Linnet's same fury, she thought.

'Can you eat it? Why is it called an ink-fish?' Isabelle asked.

'You can eat pretty much anything you take from the sea, but you'd want to cook it well. Some won't though, they say it's a sinful creature. If they got hungry enough, mind… Sometimes it has ink in it, black ink.'

'It's not always easy to know sinful creatures,' Linnet said, but she was also thinking about what the ink would look like, how it would write on the page and whether it would keep its colour well.

Isabelle was busy poking the animal with a stick, squealing a little as the tentacles reacted, until the creature snatched the stick and tossed it over the side.

They all stood amazed for a minute.

'I'm going to put 'im back,' Tom said suddenly. 'Any creature that knows how to do that deserves another life at least.'

He picked it up warily at arms' length, the tentacles swirling around in the air, looking for purchase, and threw it out into the dark sea.

Isabelle squealed at the splash, then ran off laughing and chattering with Pol who had been watching it all with close attention but from a very safe distance, leaving Tom and Linnet there.

'What's up with you then? Is it Maykin? We are all sad, I know—'

'I saw you with Godfreyd.'

The words came out as a low hiss, far harder than she'd intended, and he flinched as if she'd stung him.

'Saw me where?'

'The stables, you were touching.'

He sat down heavily in the beached boat, the breath knocked out of him. She could see a tinge of grey in his dark hair now, caught in the moonlight, and the shadows carved deep lines on his face. The silence between them grew, sharpening with the ever colder night air.

'What do you want me to say then, Linnet? I won't say I'm sorry, it's who I am.'

What did she want him to say? She wanted remorse from him and to have a better sense of who he was, but also she wanted an apology, for telling her secrets, and she wanted to know what he'd said. How much was she in danger? She'd trusted Tom, more fool her, but she would never have trusted Godfreyd.

'Why Godfreyd?' she settled on at last.

It was the biggest of her burning questions, one she kept coming back to. She thought Tom was a better judge of men than to be keeping company, to be sinning, with one she found so unpleasant. She didn't care about what they'd been doing. She knew it was a sin but she knew a lot of things were sins that bothered no one.

'He's not all he seems—'

'Nor are you,' she snapped, and again he recoiled.

'He's not just the arrogant monk you see. He's kind, he worries, he was crushed by his family casting him out.'

'Casting him out for what you and him do together – I'm right, aren't I?'

Tom nodded, shame staining his face, but then angry too.

'You're no one to tell me what's sinning and what's not, Linnet. You've told me about your thieving and your – whatever happened with them indulgences. You've no right to stand as priest above me.'

'You were no one special to him. I've seen him with others. Why did you trust him with my secrets? I trusted you.' It was a quiet shout, the key to why she felt so betrayed by her friend.

He flinched when she mentioned others but didn't look surprised.

'It were nothing, just words when we were chatting.'

She got up abruptly.

'It was not nothing. It was my secrets I was telling you and you were spilling out freely to your fellow sinner, your monk lover. I'll not be talking to you again, Tom, I can see I can't trust you. You're not who I thought you were. I knew you were flawed with your love of the dice, but you're sick at heart, aren't you? A sinner to the core, a shadow of a man who doesn't know the meaning of the word friendship.'

As she turned to go back up to the Priory, she bumped straight into Cassian. How long had he been standing there? A glance at his shocked face told her he'd heard much.

Tom tried to speak but Cassian held up his hand. 'I'll not be hearing from you, sinner. Spreading your wickedness about this Priory. Brother Benedict told me sommat, but I hadna taken his word for truth. Now I ken otherwise.'

And with that, the novice left. Linnet looked at Tom's

stricken face and almost felt pity but the anger overcame her again, and she left too.

The next day she resolved to avoid Tom, even though her anger was waning. She would come back to him in a few days, tell him why her secrets were dangerous, explain why she didn't want him to tell anyone, not even Godfreyd if he was always talking to him.

She busied herself with the work, getting lost in the manuscript, still working out the text but very close to finishing.

'Have you seen Tom?' It was the Prior, standing in the light from the doorway. Maybe Tom was hiding away too.

'Not since yesterday,' she replied, but that didn't seem to satisfy the Prior who wandered about the Scriptorium, picking up a dish of ink here, a brush there.

'He should have been out fishing with the others this morning and they were asking after him. They thought I'd put him to work but I've not had anything for him since our trip to Inner Farne. It's not like him, Linnet, he's a man of habits.'

She held back a laugh, he was certainly a man of habits, Godfreyd's habit for one. If she could laugh, was she nearer to forgiving him?

She nodded politely and waited for the Prior to go, which eventually he did but not before instructing her to ready a desk and chair for Brother Luke.

Isabelle came in next, Pol perched heavily on her shoulder, asking after Tom, she wanted to find another ink-fish.

'I don't think he fishes one of them out each time, but why ask me? Go down the shore and ask there. I'm busy and I'm not his keeper.'

Isabelle made a face and left, but not before Pol, hopping on the table, had almost spilt the ink, and not before Isabelle had taken a scrap of parchment, thinking Linnet hadn't seen her.

Linnet shrugged. It was too small to be of use to her and the child may as well play with that as anything else.

She was so deep in her work that she wasn't aware Isabelle had come back until she saw the scrap returned with her drawing of the ink-fish. Five arms, not eight. But she'd caught the beaky look on the creature's face and it made Linnet laugh.

Maybe she'd show it to Tom later, a bit of a peace offering, if not coming directly from her, a way back into their friendship again.

Next was Cassian. The novice was agitated, looking about him rapidly, but not catching her eye. She wondered if he'd said something to the Inspector about what he'd overheard.

'Has ye seen Tom? I'm – I have to—' He stopped, unsure about what to say next.

'No, not since yesterday. Have you asked amongst the fishermen or been to the inn?'

'Aye.' He sat down heavily. As if he'd forgotten she was there, she could hear him begin to pray, a muttering and a confusion of words in Latin and English, and then, without any warning, he slumped to the ground and began to fit. He moved violently and she could see the stain growing on his habit where he had pissed himself.

Linnet froze. Should she get Godfreyd? Call for the Inspector? Try to help him? But even as the questions flurried through her mind, Cassian sat back up, the light coming back to his eyes as he wiped his mouth to rid himself of the froth that had gathered there. He patted himself too, flinching as he felt the wetness at his groin.

He looked at Linnet, his face overcome with shame, and a touch of fury.

'Are you – do you need me to…?' She faltered to a stop.

With an effort he got up, she could see tiredness sweeping over him like a tide.

'Nay, it's nothing. Ye saw nothing, ye ken?' And with that he was gone.

Chapter Thirteen

A noise had woken her. She lay still, trying to recognise it. It was light, maybe an hour after dawn. There it came again. A thin scraping sound. There was someone in the room with her.

She sat up slowly, looking around carefully and trying not to show fear. It was only Isabelle.

The child was on the floor near the door, Pol beside her, and she was scratching at the wall with a fingernail.

'What are you doing in here? What do you want?'

She didn't look up. Scratch, scratch, scratch.

'Isabelle, you can't just come in here whenever you want.' Linnet felt obscurely annoyed that her fear was for nothing.

'Everybody dies.' She spoke in a flat, almost weary voice.

'Well yes.' Was she just simple after all?

'I don't care. I has Pol.' Her hand crept away from the wall for a moment to stroke the bird's head. He cawed affectionately and stretched his neck out.

'Why are you talking to me about people dying? Is it about Brother Oswyn? I thought we talked about that, you didn't—'

'No.' Her voice was still flat. 'It's Tom.'

Linnet shook off the last of her sleep. 'What do you mean?'

'He's dead. He did it to hisself. I don't care. Everybody dies.' Scratch, scratch, scratch on the wall.

But Linnet was already running down to the outer courtyard where people were gathered, and she kept hearing Tom's name. She tried to keep breathing but something solid was sitting on her chest.

She ran straight into the priest.

'Can't you ever look where you're going?' he spat at her.

She took a step backwards, words falling out of her like stones. Tom, dead? What was happening?

Cyrus looked her up and down slowly before answering. 'Yes, your friend is gone. He's sinned against God for the last time, hanging himself like that.'

Her shocked face must have stirred him to a little pity.

'We all knew he were gaming away his money faster than he could fish for it. It's no wonder the Devil caught him at his despair and he did for himself.'

'Where—'

'He's in the tithe barn. The fishermen will be cutting him down soon. They're not to bring him to me though, you tell them. I'll not have a sinner like him in my churchyard.'

His last words were yelled after her as she was running again, away from the Priory towards the tithe barn, swept clean, half empty for this year's harvest. It sat a short way off the road, solid and comforting. The door was half-open and she could hear voices inside, solemn and low.

She pushed her way in past the men, looking up quickly with horror at the swinging feet, the blackened face, the clumsy knot tying him to the beams, before she turned away.

'Sir Cyrus says not to bring him to the church. Where will you take him? You won't leave him—' The words were coming out in a rush, as she tried to catch her breath.

'No, no.' One of the fishermen stopped her. 'We'll take care of him.'

'And it's Tom? It truly is Tom?'

She couldn't bear to look up again, she'd seen nothing of the man she knew when she looked up. Was it someone else? Was Isabelle mistaken? Oh – Isabelle. Her heart lurched as she thought of the child huddled up against the wall.

'Yes, yes it's Tom.' The same man, Peter, was talking to her kindly. 'We'll take care of him, he'll be with us at the end.'

The walls of the barn felt like they were crushing against her and there were too many people. She started to leave but had a sudden thought.

'Who found him?'

'It were Isabelle, that child with the raven that runs around. She'd followed her bird here I'm guessing.'

She was outside again, standing with her feet touching the sea, looking out as if to see Tom on his boat, although she knew that couldn't be. She knew she needed to go to the child, comfort her, but she couldn't move right now. If she moved, she'd be travelling through the air and even the air felt like it would hurt her.

She didn't know how long she was there but she saw the women coming up from the village, carrying a winding sheet. She saw the men carrying that sheet, solid with a man's shape, back out into the thin, cold winter sunshine and place it down by the boats.

There was a low discussion, then the men began to carry it again, away from the beach, taking shovels with them. She followed, she didn't know why. They were walking the path between the island and the land, walking without speaking. Following the tide as it receded. They set the sheet down and began to dig. A phrase came to her. 'Between the sea and the land.' That's where you buried someone who took his own life. And how right for a fisherman.

Back in the Priory, Linnet almost felt as though she were at sea, the floor rocking beneath her. She'd looked everywhere for Isabelle but no one had seen her. The monks were gossiping about the death but most hadn't had much to do with Tom. It was the sin, not the person they were talking of. Not a friend. Oh God, had he done this to himself thinking she despised him? Guilt washed over her.

Godfreyd came out of a doorway rubbing his eyes and yawning. If he'd worked late in the Infirmary, the Prior let him miss Prime for a little more sleep, something he took full advantage of. She saw him look around at the gossiping monks, confused, and then watched his reaction as the information fully reached him. His face revealed nothing but his hands were twisting the cord of his habit, over and over again.

'Ah. A fisherman was it? A dicer? The devil finds those…' He coughed and looked away. Was it his sin that had driven Tom to kill himself? She hated him then for his perverted desires which had corrupted the man she cared for, and she hated herself for the friendship she could no longer mend.

Benedict came to him and whispered something in his ear. Godfreyd's mask slipped slightly, and he pushed him away, hard, but Linnet couldn't bring herself to care about the quarrels and botherings of the monks now. As she was thinking this, Godfreyd looked up and caught her watching. His eyes sharpened, glaring at her, demanding something from her.

Pol flew past and she followed him, out of the Priory gates up to the Heugh and onwards, clambering down the little bit of cliff there and across the wet sands and the slippery black rocks to Cuddy's Island, where she saw Isabelle staring out to sea. It was barely an island, just a lump of slightly bigger rock, and then the small shape of the child hunched up, surrounded by the sea and the sky.

She sat down next to her on the cold stones of the ruined chapel, the half walls providing a little shelter from the wind cutting across the sea. Pol butted the child's hand gently again and again until she stroked him.

'I'm sorry, I didn't understand what you were telling me before,' Linnet said, putting out a hand to comfort her but withdrawing it as Pol hissed.

'Sir Cyrus says he were a sinner. He were a sinner. It were self-killing. I hate him now.'

Isabelle's words came out evenly, no emotion behind them at all.

'He – he was our friend, Isabelle, wasn't he?'

'Friends don't leave you.'

It was as if she had closed herself off. She seemed to have grown overnight and her face looked more pinched. She was older, a hard little soul in her small body now. The only sign of warmth, the hand on her raven.

'Isabelle!'

The voice was loud, carrying across the waves, the Prior calling from the beach below the Heugh. They looked up.

'Come now, Isabelle, and you too, Linnet. There's work to be done for both of you.'

They picked their way back across the muddy causeway to the Holy Island and the Prior, the waters were rising and they were only just in time. The rocks were half-submerged and Isabelle slipped more than once, but although she must have hurt herself, she didn't cry out.

Linnet worked on the last pages of the prayer book, shutting out everything except the clean lines and swoops of the ink on the page. When her back ached or her wrist felt strained, and she was brought back to the room, Tom's death overwhelmed her anew. She pushed back hard to drive it from her thoughts and force herself to work.

Although her father's work had been all about death, she'd been protected from it. He carried rolls, in honour of the abbots or priors, and the monks wrote their prayers on them, but none of it meant anything to her. They'd not seemed to mean much to the monks they met either, it was all about what prayer or turn of phrase they would add to the rolls, how they could show their best Latin and their best inks.

Her mother had died when she was small. She had no memory of her at all, just living with her father in Durham until she was big enough to travel with him. She wondered sometimes if her father was dead. Would she find out? A ship could sink, a horse could throw you. Or someone could have killed him. Everybody dies. Isabelle's words came back to her again.

There was a cough from the doorway, Linnet jumped, her pen skidding across the page and making marks she didn't intend. It was Brother Luke.

'The Prior told me to come and you would show me the prayer book,' he said.

She sighed and then stood up to let him come closer to the desk, welcoming the chance to keep her mind away from what grieved her.

'It's nearly finished but you can see how I mark the lines first to keep the words level.'

He looked interested, bending down to look more closely at her writing. He was young, only on the island some months. She'd not spent much time with him before.

'What are those words by themselves on the bottom of the page?'

'Those? They're catchwords, to show how to put the quires

together, it's the first word on the next page that follows on from this one when it's all sewn together.'

Linnet kept her catchwords small, almost hiding at the bottom of her page. Some trimmed theirs off after the manuscript was bound, some made a spectacle of them, little rabbits on horseback carrying a pennant with the word, or a dog chasing it like a squirrel.

She gave him a scrap of parchment and a nearly worn-out pen and told him to try the Pater Noster on it. He would have to make his own pens soon too. After she had scraped off her errors, she started on some new gall oak ink as she would need more in a few weeks. Grinding the oak galls again and again, finer and finer, letting the movement take over from thought.

She lit a candle – one of the ones she'd stolen from Brother Oswyn, and the Scriptorium became a warm, small place of safety. Peaceful working, no talking, no thought beyond what they were making.

Suddenly Godfreyd was there and it felt like the world outside was crashing in, like waves on the shore. She saw his face was stern and sour as he told Luke to go to the Infirmary.

'But the Prior said I was to learn from Linnet to do the—'

'You're practising script, aren't you? You can do that with my physyk book – I need some herb names entered there.'

Luke left obediently following in the wake of the taller monk as he swept out of the room.

The peace shattered, Linnet went to get some food. The kitchen was unusually quiet. Tom had been well liked. People touched each other lightly on shoulders and nodded but there wasn't a lot of talk. Three deaths in such a short time had made them uneasy.

'Where's Isabelle?' she asked Ann.

'The Prior has her doing something for that duck of his.'

Ann rolled her eyes. The kitchen women didn't think much of making pets of food.

Jack sat down next to her, forcing her to make herself smaller to give him room. She dropped her eyes quickly but he was pressing his elbows up close as he tore into his food.

'Pity about your man Tom,' he said, mouth open and chewing. 'Still, he should have known his bounds, dicing with us.'

She stopped herself saying what she wanted to throw back at him. Remember, Linnet not Mary.

'Did you win all his money then?' she asked mildly, with what he took for admiration.

'No, he had plenty more – he were still moneyed after he paid us back. Wouldn't have lasted, mind.'

'So he hadn't lost all his money?' Maybe it was the sinning with Godfreyd that had driven him to despair after all.

'Nah – I said. He had more.'

Jack was tired of talking about Tom and his money, but talking to Linnet had him thinking about Mary again.

'You're not related to a Mary are ye? You do look awful like her.'

'No, only my mother long dead,' she said quickly. Everyone had at least one Mary in their family.

'Only that Mary I was telling ye about, she could scribe a little too, and I fancy it were Guy who had taught her.'

Linnet had taught Guy everything he knew. She bit back on saying that. They didn't let others know, much safer for him to be the one everyone knew and paid.

'My father and the monks we met taught me to scribe,' she said. Stick to the truth as best she could. 'From when I was a small girl, scraps of parchment and small feathers.'

He didn't really care, grunting and turning back to his food. He was still taking up more than his space on the bench though, his legs spread, one pressing against her, and Linnet finished off quickly to be gone.

The door to the Prior's parlour was open. She looked in as she went past. Isabelle was crooning gently to the duck, her face still numb but her body more relaxed. The Prior was in his chair, eyes shut, his fingers tapping on the side of the chair in time to the child's crooning, a tear or two falling unnoticed down his face.

Chapter Fourteen

Brother Luke was in the Scriptorium again the next morning.

'Did Brother Godfreyd not need you?' Linnet asked. She didn't want him coming in again to disturb them if they were working.

Luke looked ill at ease.

'The Prior said I must be here. The Inspector agreed too. Did you hear him talking about that fisherman last night?'

Linnet supposed that had been in the Chapter House so no, she would not have heard that. She wondered if Cassian had told the Inspector about Tom's sins yet.

'He talks a lot of sense, that Inspector does. It's not enough to be a monk and be praying, you know, it's about letting God see you, truly see you, see into your heart and trust Him to be testing you. He talked of Maykin too, but the Prior stopped him then.'

That didn't sound anything more than general praying, if Cassian had said something, that would be all the monks were talking about.

Luke's voice had risen and he was almost preaching at her. Then he seemed to remember she was only a woman, not a monk, and he looked down at the desk.

'You'll need to make your own pens, I can't be giving you

all mine.' Linnet wasn't going to be making pens for the two of them. 'You can have these feathers though.' She gave him half of what she'd collected recently, and showed him how to pare back the edges, give the nib a slit to draw in the ink, how the shape made the curl of the letters different. She told him swan feathers made the best pens but they could make do here with goose feathers, or any of the larger birds.

While he worked, she went back to the prayer book. It was nearly done. She'd be paid for it when Lady Margaret came to get it and then she could pay for her cloak. Tom hadn't asked for payment but she usually gave him a few coins as thanks if he did a favour for her.

The thought stabbed her as Tom's death came crashing back in again. Her cloak would be at Tom's. She didn't know if he had mended it or, what did it matter now? Tom was gone. No. She needed that cloak. She would get it now before his cottage was given over to someone. She'd not troubled to steal it only for it to get stolen from her in turn.

Leaving Luke at his pens, she left the Priory by the front gate, and walked into the village to Tom's house. No one was there, everyone busy with everything that needed doing. Nothing stopped needing doing just because someone had died.

The cottage was small, swept and clean. Not more than a room really. His nets were piled up in the corner, but in order, ready to be used again. She touched one. The rope was still damp from his last time out. Nothing looked different from when she used to stay here as a child, except for the emptiness.

He didn't eat here much, there was no food in the place, always going to the tavern or the Priory, she supposed. On his bed, her cloak, folded and mended. Tracing the stitches with one finger. Careful almost invisible stitches.

Holding back her tears because things needed doing, didn't

they, she picked it up and pulled it around her. She began to warm up properly for the first time in days.

She looked around the rest of the cottage, looking for signs of Tom's despair maybe? She didn't find much, although he had a nice little wooden box she was tempted by. She looked inside, it was empty. Take it? Best not. In a place this small, it might be known as Tom's box. From a shelf she took a few smooth black pebbles that felt pleasing to the touch. It looked like he'd been collecting them.

Back at the Scriptorium, Luke was reordering all her inks. She'd had them in their right place, the order she used them in with the oak gall at the front, then the colours behind. A few pots ready and some clothlets for when she started illuminating again.

'Stop that!' The words came out sharply before she could think.

He was startled but not sorry.

'The Prior told me I'd be in charge in here.'

'That as maybe, but you still need to learn and if you move my inks, I can't teach you, can I?' Even to Linnet that wasn't a good reason, but she didn't want everything touched, everything messed with.

It was enough for Luke though, and he put it all back, sullen but submitting to her wishes for now.

It was men again, taking up space wherever Linnet was. Even in this remote corner of England where she had fled to, she was still being made to feel smaller every day.

As Luke had started with the inks, she showed him her simple recipe for gall ink, not her special one that wrote so smoothly. He could have the bare information he needed, but her secret knowledge was another matter.

'You can use small ale or wine – wine writes better if the

cellarer will give you some. The longer you leave the crushed oak gall with the iron pieces and the wine, the darker the ink will be.'

He nodded like he was listening but she could tell he was only paying half a mind.

'Cover it with a cloth to stop flies getting in,' she showed him with a rag she kept for that purpose, 'and then your ink will be brewing.'

His high-minded look would do him no good. A scribe needed to be close with the kitchen and the stable and everywhere to get the materials they needed. Sure, some came with the pedlars and others, but it was the common items that made it easy to make the ink. A jug of wine here, an egg white or two there. He'd learn though, if he tried.

Linnet returned to the prayer book. She was on to the last page now. After the text was complete, she added a tiny linnet bird to the margin as was her custom. Luke was watching.

'Why did you add that?'

'Scribes often add something of themselves to their work,' she said. 'You should think about what you'd like as your sign. You could have a winged bull perhaps, like the Gospel Luke. Or a candle flame – Luke like light.' She'd seen some manuscripts where a scribe had put their name, but she thought that was wrong, too much interfering with the text on the page.

Luke liked that idea and spent a few minutes drawing small winged oxen and flickering flames on the scrap of parchment she'd given him the day before.

She went to find the Prior to let him know the prayer book was finished. She needed a new task to keep busy. Before she could knock at his parlour, she heard a loud noise, a lot of shouting and squawking and a fluttering from the inner courtyard.

'You shitting bird – you bit me!' Godfreyd roared, his usual smooth demeanour cracked.

Pol was perched triumphantly on the edge of the water basin, preening and smoothing his shiny black-blue feathers. The basin was set into the wall outside the Chapter House. A short line of monks were regarding him warily. There was water everywhere.

Cassian stepped forward to shoo the bird away but took a hasty step back when Pol went for him, wings flapping, claws outstretched. Faster than Godfreyd, he escaped injury.

The Prior came out of his parlour. 'What's going on here?'

He saw Godfreyd nursing his hand, a small, red gash showing that Pol had indeed pecked him.

'Well he has to get his dust off, don't he?' Isabelle said, defending the bird. She had turned up suddenly, as silent as a cat.

'Child, we cannot have birds in the Lavatorium basin, it's for monks to cleanse themselves before prayers.' The Prior was stern, glaring at Isabelle, who glared back.

'He allus does. It's his basin,' she said.

'Explains the feathers we always find here,' one of the monks said dryly.

'Take him away.' The Prior was implacable, not a trace of his usual fondness for the child in his voice.

'He's clean now anyways, come on, Pol.'

The bird stretched his neck to one side, and with what Linnet could only think was an evil smile if a beak could smile, squirted a stream of shit into the basin, before flying to the child and they ran, leaving fury behind them.

Godfreyd protested to the Prior, loudly declaring that the bird and the child were given too much freedom in a holy place. The Prior's face gave nothing away as he nodded. The Inspector came out of the parlour too, looking disdainfully at the dirty water and the monks now scrubbing out the basin.

In all the uproar, Linnet picked up the feathers Pol had plucked out. They would make good pens and having given Luke a share of her store, she had few left.

'There is no place in this Priory for an evil bird like that raven,' the Inspector said. 'I shall have to put it in my report if you don't take steps to remove it. They are the birds of doom and death.'

Cassian crossed himself, head bowed as he drank in the Inspector's words.

They'd had enough death recently but Pol wasn't to blame. But something was at the back of Linnet's mind, always just out of reach.

'*Deus pascit corvos*,' the Prior muttered, 'let's go back to the papers, shall we?'

He beckoned Linnet over. 'Do you have the prayer book for me? Bring it to me in the parlour.'

Linnet put the prayer book on the table, a feeling of pride running through her. The Inspector picked it up, turning it over and examining the text and the illuminations carefully. He hadn't noticed the linnet she'd added. She didn't think he would approve of a scribe leaving their sign.

'This is good work. You'll be teaching the monks, yes?'

'Yes, Brother Luke is working on inks and pens today. He needs to get his tools in order before he can start scribing in earnest. What's my next task, Prior?'

He dug through the chest of books, looking for something small.

'Ah yes, here it is, we need a copy of this book of the Gospels. It will have illustrations and we'll include the lapis lazuli when that comes.'

Linnet took the book carefully, looking through it. A typical Gospel manuscript but no illumination in this one.

'You must add the drawings and have five full pages for each Gospel, as well as their title pages. And Brother Luke can work on the text.'

Linnet would have felt more aggrieved but she was already lost in ideas for the pictures. Yes, she could get Luke to scribe the text. She could surely train him to do that well – he did have a good hand.

'Father, is that a book we will be paid for?' Brother Marcus, still pushing for his place as the new bursar.

'No, this is for Bishop Foxe. Sometimes we cast out a gift to get greater riches. Now, did you want to start on a new bursar's book?'

Finally, Marcus's patience had paid off. As Linnet left, she could see him pushing down the bubble of his joy as he tried to seem humble and grateful.

Linnet was turning into the Scriptorium when a hand grabbed at her wrist and sharply pulled her into the side of the passage, a dark corner away from the courtyard and the guest room.

Chapter Fifteen

'You bitch, you shamed him and now he's dead. He spent that last day hiding and praying and it was all because of you.' The words came out in an angry hiss and she turned to see Godfreyd glaring down at her.

She could feel the heat rising in her cheeks despite the cold of the day as she struggled to keep looking him in the eyes, and started tugging her wrist to get free. Her pride in the prayer book had let her forget about Tom for a little, but the worry that maybe she had driven him to kill himself came flooding back now.

She was wondering what to say but Godfreyd wasn't waiting for a reply, he had a message for her. Grabbing her other wrist so he had both of her hands in a painful grip, he bent down to her level, close to her face, and spat at her. The shock of the spittle hitting her face made her gasp.

'You will not last here, I will make sure of that. Watch your back, I'll—'

Linnet was scrabbling with her hand in his and managed to catch the wound where Pol had pecked him, and dug in a nail. Swearing and shaking his hand, he let go of her and brought it up to his mouth. He slapped her sharply before she could defend herself. She didn't wait for him to resume, but fled, heading for the relative safety of the Scriptorium.

Luke had gone, leaving scraps of parchment scattered over the desk. He must have got tired of practising and started to tear up what he'd been working on.

Annoyed and shaken by Godfreyd, more by his words than his actions, Linnet gathered up the scraps. They could have scraped them clean and used them again, but they were not much use in strips like this. The marks put her in mind of something, but again, it refused to come to her.

She used the back of one scrap to start noting what illustrations she would use for the Gospels. The traditional angel, lion, bull and eagle. And the lapis lazuli of course. Skies, Mary's dress, what else could she use it for? Maybe the Sea of Galilee – with the storm gathering above it.

Wait, what had happened to the scrap of paper in Maykin's hand? She ran quickly back to her room and felt amongst her clothes. It was there, in with her nightshift of course. She brought it back to the Scriptorium and spread it out carefully on her desk.

– Come and –

So someone had summoned him. To the kiln room perhaps? Why? Did this have something to do with his death or had the young monk been careless with the stones while he waited?

She looked at it more carefully, a coarse scrap of paper, such as was used all over the Priory, nothing from her Scriptorium, and a standard ink too, she could tell. As for the hand, it was cramped and mean, fitting into a small space for sure, but also tight in its letters. She resolved to remember the form of the letters in case it meant anything and what had happened to poor bright Maykin was no accident.

She shuddered. It had got dark. She needed more candles. Maybe the Prior would let her have some if this book were to help him set up the Scriptorium. And she remembered that she'd not got the coin for the prayer book.

The parlour was empty, just the mournful cuddy duck, still in its place by the cold fire. She thought it looked a little better. She was surprised the Inspector hadn't insisted it was put out, but maybe he'd not noticed it sitting there; cuddy ducks were very still and quiet when they wanted to be.

She walked past the Chapter House, but stopped as she heard the Inspector thundering at the monks.

'Be vigilant against the appearance of piety that does not hold piety in its heart. One thing may look like another, be wary.'

She could see Luke at the back of the room, face strained, eyes fixed on the Inspector, drinking in his words. He looked very young suddenly, he probably was. She thought he couldn't have rich or powerful friends, not to start his time here at this remote place – this Priory was full of the least wanted monks from what she could see. He was sitting a little way apart from the others. He'd not made friends yet apart from Maykin, who had been friends with everyone and was now gone.

'A fair face can hide the devil's snare!'

The Inspector was still talking, his eyes fixed and staring. The Prior stifled a yawn next to him. He was probably thinking of the comfortable evenings they normally had in here, with the fire warming them and the gentle talking, maybe with some reading of the Rule. Many of the monks plainly felt the same. Godfreyd was clearly not listening, his face sorrowful, his mind elsewhere. His earlier anger had left him, she could see. Had he loved Tom? She didn't think men loved men, even if they sinned together, but his face said otherwise.

Godfreyd looked around at his fellow monks before his eyes fell on Luke, who was sitting slightly forward, mouth open, eyes shining. Like a hawk spying a mouse, Godfreyd was suddenly still, and totally fixed on him. And behind Godfreyd, Benedict. Watching Godfreyd but with open-faced adoration and longing.

Cassian was next to Benedict, and Linnet saw him whisper something to him. Benedict's face showed a flash of irritation, then a crafty look. He pointed to Luke, discreetly, and Cassian nodded slowly.

What had Benedict indicated to him, Linnet wondered. She shuddered and walked on. She could go and sit in the kitchen, warm herself up, have a bite to eat, all in peace. But she was stopped by Jack, arm across the kitchen doorway, blocking her entrance. He leaned over her and grinned a little, moving one way and the other to stop her coming in. She wriggled quickly under his arm, remembering with pleasure when she had bit him, and imagining new ways to cause him pain. She looked around at the other masons, but didn't have the strength to try and find anything out tonight.

Ann was banging pots, provoked by the Priory rabble, those masons, who had to be fed but in her eyes clearly didn't deserve it. Linnet could see Isabelle in a corner, with her usual plants and shells all around her, muttering to herself, until the Cook swept down on her telling her to get that rubbish out of her kitchen.

Isabelle stuck her tongue out, but only after she had safely gathered her bits and was on her way out. She saw Linnet but didn't acknowledge her. Suddenly tired to her bones and missing Tom, she went to bed.

Linnet was aware of the monks during their night prayers and psalms, she could hear them going back to the dormitory, she could hear some of the masons having a loud argument about who could piss furthest, a hotchpotch of different languages, like all masons, somehow understanding each other though.

Finally, nothing could hold her back from falling into a deep sleep.

It was the quiet that woke her. She could see a few candles lit in the village houses as some were awake before their second sleep. The two sleeps that most practised here were seen as old-fashioned in the towns and cities, but she liked the peaceful middle of the night moments when one could hear quiet sounds and talking, without all the bustle of the day. And the thought that had been fluttering nervously out of her reach had finally come to her.

Of course Pol the Raven wasn't responsible for the deaths, but then maybe someone else was? She was thinking back to the way they died, the scratches on Oswyn's hand, the rope around Tom's neck. The scratches hadn't looked right to her at the time – they didn't seem natural. And what of Maykin? Why was he in the old kiln room in the middle of the night for no reason? What did that scrap of paper mean? Why would Oswyn drown where he usually started his swim – not when he was tired through at the end of it? And Tom hadn't killed himself because of his debts. He'd had money, he'd been spending it freely at the tavern the night before, but there was something else.

She let herself remember the swaying body in the tithe barn, the blackened face, the plain clothes, the staring eyes, the rope frayed and cutting into his neck – the rope. What was wrong with the rope?

She got up quickly and went through the inner courtyard, out of the small gate and down the road to the tithe barn. With the wind up and the darkness all around, it felt a much longer walk than in the daylight. She nearly fell once or twice but managed to right herself. Inside the barn, she felt around carefully, a splinter catching her as she found the stool still lying knocked over where they thought Tom must have kicked it. A large spider made her cry out as it crept away. And there, in the corner, the rope they'd cut when bringing his body down.

She brought it out of the barn to look at it in the pale moonlight. It had been cut above the knot, no one wanting to stand near the body untying it as it swayed there, and the noose pulled over his head. She traced the knot with her fingers, a simple, rough knot, strong enough to hold him for sure, but not the kind of fisherman's knots Tom tied.

She walked back into the village to his cottage, to go through the nets there. A few lights showed in the other nearby houses so she crept along quietly, not wanting to draw attention to herself. She knew Tom had different knots for different uses. He'd talked enough about them to her but she'd not really listened, just let him talk fondly about the many ways he could twist a rope. The nets were gone. Of course, the other fishermen would have taken them for their use. Foolish to think they would still be there.

The knot wasn't proof, she knew, but it didn't feel right to her, just as Oswyn's death didn't, just as Maykin's didn't. She thought back to what she'd heard between Tom and Godfreyd, Tom saying that others had hated Oswyn. Who else had hated him and why?

She hadn't hated Oswyn, but if he'd stumbled across her dangerous secrets she might have done. She'd certainly not liked him. What other secrets had he known? Godfreyd didn't think he knew about him and Tom, but if he'd suspected Oswyn knew, he was strong. He'd easily have been able to hold him under the water. But Godfreyd wouldn't have killed Tom and he blamed her of course. Maykin was often annoying, but she couldn't imagine anyone to have killed him purely for that.

And what about Cassian? She knew that those who had fits, they were sometimes not themselves, in a daze. Could he have harmed Tom? Was he so horrified by the sin that he had taken redemption into his own hands?

She sank down onto Tom's bed, weary with all this thinking. Was she just scratching around, trying to acquit Tom of self-murder? And herself from blame? It was too late for his soul if he'd been killed anyway. He'd been buried without rites and without sanctified land.

She wondered tiredly if God would find him anyway, if it wasn't his fault he wasn't in the right place. Maybe she could write him out a pardon. She was good at pardons, one of the main pieces of work she'd done for Guy. But of course it wouldn't help.

She roused herself, she couldn't sleep here in Tom's cottage. She needed to go back to her room. She looked around the room and took the two candles she found under the bed. She looked at the box again, empty but sturdy. The men had left it when they took the nets – it was no use to them. She'd take it and keep Tom's knot in it.

Early the next morning Linnet ran down to the boats drawn up on the shore, hoping to see more knots in the lines and the nets. Some fishermen were coming down to prepare for their day and she got a few curious looks as she examined the ropes but not much attention.

Tom's boat was by itself – pulled up onto the shore and carefully upturned. Linnet wondered if anyone would take it, or was that bad luck?

The Prior had come down too, getting into another boat for a trip over to Inner Farne. One of the men yelled over, 'No more cuddy ducks this time, eh, Prior?' and they all laughed. Linnet had a sudden memory of Tom scrubbing out his boat but she pushed it aside. She had to force herself back to the knots and ropes.

She couldn't be sure but she didn't think the knot on Tom's hang-rope matched any of the fishermen's knots. Even in the depths of his despair, she couldn't fathom Tom forgetting how to make knots. If a fisherman had strung him up, they would surely have done a proper knot too, so they couldn't be responsible.

Trudging back up to the Priory her mind was whirling. Who could she talk to about this? The Prior himself maybe? But he wouldn't want to think about the dreadful idea that Tom had been killed while the Inspector was still here. And she had no idea if he was behind any of the deaths, why should she trust him?

At that moment the Inspector stepped out of the parlour and beckoned to Linnet.

'I need dictee again,' he said abruptly and turned back into the room. Linnet had her tools on her, her little bag with inks and her pen and her knife, so she followed him in, exchanging a quick glance with the cuddy duck as it huddled down still lower to the ground. She wouldn't draw attention to it. She knew the value of being a quiet part of the room in dangerous places.

This time, he wasn't writing a report, it was a register of what he felt was wrong with the monks. Not just the monks here, but all monks. He talked so fast, Linnet struggled to keep up with him. Gaming monks, careless monks, dirty monks, lecherous monks. Or was he just marking what to look out for on his inspections?

Cassian was in the room, and when the Inspector stopped for a while, deep in thought, he stood up and came over.

'Father, may I tell 'ee about the evil I have—'

But the Inspector cut him off. 'Don't be talking to me about evil! I'll not be taking lessons from a foul-tempered novice who can't form his letters yet. I thought the Bishop must have seen something in you, something noble, to be with me on my travels, but now I see he wanted to send me with a dolt, a fool. Just to keep me mindful of how far man has to travel from the dull mud to the heavens.'

Cassian stood there, shame-faced, head down but with a determined set to his shoulders. She could see the rage he was holding in, but the Inspector continued, moving seamlessly from the string of sins about the Priory to the sins he saw in Cassian.

Eventually he petered out, and with a small nod to Linnet, unwilling witness to it all, he left to go back to his rooms.

Cassian made a noise, a strangled oath, and Linnet wondered if he would fit again, but he simply glared at her, as if she had had a hand in this scolding, and left too.

Linnet returned to the Scriptorium. No Luke this morning, so she took the chance to write down what she'd found so far. She had her own household book she'd found in another monastery. She'd torn out the few pages of notes the Bursar there had made, and it was hers now, where she could think on the page. It wasn't as good as talking it through but the only person she would have trusted enough to talk about something like this was Tom.

So she must work this out alone. If she were right and Oswyn and Maykin and Tom had been killed, or even if only one of them had, there was a murderer on this Holy Island. All three times, the causeway had been flooded so no one could have come over and gone back again, unless they had hidden somewhere before going back to the mainland. She felt sure the answer was closer to home though.

A fluttering at the door made her look up. Pol was walking towards her with his awkward rolling sailor's gait. He had something in his beak, something shiny. Was he bringing her something?

The raven stopped a little way into the room, keen black eyes watching her. She pretended to be occupied with her papers again and he came a bit closer. The floor was rough earth, strewn with a few rushes but not very clean. She had no urge to keep the room spotless, it was a good place to scribe in, that was all. Warily looking at Linnet from time to time and reassured that she wasn't paying attention, the bird dug a little into the floor and dropped the shiny thing into it. He covered it up again quickly, using his beak and his claws to pull the rushes back over it and then walked out again, watched by an amused Linnet.

She waited a few moments before going to see what he'd hidden in case he came back. It was clearly a hiding place he'd used before – there was a dead mouse which she moved carefully with the toe of her boot, and then the shiny thing. It was a fragment of parchment, a gilt letter. It seemed to glow in the dark room.

Linnet knew at once this wasn't a new piece of work, although the ink colours were bright and alive. It was too fragile for that and the hand was not current. Where had the bird found it? She smoothed it out carefully and put it to one side, and scraped at the floor to make good the bird's hiding place. She'd avoid that bit of earth now, she had no interest in rotting mice.

She went back out into the courtyard and then up the stairs to her room where she hid the fragment in Tom's box. Another mystery to untangle. She took out the bag of paper scraps she'd found in Oswyn's room. She would keep those in the box too, along with the scrap from Maykin's hand. Little pieces, little scraps, but maybe if she could find out how to put them together, she might have the answer.

On her way back to the Scriptorium, she saw Luke coming out of the Infirmary. He was moving stiffly and carefully, not his usual easy walk. She stopped him to ask if he was well.

'Of course.' He didn't meet her eye, hurrying away to join the other monks in prayer for Sext. As she looked after him, Godfreyd pushed past her carelessly, pausing to glare at her as he passed. Benedict jostled Luke roughly and caused him to gasp in pain as he caught the back of his heel, but the younger monk didn't say anything, just swallowed hard and bent his head in prayer.

That night Linnet went to the tavern. The Prior had given her the money she was owed for the prayer book when he returned from Inner Farne and she needed some warmth and comfort.

She took her tankard over to a dark corner, avoiding the villagers with their quarrels and their bawdiness, and the masons who were starting on another game of dice – this time with the parish priest.

The room was smoky from the fire, and smelled of warm bodies and their work. The fishermen smelled clean and salty, the farmers of the animal shit they'd been shovelling, the masons of their dust. She wondered if she smelled of ink and parchment. She'd seen them make parchment. It stank worse than anything she'd known, a far distance from a pretty Lady's prayer book in a sweet-lavender-scented room.

One of the masons, a big man they were calling Mice, gave Linnet a broad smile, and she remembered he came from the Low Countries. A Dutch mouse. She sat down next to him, ignoring Jack's raised eyebrow.

'Is your name really Mice then?' she asked, as she picked up a piece of bread.

'Mees,' he said sternly, but with a grin that belied the tone. 'It's a name in my country, as Bartolemew is here, I think.'

'When were you last in your country then?'

'A year or so back. The money is better here. I carve stone good – that right, boys?'

A distracted cheer from the rest of the masons who had lost interest in this boring talk.

'Which is your country then? Is it as beautiful as around here?'

That was enough. Mees settled into what sounded like a familiar litany of how wonderful his birthplace Bruges was, how the buildings were better, how many learned men and artisans there were.

'And have you ever heard of a scribe, John-the-Lies? I heard he'd gone there.'

Jack wasn't listening and she was careful to keep her voice low.

'Yes, yes, Fader John-the-Lies, he is a monk, yes?'

Struck dumb by what he was saying, she just nodded, hoping he would say more.

'He is working in a monastery there, in their library. Working with papers, soft work, not like stone. This mouse—' he poked his chest then – 'can nibble away at stone like a good cheese!'

With that, he turned back to the rest of the masons and Linnet sat, bread forgotten, while she tried to work out what her father was doing, was this what Oswyn had found out? And who her father was – a monk? That couldn't be right.

Suddenly Jack was too close to her and swaying.

'Now, I'm not saying you are Mary, but if you were,' he paused significantly, 'you might want to know that Guy's had his debts paid off and he's out of prison now.'

Linnet struggled to stay still and unmoved.

'I don't know a Guy,' she said.

'Well, as I said, if you were to, you might want to know he's freed. He's looking for whoever betrayed him – and he's all of a rage. So I've heard. If I were to pass on word that I thought Mary was here on this island, I reckon he'd run all the way up here just to have a word with her. A word with his fists.'

She couldn't help it – she flinched a little at that. Guy had always been ready with his fists. She looked up at Jack and made her mouth go slack with confusion.

'He might be coming up here anyways. I told him we were going to be doing a job for the Priory and we could take some ale with him.'

He laughed, enjoying goading her. He'd hit a mark if she were Mary or tormented some simple girl if she wasn't.

Linnet finished her drink and left, walking through the graveyard to the Priory. She was shivering despite the warmth of the last half hour. One reason she'd been feeling almost safe up here was the thought of Guy being locked away. She'd not betrayed him, but he would think she had. If he did find her, would she have time to explain? And anyway, what she had done hadn't been much better than betrayal.

Despite Mary's misgivings, they continued to make the indulgences for St Mary's-By-The-Sea. She wondered where Warham sold them, no one local would be buying. He didn't ask her to do any other work for him, not after the family tree which she had aged with a pale yellow ink, using different gall inks to make it look like different hands had filled it in over the years.

The money he paid for the indulgences was good, and Guy spent most of it on new clothes. She managed to get some from him for ink materials, telling him they were more expensive than they were, so she could keep some for herself, hidden away. She had the money for the family tree too that he hadn't known about.

After the first couple of times, Warham sent his men to

order and collect the indulgences. Broad, heavy-set men, they didn't speak much and showed no interest in what they were given. It was regular, once every five or six weeks, and soon Guy was spending the money in expectation of the next order.

He came in late one night. It was many months since she'd worried when he wasn't home by dark. He liked to think she was pining for him and fretting about who he was with, but she relished the peace, using the time to work quietly by herself. She had fallen out of love with him. She knew him now as the vain and spiteful failed scholar, lashing out at others when he felt small. She wondered if he missed his family but he rarely spoke of them, just a passing word or two about their lands in Buckinghamshire. He must have been a second or third son, or they would have kept him regardless of his manner, she was sure.

When they'd met, when she thought he would be a life for her, he had flattered her, spoke with genuine pleasure about her work. She'd mistaken that as admiration for her, not respect for a talent he was hoping to use for his own gain.

Crashing about in their rooms, she knew he was drunk, even before he opened his mouth and breathed ale into her face.

'Damn it, Mary, we need that money you have!'

She lay still, breathing carefully to feign sleep, but he wasn't fooled.

'I know you're awake, you subtle bitch.' Delivered in a low hiss, it was still a shock to find his hand on her throat, shaking her like a dog shakes a rat.

Scrambling away from him, she tried to speak soothingly, to find out what the urgency was. It was a liturgy of complaints, of small people who had no idea of why a gentleman like Guy might have to wait on settling his debts. She realised the men Guy owed had been threatening him, and he was scared.

'Why haven't Warham's men come this month? They've come every other time, once a month for more work.'

He'd spent the money then, the money they didn't have yet. In expectation of promises not made.

'But I have an idea!' Even in the gloom of the room she thought she could see his eyes brighten.

'If Warham can do it, we can too, look what I have here for you.' And with a flourish, he threw some cloth at her. She shook it out, trying to understand what she was seeing. Could it be a nun's habit?

She said, 'No, no, I'm not doing that,' and he was at her again, this time grabbing her hands hard. He looked carefully at her fingers, then up at her face and said, 'Which one do you want to lose?'

Before she could understand what he'd been saying to her, the sharp, hot-white pain took her breath away as he casually snapped her left little finger. As she sobbed and gasped in shock, he said simply, 'Next time, it will be one you use for your scribblings.'

She knew he needed her to scribe and illustrate, but she couldn't bear the thought of having that taken away. That was the last time she said no to him, until she left.

Guy scared her as did those who might follow him. She knew how to travel around the country keeping quiet and low to the ground while he couldn't enter a town without making a shout and a show of himself. What if Warham's men were looking for her too?

This group of masons were dangerous. They were constantly on the dice. She'd seen them cheating some of the other islanders for small sums. She could spot a thief when she saw them and at least one of them was a thief.

The Prior had hired them anyway, getting them cheaper

by providing 'table', the meals Ann made for them. He had the new floor to lay that the last gang of masons had got halfway through before a cathedral in the south had offered them more for urgent work on some new pillars. They were probably cheap. He liked to hire cheap. She wasn't always sure if the account books had the right sums in them. He and Oswyn had worked on those books together very late some nights.

All this musing was just her looking away from the danger she was in. Would word that she was here reach Guy? How did the masons pass the word along? Her father had been a great passer-on of messages. He'd always had what he called his message book, a love note here, a minor death there, some monies owed or a summons to a relative. And then he'd had the other messages, the hidden ones, the ones she wasn't supposed to know about, the ones set down in his own code that she'd never learnt to read. Would Guy need to have a message passed down or was he on his way already?

One of the faces in the tavern came to mind – the pedlar who was to see the Prior tomorrow. He'd come tonight before the tide cut the island off. He must be the one who had brought Jack the news that Guy was out of prison. There was no other way.

The black cat strolled past her, showing not a care. There was nothing she could do tonight. Maybe she could listen to the pedlar tomorrow and see if she could find out where he'd been. Then she could decide what she had to do.

She didn't sleep well. She woke up early, before the morning light and went out walking on the shore. She wasn't alone – the fishermen were gathered there, and Isabelle and Pol.

They'd dragged Tom's boat out to the shallows and were filling it with brush and dried leaves. Peter, the one who'd been kind to her in the tithe barn, saw her looking and came over.

'We're burning his boat this morning, at the dawning.'

She looked at him for more explanation.

'It's bad luck to take a dead fisherman's boat, if he died not – right. Anyway, there's no one to take his craft, what with him not having children and his mother dying last year.'

'So you burn it?'

'Aye, we send it off burning, to the sea. It's been the custom here for many years, I dunno if other places do the same, but it's the custom here.'

Isabelle was nearby, watching and listening. She darted to the boat and tucked something in the bracken before kicking through the waves back to the shore.

'What did you put in?' Linnet asked her.

The little girl shrugged. 'Just somefing. In case he weren't a self-killer after all.'

Linnet looked at her thoughtfully. Should she let her know she was wondering about Tom's death? No, she was just a child and anyway, it was a mishmash of thoughts right now, nothing firm as yet.

She stayed there on the shore, watching as the fishermen gathered more bracken and dried grass, and some put shells and stones in the boat. No words were spoken. This wasn't a funeral rite or a ceremony. It was a thing that needed doing, that needed doing right. She glanced over at the spot where they'd buried him, hidden now below the morning tide, and she thought his spirit was in his boat, if not his body.

The oldest fisherman stepped forward and lit the fuel on the boat with his candle, which he'd been carefully shielding against the light morning wind.

The sun hit the far edge of the water, turning it golden, mirroring the boat as it took light. They pushed it off and it steadily bobbed. The leaves and bracken caught fire and briefly flamed but it took a long time before the boat itself caught. The fuel kept it going, even as little waves put out the odd flame, and finally it was fully alight – burning strongly as it drifted a little further away, before it was nothing but a blackened hulk, slipping under the waves.

Once it was over, the fishermen got their nets and rowed away like any other day, leaving just Isabelle and Linnet on the shore, watching them go.

The tide put Linnet in mind of the pedlar. It was beginning to go out and he'd be leaving once he'd seen the Prior. She hurried back up to the Priory, slowing near the parlour to see if the door was open, if she could hear anything. But the door was firmly shut and although she could hear voices inside, she couldn't catch anything clearly this time.

Where would the pedlar go after he'd finished his business? The stables or the kitchen? She thought the kitchen for food to take with him on his way. He was plump, not one to wait for food to find him, rather on the hunt for it wherever it could be found.

She found Ann in the kitchen, her usual bad-humoured self. 'Coming to help or just for picking as usual?'

Information would have to be paid for so Linnet sat to peel and chop turnips. She hated turnips. Hated using her good knife on their scabby skins.

'Has the pedlar been here yet this morning?' she asked.

'No, he's coming in after he's seen the Prior. You got coin to spend then?'

If she wanted a reason to talk to him, she might have to spend, perhaps some gum arabica for a new ink.

'Where's he been before here?' she asked, trying not to sound concerned as her knife slipped on the stubborn turnips, almost catching at her hand.

'How would I know that then?' Ann was in no mood to chat, that much was clear. Linnet went back to her turnips.

She'd nearly finished the chopping when the pedlar came in, pulling his bags through the door, cheery and loud.

Ann did a quick bit of business with him, selling him some small pies for his trip. Linnet tried to get a little closer.

'Got far to go?'

'I'm bound for Newcastle down the coast,' he said, sitting down next to her. 'But I'll be doing all the towns and small places in between. I seen almost everywhere, you know.'

He smiled at her as if she were a simple, taking her for an islander no doubt. She decided to keep it that way, no need to go and get coin.

She gave him her best try at an admiring look. 'You must have been even down South I should think?'

'Oh yes, I've been down as far as Kent. That London isn't for me though, too many others with their buying and selling. You'd be amazed at the folk and the smell! Oh my God, the smell!' He laughed as he wafted his hand in front of his nose.

She laughed along with him. The smell in London had never troubled her. It was a different kind of place to hide in, all those people everywhere, but after a few months she'd learnt that each busy street was its own village. She could only stay unseen if she moved all the time. That's when she'd decided to come to Holy Island.

'Where were you last?'

'I've come last from Seahouses,' he waved more or less towards the mainland, 'but I've been on the road from York for the last few months.'

York. It was York she'd last seen Guy, York where he'd been taken into the prison. Yes, that was probably where the news had come from. Could she get him talking about the area without making him suspicious? She was trying to think of a way when he got up, thanked Ann for the pies and headed off briskly towards the stables.

She gave Ann the chopped turnips and followed him. She could pretend interest in some fairings maybe.

He was still cheerful when she caught up with him, but his mind was on the tide. His cart was full to bursting and she cast around for something she could want. There was a soft leather pouch that would take her pens and knife.

'How much for that?' she asked.

The price he asked was too high. He shrugged as he said it, knowing she couldn't afford that, especially not as the ignorant kitchen girl he was taking her for.

'Tell me more about York,' she said eventually, despairing of getting the information out of him any other way.

'It's a busy place, full of all sorts of folks.'

'And the prison there?'

He laughed. 'And why would you want to know about that?' Then he looked more suspiciously at her.' Are you after getting me into trouble?'

And with that he turned his back on her and finished his packing.

She loitered anyway, picking up ribbons and putting them back until he shooed her away. He didn't see what she took, or the little hole she made in his packs, something for him to blame the loss on later when he discovered it.

Returning to the Scriptorium, she found Luke busy cutting parchment for the new Gospels book. She'd left a note of the sizes and he'd taken it on himself to start. She was pleased but didn't show it.

'Mind those holes in the skins,' she pointed out. 'We'll have to work around those so better on pages with text where we can encircle them.'

He nodded and kept working.

She went along to the Prior's parlour, to see what inks or gilt he may have got from the pedlar.

He was sorting through a small heap of powders in twists of paper and cloth, and little clay pots.

'Ah, Linnet, I have some more of that gum arabica and some oak galls, and this packet of shell gold for the new Gospels. I'll keep the shell gold here until you need it, you'll have to ask me for it.'

'And the lapis, the aquamarine?'

'Yes, yes, he brought that too, I've got that safe. How is Brother Luke's work?'

'He's learning well, he'll be a good scribe.' She just hoped he wouldn't replace her when he was good enough. 'Do you want me to enter the goods in the Bursar's book?'

Marcus stopped her. 'No, I'll be doing that,' he said but as he bustled her out of the way, the Prior stopped him.

'Linnet's hand is better.'

Marcus shot Linnet a glance of pure malevolence, but as the Prior looked over, Linnet saw it vanish. She'd made another enemy there, without even trying. Although the Prior seemed to be using her more, that might protect her.

'Is there a receipt for the lapis?' she asked after a while, when she couldn't find it in the column.

'Negligent man,' the Prior muttered. 'No, I think the pedlar forgot to put it on.'

He gave her the figures and she made a new line for it, blotted the page and closed the book. The duck was looking better, more bright-eyed if still very quiet.

'How is the duck, Prior?' she asked.

His face lit up. 'She's doing very well, she takes her bread and milk and I think her wing is healing. The cat isn't very happy though, I've caught him trying to strike her before.'

The cat probably felt the spot next to the fire was his by right. No wonder Linnet had seen him about more.

Chapter Sixteen

The Prior looked at her attentively as she dipped her finest brush into the pot. She'd thinned the paste he'd brought in with a little egg white. It smelled strange, but not unpleasant. She swept it across a tiny corner of the test parchment. They both looked at it carefully, the Prior moving the candle closer.

Linnet felt disappointed. Where was the beautiful glowing blue? Had the pedlar tricked the Prior? The Prior didn't look angry, just thoughtful.

'Ah well, nearly there. Just needs a bit more from the other packet, I reckon,' he said.

She didn't know much about lapis but she offered to look at the powders and help him. The Prior brushed that aside.

'We'll try again tomorrow.'

'What about if we leave it to stand overnight?'

He shook his head, he didn't think it would make a difference and she didn't either. The muddy colour had no hope of becoming sparkling. Light colours could go darker, it was rare for them to go the other way.

The Inspector stood at the door, beckoning the Prior away, indifferent to the finer points of the manuscripts they were talking about. How much longer was he going to be here anyway? How long did inspections usually take? The monks had been strictly pious since he came but perhaps he was staying so long to catch them at their ease. Linnet had only known Inspectors to stay a few days at most, but he'd been here over two weeks now. They surely couldn't keep it going for that much longer.

Luke looked at the little mark of blue. 'What's wrong with that? It's a lovely colour.'

'Not proper shining lapis,' she explained. 'It almost needs to glow like gilt.'

She found it hard to put into words the glory that the lapis could convey. They got back to their preparations, Luke refining his pens ready to start the text of the Gospels, Linnet drawing out her first ideas for the pictures. She'd seen a window in Ely Cathedral with Jesus walking on the Sea at Galilee, and she wanted to copy that on a full page in her book. The boats she was drawing looked like the fishermen's boats on the island, stubby and solid, working boats. Perhaps she could add a bit of Tom? She took special care over the nets, working in the patterns she'd studied by the shore. Yes, the pattern of his nets would be in the Gospel, her own tribute to him for years to come.

Luke had gone to prayers and she was alone in the nearly dark room when Isabelle and Pol came in. The girl looked at the drawings, tracing the boats and the waves with a dirty finger. She didn't say anything but she nodded, once, deliberately. She'd noticed the nets.

'How do you do that?' she asked.

Linnet gave up another scrap and an old pen, and let her do some scribbles. She helped her to make her mark, easy to draw an 'I' but the other letters were harder. Pol watched quietly for a while then hopped down to the floor and threw the rushes around.

'Does he often hide mice?' Linnet asked, thinking of his hiding place.

'Yes, he can keep them, and they get with maggots then, so he can eat more.' Linnet shuddered. So now she had a maggoty mouse hidden under the floor of her Scriptorium. Well it was the Prior's Scriptorium by rights. It just felt hers and some part of her wanted it to be hers. Maybe it would be Luke's. The thought prickled her like straw in her bed.

'Does he bring you things too?' she asked. 'Like paper scraps?'

The girl nodded, preoccupied with getting a 'B' down perfectly. 'He likes what the Prior thinks he's got hidden,' she said, then looked up, afraid she'd given something away.

Linnet pretended she hadn't heard and continued arranging her things. So the Prior was hiding things? Another scrap of a secret to add to her pile of scraps.

It was too dark to see properly so she pushed the child and bird out, and they went for food. Luke saw Isabelle coming out of the Scriptorium and scowled.

'That's no place for that little bastard or that evil bird,' he said sourly.

Linnet was dismayed but Isabelle paid him no attention, she'd heard it all before. She supposed Isabelle might well be a bastard. She'd not heard much about her family apart from that they'd all died of that illness years before. If she was a bastard, could a monk be her father? That wasn't unusual, especially in small places where the monks acted like lords of the manor. Perhaps that was why she got special favours, staying in the kitchen, the Prior watching over her. Could the Prior be Isabelle's father?

The thought pricked her then, her own father a monk? No, he couldn't have kept that hidden while they travelled around the holy houses, someone would have known him. She couldn't imagine he would have become a novice in his later years either. Either Mees was mistaken or he was hiding as something he was not. A spy, she thought, feeling the idea settle, and herself a spy's daughter. A chill whisper of danger travelled down her spine but part of her welcomed it.

When she went across to the tavern that evening, there was the priest, drinking alone this time. She sat down nearby, waiting for him to start on one of his harangues. It wasn't long coming.

'Don't think I didn't see 'ee, down by the shore yesterday.' He was stabbing his finger wildly in the air again but his eyes were fixed on her. 'Those fishermen don't do things the Christian way, you know, I've told 'ee, your soul is in peril.'

If her soul was in peril, his must be pickled by now, she thought sourly, but she tried smiling at him.

'Has the island changed much do you think, Sir?' she asked. It was customary to call priests Sir, but it stuck in her throat all the same, he was no great man this one.

'Not for those fishermen,' he grumbled. 'That's pagan what they do with their boats. The Priory isn't what it was mind, that was a thing of beauty before. The lords and ladies used to stop by to see it and pray, not like now.'

'How long has Prior Richard been here then?'

'About five years. He came just after that big frost, I remember.'

Five years, not long enough to have been Isabelle's father.

'And what of Isabelle's family? You were telling me they all died around then.'

At the mention of Isabelle, he moved swiftly on to denouncing Isabelle's mother, a loose girl, a girl with too many ideas, a girl with a fancy for silly names, Isabelle for the love of God. What was wrong with Mary?

Plenty, Linnet thought, plenty was wrong with Mary, but she kept listening.

'No one knew who the baby's father was, but she didn't

care, flaunting her belly and then her baby, alus carrying her about like she were a princess, not a dirty little bastard.' He spat at the last word, just missing the table and Linnet.

She'd been loved then, at least at the beginning, that was something, Linnet supposed. Why did the Prior favour her so much then?

Cyrus had started again on the evils of women and how they poisoned the souls of good Christian men. Linnet moved away. She'd got all the information she could for now.

Nothing was clearer yet, but there were mysteries to uncover on this island, and she felt sure the three deaths were neither accident nor self-harm. With Oswyn, she just wanted to know who killed him and why. Maykin's death felt so sad, but she burned to find out who had killed Tom, destroyed his good name and condemned his soul. If she could prove he'd been killed, the guilt she was feeling might finally leave her. The sting of the words she'd last said to him.

She lit another stolen candle stub in the embers of the fire in the kitchen, and carried the flame back to her room. The knot, the gilt letter, the scraps of paper from Oswyn's bed, the black pebbles. What could it all mean?

She smoothed out all the scraps of paper, laying them one above the other and began to see a pattern. Loops and curls and little stubby marks. Almost someone's rough hand here. What had made her think of this earlier? Luke's practice scraps when he'd ripped up the letters halfway through and she'd been angry at the waste. Half a letter. That was it. These were half of a line of text, torn away from the other half.

She spent a long hour matching up the scraps but although she could sometimes discern what she thought might be an 'S' or a 'U', there was nothing like full letters there. Maybe she was wrong but it had seemed the answer.

Too late now, she put it all back into Tom's box and settled for the night. The cat was back, still sulking about the duck no doubt. He rumbled a purr and she felt almost at peace for the first time since Tom died. Yes, she was probably being sought by Guy, and others too. Luke was going to take over her Scriptorium, and there was nothing she could do. Still, she felt some peace. She had a quest, a search to rescue Tom's honour and his name.

Chapter Seventeen

Isabelle was shivering, she'd been out in the rain and was holding a handful of yellow weeds. She dripped water in a corner of the kitchen until Ann chased her out, complaining.

The Prior approached her and took the plants, talking to her in a low voice but Linnet could hear his annoyance from where she was standing outside the Scriptorium. Was he just finding busy-work for the child to do to keep her occupied?

He saw her watching and came over.

'Can you show me your drawings for the illuminations for the Gospels? Bring them to the parlour.'

Linnet collected her papers together, glad of a chance to go into a warm room. Leaving Luke in the cold Scriptorium, she went straight into the parlour.

The Inspector was there, staring into the fire and evidently unaware of both the Prior and the duck. The Prior was arranging the various weeds and shells that Isabelle had been collecting into a large, wooden bowl. As Linnet came in, he pulled a cloth over it all. She could see Cassian in the corner, grimly studying his lessons.

The Prior liked her pictures, but he suggested a few minor changes.

'Who is this book of Gospels for?'

'Bishop Foxe.' The reply came from the Inspector. He didn't look impressed with the thought.

'Yes,' Prior Richard said, 'I'll be sending him an example of our work as a gift and to show how a working scriptorium here could be of use.'

For such an important gift, Linnet would have to pay special care. She wondered if she could thread some small foxes into the initiums, the decorative letters at the beginning of each page. It might help find favour with the Bishop.

She asked if she could stay in the parlour for a little while to make notes on the changes to the work while it was fresh in her mind.

The two men resumed their talk.

'Father Nicholas, I do understand there is more to see, but how much longer do you think we'll have the pleasure of your company?'

The Prior was using all his charm, but there was a steely edge in his voice. Cassian began to speak but the Inspector quelled him with a wave of his hand and replied, 'As I said before, Prior, this is not something that can be hurried. I am working on my report on your Priory but it is only part of a larger reckoning for His Grace, more than you can understand in such a small, holy house.'

Mocking the size of the Priory must have pained him but the Prior showed no sign of it as the Inspector carried on.

'I must examine the souls of those monks who are in danger of sinning, as well as making a note of those who have sinned.'

'What would you like us to change? Are we not following the Rule, Inspector?'

'Many, many things.' He sank his chin further into his chest and gazed again at the flames but said nothing more.

The Prior sighed, clearly his guest was not leaving anytime

soon. Cassian looked as if he had something to say, but bit it back. He looked at the Prior; Linnet thought he was willing him to catch his eye, but the Prior wasn't paying attention.

Someone knocked and a messenger, still dirty from the road, came in. He stank of horse but looked well dressed.

'Father, I bring word from Lady Margaret. She is eager for her prayer book and is lodging at Neasham Abbey.'

The Prior looked at him warily. 'Have you had food and drink yet, man?'

'No, Father, I was to come straight to you to deliver my message before any ease for myself.'

Neasham Abbey was a good day's ride away, or two days' walk or more. The man looked cowed. His mistress must be harsh if he didn't even dare to get an ale before delivering his message.

'She wants you to deliver it to her by hand.'

The Inspector and Prior both looked at him, perplexed. Lady Margaret was not a great lady that should command this kind of respect. Linnet wondered why she wasn't at the family seat.

The man looked wretched. He must know that this was highly unlikely but it would mean punishment for him if the prayer book did not come to her promptly.

'Well, man, let me think about it. You go and get yourself washed and to the kitchen. The tide is turning so no one is going anywhere for a good few hours now.'

After the man had left, the Prior was lost in thought for a while. Linnet gathered her things to leave and the noise drew his attention. He muttered something to the Inspector who nodded, and called her over.

'You are to deliver the prayer book to Lady Margaret, and you can borrow the copy of Juliana Berners' book of 'Hawking and Hunting' while you're there. I know the Abbess at

Neasham has it and she will send it back with you if I give you a note. We can then make a good copy of it for future books.'

Linnet didn't hear much after the instruction to deliver. She had been safe on this island but now she was being sent out.

'Would one of the monks riding not be quicker, Father?'

'You can act for me, Linnet. You can answer her questions about the prayer book and maybe persuade her to ask for another? Anyway, best to go now.'

Of course she couldn't refuse. It might be good to leave this place anyway.

She set Luke up with the beginnings of the Gospels book. He'd made his own pens and had the rest of her gall ink now so he would be busy for a few days.

Before she left the Scriptorium, Cassian came in with his book of lessons, and took her seat. He didn't look well, she thought, dark circles under his eyes showing even on his tanned skin.

As she soaked a clothlet in a little ordinary ink so she could write while travelling, and gathered her coloured clothlets, she could hear Cassian whispering to Luke. She tried to look as if she wasn't listening, but she could make out the odd word. Was he asking about which of the monks would sin, trying to find Tom's lover?

Luke flushed a deep red and shrugged, refusing to answer the questions. Cassian looked frustrated but not surprised, glancing up at Linnet as if to see if she had heard anything. She left without catching his eye. If she'd liked the man more, she would have helped him to ask without asking, let conversations wander, not always plough straight in and send the information scattering before it had a chance to settle.

Lady Margaret's man left for the camp further north, he was going to pass on messages to Lord Edmund and bring supplies. The Prior gave her some pence for meals and a room on the way. One of the stable boys guided Linnet across the low tide to the mainland and set her on her way. The stable boys always took a clear route, unlike the Beale boys. They followed the stones that showed at low tide, set out years before and still a guide for walkers. It took skill to find them amongst the natural rocks. They sometimes went right of the stones, and sometimes left, she tried to keep it all in her head but it was too hard to remember. She noticed a long stick of cured white ash had been planted in the spot where Tom had been buried and crossed herself as they passed it.

After all the journeying with her father, she was familiar with the main routes and knew she was walking down the coast and Neasham Abbey was near Bothal. She remembered the story her father used to tell her about the Abbey, the fight they had with the Bishop over their Abbess. The women's holy houses always seemed to be at the mercy of the local bishops.

She stood watching the stable boy pick his way back across the wet sands for a while. The birds looked almost like people walking across at this distance, it was hard to see properly as the winter sun was slanting across the mud. Holy Island sparkled in the sunlight like a tempting jewel she'd owned but lost. She did feel safe there, safer than elsewhere, despite Jack and his threats.

She started to walk. The prayer book was well wrapped in a linen cloth and she had letters with her. One was for Lady Margaret offering the Prior's fulsome apologies for not coming himself and presenting the Holy Island scribe in his stead, the other a demand for the book he wanted from the Abbess. Neasham did not have a lot of standing, not since the Bishop's investigations from fifty years ago. Linnet had heard some stories of the disobedient Abbess Agnes and the nuns' refusal to heed the Bishop from long ago. All was quiet with them now but the present Abbess would not be able to refuse the Prior's request.

The way was rough and Linnet grew tired of picking her way. She came off into a hollow path, moving more easily through the green paths than on the dirt. Even in winter, it was more peaceful on the eye and smelt better than the busy roadways. She could hear birds calling and small creatures rustling. And the harsh note of a raven calling…

She turned around abruptly. Isabelle. That wretched child. There was no sign of her but Linnet sensed a sudden stillness and she waited.

Looking guilty, Isabelle came out from amongst the trees. She looked cold and tired already.

'I wants to see where you're going. Is it right about the Lady? I've never seen a Lady.'

'And you're ready to walk for two days or more – and with you it could be longer? And that's just to get there.' Linnet surprised herself by not feeling as angry as she thought she would.

'I can walk. I do it all the time, don't I?'

Linnet looked at Isabelle's feet. Poor felt shoes and worn thin.

'Where's the furthest you've been?'

Isabelle shrugged. 'I've been off the island twice.' She was trying to look as if that was not a big thing for her.

Linnet sat down. She needed to think. She threw Isabelle an apple and they sat in silence for a few minutes, eating. She couldn't take her back, that would mean she took far too long to get to Bothal. Could Isabelle find her own way back? Probably, but would she go? If she were resolved to follow, it would be better to let her, or God knows what might happen. She wondered whether the child would be missed back at the

Priory. Perhaps not, only if the Prior was looking for her and no one could find her.

'All right. You can come with me. But you have to do what I say.'

Isabelle opened her mouth to argue, then thought better of it.

'We'll be walking fast and I decide if we're going to stay in inns and the like. When we meet the Lady you can be my serving girl.'

That last was too much for the child who laughed out loud.

'I'm in earnest, Isabelle. The Lady isn't going to be interested in why I'm travelling with a disobedient child. And what are you going to do with Pol?'

A child she could explain or could be overlooked. A child with a raven was going to be a lot harder.

'Pol will fly back soon. He don't like it on the mainland. He'll be waiting for us when we get back.'

They started walking again. Linnet explained that walking too fast took longer than walking steady. All the old habits were coming back to her. It got dark too soon for the best walking but they could keep going if the moon was up and it was a clear night.

Isabelle began singing, little made-up songs, snatches of the island songs that she must have heard since she was a baby. Linnet hummed along a little. The noise felt comforting.

The last time she'd been travelling, she'd been by herself and kept away from all the main towns and villages. This time she should be safer. The child would divert any suspicion too. No one would think of Mary travelling with a child.

As it grew dark, they began to make their way back to the main track, the one by the sea. They'd made good progress. Isabelle liked it when the way was harder, going up hills or having to get through brambles. Easy walking made her whine and complain.

As they entered the town, it must be Beadnall, Linnet thought, they could hear people talking and laughing, and smell the fires and the dinners cooking. Isabelle gave Linnet a hopeful look. The money the Prior had given her wouldn't go as far if she had to get food for two.

They walked into the inn and Linnet asked for half a bowl of pottage. The woman serving looked motherly, and gave her a full bowl with two spoons, winking at the child. Another unexpected advantage. She also offered them a place in the room overnight for another penny, which Linnet accepted. She wrapped herself in her cloak, putting her bag underneath her – she'd be woken if anyone went digging through it. Isabelle curled up next to her, like a cat. Pol had flown off a few miles back.

They slept through the late-night drinkers and their talk, but Linnet woke when she heard a voice she knew. The pedlar was here, of course. This was the route he was taking. He'd obviously been drinking all evening , boasting about the good sales he'd had, and how the monks at the Priory had paid too much for his wares, but he'd be offering them to these folks for good prices. She thought that was unlikely, the Prior had a sharp eye for every coin spent, even if they were without a bursar at the moment. Still, everyone liked to hear about the monks paying more.

One of the local men asked him about the masons. They'd come through here before arriving on the island and not made many friends. There was some laughter at a lad in the corner, he'd lost near all his money to them and was still sour about it, not joining in with their sport.

It turned to abuse and ever stronger curses on the masons. It was partly envy for those in such a good trade, she supposed.

'The things I could tell you about them and their 'complices.' The pedlar was full of his own importance, the centre of attention.

'Go on then, man.' It was the lad asking, sitting forward more eagerly.

'Well, they were very interested in where they could find a released felon I know of.'

The barmaid shrieked with pretend fear and one of the older men promised to protect her, for a kiss. Linnet lay tense, ears straining.

Speaking over the laughter, the pedlar tried to gain attention again. 'He wasn't violent, a book-learnt man who'd not paid his debts, although he told me different, coming up from York, looking for his wife, who'd run off for some reason.'

Wife? Was that what he was saying? She'd never married him, she didn't want to marry anyone. They'd worked together, even if he'd always told everyone the scribing was his. She became aware she was shaking slightly and Isabelle had woken too. The child was lying still and breathing very quietly, aware as if by instinct of some unknown danger.

The men in the inn weren't listening to the pedlar any more, he'd lost their interest. If he'd had a story about a murderer or a thief, they'd still be listening. Otherwise it was of no real consequence to them.

There was low talk then about the great men in London and what the King was up to, but that was of no interest to most, and the pedlar found no listeners to his tales. The people in this area were wary of the squabbles of these Lords. Henry had been King for ten years now, that felt like an eternity after all the battles and illnesses and skirmishes of the years before. Linnet knew there were some who doubted his right to the throne, and she was sure if someone came along with a bigger army, that would be that. An older man, sitting in the back, eventually held up his hand and hissed, 'We'll have none of that whispering here.' Linnet noticed the scars on his face and wondered which battles he'd been in and which side he'd been on. His word was respected and the pedlar took the message and stopped trying to pass on the rumours he'd heard.

Linnet put a hand into her bag, feeling the leather pen pouch with some satisfaction. It had been a last-minute decision to take it and the pedlar had evidently not missed it yet.

The inn became quiet as the local folk finally made their way back home. The pedlar went upstairs to one of the good rooms. They would leave at first light tomorrow, best to keep out of his way in case he did discover it was gone and suspect who took it.

Chapter Eighteen

It took Guy a week to wear her down. He began with long speeches, talking about how their skills were wasted, how there was no shame in owning that. Then little bursts of violent impatience, veiled threats and finally begging her. Tears rolling down his fine-featured face as he implored her to think of him, of his debts, of how they could start again once they did this one thing.

Mary thought it was probably the lack of sleep that had made her give in. She was so tired. Kept up late by his raving and ranting, woken early by his cheerful descriptions of how their life would flourish soon.

Once she had capitulated, it all happened very quickly. He'd already got them spaces on a cart going to Bishop's Lynn, a promise of money later for the carter's trouble. She wondered sourly if he'd have gone by himself if she'd not agreed. And it must have been tiredness that had her laughing at the thought of him, dressed as a nun with his scratchy hand churning out indulgences, simpering at the good merchants and gentry. Maybe it was partly her pride, if they were to sell forged indulgences, she wanted them to be so good that none would tell they were not the real thing, not some pale thing that Guy would scratch out.

She travelled as Mary, changing into the nun's habit when they arrived.

'I'll call you Sister Maude and I'll play the part of a pardoner.' Guy was all charm now, now that it was going his way. She hated the name Maude, it sounded ugly and plain and a boring woman to boot, but it was close enough to Mary, if he slipped up. She stayed in the room he'd paid for, while he worked his way around the inns and taverns, spreading the word of indulgences for sale, a holy woman who travelled to write them.

It wasn't long before they had their first customers, and she was soon too busy to think further of the sin they were committing, or the danger they were putting themselves in. When they worked for Warham, she could tell herself that as a man of God, he would be absolving them of sin. Working for Guy there was no such assurance. A fussy woman who wanted an indulgence for her sin of greed insisted on meeting Sister Maude, and they were sat in the inn, with Mary keeping her head down and quiet, Guy doing all the talking, the woman warming up to his chatter, and some of the lines of worry leaving her face, when Mary saw Warham's men come in.

They recognised Guy at once, and could see the indulgence in front of him, ready to work on for the woman who was talking freely now, confessing her sins all over again to Sister Maude. Mary tensed but they didn't come over, just drew one finger across a throat. Guy hurried the woman up, took her coin and they left.

'We have to stop now,' Mary hissed as they hurried down dark streets to their room. 'He'll know, he'll come after us.' They had promised early on not to write indulgences for anyone else, only for him. Let alone doing them and selling them themselves, and keeping all the money. If there was money to be made, Warham wanted it all.

Guy had blanched at first, but the ale he'd drunk had emboldened him. 'They won't do anything without Warham's orders. He's not in the town, we'd have heard if he was. We can finish off then leave. Mary, we don't have to go back to Ely, we can move away and he'll not find us. You worry too much.'

She knew that wouldn't be it, but hoped that Warham was too busy in London with the court to come after them. Guy didn't know about the family tree she had written out for Warham too, the proof of his nobility, that last step he had needed to get into the room with those in power.

The fire was long out by the time Linnet and Isabelle woke up, the thin morning light coming through the gaps in the door as a maid came in, yawning, to sweep the floor. Isabelle's pleas for a bite to eat before they left were in vain, and they quickly went, following St Oswald's Way, the coast path.

It threatened rain all day and the wind was savage. After an hour or two of tramping on shingle and mud, they moved a bit further inland to get some protection from it. Isabelle tired more easily today, but Linnet forced her on. If they could get to Alnwick, they could stay at the monastery at Hulne for no cost.

'What were that pedlar talking 'bout last night that made you feared?'

The question startled Linnet. She was thinking about nothing but the walking, but it was clear Isabelle had been fretting about it for some time.

'I just didn't like him, that's all.'

'Did you know him afore?'

'No. We don't all know each other on the mainland, Isabelle.'

The child actually looked perplexed at that. She walked on for another few miles in silence, thinking about it.

'Why ain't you married, Linnet?'

Had the talk about the prisoner's wife stuck in Isabelle's head then?

'I never wanted to. My father wanted me to marry a groom at an inn in Durham.'

'Did he smell bad then?'

Linnet laughed, thinking back to George. He smelled of the horses, but that was a clean smell really, hay and sweat.

'No, he didn't smell but I didn't want to be married to anyone.'

She allowed herself a moment's dream, seeing herself helping him with the stables, selling eggs, perhaps a child or two. But no scribing. He'd said no wife of his would do that book stuff. He was one of those who thought writing was next to magic, to be feared if it happened in the wrong place, outside of a church or a court.

She remembered the dismay she'd felt when her father said he didn't care about her wishes, didn't want her to keep scribing. She had learnt to write and read by chance but this was not part of his intent for her. He was going away, he would be busy and couldn't take her with him. Not that she'd wanted to go, but she'd not wanted to get married either. Well, she'd chosen a life where she could write, even if some of it had been wrongful.

Her mind wandered as she did, fighting with her father again all those years ago, the moment when she realised her skills had not been part of his plan, just an accident he'd not been bothered to attend to, remembering his anger at her lack of gratitude, and her anger at his lack of care for her.

The child, still hungry, had gone on ahead and was now carefully picking a mushroom or two to eat from the dank roots of the trees.

At the monastery they were taken in by a stern cellarer who gave them solid but plain food, yesterday's bread and half a cup of yesterday's soup.

'It tastes so much – more – when you've been walking, don't it?' Isabelle was eating with real pleasure.

Linnet smiled, yes. Walking did make everything better, even yesterday's food. She asked the cellarer if there'd been any pedlars recently but he just shook his head, eager to get on with more worthy work than feeding travellers.

They had a better place to sleep this time, with a soft stuffed sack to rest on and some water to wash with, although Isabelle whined when Linnet scrubbed her face.

'You'll have to look proper for the Lady.'

The magic words, 'the Lady', did it and Isabelle sullenly accepted.

Chapter Nineteen

'Well now, isn't this disappointing?'

It was a question but it wasn't a question. Linnet and Isabelle both kept their eyes down. Lady Margaret was annoyed that the Prior hadn't come and his letter hadn't smoothed things over enough.

They'd walked the day from Alnwick and had time to wash quickly before asking to see the Lady. The nun who had shown them in had rolled her eyes when they said her name, although she quickly adopted a look of piety and took them to the best parlour.

Unlike the rest of the nunnery, this room was sumptuous. Lady Margaret had clearly made it her home, laying good coverings on the floor and lighting it with fat creamy beeswax candles. There was a little table with wine and fresh bread which Isabelle kept looking at in vain.

Clothes and trinkets were scattered around, as if she'd unpacked by throwing everything into the air and leaving it where it fell.

'Show me then.'

Making the best of it, the Lady held her hand out impatiently.

Linnet opened her bag and took out the book, carefully unwrapping the cloth before laying it into the small white hand.

'Very nice.'

She turned the pages idly and without care, not even really looking at the words and pictures Linnet had toiled over.

'Scribe, read me this page.'

She'd stopped at one of the first prayers. Linnet read it out trying to sound well spoken. Why was she asking her to read it?

'The pictures are very pretty.'

Lady Margaret hadn't waited for Linnet to finish before she took the book back and started looking through it again, stopping at the little cat on the page of prayers for serenity.

Maybe she couldn't read? Why ask for a book you can't read? Stupid question, Linnet chided herself, it was about looking as if she could read.

'And you did it? But you're not a nun?'

The woman's attention span and caught at Linnet. Isabelle opened her mouth to tell the story of John-the-Lies but Linnet took her hand quickly, pinching her skin to keep her quiet.

'Yes, my Lady, I was brought up with the monks and they were kind enough to teach me.'

Lady Margaret was examining her carefully now so Linnet took the chance to look at her too. She was young, a second wife for sure, but no swelling at the waist. She looked pretty and sleek, like the cat Linnet had drawn for her, but her manner was peevish and testy. At a closer look, Linnet could see how very young and thin she was. Her lavish clothes were weighing her down, much as she tried to move with grace in them. How long had she been staying here with the nuns? And where was her husband? Linnet made a note to find out.

'You can go now. Get some food in the kitchen, tell them I sent you.'

Giving them an order as if they needed her word to get fed by the nuns.

'And I'll want you to read to me more tomorrow morning before you go back to the Priory.'

And with that, they were dismissed.

Isabelle was bursting with questions as they went back to the kitchen but Linnet stopped her again. They would wait till they were alone before she started. The food was much better than at Hulne, fresh coddled eggs and even some blackberry pie, and the young nun serving them was a gossip, ready to talk to anyone new.

After Linnet had told her all about their journey, which very much impressed the nun, she asked about Lady Margaret.

'Oh she's a right—' The nun caught herself in time. 'She's been here months – Lord Edmund left her here while he was called back to fight the Scots.' The Percys of Northumberland were known as fierce fighters on the side of the Crown. That side had shifted over the years, as the Crown had of course.

She started on a litany of complaints. Lady Margaret was treating all the nuns like servants, she kept changing her mind about what she wanted and she slapped anyone who displeased her too often.

'But what do she do?' Isabelle was confused by the idea of a person without definite work.

'Why, my sweet, she don't have to do nothing!' The nun laughed at her. 'She's a Lady and they just be, that's enough. And make little babies for her Lord. No chance of that for now though!'

They'd finished eating and Linnet asked if she could see the Abbess. She needed to give her the letter about the book the Prior wanted. The Abbess was not in the nunnery now, she was told, but would come back later today, so they would wait.

'And your girl can card some wool while she's waiting, yes?'

Despite her pleading glances, Isabelle was led off. The nun came back, still in the mood to talk. After Linnet asked, she started on the story of the Abbey's disgrace from all those years ago. Linnet knew some part of it, but it was a new way of telling the story. She was always interested in how the holy houses fought amongst themselves. Her father used to say 'fighting for the spoils' but there wasn't much here at Hearsham – aside from the book of course. The nun started talking with relish about how after the Abbess Margaret Hawk had left 'all of a huff, not sorry to see that one go', the women had chosen their Abbess, back in 1437, Agnes (and the nun crossed herself).

'But because the Big Man—' She paused to check Linnet's face as the way of referring to the Bishop of Durham, and took her amused silence for encouragement – 'The Big Man hadna chosen her himsel', he turned it down. Came here all of a lather, demanding this and demanding that – stayed in Madame's room that she's in now of course – and then after all the fuss, it were Agnes he picked! We all went "aye lad, ta for that" and off he toddled and on we got on wid it all.'

Linnet joined in her laughter, charmed by how the nun talked about events that happened well before she was born. She went off to pick some herbs from the garden, pleased with her telling of the tale, and Linnet took advantage of some quiet to stretch her legs and warm herself in front of the kitchen fire, shutting her eyes, just for a minute, to think.

'Sleeping in the day?'

The voice was sharp and impatient. Lady Margaret. She stood in front of Linnet who rubbed her eyes and tried to clear her head.

'You can help me scribe a letter, the nuns here are too stupid to write properly what I tell them.'

Back in the Lady's room, Linnet found a small writing desk, candles lit, paper ready for her. She got her ink and pens out of her pouch and sat waiting, but now that she was there, the urgency seemed to have passed.

'Are you married, scribe?'

'No, my Lady.'

'How strange. You must be about thirty?'

Linnet nodded, although she was some years off.

'I'm nineteen and I've been married two years already.'

It was an empty boast from a girl with nothing to do, stuck in a dull nunnery. Linnet tried to look as if she were envious but she seemed so young. Linnet would not be nineteen again if she were paid for it.

Lady Margaret prowled around her room, picking things up and putting them down as she talked. She spoke of fine food and her clothes, and her husband She strayed into talking about her life with her sisters, she was the eldest of five, no brothers, and it was clear she missed them, even if she was now a Lady. Linnet knew she would have been one of those big sisters who the others trailed after, the head in all but name of a large family, and now so dreadfully bored here alone in the nunnery. There was something that reminded her of Maykin, poor broken Maykin, something she could see that would have others smiling with her lively words and maybe imitations of others around her.

Linnet noticed with a pang how the prayer book had been tossed aside on a pile of dirty linen. One day, she promised herself, she would start stealing books, not just a half-broken copy of the *Divers Arts* but actual complete books. She would have her own secret book closet and keep them properly, safe from harm, somewhere they'd be treasured.

'Well, scribe?' The sharper tone broke into her thoughts and she looked up. Lady Margaret was ready to start.

'My Lord – no – My Dear Husband, I trust this letter finds you well and your action meets with success. I am – no wait – Your Lady is well. Indeed she is well enough for two.'

Linnet looked again at Margaret's waist, which was slender and gave no sign of her being with child.

Margaret blushed a little but continued boldly, 'It is early of course but the signs are fair.'

Linnet considered. Lord Edmund had left here months ago. She couldn't be in the early days of pregnancy unless she'd seen him at least in the last couple of months. She coughed.

'Yes, scribe? You have something to say?'

'I was just wondering when you'd last seen the Lord.'

'How dare you ask that kind of question?' She came over quickly and angrily slapped Linnet's hand away from the page. 'You're writing the wrong thing, that's not what I told you to put. Throw that away and start again!'

Linnet folded over the spoiled page and put it to one side. She'd take it with her as she left.

'My Dear Husband, I trust this letter finds you well. Since I last saw you, I have had my hopes dashed of a happy event. May I ask how long it will be before you visit me again? I wish to be a good wife to you and can come to your camp if you send for me.'

The longing in her voice was obvious. This was not the life she'd boasted of to her sisters when she'd been picked to be a Lord's wife, not even head of a household of her own. She finished the letter with some complaints about how badly the nuns were behaving towards her and then signed her name in an uncertain hand. Linnet wondered again why she was here in the nunnery.

She went back to the kitchen where a rebellious Isabelle was sitting in front of a big pile of dirty wool that she was slowly carding. The gossipy nun was there too, kneading dough for tomorrow's bread.

'Is the Abbess returned yet?'

'No, she won't be back till late now. She's visiting her sister in the village and they talk a lot that pair. You and your girl will be staying tonight though? You can see her tomorrow after morning prayers before you get on your way. What did that Lady Margaret have ye doing?'

She managed to make 'Lady Margaret' sound like a curse.

'Oh just some more to do with the book,' Linnet said. 'You said she's not with child, did she miss a baby while she's been here?'

'No, she can't have done, we do all her linen for her and there's been nothing but the ordinary.' She pointed towards her skirt.

So Lady Margaret was lying then. Trying to sound like a baby had started but not stayed, and another might be on the way if only her Lord was to pay her some attention.

Linnet was relieved she'd never caught for a child when she'd been with Guy. He'd been all over her to start with but lost interest quickly and she hadn't cared by then. She had wondered if she was barren. It didn't give her any pain to think that. But if Lady Margaret were barren, that would be difficult for her. She'd probably be left in the nunnery to moulder for a lot longer.

The nun was talking still. 'Her Lord has two sons already, you know, from his first wife, God bless her soul, a gentle woman – nothing like this one. They're only young though, and don't look that strong, I've heard.'

'Why isn't she at the family home?'

'They've not got one built yet, he's not a big name in that family so he's out to get glory agin the Scots first. The boys are with his mother, and she could be too but I heard she quarrelled something fierce with the old lady when she first was there, so she's gone off to find him, only he keeps on the move.'

She showed them to a small guest room, empty this time. The nunnery didn't get a lot of people staying. Isabelle bounced on the tick and poured out a stream of questions.

'Were all those clothes on the floor in her room for the Lady? Why did she look so angry? I'd be happy like a pig in mud if I had all those clothes, so many different colours an' all. Where's her Lord gone? Why does she want a babbie? How do you get babbies anyway? Is it like the pigs? Why don't Ladies have a litter? I don't think she can read – can she, Linnet?'

Linnet latched on to the last question with some relief, trying not to laugh at the idea of the elegant young Lady Margaret suckling a litter of pig-like babies.

'No, I don't think she can read, nor write. She wants the prayer book so she can look like a proper Lady, I think.'

'I want to write, can you learn me how? You showed me letters but there's more, I know. The Prior says I'm too little but I ain't, am I?'

Linnet thought about it. Yes, she supposed she could continue to teach her to write. Why not? It couldn't do any harm. Maybe something to keep from the Prior though.

'Yes, I'll teach you more of your letters, but not now – we've not got enough candle for tonight and we need some rest before starting the walk back tomorrow. Can you settle down and hush now, Isabelle?'

In the dark, Linnet was startled by a brief hug from the child before they fell asleep.

The nun was too busy to gossip the next morning, a shame, Linnet thought, she'd enjoyed their talk last night. As promised, she took Linnet to the Abbess, who read the Prior's letter with almost as much annoyance as Lady Margaret had. They both knew that although the letter was phrased as a request, the Abbess had no choice but to send the book back with Linnet. The book had been written by Dame Juliana Berners from St Albans, they had been novices together and that was how this nunnery came to have it.

She took a small key from the chain at her waist and unlocked the book closet and took it out. Linnet managed to keep her face blank, merely a scribe carrying for the Prior, but inside she was jumping with excitement at the thought of seeing this book.

The book of 'Hawking and Hunting with all the Properties and Medicines that are Necessary to be Kept' was written in elaborate script across the frontispiece above a drawing of birds, maybe ravens or hawks, lecturing to sparrows, as if the words within came from the birds themselves. Linnet held it carefully and gently turned the pages. It was, as she'd heard, a goodly bit on hawks, then hunting lore, and then the nouns of venery, the groupings of animals and others. She spent a long time looking at the pages, seeing the want of illustration. If she used it for another book, she would add pictures of the different hawks at least.

'I'll not have you keep it for long, mind, you're to do a quick copy and we will send someone to take it back, maybe by St Benedict's day?'

Linnet thought for a bit, then countered with St Barnabas, and they agreed finally on St George, somewhere in the middle. She could get a rough copy done earlier, but she really wanted to have the coats of arms done properly. Maybe the Prior could give her another monk to help with it.

'We've done the binding for it so you can see my nuns' work. Tell your Prior that we can do bindings for his books if he is to set up a scriptorium.'

Linnet was interested and they spoke about prices and

what cloths and leather they might use, what kind of time it would take. She made some notes to show the Prior when she returned. The Abbess had unbent a little, even smiling as she wrapped the book for her, this could be the beginning of useful relations between the two holy houses, and would help the Prior with his ambitions.

They left without Lady Margaret demanding any more from them. She was busy shouting at a stable boy for worrying her horse in some way so they slipped away unnoticed.

It was raining lightly with the promise of more to come and the wind was getting stronger. It was going to be a difficult journey, heads down and faces set until they could find shelter. Linnet showed Isabelle how to play 'slug or leaf' and 'bird or leaf'. They kept count. Linnet was much better at looking down and picking out slugs, years of walking, sometimes barefoot, had taught her well. Isabelle, with her face turned upwards, was always right on birds.

'Will Pol know you're gone?' Linnet was curious.

'Yea – but he's off enough hisself. He has other ravens he likes – he goes off with them. I don't mind though. It's his nature innit?'

They didn't see any ravens, just a few rooks soaring near their nests, high in the trees.

Linnet was keen to get to a place of shelter so she could examine the book more. She'd heard so much about this book of 'Hawking and Hunting', one of the first printed books, and she was longing to look at it further. They aimed for Alnwick but they must have taken the wrong way somewhere, and they were now near the sea.

The road was getting busier as it grew dark. People with carts, people with bundles, a flock of sheep here too. Linnet was told they were bound for Alnmouth for tomorrow's charter market, so it would be Alnmouth for them too.

She wondered if they would find anywhere to stay. The church rooms would be full already with a market coming, but there might be a few inhabitants who would cram in a few more for just a few coins.

Isabelle had grown silent, looking around at the crowds in awe and perhaps a little fear. She was walking a lot closer to Linnet, even holding her hand at one point when the throng began pushing in the narrower streets. There was a weekly market on the island, but only a smattering of folk – nothing like this.

Linnet took them to the sea side of the town. It was a bit quieter there. The fishermen were stowing their nets and pulling their boats ashore, a bit quicker than normal perhaps, wanting to get to their place in the crowded market day taverns. She stopped one of them to ask where she might find cheap lodging. He directed them to his wife's sister's house down a small lane. Her room was nearly full already but clean, and she gave them pottage and a spot by the door to sleep.

With no one paying them mind, Linnet got the book out and opened it to feel the pages, and admire the words. The printing was done well, she conceded, but she felt something was lacking from a proper book. Isabelle pointed at the words, asking, 'What does that say? And that? And that?' every time she turned the pages.

Linnet turned to the part that explained which birds were for which rank, and read aloud to her quietly for a few minutes. 'And this is a falcon genteel and this is for a prince. This is a falcon of the rock and this is for a duke. And this is a sacre and this is for a knight.' She thought the quiet repetitions were soothing Isabelle to sleep but as she put the book away, the child murmured, 'And this a raven and this is for a child.'

*

They got up early the next day. Linnet wanted to start away but Isabelle was lingering, eyes wide at the stalls and people preparing for market.

'Can't we bide a wee while? I've not seen a big market afore, only the usual one on the island.'

'I've nothing for you to spend here, Isabelle. You can only enjoy the market when you have coin.'

The child didn't heed her warning and skipped off, stopping to look at piles of cheeses, stalls with pins and hair clasps, and a monkey! Was it a monkey? Linnet had seen pictures of them in her books and she was sure it was. It was held by a string, shivering in this cold English winter, very far away from its warm home.

Linnet found Isabelle chatting to the man holding the monkey's string. He was dark-skinned and spoke halting English but he was smiling at the child who was trying to touch the animal.

'He bite! He teeth!' he warned, but that didn't stop her.

The monkey was thin with patches of fur missing. He looked ill. Isabelle held out an apple core she'd been saving and he took it with tiny human hands and began nibbling on it daintily, for all the world like a bishop at a feast, Linnet thought.

As people began to gather, they crowded around the monkey and he dropped the apple core and jumped onto his master's head, sullen now.

The kind man of a few minutes ago vanished as he began to shout a string of commands, pulling sharply on the string to make the monkey dance and collect coins from those watching.

Linnet and Isabelle moved back out of the way.

They came to a stall selling cakes, toasted and full of spices, even the smell was warming in the cold air. Linnet sighed.

She took out her purse and counted out a couple of coins and Isabelle bought them each a cake.

'Let us carry the purse, Linnet, I can do it.' Isabelle wasn't quite whining but she was clearly tiring of the people and the noise.

'No, the Prior gave me the coin and he'll be expecting a good account of how we spent it. We can't lose it.'

Isabelle paused.

'We'll say last night cost a little more.' Linnet was used to working accounts, a penny here, a penny there, it made life more agreeable.

Isabelle looked reassured but as they finished the cakes, she seized Linnet's purse and ran off laughing.

It took Linnet a few minutes to swallow the last mouthful of cake. She started after Isabelle. It would be time to move on after this, enough market time now.

She rounded a corner expecting to find the child taunting her with the purse but Isabelle was sitting on the ground, stunned and gasping for breath. No purse.

Damn! Damn! Damn! And this was another reason she didn't like markets.

Isabelle was almost weeping with rage. 'He tripped me up and just *took* it.'

'Who was it and where did he go?' Maybe they could still catch him and get it back.

'I dunno, do I? I don't know these folk. And he just – he just *went*.'

Probably a regular cutpurse then, he wouldn't be able to believe his luck when he came across a young girl waving money around like a queen.

Linnet helped Isabelle up, although she wanted most of all to just sink down in the mud beside her. They had a few coins left – she was not so green as to keep all her money in one place – but not enough for tonight's lodging and not enough to explain their expenses to the Prior.

Isabelle showed little remorse, hanging on to her fury at the thief. Linnet would have liked to have seen some at least but none was forthcoming and she had to think what they could do next.

They wandered back into the market. The commotion around the monkey man had died down, he'd thrown a brightly coloured scarf over a basket and Linnet supposed the monkey was in there. She hoped he'd been able to finish eating his apple core.

The people were now thronging around the ballad singer, who was telling his bawdy tales and promising an utterly filthy ballad for later. Isabelle didn't look startled, she'd probably heard worse from the fishermen and the stable boys on the island.

The ballad singer was young, barely twenty, but with the confidence of a man twice his years. He only had a few ballad sheets though, which he was trying to sell. No buyers, not before he'd sung; they were scrappy bits too, and not worth that price. It gave Linnet thought.

She pushed to the front to catch his eye.

'Ah, we got an eager woman here – husband away is he? Want some attention from a fine young man, ready for a good time?'

The crowd roared, but Linnet frowned and made a discreet money sign at him. He may have been new to his craft but he recognised when someone wanted to talk about money. Then he quickly turned to a blushing hulk of a farm boy, telling him it was time for him to be ploughing the lovely ladies around him as well as the fields.

As the laughter rose, the ballad singer called for quiet.

'I'll be here a little after noon, so bring your coins for the dirtiest stories you've ever heard – the more coins, the filthier they'll be!'

Jumping down from the stone he'd been standing on, he came over to Linnet.

'What are you after then, mistress? Not my stories, I reckon then?'

'I see you've only got a few rough sheets for sale, and you'll never sell them at that price.'

'Maybe after they've heard the songs I might,' he said, but they both knew that was talk.

'I can help you. I've got some paper and inks with me and I'm a scribe travelling through. We've time before your songs. You pay for me and the child to have some pottage in the tavern with some warm ale and I'll do you some copies. I'm fast and good and you'll be able to get twice what you pay me for them.'

She showed him a couple of pages of her work she had with her and he nodded in recognition of her skill.

The size of the crowd had been encouraging. The ballad singer tried to bargain for a bit but he wasn't used to it and Linnet got more or less what she'd wanted.

They went to the tavern and he got them the drink and a table for eating. Isabelle fidgeted a bit but was soon warmed by the drink and even fell asleep for a while.

Linnet got out her pens and plain ink, and the paper she'd taken from Lady Margaret's desk. She knew the Lady would have missed jewels or silks but she'd paid no attention to the paper and she would never use it herself.

The songs were dirty, but nothing Linnet hadn't seen or heard before. She put her head down and worked fast, becoming more oblivious to the hum and chat in the tavern. She made ten good copies and then playfully added a grinning man and a fine lady in the margins of a couple of the sheets.

When the ballad singer came back that afternoon, she persuaded him to give her more for the two with pictures and the price they'd agreed for the rest. She woke up Isabelle and they started out of the tavern. Linnet hoped they had enough time to get to a nearby monastery before dark and then it would be a long walk for the last day and they'd be home.

The people were still thronging around the stalls, buying and selling and quarrelling, as Linnet and Isabelle pushed through. The bats were starting to flitter in the darkening sky. Isabelle still looked very tired, too much for a long walk.

She considered quickly what was for the best. If they slept another night here and started early, they could get to the shore near the island by the end of daylight tomorrow, and the place they stayed last night had been clean and warm.

Isabelle revived a little when Linnet told her they'd be staying and they turned back to the market where people were beginning to pack up. Linnet bought a broken meat pie for them for half the price from earlier in the day.

The ballad singer saw them eating their pie. He was red-faced and sweating, he'd been singing and shouting and jesting for over two hours. He called them over. 'I sold all my sheets, you're not bad for a woman at that scribing. Want to do me some more?'

Why not? They were here for the evening anyway. He asked her to do more of the pictures on the sheets and they settled back in at the tavern again.

Isabelle befriended the tavern kitten, playing with a piece of torn skirt and letting her spring at it, on and off. It was peaceful, most had left for the day not wanting to spend any gains on another night's lodging. The remaining drinkers looked pleased with their day's work and were counting coins, or drinking away what they'd made.

Linnet let her mind wander back to George, the marriage and the life she'd refused. And for her own satisfaction, she gave the man she was drawing something of George's face, and the woman Lady Margaret's.

They walked out into the night air, colder than ever after the warmth of the tavern, back to the house they'd stayed in before. They were too late though, and she was full, sorry to turn them away but she had not an inch of space left.

Linnet had a thought so they carried on down to the harbour. As she had hoped, some of the boats were overturned on the sands, so they crept under one to use it as shelter. She stopped up the gaps with stones and mosses and it soon grew warm enough for them to stop shivering.

Isabelle was off asleep straight away but Linnet couldn't seem to quieten her mind. She counted the money she'd made and what she owed the Prior. She should have some left she could keep.

As she was falling asleep, voices outside the boat woke her up again. Two men talking, stumbling a little on the pebbles, low voices, stopping for a piss, she thought.

'But did ye see the monkey? Like a little old man he was! Never seen the like.'

'Ah, he were nothing more than a child dressed up I reckon.'

'A child with a tail? Get away with ya!'

They laughed then sat down, backs against the boat. Linnet held her breath, she didn't want to be found here.

'And that singer – what he was singing about, eh?'

They talked for a while about what they could do to the women they knew, laughing about their friend who was too shy to do a thing.

'Should have bought him one of the ballad sheets – that'd learn him what he needs to do!'

'Did ye hear the singer saying it were a woman scribe who'd

drawn them up for him? Bet she were blushing by the end of it.'

Linnet nearly sat upright but the size of the boat stopped her just in time. How stupid she'd been. Now this would be part of his performing, a woman scribe writing these filthy words. If Guy heard of it, he'd know she'd been nearby.

The men walked off and Linnet lay there, in the dark of the boat, confused and trapped, with no clear path ahead of her.

Isabelle was whining again, asking for food before they left the town, dragging her heels, coughing a little too. This adventure was proving a bit too tiring perhaps. They passed by the tavern and Linnet asked for some stale bread.

They were finishing it when a voice called out.

'Scribe lady!' She'd not given the singer her name. She wasn't sure why, maybe just out of learnt caution.

'You bound for Berwick? Want to travel with me? I could use a scribe and a pretty one at that.' That last was courtesy, not especially sincere.

'Bring your daughter too, of course.'

Isabelle opened her mouth and Linnet pinched her.

'No, we're going south now. My girl and me, we're off to find my aunt and bide with her a while.'

'Pity, well if we chance upon each other again, I'll take more of your sheets. I did well out of those yesterday.'

She had sown a seed. In case Guy was asking, he'd hear about a female scribe, yes, but one with a daughter too old to be his, and one going south.

They went out on the south road, before circling round by the sea and turning back up to Lindisfarne again.

'You tells a lot of lies, Linnet.'

'Well sometimes you have to, to keep safe.'

The child nodded. That was common sense to her.

The walk was long but they made good time and arrived at

Seahouses before dark where one of the island fishermen was visiting a friend. He offered to take them back up the coast to the Priory next day on his boat, tides not right now, and his friend had room, so they stayed. The talk was all of the Inspector. He appeared to have settled in to the Priory and made himself very much at ease over the last few weeks, as if it were now his home.

'He's got sores on his bum, can't ride, so will be staying a while. He's putting Prior Richard's nose out of joint. That novice, he's been causing all kinds of strife too, allus wanting to know what all the Brothers are up to, reporting back to his master na doubt.'

The fishermen were like the rest of the islanders, always ready to gossip about the monks who thought they owned the whole isle.

Linnet asked more questions, wondering what had been happening while they'd been away nigh on a week. Apparently the Inspector was giving talks every evening in the Chapter House. Most of the monks were attending but those that didn't had to explain their absence the next day.

'And Prior Richard is letting that happen?' She had always thought of him as a strong leader of the monks, using discipline lightly, only where needed.

'He's in a black humour, for certain. Always in his parlour doing something with herbs and that. Some say it's the deaths there's bin. A drowning, poor Brother Maykin and the stones, and a self-killing in short order is bad luck, isn't it? And he's been looking for you, missy.' He poked Isabelle. 'Didn't know you was travelling with Linnet here, did he? And away nearly a week!'

Isabelle wasn't paying a lot of attention. She was looking out the door, whistling lightly, hoping for Pol to hear her, Linnet realised.

The boat ride the next day was smooth. The Priory rose up from the gentle hills of the island like a commanding voice, if one dwarfed by the rocky outcrop behind it. Linnet admired the shape of the island, that long spit of land and the curves about it. Even in winter there were evergreen grasses on it, mosses and shiny stones, birds and the rabbits from the coney. Isabelle bounced about in the boat, delighted to be coming home.

She felt a pang of envy. Even though Isabelle was alone amongst the islanders, she belonged to them, and to the Abbey and the fields, to the island itself. Sometimes Linnet felt her journeys had added things to her – like the words on a parchment roll. Sometimes she felt like she'd lost parts of her everywhere she'd been, a drop of blood from a blister here, a fragment of shoe left on the road there, people who could have been friends.

Chapter Twenty

'And the Lady was pleased with her prayer book?'

'Yes.' She'd not shown pleasure but Linnet knew she'd made something beautiful. Lady Margaret had said she would send the money back with her man, not trusting Linnet for some reason. With the theft of her purse, this was a relief.

Linnet got out the book of 'Hawking and Hunting'. The Prior examined it carefully, turning the pages. Marcus strained to catch sight of it but was a bit too far away. He was always in the Prior's parlour now, puffed up with the importance of finally becoming the Bursar.

'Is it the first printed book you've seen, Linnet?' the Prior asked.

'No, I've seen some others.'

'But you can copy this, and make it look printed?'

Of course she could. She could make it look exactly the same, or better if he'd rather. She wondered if someone already wanted a copy or if he just wanted one for the growing Scriptorium library.

He examined it, counting pages, exclaiming at the script.

She told him what the Abbess had said about binding books. They had done their own for the prayer book but it was just a simple bit of leather that she'd sewn on to the quires, this would get them more money if they were properly bound. He took her notes and made his own on the margins, adding a word or number here and there but looked very pleased. She asked him about more monks to help her but he brushed that away, impatiently.

He looked up finally. 'And you took the child with you? I had need of her here!' He was not pleased about this at all, it was clear. She felt a stab of fear, she mustn't make him angry with her.

'No, she knows the causeway so I think she followed me and the boy over. I couldn't leave her in the forest and the tide was coming in so she couldn't get home.'

The Prior went to the door of his parlour and sent a novice to go and find Isabelle. Linnet hadn't seen her since early that morning, happily playing with Pol who was cawing and almost purring like an eager kitten.

Isabelle came in, the raven hopping behind her, staying close in case she left again, Linnet supposed.

'So you disobeyed me and went after Linnet and stayed away near a week?' His voice was dangerously calm.

'You never said I shouldna,' she said, pouting.

The slap, when it came, shocked Linnet as much as Isabelle. She'd never seen the Prior hit anything, not even spur his horse that hard.

Isabelle looked at him startled and in horror, still but not crying. By contrast the raven flew into furious action, cawing and pecking at the Prior in retaliation. He waved his arms around to deflect the bird, and over the commotion, continued to scold the child.

'I have work for you here, Isabelle. You are not to go off. We feed you and clothe you and house you here at the Priory, don't we?'

She nodded slowly, the red mark on her cheek beginning

to bloom. The raven settled down near her but kept a glaring black eye fixed hard on the Prior.

'Now be gone with you, and I expect you to be here at first light tomorrow morning, I have need of your gathering skills again. You're old enough to earn your keep properly now, you hear?'

She ran, bird flapping behind her, and vanished into the fog and murk of the day.

'And why are you still here, Linnet? Go to the Scriptorium and see how Brother Luke has been faring. And I'll expect your accounts and monies from the trip. If the child cost me anything, you'll be paying that.'

The fisherman had been right about the Prior's mood. Linnet left quickly but not without a quick glance at the hearth. The cuddy duck was still tucked up on the blankets, looking for all the world like it was carved out of wood. He was still taking care of her then. Marcus followed her glance and again, she saw that flash of disdain. If he wanted to be a favourite of the Prior's, he would need to heed his love of animals, she thought.

The Scriptorium was empty but Linnet could see the Gospel Luke had been working on. He'd done well. His desk was tidy, the candle stub far enough from the parchment to be safe, his pens arranged and his ink covered. There were a couple of small errors but she'd teach him how to scrape those out and rewrite them.

She got out the money she'd earned and the scrap of paper she'd written her accounts on. She needed a good story to cover up what had happened, and she had to make certain Isabelle kept quiet when she said they'd stayed a second night in lodgings at Alnmouth, for example.

She made a fair copy, costed the child's expenses at a couple of pence, which she put separately from the Prior's money, and brought it all back to him. He looked through it with sharp eyes but nodded, and put it carefully into his money chest.

'You can give the figures to Brother Marcus,' he instructed her. For once, Marcus wasn't in the room. Nor was the Inspector.

'Is the Inspector still here?'

'Yes, he's – unwell.'

She wondered if the Inspector truly did have sores on his backside. He was too big a man to ride lightly if that were the case.

She saw him through the door of the Chapter House that night, but he looked no different from when she'd last seen him. He was preaching with the same fervour as last time too, thundering at the monks, more of whom seemed to be attentive now.

'What God intends for you, is your duty to obey. He works in ways of mystery, we know, and he will raise up those the worthy. Ask yourself – are you worthy? Do you keep God in your heart as you go about your day? Is God part of your work here in the Priory? Is it God you take to sleep with you and wake with? If not, you will be damned, and you will deserve it!'

Luke was at the front, his eyes alight. She'd not seen him since she had come back, but nothing would take him away from the Inspector's words. Cassian was sat at the Inspector's side, watching him closely. She wondered, not for the first time, why the Bishop had sent this novice with the Inspector on his travels.

She went back to her room, and stopped in the door, on edge. She'd left it in order, her blankets piled up on the tick, her special things in the box at the end, but something felt amiss.

The blankets were all still there, no one had taken the good one she'd had from Brother Oswyn, but they weren't folded the same. Had someone been looking for something?

Her box had all her usual things. Her money she always kept with her so that was safe, the pebbles from Tom's cottage were there, the small twists of paper she'd found in Oswyn's things and her spare candles. But Oswyn's household book was gone.

She sat down heavily. Was nowhere her own space? All those years of living with Guy at his mercy, after fitting into spaces around her father, she'd loved this little room that was all her own. It felt different now, stripped of something that made it feel safe. And now the household book. She couldn't ask anyone about it – she shouldn't have had it anyway. She wanted to have another look at it this evening. She'd had another thought about the paper twists.

After all the walking, she fell into a deep sleep with no trouble for once, dimly aware of the monks' night-time offices, and of the cat, settling on her. And she slept without dreams.

Luke looked pleased she was back, eager to show her what he'd done. She praised him, then pointed to the few errors. He tried to argue they weren't but gave up after she held his gaze for long enough. She showed him how to use a sharp stone or a knife to gently scrape ink off, and how long to leave it before writing over. He had his own knife but it was none too clean so she gave him a sharp stone instead. She wouldn't let him use her knife, of course. He was soon caught up in the process, his earlier objection forgotten.

She started on the first of her illuminated pages with the *Gospel of St John*, pricking out a rough eagle shape to paint in dark colours. She intended to use a little shell gold on the tips of his wings, perhaps the light of God shining down to pick them out.

It was hours later, and she was cold and stiff, when she saw that Luke had gone. It wasn't dark yet but soon. Where had he gone? Had he spoken to her before he left?

She put away her inks and her tools, pleased with her work so far. The eagle had a hungry look but still noble, a bird of prey and pray she thought to herself.

The kitchen was full, and Ann almost looked happy to see her.

'Why did you take the lass with you?'

Inevitably the word had spread around – Isabelle hadn't just run off, she'd been on an adventure. Linnet would need to tell her firmly what she should and shouldn't say.

'She just followed me. I think she was curious.'

Ann shuddered at the idea of travelling off the island. 'She said she saw a monkey? Do they have flaming eyes like she said?'

Linnet laughed, then regretted it immediately as the older woman looked shamed to be fooled by a child's unlikely tale.

'No, but it did have a tail and it did do tricks. And its eyes were red, so that's probably why Isabelle thought they were flaming.'

Ann nodded, slightly appeased, and put out a bowl of hot soup for her, which Linnet ate gratefully before setting out for the tavern.

Back on the island, Tom's death was hitting her hard again. When she'd been walking, she could pretend he was still here, fishing and drinking and dicing, but as she walked into the tavern, his absence struck her like a cold blast of wind.

The masons were still there, spreading themselves over the benches and tables. The islanders were used to visiting craftsmen and other guests crowding them out. The innkeeper always kept the better ale for them anyway, so they could suffer a few elbows in their faces as they drank. None of the monks were in here, still staying away with the Inspector on the island.

Jack caught sight of her and raised his tankard in a mocking gesture. She ducked her head, meek Linnet, not fighting Mary, remember.

After a quick cup of mulled ale, she left and walked down to the fishermen's beach. It was cold but a clear night, so she sat, wrapped in her cloak. She'd done nothing about Tom's death but she felt more and more convinced he'd not killed himself. He had black days – she could remember when he wouldn't meet anyone's eyes, hurrying from boat to house to tavern without a word – but he wouldn't have done it. She was sure. But was she just trying to make herself feel better?

She forced herself to think about what she'd said, like rubbing a lemon over a cut, letting the sting last.

'What you musing on?'

Isabelle sat down and leaned against her. The journey had made her more comfortable around Linnet, happy to use her for warmth at least.

'I'm thinking about Tom.'

Isabelle felt in her skirts and fished out a small rag creature to show Linnet. 'It's my mousie. He made it for us. I was to put it in his boat when we sent it off, but then I thought a stone would do as well. I used to find good stones for him to keep, the blackest ones, and I found one looked like mousie.'

So that's what she'd taken over to the boat that day, and that was why Tom had those stones in his cottage. Linnet looked at the child's face, bleak and resigned, and spoke on impulse.

'I think someone killed him, Isabelle.'

The child didn't move or speak. She sat, the rag mousie in her hand, turning over in her mind, like pebbles on the beach, what Linnet had said. Finally, she gave a slow nod.

'You might be right there. If we find out who, I'll kill 'em for it.' Her eyes, bright button black in the moonlight shone with grim purpose.

Having said those words aloud, Linnet was finally sure she believed them. It was now clear to her. She had to find out who had killed Tom and why.

But she also had to keep an eye on the child and what she might say. Linnet spent a long while schooling her on what she could and couldn't say about their journey, leaving her clear to talk about the monkey (without flaming eyes), the wonders of the market (nothing about the ballad singer), the nunnery, and Lady Margaret's incredible collection of silks. That should keep the women on the island interested for a few days.

She would spend the next day illuminating as usual, but would also take time to look for Oswyn's household book. She thought the strips of paper she'd found might have been torn from it. She'd not found words when matching them up with each other but maybe they matched the torn edges of the book. Oswyn was such a keeper of secrets and there might be something in his notes to point her on the right path. She wondered who had taken it and for what purpose. She'd kept the scrap from Maykin's hand too – but that couldn't have been Oswyn, he'd drowned before the accident. If it was an accident, of course.

The Prior spent the morning in the Scriptorium with her and Brother Luke. He'd mixed up the lapis powder again but it still wasn't working as it should. The colour would go on well, but even within minutes she could see it dulling and fading.

She used a little on St John's page, carefully with a tiny horsehair brush, just to add stars around the border, but it was hard to keep her hand steady with him breathing over her.

At last he sat down with a scrap of parchment and started making notes. He looked up. 'I'll need more monks to start on copying the book from the nunnery. I'll see who I can bring over from other duties.'

Luke sat up a little straighter. As if they were drawn on the parchment in front of him, Linnet could read his thoughts – him in charge of a set of scribing monks, the head of the Scriptorium. The Prior would be taking them away from other duties though and there weren't that many of them. Maybe he'd ask for more from Durham, to build the Priory up to its former glory.

A shout from outside disturbed them. The Prior hurried out, then quickly returned.

'It's the Brothers on Inner Farne. They've sent up a beacon. I thought Brother Aldus wouldn't last the winter. I'll get Tom—' he faltered, 'a couple of the fishermen to take me over. Linnet, we shall need Brother Godfreyd too, perhaps it's not too late and he can still help – go fetch him quickly.'

She went looking for Godfreyd. The Infirmary was empty but she soon found him near the stables. He scowled when given the Prior's message.

'You can come too – you can help with any cleaning and the like.'

An old, dying or dead monk was certainly too odious for Godfreyd. Linnet was curious about the cell on Inner Farne. Once the refuge for St Cuthbert, who'd died there, it was now a small cell of just two monks keeping his memory alive.

There were seven of them in the boat in the end, the Prior, Godfreyd, Linnet and another monk, Brother Adam, and two fishermen rowing. Cassian offered to come to help with the rowing, anything to keep him away from his lessons. The Prior would leave Adam there if they took Brother Aldus back. The cell had to be maintained.

They were all silent, the fishermen and Cassian concentrating on the journey. It was a long rough trip and

Linnet was soon lost in her thoughts, huddled in her cloak as the sea-spray splashed around them.

She was thinking back to her life with Guy when she was startled by the sound of Godfreyd vomiting copiously over the side of the boat. He had been going green since they left Lindisfarne and eventually succumbed. The Prior looked disgusted, drawing his robes about him and glancing away. Brother Adam tried to help, offering him water from a flask until Godfreyd swore at him and knocked it away.

At last they reached Inner Farne. Barely an island, more a small outcrop in the dark and gathering sea. What had made St Cuthbert pick this tiny pile of rocks, rather than the other few dotted about within sight?

The boat moored at the bottom of a pile of rough stones, just below the little chapel, tying up at a post there. Linnet was startled by how dark everything seemed, the stones, the ground, the sky. Edwin, the other monk, stood at the top of the small slope, his face serious.

They scrambled up to the chapel, slipping on the moss and the dank stones and the bird shit. The island was littered with ducks and puffins, their orange beaks adding a flash of colour. None looked worried by the strangers coming up the path, grudgingly shifting out of the way just in time if needed.

'Thank you, Prior. He's still breathing and waiting for you to hear his confession and anoint him.'

They went into the dark chapel where Brother Aldus was lying, the light from the candles making his white hair the only bright spot in the gloom. Linnet could hear his rough breathing, he kept pausing for longer and longer gaps. The Prior bent over him to hear his confession.

Aldus's voice was thin and light, almost childlike. Linnet looked away, distressed to be seeing him at the end of his life like this. She took a few steps back, away from the dying monk, and almost fell over a small wooden chest. She opened it slightly and looked inside.

Candles, cassocks, some bundles of kindling, but at the bottom, half a page from an old manuscript. She looked more carefully, the initial letters glowing a little in the dark but it was too gloomy to see what was written. A sharp cough made her shut the chest as quietly as she could. Cassian was looking in her direction. Had he seen her with the open chest?

Godfreyd briefly examined the monk and shook his head.

'I think he'll not survive the crossing back to Lindisfarne, Father.'

The Prior nodded and led everyone outside. Brother Edwin looked calm now that he'd seen Aldus's confession.

'I don't think he'll last much longer, Father. Thank God you're here for his end.'

Linnet walked around the rest of the island as the monks were speaking. There was a small hut above the chapel where the monks lived. As well as the birds, she saw rabbits hopping about, food for the monks, and the small kitchen garden they had grown next to the chapel.

She sat on a rock and shut her eyes, trying to imagine St Cuthbert here, hundreds of years before, battling demons and hiding from the world.

They heard a cry from Edwin inside the chapel and went in. Brother Aldus had died. The Prior led the others in prayer for the soul of their brother monk. They would be able to bring Aldus back now, rather than having to make another trip.

The fishermen were keen to start back. They were talking about tides and the like, which Linnet could tell meant nothing to the Prior but he nodded like it did.

Brother Adam got the winding sheet from the boat and Godfreyd gestured to Linnet and Cassian to come and help.

They wrapped the frail old man, and carried him down the path slipping and sliding and struggling to carry him safely, but finally laying him in the bottom of the boat. His body was still warm, but so old and frail it was the last gasps of warm wax in a candle freshly put out.

The trip was calmer on the way back. Godfreyd didn't vomit this time but had his eyes shut all the way. The Prior was intoning prayers over Aldus, but his mind was clearly elsewhere.

Home on Lindisfarne, monks came to get the body out of the boat and Aldus was taken to the Priory.

Free from the boat, Linnet had time to think about what she'd seen in the chest. Was it more of what Pol had brought her? She went up to the Scriptorium but Luke had gone to help the others and then it would be evening prayers.

She carefully uncovered Pol's hiding place, but there was only a dead vole this time, and nothing else of value.

Chapter Twenty-One

Isabelle was waiting for Linnet as soon as she was up the next day. She was paler than usual, Linnet thought, and coughing a lot.

'Pol and I has something to show you,' she announced with great importance.

'Do I have to come now, Isabelle? I have to get to the Scriptorium.'

Isabelle looked offended as though she couldn't believe she'd be made to wait. Linnet gave in. It wasn't as if her absence would be noted anyway.

The girl, with her raven perched on her shoulder as if he were light as a sparrow, led her out of the Priory, up to the Heugh, over the side and down the path to the shore. The tide was out so it was a muddy walk across to Cuddy's Island, where Linnet had found Isabelle after Tom's death. Less of a walk and more of a scramble, each rock and stone covered in dark green seaweed and slime.

The simple stone ruins on the island reminded Linnet of Inner Farne. This had been Cuthbert's first attempt to move away from the querulous, busy world of the monks. The more time Linnet spent with them, the more she felt the saint had had good reason.

Isabelle was walking with purpose, stopping every now

and again to catch her breath, leading her to a small mound of stones just out of view from the mainland, in what had been the nave of St Cuthbert's-By-The-Sea.

'We found these here – you can read 'em.'

Under the stones, wrapped in cloth, were more of those manuscript pages. Linnet gasped. They were so fresh and clear, as if written yesterday but they were much, much older than that and she wondered how they'd been protected.

She touched the pages carefully. They couldn't have survived out here under this pile of stones, even wrapped up, for more than a few months. They were torn and holed in places, but dry and well preserved. The hand was similar to that in St Cuthbert's Gospel, she was sure of it, even if she'd only seen that once for such a short time. It was an old joining-hand style that hadn't been the fashion for hundreds of years. It wasn't another Gospel though, more a book of prayers.

Her mind was racing. Could these have been written by St Cuthbert? She was setting her imagination free, she knew it was unlikely, even incredible, but they could be as old as the saint's time.

The prayers were simple, inspired by the sky and the sea and the animals and birds around the island. Amongst the prayers she found notes and scribbles in the hand of that monk of long ago, complaints about his aching hand or his head, a jest about a duck, grumbles about the weather. It was all in English but with many old words and she found much of it hard to understand.

She'd been looking at the pages for a long time, with Isabelle sitting patiently next to her. Pol had hopped off to scratch in the dirt for grubs.

'How did these get here, Isabelle?'

The child shrugged. She might know more but she wasn't

going to tell everything. After their journey together, she trusted Linnet more, but she was naturally wary.

'Should we take them somewhere?'

'No, or whoever put them here will know. I'll come and make a copy when I can. Thank you, Isabelle, this might be important but we mustn't talk about it to anyone for now.'

'Does it say who killed Tom?'

That was why Isabelle had shown her.

'No, not this. I am looking for Brother Oswyn's household book though, have you seen it?'

Isabelle seized on the chance to do something and ran off immediately to look for it in all sorts of unlikely places, Linnet thought. She watched her clamber back across the rocks and the low tide coming in, heedless of her clothes and her safety, with Pol flying just above her, circling round and back lazily.

She put the manuscript pages back carefully, hiding them just as she had found them. They looked like the ones she'd seen in the chest on Inner Farne but she'd only seen those briefly in the dark so she couldn't be sure. If they were the same, then it had to be the Prior. He was the only one to visit Inner Farne regularly and she knew he loved the manuscripts and books that the Priory had. Was he taking them from Cuddy's Isle to Inner Farne, or was he moving them from Inner Farne to here? Why wouldn't he display them in the Priory?

But the next day, Isabelle wasn't running around looking for answers. Linnet found her in the corner of the kitchen, curled up way past the time she was normally up. She shook her to rouse her but the child was hot to the touch, coughing and not awake, her eyes rolling around in her pale face.

Ann saw her looking at the child and said, 'I tried her with a spot of warm honey last night but she's got that cough. She needs some of the monks' dose, I reckon.' She looked worried, more so than usual. She knew all too well how quickly a child could fade and die, she'd buried three of her own, leaving her with just Judith, now married to a farmer on the isle.

Linnet knew Ann was right, but the person to ask was Godfreyd. Would he listen to her? She found him in the Infirmary looking over his leech book. Luke was in there too, grinding some seeds, looking sullen and unhappy. He much preferred being in the Scriptorium, she knew.

'Brother Godfreyd, the Prior has asked if you would make a dose for Isabelle for her cough and fever.'

Godfreyd looked up, eyes narrowing as he saw who it was. 'The Prior? Are you sure about that? Maybe I should ask him. I don't think he'd want my skill wasted on a kitchen brat, do you?'

She opened her mouth, trying to think of something that would persuade him, and stop him from seeing the Prior. 'Yes, he is using her for his purposes, so it will not suit him to have her sick. But I can tell him that you are unwilling if you like?'

They stared at each other for a minute, Luke looking from one to the other in the silence. Godfreyd broke it with a snort, almost a laugh as if something had just occurred to him. 'Yes of course, I will get Brother Luke here to mix it up, the remedy for fever in the leech book, I'll find the page for you.'

He was smiling broadly at Linnet as she left, although she was sure she had the better of him for this.

The rest of the monks were preparing Brother Aldus's funeral. The Inspector had taken charge, ordering a day of sung prayers for the venerable monk, more than the other deaths had warranted. Linnet thought that Aldus had become wiser and more venerable by the hour since his death. She had heard of him as a rather simple old man, a monk since he was a boy, good at catching rabbits but not able to read or write, singing all his prayers from memory.

Linnet had been sent to help in the kitchen with the funeral food. Isabelle was still curled up in the corner, coughing violently from time to time but not showing any other sign of life. She would make sure Luke did give her the dose today, she was sure that would help her. She was half-heartedly chopping when she heard a loud, arrogant voice from the courtyard.

'Fetch me the Prior. Lady Margaret will be here soon and she will need a room.'

She dropped her knife. Stricken.

'What's with you? Too proud to chop when you've been told to? It was the Prior promised me you would help today.' Ann was not impressed by Linnet suddenly stopping work. Unable to think what to do next, Linnet started chopping again.

She tried to hear what was happening outside but there was just general noise. She could hear a horse being led to the stables and the Prior talking but she couldn't hear that voice, the voice she hoped never to hear again.

At long last she was able to escape, although Ann was still complaining as she slipped out of the door.

She went around the side of the inner courtyard, moving slowly and carefully, keeping to the walls for fear of being seen. Then she saw him.

Guy looked almost the same as the last time she'd seen him, being led into debtor's prison, but much better dressed. He was looking around with that air of confidence he'd always had, the slight smile on his face as he talked to the Prior, who was listening to him as if he had something worthwhile to say.

He was slender, not as tall as Godfreyd, but handsome. She had wondered if anything had lasted of what she'd felt for Guy when she was a girl, but now she knew it had long ago died. What was he saying? She crept a little closer to listen.

'The Lady will need a room, of course, and somewhere for her maid.'

'Forgive me, but why is she coming to stay with us?'

'She is bringing the money for the prayer book and wanted to see your Scriptorium. She is only passing. Her Lord has called her up to Berwick where he is encamped.'

'And you are her new man? Where's the other one?' The Prior had clearly forgotten his name.

'He's with her, I am to go north too with my Lady to take up the office of secretary to Lord Edmund. I came across her on the journey to the island and was glad to be of use to her, saving her from troubles on the road.'

This would be perfect for Guy, Linnet thought, to be a secretary again where he could get his feet under a fine table, feted as a literate man, letting everyone think he was counselling those he was merely scribing for, and known as a hero. But what could she do now? Did he know she was here? Was this just a very unlucky chance?

As she was considering desperately what choices she had, Guy looked up and saw her in the shadows of the wall. He looked directly at her, smiled slowly and then winked. He'd obviously been thinking he might find her here, but she would have to wait to find out what he intended to do.

She lost the argument. They stayed and sold three more indulgences, but Guy, despite his bluster, was quieter in the taverns now, and Mary stayed in their rooms, working and only coming out for food.

The money was good. Guy let her take half to carry, in case he was robbed. He was poor at counting and she continued to take a coin here or a couple there, building up her own money.

Once Guy had teased out all the wealthy sinners who were looking for indulgences, he agreed they would leave.

'But we must go back to Ely, all my things are there,' he insisted. She was scared to go back but had no choice.

No one followed them out of Bishop's Lynn. The farmer who took them the first few miles was taciturn, not interested in their reasons for travel or anything about them at all. Guy did at least take the quieter paths, avoiding the main market towns.

When they reached Ely, Mary was eager to get their things and leave. They had been arguing about where to go next. Mary thought London would be safest but Guy wanted to go back towards the north, maybe Lincoln or York. A fine cathedral town that would work for them.

She stopped outside their lodging. She didn't need to go inside to see the men had been there. That was the first warning then, who knew what else they would do to them.

'Shit, shit, shit!' Guy kicked the door as they went in. His clothes were scattered all about, her inks – the ones she'd left here, curing while they were away – spilt all over the wooden floor, a swirl of muddy colours, and nothing was in its place.

They didn't speak to each other as they gathered their things, packing up to leave. The woman they had the rooms from came by. Angry about the mess. Guy threw some coins at her and snarled at her to get out, they were leaving soon, the rooms were damp.

Mary followed her out. 'I'm sorry,' she said. 'He's—' What could she say?

The woman brushed aside her apologies. 'Never mind that, he's an arse-spittle – always was so. You'd be better to find someone else.'

'Did you see who did this?'

'I'd have told the arse but he don't want to listen. It were those two men that used to come and see you. I expect you know why, none of my business. Anyways, they said to tell you that they'd be back. And they asked if you knew about that young scribe – the one who got his throat cut in a brawl after market day.'

Chapter Twenty-Two

She couldn't help it – she ran. She ran to the Heugh, tears coming in spite of herself. This was supposed to be her place of safety, but now Tom had died and Guy was back.

She slumped with her back to the stones of the little ruin, looking down on the busy work of the Priory continuing as if nothing was wrong, and tried to steady her breathing. It was warmer than it had been for the last few days, the sun steadily heating the ground.

'Hello, Mary.' He'd followed her up. 'I thought you might have come here. I remembered you talking about your visits with your father years ago. See, I know you, Mary, I know how your little flittery mind works. Lucky that Jack suggested we meet on the island once I was free. He visited me in York Prison, which was more than you ever did, so I knew he was likely to be here. And then when I happened across Lady Margaret on the road to here, hearing about the ugly little scribe who'd done her book, I knew I'd find you.'

She didn't reply.

'So am I calling you something else now?'

She stared at him but still said nothing.

'I think you know what I want.'

'There's no money left, Guy, I spent it on travelling, on getting here, on feeding myself this last year.'

'Well then I think you owe me, don't you?'

She didn't. It was her money, damn him.

He took a step closer, his eyes gleaming with a sudden spite.

'Not told your Prior about any of this, have you? Not told him you were living as my wife, or that I was in debtor's prison.'

She'd not told the Prior, no. But then –

'Do you want me to tell him how we know each other, Guy? Aren't you here with Lady Margaret? She'll not be taking you to be her Lord's secretary if she knows you were in prison now, will she?'

His sallow face grew red with fury, always the only sign. He never raised his voice or readied his fists. When he used them, his punches came from loose hands with terrifying swiftness. He wasn't like Jack and the masons, with their love of a good fight in the tavern. His violence was sudden and unforeseen, with no build-up, no time for him to savour the moment.

She shrank back, her hands clawing at the stones behind her so she could find something, anything, to protect herself with. He caught the movement, of course he did.

'Don't worry, Mary, I'll not be hitting you now,' he sneered. 'No, you're right, I don't want you to ruin my chances. But you owe me and you know I'll never forget that. You'd better be thinking of how you can pay me back.'

'I earned that money!' She was the old Mary again, the one who did talk back, at least to start with.

'Both of us earned that money, and what you earned was mine, my darling, or should have been. And if you'd given it to me like you should, I'd never have spent time in that stinking hole.'

'How did you get out?' She was curious.

'All you need to know is I made some friends who wanted to help.'

He'd charmed someone, of course he had. She'd been charmed too to start with, thinking he loved her as well as her work. He had just seen her as a way of making money. But he'd misjudged her. Charm fades after a while, and the truth shows through.

She was angry now. 'Who knows you're here?'

'Who cares?'

God, he could be stupid. She'd mistaken his sharp phrases for wit when they'd first met. Given him more than he should have.

'Warham's men.'

He gave her a blank look. Even now he had no idea of the danger they faced, the danger to her now that he'd followed her to the island, openly in the service of Lady Margaret.

'Why worry about him? We did him a job, he paid us.'

'You know what else we did.'

He shrugged, not caring.

He seemed sure that his explanation to Warham's men would be the end of it, that after their excuses Warham would forget. If she impressed the full danger on him, though, he would turn on her and use it to bargain with. She'd be better to rely on his stupidity and hope it could help her for this time, at least.

'I've other work we should do, Mary. I know you've promised some time to the Prior here, but you'll be coming with me soon, you owe me. And you'll be writing a letter for me too, a letter of introduction for the Lord. Your finest work, Mary, and I'll know if you scrimp on it. I've a name it's to come from and all the details you are to put in it.'

And with that, he started back towards the Priory, whistling, a man in his prime, with his fine clothes, with a fine place ahead of him. A man who had made himself anew, yet again, to be what people expected to see.

Linnet came slowly down the hill. If she was right, he wouldn't say anything to the Prior. And he could hang before she'd follow him anywhere again. She might have to write him that letter though, a good way to make sure he would be gone maybe. He'd need to be putting on a good face for Lady Margaret. Oh God. That pampered baggage again.

The Priory was in confusion, prayers for Brother Aldus in one corner, preparing lodging for Lady Margaret in the other. The Inspector was staying in the rooms next to the Prior's parlour so they had to clear out an old guest chamber for her off the outer courtyard, and make it fit for a Lady or she'd be sure to complain.

Linnet took advantage of the busyness to find Luke and urge him to make the dose. He was halfway through the receipt for it. He handed it to her curtly and she took it to Isabelle who she could barely rouse enough to drink it. She spooned it into the child's mouth, who didn't even grimace at the taste, a limp rag doll of a child for now. She left her in the kitchen with Ann who barely glanced up from the furious cooking she was doing for all the guests.

Linnet took refuge in the Scriptorium as Luke came back in. He had been working steadily between prayers and whatever else Godfreyd had him doing. His work on the Gospels was going well but she saw he had a habit of not quite finishing a line with the right spacing.

'You need more space here, see?'

'I think it looks better without that space. Isn't it the choice of each scribe how to lay it out?'

She rolled her eyes and explained, yet again, the difference between a scribe's own hand and the needs of those that would be reading the page in time to come. How a word running on could change the sense, even make a mockery of

God's words. He didn't admit to his fault but he did begin to keep the spaces as she'd told him.

As always, the scribing calmed her and cleared her mind. As she returned to her illumination, she pricked out patterns for the margins, thinking about what she needed to do.

Guy wanted his money. She'd thought they were partners, they worked together. But that day, the one when they came for him for the money he'd spent and the money he'd owed, she'd realised he truly was the man who hit out. The one who liked inflicting casual pain. Who thought of her not as his Mary, his partner, but his thing, his skilled but senseless thing. The dull shock of realising she'd not been seen as she truly was, giving way to a burning anger.

He'd shoved her towards the men, said he'd not known what she'd done, that she must have been stealing, that she was the one who owed the money – tried to get them to take her not him, but they'd not been fooled. She'd frozen, not able to speak up for herself as he casually hit her on the back of the head, tore her dress to show what a skinny, ugly thing she was, how the men could do what they liked with her if they'd leave him alone.

Despite his efforts, he'd owed too much for them to be distracted. Eventually he had told her to get the other coins that he owed, and she'd played dumb until he'd been taken away. It had not taken much play-acting. She was numb at the way he'd thrown her out like a scrap to be used instead of him.

She would never give him the money and she would never go with him again. He wanted this place with Lord Edmund, it would be perfect for him. Betraying her would betray himself, unless he could make them believe his lies. He could easily lie, but so could she. She would have to watch and wait.

As if in answer, her little finger set up its familiar ache. She knew he'd never harm her scribing hand, not now he needed her to write that letter for him, but the fear remained, what if his temper got the better of him again.

Meanwhile she would try to avoid Lady Margaret. She must be keen to be with her husband after all this time. It could only be a short stay.

So what else could she do for now? Nothing. That was the simple truth of it. Only hope Guy blundering about the country hadn't brought more trouble after him.

Everyone heard Lady Margaret arrive. She had complained for the entire ride over to the island. Why wasn't there a better road, why was there a flood half the day, why hadn't the Prior come to the mainland to accompany her? How lucky she had been to come across Guy just as they were to take a dangerous route through the forest. Without his guidance, who knew what would have happened to her. She was sure her husband would be very content to have Guy as his personal secretary. She was so clever to have seen the need for him. Her maid kept quiet, her head down, trying to get them across as soon as possible. The Beale boy, one of the younger two, Linnet thought, who took them across looked in awe of her, and had taken them a truly direct route for once, but his face darkened at the lack of coins at the end and Linnet knew that there would be a lot more mud to come when Lady Margaret returned to the mainland if he had anything to do with it.

The Lady dismounted gracefully and greeted Guy with warmth, a friendly face on the island, but was rather disdainful towards the Prior and the Inspector, perhaps a touch of timidity she was covering up. She demanded to see her room and her maid came running out shortly afterwards, sent on a quest for more blankets, more candles, more rushes.

Linnet thought back to Lady Margaret's room in the nunnery. Nothing on this island was going to satisfy her.

Once the maid had hurried back, laden with all she could find to make her mistress at ease, the Lady herself emerged, graciously allowing the Prior to take her into his parlour. Guy followed them, glancing around to catch sight of Linnet again, to make sure she didn't forget he was watching her, even if he was preoccupied with his advancement.

Jack had caught his eye too, but they did not acknowledge each other. Jack must have realised Guy was rewriting his history again, and wouldn't want to be seen talking with the masons. He didn't look offended. He knew how it was.

Linnet went back to the Scriptorium. She didn't want to be caught by Jack. Doubtless he would confront her again now that Guy was on the island, and she didn't know what to say to him.

The room was empty, a neat stack of Gospel quires, a few ink blots and some scattered pens showing where Luke had been. Maybe Godfreyd wanted him again.

Isabelle appeared at the doorway, she looked frustrated but her colour was better than before. She was still coughing a lot and moving a lot more slowly than usual.

'What's the matter?'

'The Prior won't let me take his duck.' The indignation flowed from every inch of her.

'Well why should he?' She was trying not to smile.

'I wanted to keep the duck safe from that Lady. She had duck-down feathers in her room, I saw.'

Linnet was impressed by how much the child had observed.

'And he wouldn't let you?'

'He waved me away. Anyways, he wants you in there. You can get the duck out, can't you, Linnet?' Isabelle would have said more but the coughing overtook her again and she slowly walked back to the warmth of the kitchen.

The duck was the first thing Linnet looked for when she went into the room, still nested by the fire, still trying not to be seen. In the late afternoon light, with the flickering candles, she didn't think anyone would find the duck unless they were looking for it.

'Ah, Linnet.' The Prior was in a welcoming mood, resolved on charming Lady Margaret. *Good luck with that endeavour*, Linnet thought sourly.

'You wanted me, Father?' she asked, trying not to catch anyone else's eye.

'The Lady wanted to thank you again for your work on her prayer book,' he said smoothly.

She smiled courteously at her. Lady Margaret didn't look thankful so much as annoyed. Her robe was very elegant, too grand for travelling, surely, so she must have changed. Linnet tried to think what the Lady was wearing when she arrived, but she rarely noticed clothes.

'I love that little book, I keep it with me always.' The words were full of praise, but the manner showed little sincerity.

She spoke a few lines, looking at the Prior but speaking to Guy. Maybe she had more than one purpose in bringing her husband a secretary. Linnet and Guy used to laugh at the way he could get the gentry to believe anything he told them. She was on the edge of laughing aloud now and avoided catching his eye.

'The Lady wishes us to make her a little book of how to look after a hawk, for her Lord as a gift.'

'But he's not to know about it, or I'll not pay!' Her attempt to amuse was met by an awkward silence. Linnet wondered if she'd paid full price for the prayer book or found some excuse to hold back a few coins.

'Can you compile such a book, Linnet?'

'Yes, Father, I'll begin immediately.' She could use the text in the book of 'Hawking and Hunting'. It would give her the chance to see it properly. She would put the Percy coat of arms at the start.

The Prior and Lady Margaret discussed the price, and Linnet took note of the agreements – no gilt on this one, just plain ink drawings to join the text. The Prior unlocked his book cupboard and gave Linnet the book of 'Hawking and Hunting', with strict instructions to be careful with it. As if she needed those.

They left for the Refectory, still talking about the book Linnet would be making, but seeing no need for her to participate.

Alone in the room, Linnet determined to rescue the duck. It could sit in a corner of her room, at least until Lady Margaret left. She picked it up, heavier than she was expecting, but so, so soft.

The duck tucked its head under its wing, hiding from whatever was happening. Sadly, she wished she could do that too.

Lifting the duck up, Linnet saw it had been sitting on something. Something familiar. It was Oswyn's household book. She grabbed it quickly, hoping the Prior would be too busy to see it was gone.

She was finally holding the book she'd been looking for but where could she put it? Her room wasn't safe, that's where it had been taken from. Where could she take it so she could get it later without arousing suspicion? She was also still holding the duck and the 'Hawking' book.

Both in the Scriptorium for now then, the place she could hide a book without it looking suspicious – and enough dark corners to plant a duck.

Luke was working, his head down and he didn't see her, as she came in carrying the duck and settled it on a pile of soft rushes. The wing had mended but it still didn't seem to want to waddle off.

She had the household book under her skirts and set it down in a dark corner, with a pile of parchment and some half-completed quires, leftovers from the last time a Prior had tried to establish a scriptorium on this tiny island.

She told Luke about the book of hawking for Lord Edmund that she would be working on, but he needed to continue with the Gospel.

'I think we should only work on God's words, not man's,' Luke said, piously.

She was sure he didn't think a woman should be scribing at all, but while the Prior had her doing his bidding, he wouldn't say it out aloud. Fine, she wouldn't show him the wonders of the hawking book then, she was itching to look at all of it. She wouldn't tell him it was the work of Abbess Juliana Berners either.

Luke told her there would be two more monks starting soon. He thought they could read but he wasn't sure.

Linnet sighed. They might copy the shapes well enough even if they couldn't read, but without the meaning, errors would certainly creep in. She would have to oversee all their copying.

Before she started again on her drawing, she looked again through the 'Hawking' book. Past the instructions for birds and past the hunting talk, there were the terms of venery.

She held the pages down as she dipped in and out, copying the fragments she loved most into her household book. She would choose for this Lord's book anything she liked. She was sure Lady Margaret wouldn't be able to read any of it, and the Prior would be looking at the book as a whole, and who knew if the Lord would even look at it.

The nouns of venery were her favourite. It started with herds, a herd of harts, a herd of swans, a herd of harlots.

Then an eye of peacocks – she paused, imagining a beautiful peacock with all the coloured inks she had – tail aloft over all the veneries. A shame there weren't to be illuminations in this one. A clattering of chuffs, a flight of doves, and an unkindness of ravens. She made a note to tell that one to Isabelle. A rout of knights, a pride of lions, a kyndyll of kittens. So many beautiful words in this book. Before she shut it up she came across two more that had her laughing out loud – a rage of maidens and a blush of boys.

Luke looked up frowning, not understanding when she laughed and his colour rose. She went back to the drawing for the Gospels book, but as she continued, her mind was on the Prior. It must have been him who took Oswyn's household book. Only he, and perhaps Isabelle, had anything to do with the duck. But why hide it? He had every reason to have it, on his desk with the other books. There must be something hidden in it and it must be something he didn't want known. Once Luke left for prayers, she would look again at the entries to see if she had missed anything.

She also wanted to get those scraps of paper and see how they matched.

Luke lingered – or so it felt to Linnet – but finally the call to Sext summoned him.

Alone in the Scriptorium at last, Linnet opened Oswyn's book and read the entries, one by one. He had marked with a star those purchases he and the Prior had intended but not completed. She looked through them carefully but it seemed to agree with what she knew already. She saw Oswyn had kept a tally of 'scribe expenses' too, far above what she was eating and costing them she thought sourly.

Unless it wasn't a case of what was in the book but what was missing from it. Where was the entry for the lapis lazuli? The Prior would have told him he was planning to buy it so it should be in here. And why hadn't the pedlar given a reckoning for that? She remembered the Prior calling him careless but it would be one of the most costly items on his cart. She could see him forgetting a note for pins or the like, but not for a precious powder.

She'd entered the cost of the lapis into the accounts as the Prior had instructed but if he'd not spent it on that, he could do anything with that money. But there had been a note in the accounts – the Inspector had found it when they were talking the other day. Why hadn't he noted it into his household book first as he had with everything else?

She looked around the desk. The lapis was certainly there but still not making the beautiful blue colour she expected. So if he'd not bought it from the pedlar – where had it come from?

She started to trace the occasional torn edges, with their scraps of words falling away. She needed that bag of paper scraps to see if she could match them

Luke came back in and went to his desk with an assured stride. As he settled down to the scribing he looked up at Linnet disdainfully.

'Is there something…?'

'I was thinking about how kind the Prior is to let you scribe.'

She bristled. 'Why so, Brother Luke?' she asked, trying to keep calm.

'Well you're not in holy orders. You may have some skill but that's not the same, of course. The Inspector says women should spend their time beautifying the church for God, but in embroidery and the like, not in books.'

'Does he?'

'Yes, women are to support our true purpose, but they should keep to their allotted tasks.' He was leaning back in his chair, waving grandly around the room, like a man twice his age instructing a child.

The duck let out a loud quack, perhaps adding her voice to the argument, and Luke, startled, nearly fell off the chair.

'Why is that duck here?'

'The Prior wanted it out of his rooms while Lady Margaret was here,' Linnet said. Well he might have done if he'd thought about it.

'I don't know how I am supposed to do my work with birds and women in every corner,' he said.

She'd finally had enough, but she still strove to keep her voice calm.

'This woman has shown you how to scribe and is busy correcting your errors. I think you'd find it a lot harder without me here.'

Offended, he turned back to his quire. She would look at it carefully later. This kind of pompous pride often led to careless errors.

'Brother Luke! I need you for the priest's boils, they need lancing.' It was Godfreyd, and in a trice, the young monk seemed to shrink, all pomposity gone.

Linnet tried and failed to conceal a smirk at the thought of him dealing with the irascible priest, and Luke glared as he left.

Chapter Twenty-Three

It was too dark to continue so she went to get some food. Ann was in a worse mood than usual. As Linnet had expected, Lady Margaret had particular needs.

'Cook her own food she could, if she needs it done special,' Ann hissed as she basted a chicken.

Isabelle was back in her corner, slumped over. Linnet went to look at her. The child was breathing very shallowly now and cold to the touch. She shook her but she didn't rouse at all.

'Isabelle!' she shouted at her, trying to wake her but there was no change. She'd been so full of life trying to save the duck just a few hours earlier. This couldn't be right.

Ann looked over, disturbed by Linnet's noise, and looked alarmed.

'That's not right – did you get the monks to give her the dose?'

'Yes, they made it up for her earlier – Luke did.' Linnet was lifting up the little girl who was dangling, heavy and inert in her arms. She needed to get her help.

Running out into the courtyard, she saw the Prior who looked at her with concern.

'What's the matter with the child?'

'She was sick, Father. Brother Luke gave her something but now I can't rouse her and I'm—'

He reached over roughly and took the child from her as lightly as a bundle of cloth and was running to the Infirmary. Pol arrived, swooping down and chattering and cawing loudly but the Prior batted him away and kept running. Linnet followed him as he shouted for Godfreyd who appeared minutes later.

'What did you give the girl? What ails her now?'

Godfreyd bent over her – the Prior had laid her on a bed – and listened to her breathing, then shouted for Luke. Linnet thought the girl's breaths were coming further and further apart, and more and more shallowly.

'Don't wait for Luke,' she pleaded, 'she's stopping breathing, I'm sure of it.'

Godfreyd shot her a quick look, hard to read, and then reached into his bottles for something and forced a spoon of liquid into the girl's mouth. They all watched her and Linnet jumped when Isabelle sat half up, retching and spitting and vomiting a thin, pale liquid.

Godfreyd took a careful step back but made soothing noises, one eye on the Prior who was tenderly wiping Isabelle's mouth and eyes as she came to.

Luke had arrived by now, looking bewildered and afraid.

'What did you give her?' the Prior demanded.

'The… the dose Brother Godfreyd told me to make up, from his leech book,' Luke stammered – pointing across to the book on the table.

Godfreyd opened it to the page and looked carefully at the receipt. 'And you made it up as it was stated here?'

'Yes, I promise I did, I didn't mean the bairn any harm.' He looked terrified.

Godfreyd looked closer at the page, then smiled, and turned to the Prior. 'I see what has happened, Father, the receipt calls for one spoon of poppy elixir, but here – see?'

He pointed to a word and the Prior's already troubled face darkened further. 'There are marks for four spoons, aren't there, Godfreyd? Was this an error on your part?'

Godfreyd looked up and straight at Linnet. 'No, this was scribed for me. This scribe here. She must have made the error. Almost enough to kill the poor bairn.'

The Prior swung round to Linnet, fury evident in his low, controlled voice as he said, 'Carelessness, Linnet? A slip that nearly cost Isabelle here her life? I thought you were a good scribe.'

She tried to get a look at the page but Godfreyd had shut the book already. She didn't think she'd make that kind of error, but what if she had? What if she had injured Isabelle – or worse, what if the child had died?

She couldn't find words to speak as the Prior continued to glare at her. The silence was broken by coughing. Isabelle looked confused and only half awake still. There was a timid knock on the door and Ann was there.

'May I take the bairn, Prior? She needs a clear up and a look after, don't she?'

The Prior handed her over carefully, wiping the last of the spittle from the child's mouth carefully with a corner of his habit, his concern for her overcoming his usual fastidiousness, then held Ann's shoulder before the woman could turn away.

'Mind she gets good food and drink now – and keep her near the fire – until she's quite well.'

Ann nodded. Linnet could see she was shaken by the events of the evening too.

The Prior swung round to Linnet and said, almost in passing as he left the room, 'A bad scribe is no scribe I want in my Priory. You can finish the paintings but that will be all.'

Luke left straight after him, not looking at Linnet who

was still standing there, aghast at what had happened. Godfreyd gave her an amused smile, and it dawned on her what had happened. It wasn't her who had made the error, he'd deliberately changed the receipt. She made a lunge for the leech book and managed to get it open on the page before he tore it back from her. Not before she saw that the number had been changed, written over in a different ink.

'But, you could have killed the child?'

He shrugged. 'She's not my concern. I had a remedy to hand in any case, I thought you'd probably notice her fading. But bringing the Prior in too, that saved me time.'

Linnet felt as if the breath had been knocked out of her. The Prior had no trust in her now and she would have to leave when the illustrations were done. She could show him it was in Godfreyd's hand but he probably wouldn't see the differences she could see. Worse, if he told others that her scribing was careless, she would struggle to get more work in holy houses. What was she going to do?

'I'll tell the Prior.'

'And why, tell me, would he listen to you?'

She went back to her room. Shaken and trying to think what to do next. She looked through her things again. Her coins were safe, she'd hidden them under some dirty linen. Men wouldn't go looking under a woman's rags, she'd learnt that early on. Tom's box was also still there. Whoever had gone looking for the book hadn't troubled with what looked like a few stones and a tatty bit of rope. But the little bag of paper scraps had been emptied all over the floor.

She cursed and gathered them up. She thought they were all there but it was like some wild game – she'd got the book back but now half the scraps were gone. If someone had been looking through them, they'd not seen the significance. She'd only just seen it herself so that was understandable.

Tomorrow, as soon as Luke was out of the room, she'd try and see if she could match up the scraps and the book edges. If she had to leave soon, she would try and solve this puzzle first. She owed it to Tom.

Chapter Twenty-Four

She couldn't have been asleep more than an hour when Tibet woke her, jumping full on her chest. She put her hand up to stroke him only to touch – urgh – a live mouse which he'd dropped on her. She almost screamed but pushed the cat and its prey off the bed.

The cat looked offended to be pushed away after offering her the mouse, but sat by the bed washing itself while the mouse quickly escaped.

She was fully awake now. She could hear the monks coming back from Nocturnes. She looked out of the window and could see a few stragglers at the back. Most had already gone up the dormitory stairs for a few hours' sleep before the next service. One of the monks at the back, much taller than the rest – it had to be Godfreyd – held back one of the others, and after a short conversation, they hurried to the stables, Godfreyd pulling the other who was reluctant, she could tell. She slipped out of bed and crept across to the courtyard.

The two monks were talking quietly, but she could see Godfreyd leaning threateningly over the other monk. She immediately thought of the time when she'd seen him and Tom in the same place, but their bodies had told a very different story. Then the two men had been standing close and reaching out to each other. Now Godfreyd was forcibly holding the other monk with one hand while reaching under his habit urgently.

The other monk was talking very quietly, protesting 'no, no, no' but with no hope of Godfreyd heeding him. As he turned his face, Linnet recognised him. It was Luke.

She gasped aloud and he heard. He looked at her with shame and rage but Godfreyd hadn't seen her, busy with his sin. She left as quickly and quietly as she could. Could she use this against Godfreyd? But as he'd said – who would believe her? As she slipped through the courtyard, keeping to the shadows, she thought she saw another monk, walking quickly from the stables towards the dormitory. It was too dark to see who it was.

Chapter Twenty-Five

Lady Margaret was causing a commotion. She had had enough of this island with so little for her entertainment. Linnet thought she was probably missing the crowd of nuns she could make run around after her. The few female servants at the Priory were too busy and too old to care about an upstart Lady trying to make busy-work for them.

She was berating her maid, who was trying to explain that she may wish to leave the island now but the way was under water, when Guy stepped into the outer courtyard in his rich suit, face washed and hair combed.

'My Lady, can I help?'

'Yes! This idiot won't follow my orders! We need to leave now and go to Berwick to meet my Lord. I will not wait any longer.'

Guy looked at the servant with some pity.

'Of course, Lady Margaret, you are eager to see Lord Edmund again, I understand. We can leave now if you wish, I will ask one of the fishermen to use his boat. Does your horse travel well in a boat?'

Lady Margaret looked unsure. No horses travelled well on boats, that was the truth of it. In a small fisherman's boat, they would be sitting next to a frantic heap of kicking horse, probably shitting itself in fear.

'Well maybe we can wait a little longer. When can we leave? I must be on my way.'

Guy spoke to one of the servants who was passing.

'We could leave this evening but it will be too late to head off to Berwick then. The tides are right tomorrow after Lauds and we could then ride straight on.'

'I suppose I can spend one more night here if I must. But, Guy, make sure I have more blankets, the room they've put me in is too cold! I am too thin for this climate.' She made a pretence of shivering, looking at him with pleading wide eyes.

He took the bait and promised 'the softest blankets I can find for my Lady's delicate skin', which had her preening like a pampered child.

She went back to her room, to change her clothes again no doubt, and Guy saw Linnet watching. They shared an amused grin, each knowing what the other was thinking. For a brief moment, it took her back to their good years. It hadn't been all violence and fear, had it? No, he'd given her a lot, not only the money she'd taken.

'What have you done with the duck?' The Prior's abrupt question startled her.

'I didn't think Lady Margaret would like to share the parlour with a duck,' she answered, looking him boldly in the eye. Would he mention the book? They both knew she must have taken it and that he'd first removed it from her room. She knew he'd lost confidence in her but then she had nothing more to lose by standing up to him now.

He smiled thinly but didn't say any more.

She wanted to ask him about the manuscripts Isabelle had shown her on Cuddy's Isle but didn't dare bring up the child's name, so kept quiet. She wondered why he was hiding them, then it came to her. If they had valuable manuscripts, Bishop

Foxe would want them for Durham. Or maybe it would increase what the Priory had to pay to Durham in dues.

She forced herself to keep meeting his gaze. He seemed taller now that she was standing right next to him and looking up at him. His hands were flexing as he spoke. She imagined those hands tying the rope that hanged Tom and flinched.

He had things to hide, but was he a killer?

'Shouldn't you be in the Scriptorium?'

She nodded and left without saying any more. She was turning it over in her mind. Would the Prior have killed Tom? Had he known something that made him a threat? He had been the main fisherman who took him to Inner Farne, was that where the manuscripts came from?

She kept thinking of those manuscript pages. If only the Prior would let her look through them properly when he did bring them into the Priory – but of course he just wanted her gone now.

Luke was in the Scriptorium. He looked like a coiled spring, wrapped around his desk and stabbing his pen down as he scribed.

'Luke, be careful, you're going to rip the parchment!' She went to take his pen off him.

'Get off me, don't touch me!' he yelled.

Startled, she took a step back.

'Bad enough that you're in here with your sin and your wiles, never, never touch me.' He was hissing now, eyes wild.

'I'm not the one who was sinning in the stables last night.' She hadn't meant to shout that out either, she was becoming careless.

He stood up suddenly, sweeping the parchment off the desk in his haste, and in two strides was shouting in her face. 'You didn't see anything. I wasn't doing anything. I am not the sinner. I am not the sin!'

She shrank back from the spittle. A noise from the door and Luke broke off.

It was Guy.

'Not interrupting a lover's quarrel, am I?' His voice was smooth as silk, a danger sign Linnet knew well.

'Don't be absurd. I am a monk in holy orders.' Luke blushed, probably at the thought of what that meant and of what Linnet had seen but controlling himself with an effort.

'I've come to fetch Linnet. Lady Margaret wants her things ready and her servant is busy elsewhere.'

Linnet was not so angry she didn't feel irked by the thought that she could be loaned out to any passing gentry as a pair of servile hands, but she took the chance to leave Luke. Perhaps he would have calmed down by the time she returned.

It was as dull as she had feared. She folded the linen once again, more carefully this time. Lady Margaret was watching her, puzzled and annoyed.

'Why can't you fold this properly? What is your difficulty? Are you getting ink on my sheets? Be careful!'

Linnet refrained from answering as she wished. She knew nothing of folding linen in this particular way because it wasn't what she did. She scribed. If Lady Margaret could do it better, then maybe Lady Margaret could fold her own linen. She thought wistfully about a preacher she'd heard at one of the market towns they'd passed through when she was a child. Shouting about how everyone was the same, why did the gentry get everything done for them? He wasn't left to shout for long.

She tried to tame the linen, straightening edges and smoothing it again, taking quiet satisfaction as she saw her inky thumb leaving a little dark mark just under the fold. Lady Margaret stared at her for a moment before turning her attention back to Guy, twitching her skirts in irritation.

Their voices were low but Linnet could hear Lady Margaret laughing and Guy's murmured responses. She wondered if Guy thought he was making her jealous. She'd hated the way he charmed other women when they'd been together but those times were long past.

As she worked on the folds, she saw more paper lying on the table nearby. She glanced up. Lady Margaret and Guy were by the window, pointing and laughing at something in the courtyard. She slipped it amongst her skirts. She could at least get something out of this stupid waste of time.

With a loud caw, Pol flew into the room through the open door. Lady Margaret gave a little screech of fear and fell into Guy who caught her gallantly. Isabelle came running after him, shouting at him to come back. Linnet was relieved to see she didn't seem any the worse for her recent brush with Godfreyd's dose. Perhaps too pale, and still coughing, but the spark was back in her dark eyes and Linnet thought Pol looked relieved – if a bird could look relieved – fluttering happily around her again.

Guy let go of Lady Margaret and started trying to drive the bird out. He came close enough to almost catch him, Pol slowing to let him get nearly there, but then he flew up to the rafters and cawed louder.

Lady Margaret looked at Isabelle. 'Isn't this your girl?' she asked Linnet. 'Why isn't she busy doing something useful?'

'I ain't her girl.' Back on her home ground, Isabelle was her usual self, insolent and confident. 'I do things for the Prior, ain't nothing I do for her.'

'And is this your bird?' Lady Margaret gave another little scream as Pol flew back across the room, before settling on the bed, waddling about and using his beak to tear at the bedclothes.

'Yes, he's mine.'

'But he can't just come in here – you just can't come in here and start wrecking my room.' Lady Margaret looked annoyed but she was smiling a little at the stubborn child and her funny pet.

'I's just following Pol, I was trying to get him out of your room, not in it.' Isabelle looked back at her with an air of angelic innocence.

'Well, can you get him out?' Guy was not charmed by her, that much was clear. He'd never liked children, never thrown a penny at a group of little boys kicking a stone around, never smiled at a small girl finding joy in a puddle.

Isabelle whistled and Pol hopped over from the bed, after a quick look up and down to make sure he wasn't missing anything, and they left.

Linnet thought Isabelle had wanted to have another look at Lady Margaret's things. Pol was a useful ally for her. She could have called the bird over any time she wanted.

Lady Margaret turned back to Linnet to resume complaining, but was interrupted by the return of her maid, so she started shouting at her to do the linen properly.

Linnet hurried after Isabelle. She wanted to see how she was. The child was standing in the courtyard looking thoughtful, Pol hopping about nearby.

'How are you feeling now, Isabelle? Do you feel sick still?'

Isabelle shrugged that off, that was another time, she was better now. 'That Lady likes that man doesn't she? I don't. He don't like Pol.'

'Yes, I think she does, and no, he's not very nice.'

'Will he do bad things to her?'

Linnet thought about it for a moment. Lady Margaret was of value to him, not like a servant girl. He'd have to find another object for his violence.

'No, he wouldn't dare. He's careful.'

Isabelle nodded, approving. 'I like being careful too.'

Linnet saw Isabelle was eating something. 'What do you have there, Isabelle? Did you take something from Lady Margaret's room?'

Isabelle swallowed the sweetmeat hurriedly and changed the subject. 'Did you fetch the duck?'

'Yes, she's in the Scriptorium now. The Prior knows and isn't pleased but he's not taken her back.'

Isabelle insisted on going to see the duck to make sure it was okay. It shrank away from Pol who seemed offended at another bird drawing Isabelle's attention. While she was gently patting it, he went over to his hiding place and started carefully pulling away the rushes.

'Did you know he hides things here?' Linnet asked Isabelle.

She nodded, still playing with the duck who was looking grimly straight ahead, not enjoying the attention.

Linnet had a closer look at what Pol was digging up. That dead vole which he proceeded to carefully tear apart and eat. He was still tearing at it when Luke returned from prayers.

He looked at the bird eating the rotten vole and the child playing with the duck and raised one eyebrow at Linnet. She felt foolish. It was hardly the organised scriptorium she dreamed of.

She drove the child and raven out, Pol protesting at having to leave the rest of his meal, although he quickly covered it again.

Chapter Twenty-Six

Linnet brought the little bag of scraps over to the Scriptorium when Luke was next away, and opened the household book on the desk. It was difficult to match each scrap with a torn edge and she soon realised she had fewer scraps than edges.

She moved them around, trying them in turn against each one. The first one to fit was from a few months ago. She was sure the first letter was a G – and when she matched it to one of the scraps she could see 'Godfreyd' and '*amor homin*'. The latter had a dot next to it – a shortening. '*Amor*' was love. Could '*homin*' be man or manly? That would fit with what she'd discovered herself.

It suddenly became plain – Oswyn had been making private notes in his book, and he must have found this the best way to keep it away from prying eyes. He'd written in a tiny hand, and then torn the edges off but kept them. He must have thought it was the safest way to keep them hidden.

Excited, she put that scrap carefully aside, marked the edge of that page with a tiny dot to signify she'd read it, and moved on to the next torn edge. This was harder. The page itself was partly ripped, and it had become damp. The letter that started the note had a loop, perhaps part of a 'B' or an 'R'. When she found the matching scrap though, it was a 'P'. *Prius furtum pecunia*. Was that the Prior?

She puzzled about that for a while. *Furtum* like furtively? Hiding perhaps? She wished her Latin was better. It was fine for copying but there was so much she didn't know. She made a promise to herself that she would try and learn more from the monks if she could.

Her examinations were brought to an abrupt halt when she heard shouting and went outside. Two of the grooms were running into the inner courtyard, calling for help.

She followed them back to the stable door where she saw a small throng staring at something inside. A monk was lying face down, not moving on the ground, very near one of the horses. Had he been struck by the horse's hooves? The horse was pressed against the stable wall, breathing heavily, its flanks damp with sweat and flecks of foam at its mouth.

The Prior came out of his parlour and pushed his way to the front. He called for one of the grooms to lead the horse away before he gently turned the monk over. The man was bloodied and bruised but he groaned as he was turned. Alive. He didn't open his eyes and he seemed to be struggling to breathe. She could see cuts on his face, blood streaming over his features.

It took Linnet a few minutes to recognise this bloodied heap as someone she knew well – Luke. She shrank back, memories of the night when Maykin died coming back again, his screaming, the blood, the gasping of his final words.

The Prior stood back. 'An accident. It seems Brother Luke has disturbed the horse in some way. Take him to the Infirmary and fetch Brother Godfreyd.'

Cassian and another monk came forward to carry Luke, who hung like a soiled cloth between them. Godfreyd had arrived and was looking at Luke thoughtfully. He told the men to lay him on the bed nearest the Infirmary door.

There was a sudden scream from the crowd. Lady Margaret had pushed her way through and had seen Luke covered in blood, being carried to the Infirmary. Guy came from behind the stables, and quickly led her away.

The Inspector was watching it all too, with a look of disdain.

Linnet felt Isabelle arrive by her side, prodding her and whispering something. She couldn't hear her so they found a quiet corner and the child said, 'That weren't a horse what did that to Brother Luke. I know it.'

'Why do you say that?'

'I ain't never seen that horse get afeard or mardy. Not even once, not even when Pol sat on him.'

Linnet felt suspicious too, doubt forcing its way up through her shock. But who would want to hurt Luke and why? She knew Godfreyd was using him, surely he wouldn't want to hurt him. But after all, he'd put Isabelle in danger so maybe he would. She remembered Guy coming out from behind the stables. Did he really think she and Luke were together? Did he still care about her so that he would harm others? Was it Cassian? What had Brother Benedict told him that time he'd pointed at Luke in the Chapter House?

After all the commotion died down, the Prior sent across the two monks who were now to be assigned to the Scriptorium. Without Luke there, Linnet could have the monks working as she wished. They started script on scraps of parchment so she could see their hand before she gave them each a quire to copy. They talked quietly about Luke for a few minutes, praying for his swift recovery, before settling down to their new tasks.

She couldn't go back to Oswyn's book with them there, so she put it to the back of her mind. But seeing Luke's body, and fearing him dead, had raised all her questions again about Tom's hanging, Maykin's accident and Oswyn's drowning. She shivered at the thought of another death. There must be a connection between it all.

The elder of the two monks, Father Thomas, was about sixty, and thankful to be doing easier work than in the gardens where he had spent a lot of his time. Neither of them could read especially well, but if she read it out to them, they understood the Latin well enough.

Linnet took advantage of their knowledge by compiling a brief Latin manual as they talked, and then saw how it could be very helpful.

'What's *pecunia*?' she asked.

'We don't see any of that now!' Father Thomas was pleased with his jest. 'It's money or coins.'

'And *furtum*?'

'Thieving. That's thieving.' He looked worried then, glancing down at his quire. 'Does it say it here? I can't see it.'

She reassured him it was from another book and they went back to their scribing.

Thieving… money…? *Prius* – that must be prior. Did it mean the Prior was a thief? If so, Oswyn would have known, which made him a danger. If Oswyn was threatening to betray the Prior to the Inspector, that would be reason enough to kill him. But what about Tom? Why Tom?

She remembered Tom talking about seeing two monks quarrelling the night before Oswyn died. Had he overheard something he shouldn't have done – and had he been seen? And she still wasn't sure if that was the same quarrel she had seen, Oswyn and Cassian. Thinking of him and now here he was, coming into the Scriptorium to see Father Thomas.

'The Prior said you could help me with my lessons.' He was brusque, passing on an order. The older monk graciously made space next to him at his desk, and set him on one of the lessons, patient and friendly with him.

'And what were you doing afore you became a novice then, Cassian?'

'Carpenter.' Cassian didn't look up as he looked down at the words, scowling at them.

'And do you have a family, are they missing you now you're in the order?'

'Ah no, my folks dinna make old bones. Nor my wife either.'

Father Thomas crossed himself and said a quiet prayer. Cassian smiled in thanks, and patted the old man's hand.

They settled in to the lesson, Father Thomas enjoying the teaching, and Cassian calm at his words for once.

It was the first time Linnet had seen him closely since the time he had the fit. She wondered if the Inspector knew of his affliction. He couldn't have said anything about Tom's sin to the Prior or the Inspector. If he had, there would be a flurry of searching and questioning. Did he know it was Godfreyd? No, she'd not used his name when she was cursing Tom, so Cassian couldn't have heard that, but again, she thought of Benedict and the way he had pointed to Luke.

She studied him while he was busy with his work, seeing those shadows under his eyes that hadn't been there before, and his hands, more fresh cuts. She thought again of Luke, but why would Cassian want to harm him? She needed to find out more about the monks.

Chapter Twenty-Seven

It was another cold, wet day and Lady Margaret and her attendants were preparing to leave. Guy was making sure her bundles were properly attached to the carts and that her servants had fulfilled their duties.

The Prior came out to bless their journey and to ask them to speak kindly of him to Lord Edmund, which Lady Margaret said she would do. She looked like a pampered child on the horse, small and wrapped up in her furs, but imperious nevertheless, no trace of her earlier timidity remaining. Linnet noticed her maid casting side eyes at Guy, perhaps suspicious of how quickly he'd become part of the party. She'd heard Ann tell one of the kitchen maids how Guy had rescued Lady Margaret from a muddy pathway he said was dangerous. She guessed he'd seen a rich woman riding and thought to get in with her for his advantage. She'd seen him do that same thing a few times in the past.

Before they left, Guy came over to Linnet.

'I'll not be far away, Mary, don't you forget that.' He held out his hand beneath his cloak and she passed him the letter. It was a fine piece of work but she'd left a little mark in it so that she would know it was hers, if she needed to point it out in the future. He could have this but she would never give him back that money.

She had to ask: 'Did you hurt Luke?'

He looked blank but he wouldn't admit to anything, she knew. She watched the small train off the island, following the middle Beale boy as he picked his way across the damp sands, a sudden turn or twist to avoid the deadly muds, and lead them safely, if not quite as cleanly as before. With a stab of fury and fear, she wished the lot of them to misstep and sink below the grey mud and the dark water rushing in, keeping her safe on this island again.

The island was quieter when they had all left. The Prior was plainly relieved that Lady Margaret had gone, but Linnet caught him looking with some impatience at the Inspector. Still here, still digging into things.

Of course he'd be very unhappy with the inspection if he was falsifying the accounts. She determined to look at Oswyn's book later to see if there was anything amiss.

The two monks in the Scriptorium had been given an exemption from the day's prayers, they told her. The Prior wanted them to work on the Gospel, especially now Luke was in the Infirmary.

'How is he?' she asked.

'Still very unwell, or *vapide* as we might say in Latin.' Father Thomas smiled at her, pleased to be teaching her. She smiled back and wrote it out carefully in her new Latin manual.

She thought about Luke and how much he'd been hurt. She'd been sure he was dead when she'd first seen him lying there. She shuddered.

'Shall I add more wood to the fire?' Father Thomas had seen her shiver and thought she was cold. She liked him, and liked having him in her Scriptorium. Until she was told to leave, it would be her Scriptorium. And now the monks were here, a scriptorium with a fire.

A thought came to her. If the Prior was stealing and she

could prove it, could she use the knowledge and make him let her stay? But, of course, that would be stupid and dangerous. Had others tried to do that – Tom, Oswyn or Luke?

In the kitchen that evening, Isabelle came and sat close to her, taking the seat just before Jack could sit there. She wondered if he'd spoken with Guy before he'd left. Jack caught her eye from across the room and winked at her. Yes. He must have done.

The room was as busy as normal but everyone seemed a bit more relaxed now Lady Margaret had left. Linnet had been to many priories and monasteries, and some were more prepared to have visitors than others. Here on Lindisfarne they seemed to be accepted grudgingly. The Priory was happy to take their money but provided little enough for it.

Even without the gentry on their trips around the country, there were plenty of people coming and going. But they were working people, lodged above the stables or in the old monastic cells, happy enough with an old bundle of ticking and a worn-out blanket, and here for a purpose.

The talk around the tables was of Luke, why he'd annoyed a horse and so forth. Isabelle kept looking at her, trying to wink but only making strange faces.

'What's the matter, child? You got something in your eye?' Ann asked, kindly enough for once, clearly watching out for her after her illness and now that the Prior had tasked her with it.

'It's the smoke from the fire,' Isabelle replied quickly, and stopped trying to get Linnet's attention.

Once they were outside she tugged at her sleeve urgently. 'I know for sure it weren't no horse! The marks aren't right, Linnet – I know the marks from a horse kicking.'

'Have you gone in to see him?'

'Yes. I took water in for Brother Godfreyd, and he weren't

there so I took a good look at him. He's not speaking, didn't know I was there. Not dead yet though. Anyways, he had all these bruises around his head – his eyes and cheek had swelled up – and on his chest, but his hands was just scratched. No horse does scratches.'

Again the child's attention to detail surprised Linnet. She thought of Oswyn's scratched hands.

'So if Oswyn, maybe Maykin, and Tom were killed, and Luke beaten, who's doing it and why?' She was asking herself as much as the child.

Isabelle looked back at her as if she were wanting answers herself, but said nothing.

Linnet sent her off to bed and went to the tavern. She wanted a hot spiced ale and to see if anyone was talking. She was immediately grabbed by Sir Cyrus, his breath hot and heavy into her face.

'Took the child off the island, did you? More trouble than she was worth, I'd think!' He looked very pleased with himself, and she couldn't deny there was truth in what he was saying. She wondered if he'd ever been off the island, maybe he was jealous of Isabelle.

'Were you born here, Father?'

'Of course I was. Born here, learned by the monks here, and then given the priesthood here, and they'll bury me here too.'

He was probably seventy or more so burying him wasn't too far off. The thought made her think again of Tom, wrapped in a sheet like waste from a sick bed and planted in the sea. Her anger came back too, white hot and satisfying, burning away some of her grief.

She looked down quickly before Father Cyrus could see it in her eyes. Why was she wasting time here, amongst these loud people with all the noise and drinking, when she could and should be trying to avenge him?

Her best source of information so far had been Oswyn's book. He'd loved his secrets, hoarding them like the fat squirrel he had been. She needed to see if she could patch together anything else that might give her more inspiration. How many more scrolls had been in the bag? Why hadn't she counted them when she had the chance?

She left abruptly, going back to get a candle from the ones she'd hidden in her room and then creeping quietly into the Scriptorium, empty and cold now that the day's fire had died down. She felt her way around in the dark, carefully retrieving the book and the bag of scraps before lighting the candle from the embers. Tucked away at the end of the Priory quarters, the candlelight wouldn't alert anyone.

The most important secret would have to be the last one he wrote and which may have led to his death. She set the candle on her desk and laid it all out. She turned to the last page. There were the usual notes about his tasks for the day, hiring the masons, what they'd be paid, a warning about their drinking and fighting. He knew why they were coming cheap.

The Inspector's arrival was also noted, which room he had been given, what they would reserve for his candles, his firewood, his food, and Cassian's name, with a question mark. Oswyn couldn't have known how long they would be here but he'd calculated a per diem sum to account for everything, including paper and ink. Her time helping the Inspector, she noted wryly, was put down as 'gratis' with a note that her current pay would suffice for any extra scribing.

And at the foot of the page, the little scribbles and the ripped-off strip. When she looked back through the rest of the book, she discovered Oswyn had only done this occasionally, not every day. So the important or dangerous secrets he didn't want anyone to see, especially perhaps the Prior, he wrote in his smallest hand, in Latin, and then ripped off to keep even more secret. It was something for him to hoard and lie on in his good blankets in his clean, bare cell. The lives of others.

She got out the little bag of scraps and started trying to match them to the last entry. Nothing fitted. She found a few others that fitted earlier pages, about Ann the cook, she thought, and about *fornicatum*, and about one of the monks whose family wasn't quite what he'd pretended – *illegitimus* or something like that. But she couldn't find what she needed.

Finally she counted. She had eleven ripped pages and eight scraps of paper. Where were the rest?

As she put it all away and went to blow out her candle, she saw the rough patch on the floor where Pol had his store. She carefully moved the rushes, looking for – well did he take paper? Still nothing but what remained of the vole, and now a shiny button, one she recognised as coming from Lady Margaret's elegant cloak.

Chapter Twenty-Eight

The man from Durham swung down in an elegant dismount and brushed away the mud from his journey. The Prior smiled at him and began to offer the usual polite greetings.

The man cut in, 'And to you, Father, many blessings upon your house, the Bishop sends his Brother-in-Christ his love and his prayers.' He took a breath. 'I've come to find out why Father Nicholas has not yet finished his report? The Bishop is keen for him to inspect more of his houses, and wishes him to be just, but above all swift.'

The Prior nodded – they were not going to beat about the bush then – and called for someone to fetch the Inspector.

'I fear Father Nicholas has been unwell,' he said, gesturing to parts of the body he'd rather not mention. 'He's been unable to ride and felt he could use his time here – ah, here is the man himself, I'll let him explain.'

The Inspector was limping slightly as he appeared, but was still a lordly figure. He greeted the messenger in a perfunctory way, half-embracing him in the formal act of friendship but no more.

'I know the Bishop is keen for my report, but I must be just and it must be true. He understands—' he began.

'Yes, yes, Father,' the man interrupted, 'but he is sure a man of your perception will have the information by now – do you not?'

The Inspector looked both affronted and superior, Linnet thought, watching from the Scriptorium door.

'It's simple enough for an Inspector to come in and see a monk is poorly dressed, that he is singing the wrong prayers, but it takes time to see a monk's soul is poorly dressed, does it not?'

The man shrugged wearily. Linnet had the impression that he and the Bishop were more concerned about the Priory's accounts than the monks' souls, but he couldn't say that here, not in front of the Prior.

'I fear the Inspector is also being too modest here,' the Prior began, with a slightly malicious look. 'Tell him about, you know.' He whispered in Father Nicholas's ear and the Inspector stepped quickly back, visibly furious.

'Yes, yes, I am also unable to ride at the moment but that problem is being resolved. I'm sure the Lord will cure any discomfort when he feels my work here is done.'

And still smarting, the Inspector stalked back into the Chapter House, making every effort not to limp. The Prior and the man exchanged faintly amused glances.

'Come, you must need refreshment and your horse needs rest before you return. The tide will change in two hours so if you're quick, you can return today.'

The man nodded and led the horse off to the stables. He'd delivered his message. It was not his fault if the Inspector refused to hear it. He saw Cassian loitering outside and beckoned him closer. Linnet couldn't hear much but the novice was protesting, she could see, angry at what was being said. Something about what he was doing for the Bishop and for the Inspector and now this man.

'The Inspector ain't going nowhere then.'

Isabelle was standing by the door of the Scriptorium, Pol fluttering down in front of her and hopping and strutting around.

'No, it seems not. Isabelle, what is the secret you and the Prior have?'

The child looked at her carefully, weighing loyalties. Linnet waited.

'I ain't telling you now but I will soon, maybe. He don't need my help no more, anyways. He tells me to go away now. He's cruel.'

That judgement came with all the hurt and indignation a child feels for the inexplicable behaviour of someone much older.

Linnet sighed. Scraps of information everywhere but never the full page. That reminded her. She looked at the raven, scuttling along the floor now with little hops and croaks as the Priory cat stalked past, keeping just out of its reach.

'Does Pol ever bring you bits of paper, Isabelle?'

She looked startled. 'Yes, he do sometimes. I keep them safe, I keep all he brings me safe.'

'Can you show me those?'

The child nodded. This wasn't telling a secret so it was allowed. She led Linnet out to a corner above the kitchen, where she often slept. Under the small heap of torn blanket rags, she'd dug out a little of the earth floor and carefully lined up her treasures.

Linnet looked at her poor collection: a polished stone, a button (again one of Lady Margaret's?), a rabbit foot, a perfect tiny bird's skull – and some scraps of paper. Isabelle gave her the papers.

'Do you know what they say then?'

There were three scraps. One was on very poor quality parchment, and appeared to be nothing more than marks and lines in different directions. The other two were the same as the ones Linnet had. She held up the poor quality piece.

'What's this, Isabelle, do you know?'

'Oh that be what Ann marks to make sure she has the right store of flour and so on. She said she got those marks from her mother and her mother before them. Father Cyrus says they be heathen but I seen them on some of the stones on the island.'

Another mystery, but it didn't help.

'Can I take these others?' The child nodded. And then, in a rush, 'He has me collecting things for him – the Prior – flowers and herbs and things from the sea.'

'Why does he want those?'

Linnet wondered if he'd contrived tasks to keep her busy or keep her from harm but Isabelle continued, 'He has an old piece of paper, but it were damp before so he couldn't read it all right. He said it had the things you nee't to make blue.'

Make blue? Linnet thought for a moment and then it struck her. Of course, suddenly it was all plain. He didn't have an account for the lapis because he'd not bought any. He was making his own. He must be keeping the money. Oswyn was right, a thieving Prior.

But it hadn't worked yet. Where had the recipe come from? She wondered what the instructions were.

Her thoughts were racing but her attention was drawn back to Pol's loud cawing, angry that Isabelle was giving away his treasures.

'You got anything you can give him?' Isabelle asked. 'You gives him something and he gives you something, then he'll be right.'

Linnet pulled out a hairpin and the raven fell upon it, gleefully plucking it delicately from her flinching fingers before waddling over and ceremoniously dropping it in

Isabelle's hand. She put it with the other treasures and drew her blankets over the pile.

The monks in the Scriptorium were busy, tucked in with the fire roaring and plenty of candles lit. Linnet remembered how bare and cold it had been before the Prior wanted his monks to work there. He'd said the fire was needed now to keep the monks' hands warm enough to write. She'd refrained from pointing out that she too had hands.

The monks were called to hear the Inspector talk again, even though it was the middle of the day. None of them looked eager to hear what he had to say. Linnet took the chance to get out Oswyn's household book and the scraps that Isabelle and Pol had given her.

The first scrap she tried didn't fit at the end, just on another page, something about one of the fishermen giving short measure on his catch. She tried the second one. It matched.

Quickly she scribbled the words into her book.

neque obliviscaris in faciem Pulsante autem, occisor dic Priorus – sed mortuus est

She could understand some of the words – *faciem* must be face, and *Priorus,* that was Prior again, *obliviscaris* something to do with forgetting? This must be the last secret Oswyn had written, and it could have led to his death. *Mortuus* must be to do with death.

Had he discovered something even more grave about the Prior? All the signs suggested it. He already knew he was thieving, but maybe he'd decided to confront him? Was there another secret he'd forgotten until now – was that *obliviscaris*?

The monks came back, Father Thomas poked at the fire and they settled to their work, gossiping happily.

She quickly hid the book and the scraps and continued with

pricking out her drawings. She felt everything was pointing to the Prior – but what could she ask him and what would she do if he was a killer?

The monks were chatting as they worked about the Inspector's sermon which, it seemed, had become a daily punishment. She half-listened as she carefully decorated the border.

'He does believe in fate, doesn't he?' Father Thomas said thoughtfully. 'You too, Brother Samuel?'

The other monk agreed.

'To a point, Father,' he replied, 'but how much do we decide our fate and how much do we merely follow the path the Lord has decreed for us?'

'Well now, that's the question. Too much for a simple monk like me to understand. But if we are already set on our path, why do anything but be carried along, like twigs in a stream, eh?' Father Thomas was enjoying the talk. Linnet thought he had probably chatted with the plants when he'd been tending them. At least here she and Brother Samuel would occasionally reply. Cassian didn't talk, head down, still fighting with his lessons.

'Perhaps we only think we stride out, choosing our own path, but it's the Lord who decides and he's making us think it's our choice.'

'Ah, now you're too learned for me.' Father Thomas chuckled and went back to his scribing.

Linnet did not believe in fate. She was in charge of every foot she put in front of the other, of all her choices, stupid as some of them had been. She was sure of it. But was she to blame for the things that had happened to her? Was Luke to blame for being beaten – or kicked by a horse as most people thought?

She looked at her Latin handbook again.

'Father Thomas, what's *occisor*?'

'Oh now, that's killer, or murderer, I think. Where do you get these words from?'

She froze. Did the paper say the Prior was a killer? No one had died when Oswyn wrote this but maybe he knew what was to come. She muttered something about Cain and Abel while inwardly she turned over what this could mean.

If the Prior were the killer, who could judge him? He was the lord of this island, and she would never leave if she accused him – not if he were ready to kill. But there was the Inspector. He was the Prior's superior. If she had evidence, she could take it to him and he could tell the Bishop.

There was a noise from the corner of the room, the duck. She'd completely forgotten about the duck. It looked around from the gloom and took a tentative waddle out.

'Oh my Lord, a duck! What else do you hide here, Linnet?' Father Thomas looked startled but then charmed.

She looked from the duck to the monk, they both had the same expression of contentment, confusion and general geniality. Was she going mad now, thinking of it like a human? It was just a duck. And of course it was hungry. As the Prior's pet, she'd been fed in her spot by the fire. She'd neglected it but she had probably come out now for food. She'd have been better treated by the Prior, but a man who could be so kind to a duck – could he really be a murderer?

She needed to know. Even if asking questions was dangerous.

'Come in!' His voice was sharp.

She walked into his parlour, carrying the duck. After its brief burst of activity, it was still again. She decided it would be the perfect reason for her to see the Prior.

'Did you want the duck, Father? I found it in the Scriptorium.'

'Found it?' He raised one eyebrow and she looked steadily back.

'Ah well, put her back by the fire, she will need some more bread before we can release her, although she's looking better for her roving.'

He gathered his papers and headed out of the door, not waiting to see the duck settled. In his haste to leave, he'd dropped a page or two so she put them on his table. One felt very old and fragile, she took another look.

It was a simple thing, a list of names and some numbers. The text was cramped, not a scribe's best work. He'd crossed out a few lines and written other words on top. They weren't in Latin but it wasn't an English she recognised. She could see the Prior's hand on a few notes on the end of the page. He'd put a query mark by the last line of the receipt – she was sure it was a receipt. She made out the words *sur it gud.*

Thinking hard, she realised what it might be. The missing lapis powder, the herbs and weeds Isabelle was always collecting for the Prior. The muddy blue she'd been trying out for him.

She put the page down and looked around. Under a small cloth she could see an ink steeping, the one that he kept bringing to her as a paste. She had a sudden thought, this might be enough to keep her here.

She took a little of the ink back to the Scriptorium, fetching a small pot to transport it, hiding it in a corner, but not before adding a little vinegar – it needed souring to keep the colour pure. She was sure that was what *sur it gud* meant – why would the Prior know what that meant? But she did.

Father Thomas came in so she started questioning him again. He answered her with evident pleasure, giving her Latin words for English ones, and English for Latin, as she dragged up as many different words as she could remember.

She slipped in the other words as she could: *neque obliviscaris in faciem Pulsante autem, occisor dic Priorus – sed mortuus est.*

Obliviscaris – that was to forget. But *neque* meant never. So 'never forget'. That sounded like Oswyn – always boasting about his memory. His frequent mentions about his memory could also have been veiled threats to those whose secrets he was hiding, if they were aware that he knew, of course.

So she had 'never forget', 'face', 'killer say Prior' and 'dead' or 'death'. But what were *pulsante* and *autem?* Father Thomas wasn't sure – 'pulsing' or 'throbbing', he thought. *Autem* meant however. She tried the sentence again, writing out the gloss below the Latin words: 'never forget face', 'throbbing however', ' killer tell Prior' and 'but he is dead'.

But was she putting the words together in the right way? Although she didn't have Oswyn's book at hand, she remembered he scribed in the old style with very few signs or marks to show the sense of a sentence, apart from some spaces. She thought back to the day before Oswyn drowned. Had he talked to the Prior?

She remembered him coming out of his room once, or was it twice? He tried to talk to the Inspector and the Prior but they had brushed him aside. Later, he'd asked her about her time in Durham and what she remembered but said she was too young.

There must have been something he'd realised. Something he'd 'never forget'.

'Knocked!' Father Thomas sounded triumphant and his exclamation startled her. '*Pulsante* can be knocked.'

She thanked him and made a note. The words now read: 'Never forget face knocking however, killer tell Prior, but he is dead.'

Another scrap of conversation came back to her now, when she was hiding in the parlour the first night the Inspector came. What had Oswyn said? She'd noticed at the time he'd said something with heavy emphasis. Something about how the Inspector should knock on the door. Had he paused before 'knock'?

It was frustrating to be so close to answering another question, but not quite close enough.

The monks went out for Compline and Linnet followed them for some fresh air. Cassian held back, waiting to talk to her.

'Ye haven't told the Prior about – ye ken…' he tailed off, looking miserable. He must be talking about the falling sickness.

'No, does it happen often?'

'Only when I be tired. Not much. It's na' worth saying about,' and he grabbed her arm hard, to make his point.

She shook him off, scared by the naked threat in his eyes. 'I won't say anything.' But her curiosity bubbled back up again and before she could stop herself, she was asking, 'Why are you here with the Inspector? Does he always take a novice with him?'

She didn't expect him to answer but he nodded carefully, fair to have a secret given for a secret kept. 'The Prior at Durham, he knew me as a carpenter, afore I took orders. Asked me to go with him and keep an eye. He didn't think that much of the Inspector, he can be—' He waved in the air around his head. 'I was ta keep him with his feet on the ground.' He looked miserable. 'And I canna get him to do his report and go, no matter what I say to him, he wants ta tell all the monks his ideas. The Bishop thinks the sun shines out of his arse for some reason—'

He cut himself off, obviously saying more than he'd meant to.

That must have been what the man was scolding him about.

So Cassian was spying on the monks for the Inspector, and on the Inspector for the Prior at Durham. She couldn't think of a man less able to spy and connive than this one, and he was spying twice over. She would keep a distance from him, she didn't know how dangerous he might be.

Chapter Twenty-Nine

She was walking across the field behind the Priory on her way up to the Heugh when she heard a shout behind her.

'It is Mary then! I knew it!'

Jack, puffing as he strode up towards her. She looked around, fearful, but no one else was nearby. The villagers didn't like this field, said it was full of old bones from before the Priory. Now full of rabbits and their burrows, it was a spread of holes and tussocks, hard to climb without spraining an ankle. She hoped he would trip but he caught up with her easily enough.

'Guy was talking to me afore he left. He's not happy with you, is he? He wants his money back.'

'It's my money and it's gone,' she said, giving up all attempts at pretence.

'It's never your money. He earned it with his work, so why did you keep it, eh? Why would you have him put in prison like that?'

He looked genuinely offended that she could have betrayed his friend. She stopped trying to walk away from him and turned to face him

'I earned that money. He never did most of the scribing, that was me – see what I'm doing now? He's not doing any scribing is he? He's prancing about on some horse, whispering sweet words to that Lady. I'm the one with ink on my fingers.'

Jack laughed. 'Ah, you're jealous are you? He told me you were that – and hot-blooded besides!'

She didn't trouble to correct him. Let him think she was a jealous lover, cast aside and wronging Guy out of some womanish sense of vengeance. The question was, what was Jack going to do now and what did she need to do about it.

'He's told me to keep an eye on you, see what you get paid and take it from you,' Jack continued. There it was.

'And what's he promised you, Jack? Why would you do his work for him?'

Jack smiled again, the fat smile of a man who thinks he's got everything sewn up neat and tidy. 'I'll be getting my share, and he'll be saying good things about me and my lads to the Lady and his Lord. If the Lady gets a baby in her belly, the Lord will be wanting to build them a good stone house, safe from the Scots, and there we'll be.'

'You could be waiting a long time and in vain for that. It's been a couple of years and the Lord doesn't seem willing,' she replied.

'It ain't always down to one man is it, though?' Jack made a lewd gesture. 'Guy'll do what's needed sure enough!'

So that's what Guy was scheming. However repugnant it was, she had to admire his boldness. If he could get a baby for Lady Margaret, she would be safe in her position, as long as she could persuade her Lord to cover her too. Then she'd never tell on Guy, he'd have the perfect hold over her forever. Lord Edmund wouldn't care. He'd have his heir if his sickly little boys from his first wife didn't survive, and he could go back to neglecting her.

She smiled to herself. Of course Guy hadn't given her any children when they'd been together. Perhaps she wasn't barren, perhaps it was him. Maybe he'd fail because he was lacking.

'Clever, ain't he? So you don't want to cross him, or me, mind.' Jack had enjoyed watching her piece it all together. She nodded, as if in agreement, but she would think about this later. He may think he had her pinned down but masons moved on. She could put off being paid as she needed, and he'd be forced to leave the island soon enough, they'd nearly finished laying the floor.

She surprised herself by how much she wanted to stay here, even with the dangers that were evidently around her, even with the Prior telling her to go. She'd begun to feel this was a place of some wild sanctuary, something from Cuthbert's time was lingering in the grasses and the stones on the beach.

Jack drew a finger across his throat as a parting warning and lumbered off towards the Priory. She made her own rude gesture behind his back, for her own satisfaction, and spat after him with loathing.

She went back towards the Priory thinking about Luke. If he were awake, he could tell her what happened in the stable.

He was asleep and alone in the Infirmary, still looking very bruised but the blood and dirt had been wiped off him and he was clean at least. He'd had his hair washed too, and it was a small cloud of bright blond about his battered face, like a thistledown puff. He looked so young lying there.

She had been so irritated by him, in her Scriptorium, annoying her and lecturing her about her sins. But looking at him lying there, she wished she'd been more merciful. She feared this was Guy's work. Hurting someone else to relieve his fury at her betrayal, and choosing Luke because he mistook their squabbling for affection. This monk who shrank from the slightest accidental touch and who was constantly raving about the evils of womanhood.

She glanced at his hands, they were indeed scratched as Isabelle had told her, and she was right – a horse couldn't have done that. Her time with Guy was probably clouding her thoughts, but who else would have attacked Luke? Had he found something out?

Lavender was burning in the fire but a sour smell lingered above it. Luke was sweating and his bruises were yellow and black, standing out against his pale skin.

'Who did this to you, Luke? It wasn't a horse, was it?'

He groaned slightly and stirred in his sleep, but didn't wake up.

'Why are you here, Linnet?'

It was Brother Godfreyd, standing in the door.

'I came to see if…' Luke couldn't tell her anything so what was she hoping to find? A signed confession attached to Luke's habit? Some sort of signature that would show her who had done this?

'There's nothing you can help me with as yet, but I will call for you if you are needed, of course.'

Clearly he assumed she'd come to offer help. She nodded obediently, let him think she was cowed now by his actions with Isabelle, beaten down by him.

'Is he going to wake up?'

'Even if he does, a kick to the head from a horse can leave a man stupid. He may not be able to write again.'

Standing there with Godfreyd talking about Luke as if he were just anyone, Linnet found it hard to reconcile this lordly monk with what she'd seen in the stables. Godfreyd didn't look at all perturbed by Luke's condition. He was merely a thing for his pleasure, not what Tom had been to him. She thought again of the look on Godfreyd's face when he'd been watching Luke in the Chapter House. A cat with a mouse it could toy with, perhaps even hurt, but a cat too well fed to want to eat it.

'Anyway, be gone.' He dismissed her and she went.

Back at the Scriptorium, the monks had gone to prayers again. Linnet pulled out Oswyn's book to see if there was anything she might have missed. There were a few notes on the next page.

Durham Door, written in English. He'd underlined it heavily. It was not in his usual neat hand, or his 'cramped secrets' hand as she'd come to think of it, but hastily written and with a scattering of ink blots. It looked like something he would have crossed out later as he did throughout the book.

Durham Door? What was special about a door in Durham? He must mean the cathedral. There was nothing else on the page.

She put the book away and took out her inks and pens to work on the next illumination. As she started on the border, she traced the patterns she remembered from the pillars in Durham Cathedral, the chevrons and other markings.

In the quiet room, the fire sputtering and the candle flickering on her desk, Linnet felt as if she were dreaming, the repeating pattern coming out smoothly on the creamy parchment. Her mind wandered and she thought of Durham, a small child again.

She used to creep quietly around the corners and the out-of-the-way nooks of the cathedral, ducking into the shadows when a monk or two bustled past, but taking no notice of the throng of pilgrims. The monks knew her, of course, as the daughter of John-the-Lies, and they knew where she should and shouldn't be. The pilgrims neither knew nor cared, weary from their journeys and in a fervour at the thought of seeing Cuthbert's tomb.

As her hand looped along the page, in her mind's eye, she walked the outer edge of the cathedral, starting on the green in front of the immense solid building. The field covered with stalls selling food and drink and tiny St Cuthbert medals and badges. Occasionally someone of importance would ride in and force their way through the throng, pausing the frantic noise and bustle, before it washed back over the space again.

Most pilgrims came in by way of the Galilee Chapel, wanting to see the rose windows before walking the length of the cathedral. Some liked to press their foreheads to the stones every few paces along the aisle.

That wasn't the biggest door, though. The north door took you straight into the nave and when it was open wide on feast days, twenty or so would come through together in one rush. But most of the time it was shut and the knocker on the giant door unused.

Linnet sat up with a start, spilling ink on a corner of her page. The knocker! That hideous face that gave her nightmares as a small child. The lion roaring with its glass blue eyes with the knocker held between its teeth. 'Looks like that to scare the evil out of you,' one of the older monks had told her with grim satisfaction when he'd caught her staring at it. But it had a name. The Sanctuary Knocker.

Before she could think more about this, there was a scream and shouting from outside. She could see Isabelle, struggling to get away from the Inspector who had her in a firm grip around the elbow.

'Get OFF me. I ain't done NOTHING. Get off me NOW.' Isabelle was shouting loudly and grimly determined to wriggle free but the Inspector seemed just as determined not to let her go.

The Prior came out of his parlour and Brother Godfreyd down from the Infirmary, pushing through a growing throng of curious spectators.

The Inspector addressed himself to the Prior. 'This child was going through the monks' quarters, a child who has no place being there, and worse – a girl child.'

The Prior's expression of surprise quickly gave way to frustration.

'Isabelle, you have no business going into the monks' rooms, you know that—'

'But I dinna and I wasn't!' She was on the verge of furious tears, Linnet could see. 'He just took hold a me when I weren't doing nothing.'

'And now she's lying. You can never trust a female to tell the truth, especially when she's caught in the very act.'

The Prior came forward, still looking unwilling to become involved. 'I'll take care of her for you, Inspector. I promise she won't be in the monks' rooms again.'

'I should hope not. If I do find her wandering around there once more, it will have to appear in my report.'

The Prior nodded and Isabelle was handed over from one to the other, like a furious spitting package.

'You're just lucky Pol ain't here. He'd have your eyes out for grabbing me like that,' she hissed at the Inspector who was brushing his hands together as if to clean off the stain of her. He went back into the Chapter House, leaving the small crowd to disperse.

The Prior let go of Isabelle who stumbled and sat down heavily in the dirt.

'Don't be coming to his notice, Isabelle,' he warned. 'I can't be keeping an eye out for you. Perhaps I should send you to Ann in the kitchen. She could do with a pair of willing hands.'

The expression on Isabelle's face made it evident that her hands would not be willing. The Prior gave her a final exasperated look and went back into his parlour.

'What were you doing digging about the monks' rooms then?'

'I weren't!' It was a furious shout but as quiet as a whisper. 'I said I weren't. Why ain't anyone believing me?'

Linnet took her into the Scriptorium.

'What were you doing then?'

The child looked a bit guilty. 'Well I weren't looking in the monks' rooms, was I? I were going to the Chapter House, that ain't their rooms – it's one room. I dinna know he was in there – the Inspector.'

'You mustn't go in there! You know that, Isabelle, what were you looking for?'

'Anything. I dunno. I were trying to help you find Tom's killer.' She flounced out of the Scriptorium, indignant that her help wasn't appreciated.

Linnet sighed. She had all these scraps of information but nothing that pointed to anyone in particular or to any reason why Tom was killed. She wished Tom was here so she could get his help, but how stupid. If he were here, she wouldn't be looking for his killer.

What had she been thinking about before the commotion? The knocker. She needed to talk to someone who knew about the Sanctuary Knocker. Oswyn had written 'never forget face knocking however, killer tell Prior, death', or something like that, then Durham Door. The door had to be the north door, the knocking had to have something to do with the Sanctuary Knocker.

The face that knocked? A killer's face? Oswyn remembered the face. He wrote this in his book the day the Inspector and Cassian came, which was also the day he'd collected the masons from the mainland. Maybe one of the masons was a killer, or was it something the Inspector had said that reminded him that the Prior had a history – where had he been before the island? Or could it be Cassian?

Linnet tried to arrange her thoughts again. There was the note in the household book that Oswyn had torn out. He seemed to have a habit of tearing out the secrets he noted down, something only he would know was written there. There had been three deaths, Oswyn, Maykin and Tom, and one near-death, Luke. She was sure the Prior had been falsifying the books and was obsessed by the Scriptorium and building his own library. Tom said he'd seen two monks arguing the night before Oswyn's death, but said that neither of them had been Godfreyd.

What if it had been Godfreyd? Tom might have lied about that, to protect him. He was a cruel man, someone who could be violent, someone who sinned. Maybe Oswyn had threatened to say something to the Prior. But would Godfreyd have killed Tom? She thought not. She'd seen real affection between the two men, and how shaken Godfreyd had been when he found out about Tom.

And Tom? He'd had so much money just before he died that he'd bought drinks for everyone. Where had he got that from? He'd not won it gaming. The masons were threatening him just before for not paying his debts, then there he was, paying them off, buying drinks, only a short time later.

Maykin and the note also had her wondering. Who wanted to meet him in the middle of the night? That would point back to Godfreyd again, surely.

What she needed now was someone she trusted to ask about the knocker, but who was there?

The two monks came back to the Scriptorium, maybe them then.

'Where were you before here?' Linnet asked them, as if passing the time. Father Thomas's lined face lit up like a worn but glowing apple, keen to talk for as long as she would listen.

It was a long list of abbeys, priories, monasteries. Some mild complaints about the abbots or priors but largely a happy recital. He'd never been at the Durham Priory though he said he had visited a few times. Brother Samuel, a good ten years younger but still fifty or so, said he'd been a novice at Durham.

'Who else was a novice with you?' Linnet was taking full advantage of the monks' willingness to talk. The Benedictines weren't a silent order, but general gossiping was not encouraged, at least not while the Inspector was still here.

Brother Samuel rattled off a long list of other novices. He was forgetful though – it was a list of 'the fat one', 'the one who lisped', 'the one who snored through Matins every day'. She knew no more at the end of it.

They talked in general terms about the pilgrims, Brother Samuel saying he welcomed the peace of Lindisfarne after all that racket. Linnet had liked watching the pilgrims, and stealing from them, which was easy. But sometimes they seemed to draw all the heat and light out of a room, particularly those who wept, wept all the way round the cathedral and wept on after.

As a child she had waited behind the pews, to see if touching the saint's tomb had cured them of the weeping, but mostly they had wailed on. She would sometimes find them, sitting crumpled against the outside of the thick cathedral walls. A few did look calmer but most were confused, as if the answer they'd been promised had gone just when they thought it was within reach.

'Oh!' she said, pretending to suddenly remember. 'Remember the knocker? I used to be so scared of that as a child.'

'The Prior was scared of it too, at least when I was there. If anyone did claim sanctuary he had to take them in, and he never liked admitting law-breakers.'

'Do they stay then? Once they've used the knocker?'

'Depends what they did,' Brother Samuel said. 'If it wasn't too serious, they could do penance, staying on to do the gardens or other work. But not if it was a sin that "cried to heaven for vengeance".'

Father Thomas chuckled. 'You were listening to the novice master when he read them all then. I remember being so afeard of being a sinner and not knowing it.'

He looked serious again. 'But of course we all sin without knowing it and we need to guard agin that, as the Inspector has been good enough to remind us.'

The other monk crossed himself piously and the conversation stopped, the sin of talking instead of working clearly on their minds.

'What are the sins that cry out for vengeance then?' Linnet asked.

'Wilful Murder, Oppression of the Poor, Withholding Labourer's Pay and Sodomy,' Father Thomas rattled off in a sing-song voice.

He went on, 'For sins as bad as these, they have to make amends. Some are sent overseas.' Father Thomas shuddered at the thought of banishment to foreign places.

'Less talking and more scribing, I think.'

The voice from the door made them all turn to their pages, the two monks flustered as the Inspector came in. He spent a few minutes examining their work then stalked out again. Linnet was relieved for once that it was only herself and the monks in the Scriptorium – no duck, no raven, no disobedient child.

The Prior came in to look over the quires, nodding with satisfaction at the borders Linnet was working on. He told Linnet to come to his parlour after the next page was dry. The Inspector had work for her.

'Take dictee.' It was a bark rather than a request or suggestion. Linnet fumbled with her pens and ink and sat down at the desk with the fresh paper in front of her.

'I am nearly finished with the arduous task of a full inspection of this Priory of Lindisfarne. The monks were lax in their dress and their knowledge of the scriptures, but my instruction has inspired them anew and they are now on the right path.

'Do you have that, Linnet?'

She almost wrote his question down but stopped just in time, nodding. The Prior was in the shadows of the parlour but she could see him scowling at the Inspector's verdict.

'I leave the day after tomorrow but I am adding this postscript to the full inspection advising that the Scriptorium be purged of the woman scribe.'

Linnet tried to stay calm but hearing the venom in his voice as he dismissed her labours and her art was too much.

'Keep scribing. I didn't say you could stop.' The Inspector's face was triumphant and he was smirking with self-importance.

The Prior's face was blank but his mouth gave a slight twitch. Marcus was about to say something, but the Prior quelled him with a look.

She looked back up at the Inspector. He was enjoying his power, knowing it couldn't be questioned.

'She is using her womanly ways to distract the monks from their work, leading them to gossip on profane topics and keeping them from their true vocation, serving the Lord.'

She was biting her lip as she scribed now, biting back the words she desperately wanted to say. He had power – and the ear of the Bishop. And the Prior wanted rid of her too, although he couldn't have told the Inspector or he wouldn't have taken such relish in telling her just now. How would she manage to stay?

'Above all, a priory should be a holy place, a holy place without women except the common sort who keep the kitchen and the linen. The deaths in this place are a sure sign of the Lord's displeasure. Now I shall sign,' he said, watching her finish. He could have written this himself but he'd had her take his dictation so he could enjoy watching her write her own dismissal.

She stood up and, keeping her voice as low and calm as she could, addressed the Prior. 'Where should I go now? Back to the Scriptorium or elsewhere?'

He had the grace to look ill at ease, and muttered, 'The Scriptorium for now, Linnet. We'll see what happens when the report is brought to the Bishop.'

'But mind, no more of your idle talk,' the Inspector said.

She nodded and went back to what had begun to feel like home. Father Thomas tried to share a jest with her but she hushed him and bent her head to the parchment, brushing away angry tears as she tried to work.

She could hear the others talking as she worked, but she wasn't really listening. Father Thomas was asking Cassian again about his family, about his poor wife. Cassian had developed a real affection for Father Thomas, she thought. She was idly drawing a rabbit in the margins as she half-listened, and she gave it Father Thomas's sweet old face.

'Now you mustn't think like that, 'twas God's will, that's all, and that's hard to take sometimes.'

'Whether it was God's will or no, I know I was the reason for her death.'

She looked over, startled, but Father Thomas didn't look shocked by what Cassian had said, simply nodding and they returned to their work.

Once her panic had started to ebb, Linnet thought of something that she'd overlooked earlier. The Inspector had caught Isabelle prying and scolded her loudly. Now he'd humiliated her and suggested she leave and stop scribing. Why was he paying them both this attention?

He'd come in the Scriptorium when they'd been talking, talking about the Sanctuary Knocker, and then he'd summoned her, in effect to write her own dismissal. Was it possible Oswyn's notes were about the Inspector? Or could it be Cassian? Had Cassian said something to him?

She found Isabelle and gave her a task to do. A short while later, Isabelle was skipping along, chatting to Father Thomas and a couple of others on their way to Compline, Pol hopping after her.

Chapter Thirty

Isabelle came running up to her as she neared the Priory. The child was bursting with self-importance but it was nearly time for dinner so they went straight to the kitchen. She wouldn't say anything in front of the others so Linnet ate quickly and took her back outside.

They sat in the quiet, dark church graveyard, the moon showing itself occasionally through the scudding clouds, Isabelle shivering but refusing Linnet's cloak.

'I found out something – like you wanted. I was talking to the old monks and they said the Inspector came with the Bishop. He were part of his other seat – I dunno what a seat is. He'd not been to Durham before, he said to them. Only one of the monks knew about sanc— That thing you was asking about. Not the one that scribes, another one. He said there was a murderer once, long before, who'd tried to get safe in the cathedral. Folks remembered as how he'd come flying through the town like a demon, with the people running after and calling for his blood.'

'Who had he killed?'

'Only his wife, but also her brother and that's why they was after him. He'd been beating his wife for years they said, and anyways her brother caught him at it one time and tried to stop him. The murderer killed him with one blow. When his wife wouldn't stop greeting and carrying on, he'd held her in the water barrel till she did.'

Isabelle was telling the story with glee, the gory details coming alive. Linnet suspected she was adding some images of her own, the water barrel lying on its side with the dead woman half in, half out, the brother slumped by the hearth, the murderer roaring in his rage.

'Then the men came running and they was going to do for him, but he took off, like a deer, dodging them all!'

Truth struggled with the temptation to make a good story on her face.

'Well the monk said he were more like a bear, lumbering about in his rage, I think. But fast, anyways.'

'Then what happened?'

'He got to the big door and grabbed the knocker and yelled for the monks. They took him in but the Prior didn't want him staying past his time. He were two weeks in the cathedral grounds in his robes with the special yellow mark on it' – Isabelle gestured towards her shoulder – 'so then he were sent to the coast to be put on a boat and never to be in the kingdom agin. They sent two monks with him, to make sure he got on that boat, and make sure the men of the town wouldn't kill him. That would be another sin, the monk said, but, Linnet, it can't be a sin to kill a murderer?'

Linnet wasn't sure of where that sat in the order of sins.

'So he went overseas?'

If the murderer had been banished, he could be back here now with a different name and barely anyone would remember him.

'No, he died. The Lord struck him down with sickness, and one of the monks with him too.' That sing-song pious phrase must have come straight from the monk who told her the story.

'Who was it told you?'

Isabelle looked uncertain. 'Brother Jacob, I think, but he said he weren't there, he were too young to remember it – it were many years ago.'

'So how did he know?'

'It was Brother Oswyn told him!' And she sat back, pleased with telling Linnet the story.

Linnet considered what she knew. Oswyn had been at Durham then, a novice maybe. When he was there he'd seen a man come in for sanctuary – a killer. He remembered his face, the one who had knocked, but he was now dead.

A thought struck her.

'What of the monk who lived?'

'Oh he went mad, they said. He wouldn't come back to his church and wanted to punish hisself. Brother Jacob said he went overseas.'

Something tickled Linnet's mind but ran away again before she could trap it. She thought again of the note, 'never forget face', 'knocking however', 'killer tell Prior', 'but he is dead?' She'd not asked herself what the last words meant but seized on 'dead' and not thought further.

She thanked Isabelle, who was busy inventing more facts about the killing, chatting away almost to herself. They went back to the Priory and both went their ways to bed.

The light outside was on the turn when Linnet awoke, that almost light, when the shapes are real, but the mind can't grasp them. She went to the Priory Church, using the door left open for the monks who would be coming in soon for Lauds. She was quiet, so the novice who was lighting the candles didn't see her.

She crept up the stairs until she was out the top, in the triforium gallery, and she could watch the monks from above, coming in now, a slow wave, some still half-asleep.

The Prior was at the head, with the Inspector behind him. Linnet let the plainsong wash over her. She felt dizzy from worry and lack of sleep but the solid stone of the pillar kept her upright. Her fingers traced the patterns on the stone, the straight lines and the little flourishes. Even up here in the dark corners, the masons had made beauty.

Not this group of masons, their work was rough but they were cheap and only there for the floor tiles. From her perch up here, she could see where it was waiting to be finished. One last section in the north aisle near the door.

The music, the incense, the flickering candles, it all lulled her. This was her childhood, hiding in corners in a cathedral or a monastery, keeping quiet, watching everyone.

Her finger found a little nick in the pillar. It had looked perfect but looked at more closely, it was flawed. She thought of the forgeries she had done with Guy, nearly perfect but with small defects that only a scribe might see. Oswyn, looking like a drowning, but hard to believe; Maykin's accident, something clumsy for a light-footed young man; Tom's self-killing but with a knot he would never tie; and the Sanctuary Knocker, the story of a killer, running through the town like a bear. Then dying on his way to the coast, and the monk who didn't come back, punishing himself.

As if drops of ink were gathering in a pot of water, the words swirled around her and she began to draw out an idea, using her finger along the edge of the pillar. There was a man like a bear – the murderer – and two monks with him. One monk who wanted to punish himself left, the others had died. And a self-important bursar who never forgot a face, away on a small island, seeing a man he knew to be dead.

The prayers were over, the monks left and the novice had blown out the candles. Linnet was sitting in the dark, holding the precious bubble of her idea to her.

Chapter Thirty-One

She was still trying to understand it all the next day with Isabelle buzzing around, pestering to let her do some more writing, when Ann came bustling in.

'Don't be wasting your time on that writing business, pet, there's work for you in the kitchen, and I'll be getting you ready for Candlemas too.'

Was it Candlemas already? Linnet felt they'd been in the depths of the dark winter for months. She'd loved the ceremony as a child with all the candles and the lights in the windows afterwards, a sign the worst of the winter was behind them.

Isabelle was pulled out of the room protesting, as Ann informed her she would be scrubbed clean, and needed to collect the candles, and do all the other chores she'd saved for her.

The monks had their own ceremony at Candlemas, but Linnet would be expected to go to the church with the rest of the islanders. She wondered fleetingly if her stolen candles were worthy of a blessing, well, why not? Stolen or not, they gave out light.

Linnet thought she would go and help in the kitchen. The monks were busy so the Scriptorium wouldn't have a fire today.

Ann set them to work, chopping apples for a hot drink she would be making later after the church service, something her mother and her mother's mother would always do, with cinnamon and honey stirred in. She was in a talkative mood for once, the promise of spring loosening something in her.

'Going to make you look neat for the church tonight, hen,' she said to Isabelle. 'Go to my cottage and ask my Judith for her old dress, it will do for you for now and it's clean.'

Isabelle pulled a face but took the chance to escape the busy kitchen.

'Isabelle.' Ann turned the name over in her mouth like a bad piece of carrot. 'Why her mother would call a child such a haughty name is a mystery. Mind you, she always was a brazen piece.'

'Isabelle's mother?'

'Aye, a right strumpet, by no means a beauty, but all flashing eyes and talk. Her mother was nothing like it, a normal, nice woman, she loved babbies. She'd have brought Isabelle on as her own, only that one wouldn't do the right thing and stay indoors when she needed, to hide her shame. Claimed her as her own, right enough.'

'Sir Cyrus said they all died?'

'Yes, it was that pestilence one of the foreign fishermen died of. It were Isabelle's grandmother tended to him and that took for the whole family. Apart from that little one.'

She stopped chopping for a minute to give Linnet a straight look.

'She's yours now, ain't it so?'

Linnet's startled face gave Ann an answer without her having to say a word.

'Well, she followed you when you went to take that book to the Lady Margaret. She's like that damned cat, she's taken to you now and you'll have a hell of a time shaking her loose.

You're more than old enough to have a child anyways.' Ann laughed with grim satisfaction.

Well, whatever they thought, Linnet wasn't going to adopt her. She wasn't one of them – not even an islander.

Isabelle came back in a faded but very clean dress, looking unnaturally shy. Ann's daughter had evidently taken a comb to her hair, which was neatly plaited for once, and washed her face too.

The villagers, farmers and fisherfolk were gathering, clutching their candles to be blessed, and one to be lit. The service would start when the last of the winter light dipped below the sea.

The church was filling up when Linnet came in, Sir Cyrus's assistant at the door lighting candles for everyone as they came in. The priest was at the altar, dressed in his best robes.

The recently birthed women were pushed to the front, holding their babies in tightly wrapped swaddling cloths, chattering about sleeping and feeding and all the things that mattered for new mothers.

Linnet's candle was lit and she stood at the back, near the old door with its rough-hewn wood she liked to trace over with a finger. One of the fishermen had showed her an old gash in it once, which he swore had come from a Norseman's axe. She didn't believe him but she liked the tale.

The church was ablaze with the candles and alive with chatter and the little mewing cries of the new babies. Sir Cyrus called for quiet and the noise stilled.

He was a surly old sot but he gave a good sermon, talking of the light Jesus had brought into the world and the light within everyone's souls, the ways to carry light forward into the year. One by one the people came up clutching their candles, some with a few stubs, some carrying armfuls.

When Linnet came up, the priest blessed her handful. Lost in the moment, he didn't glare at her for once or berate her for her failings and sins, and she went back to her place feeling almost at peace.

Linnet was one of the first to come out of the church when the service was over. She watched as the little flickerings of light flowed out of the door into the darkness of the churchyard, spreading out into the village as people put their candles in their windows and on their door ledges.

It made her think of the stars coming out one by one, as they were in the clear night sky above. One of the farmers stopped by her and pointed at the sky. 'If Candlemas be fine and clear, there'll be two winters in the year.'

His friends nodded wisely, agreeing with him and adding their own half-remembered proverbs. Linnet hoped they were wrong, it had been a long enough winter as it was.

The doors of the Priory kitchen were open and Ann was in the centre of a mass of people holding up their mugs for the apple drink. The Priory Church itself was radiant, the lights from the monks' candles spilling out into the darkness while their plainsong rose up into the still cold sky.

The villagers had moved on from the apple drink to ale and there was much singing in the outer Priory courtyard and the village green.

Linnet could see small groups going back into the churchyard. They would stop by their family's grave and drip some wax on the stone, making the sign of the cross and then moving on. She looked around for Isabelle, who was teasing the Priory cat with a twig, her candle lying unlit next to her.

'Do you want to drop some wax on your family's stone, Isabelle? We can light your candle again.'

The child shrugged but stood up and relit her candle from Linnet's and came with her. She pointed out the small grave, a simple stone with some initials on it. Linnet supposed the village had put it up, she would have been too young.

They solemnly dripped their wax on the stone and then Isabelle asked if they could go down to the beach.

The moonlight was bright and the way down was clear. The inky black sea swept in and out, slowly but steadily, like a great creature breathing, Linnet thought.

Isabelle carefully held her candle just above the spray until the water put it out.

'That's for Tom,' she said, and Linnet did the same, offering his soul to St Gertrude as she did so.

Chapter Thirty-Two

Candlemas had felt like a pause, a rest from her suspicions about Tom and Oswyn and from the thoughts that kept coming back to haunt her. Now the sun was up and the morning of the Priory's daily business had begun.

Linnet was making her way to the Scriptorium, wondering if she were right, when the Prior saw her standing and told her to follow him. She took the moment and asked him to follow her instead, running into the Scriptorium to get the little dish of the ink she'd been souring. Displeased, he came in and was about to scold her for her boldness, when he saw her use her brush to make one clear blue sparkling mark on the rough piece of parchment she had there.

'Is that…?'

She nodded. 'It's the ink you've been working on. I found the receipt and knew it needed souring to keep the colour pure. It's your lapis, isn't it?'

He looked carefully at her, weighing up what to say next.

She rushed on, 'And it wasn't me made an error in Brother Godfreyd's book, it wasn't. I don't make errors. It was his plan, he—' Then she broke off again. This was all she had. She could help him make this fake lapis, she could keep quiet about it as he charged the gentry for the foreign ink. He could get more money than he was spending, and do with it what he wanted.

'How did you get it so blue? I followed the receipt to the letter.'

She began to explain then cut herself off. What use would he have of her if he knew how to do it himself.

'I had some ideas from when I was apprenticed to make inks, this and that and the other.'

He gave her a shrewd look, knowing why she wasn't saying more, then clearly made up his mind.

'We're off to Inner Farne again. I need you to help me with manuscripts I've found. I've been taking back a few pages at a time so as not to start talk amongst the monks, but you can bring some too, hide them in your bag.'

This must be where he found the receipt from, and the gilt letters that Pol had hidden. For now at least, she could stay a little longer to help him with these finds.

She got into the boat with her pens and knife in the pouch she'd lifted from the pedlar, in case he wanted her to make copies. The fishermen were the ones who'd brought the old monk's body back the other time. One nodded at her.

They pushed off from the shallow beach towards the sea, coming round the curve at the end of the island that looked for all the world like a flourish of penmanship to Linnet. She gazed up at the granite rock at the end of the isle, and the small kilns beyond it on the land, the hamlets scattered about on the rough farming ground. There was cattle here, but none grazing at this bleak time of year, just the rabbits scattered about, thin and jumpy, destined for skinning and the pot.

Was she being foolish, being on a boat out at sea with the Prior, now she knew it all? But she was almost certain he may have been a thief like her, but not a killer. His crimes were in the aid of making beautiful books, barely crimes at all by her thoughts.

The journey out was on calm seas, but the fishermen looked askance at the sky and told them they were to be quick. The weather was on the turn. Linnet looked at the sky but saw nothing to worry about. But the Prior thought the warning was more serious and he hurried her up the slope into the tiny chapel where the two monks were waiting for them.

Brother Adam had made a hot drink for them from the herbs on the island, and Linnet sipped it gratefully, not minding too much that it scalded her tongue. At least the pain cut through the fog that had descended over her thoughts, going over and over her suspicions with nothing to hold onto.

The Prior was talking to the monks. He told Adam he would return to the Priory soon, when other tasks had been allotted and a new monk appointed to the cell.

'A bird lover I hope, Father,' Adam suggested, and the Prior laughed.

'I'd come myself but I have too much to do.' The remorse in his voice was partly in jest but partly sincere. Linnet thought of the Prior's duck, now recovered but still living in the parlour, competing with the cat for his attentions.

The Prior sent the monks back to their hut while he opened up the chest that Linnet had seen before, prising up the false bottom with the point of his knife to reveal more papers underneath. She held the candle for him as he sifted through the fragile papers, asking her opinion of some and expressing his pleasure at what he was finding.

He'd brought a bag to put them in, leaving only the ones seriously damaged by mice and damp. He gave it to her to hold, she could bring it back into the Priory without scrutiny, he would no longer have to travel to get a page or two at a time to hide in his habit. Monks were curious and always watching their superiors closely to glean their moods. If he carried papers, the Inspector might stop him and ask to see them. Linnet wouldn't be noticed.

They went to say farewell to the monks in their hut, the Prior leaving more candles for them, a jar of winter honey, and his blessing, before he and Linnet slid and scrambled down the slope to the boat.

The clear skies had darkened and the rain had begun, gusts of wind shoving them off balance as they clambered into the boat. The fishermen gave them a look of satisfaction at being proved right, but they were too busy fighting the waves to keep it up for long.

The journey back took twice as long. She tried to ask the Prior if she would be able to keep scribing for him, but the wind tore her words away before they reached him, and he shrugged, clearly in his own world. Linnet clung fast to the side of the boat, watching the wild waves and the darker grey of the skies, all the while wondering what she could do.

They were back too late for food but Ann had kept some back for the Prior, next to the fire in his parlour. He did not invite Linnet to share. He gave her the manuscript pages to lay out in the Scriptorium, 'in a dark place mind, so they're not seen', to dry out in front of the embers of the fire there.

Once she'd finished laying them out, her hands beginning to warm a little as she did it, she went out to see if she could find something to eat.

The inner courtyard was still busy with the masons gathered around a young apprentice, mocking him about his work or his love for one of the kitchen girls. Linnet tried to get past but Jack stopped her, shouting above the gathering wind, which was whipping clouds across the dark skies.

'Now this is who you need, eh?' he yelled at the apprentice, who was blushing sullenly. 'A real woman with a bit of experience who knows what to teach you! Isn't that right then, Mary – oh it's Linnet, ain't it?'

She looked around but no one else had taken notice of his deliberate mistake. She needed to find Cassian, to prove what she knew about the man now. She tried to free herself from Jack's grip but he strengthened it, with a cruel look of satisfaction.

'I ain't what you should start with, son,' she said to the apprentice, playing the part, the sooner to get away. 'You want a nice, shy girl you can frolic with.' Damn, she was back thinking like she was Mary again.

The masons roared with laughter, enjoying her reply, surprised by the quick wit from the quiet scribe, and she took advantage of it to slip away.

Cassian was walking towards the stables. She went up to him, shivering from cold and the rain which was beginning to spit down.

'I've questions to ask you,' she said, surprising herself with her own bravery.

'Aye?' He raised one eyebrow and smiled curiously. 'I'm off to get some more hay from the stables, make my bed more easeful. Hard enough to get rest in that dormitory.'

'What happened with your wife? And her brother?' She glanced around as she asked, was she foolish to just confront him like that? But she had to know – was he the man Oswyn thought was dead, but had come back somehow, ready to atone?

Winded by the question, Cassian sat heavily on the wall outside the stables, heedless of the rain which was driving down now.

'Her brother? She had none. She died, Linnet. Of childbed. It were our fourth child, none had drawn breath, and this little lad no different. I shoulda stopped asking it of her, we could ha taken in another's bairn, safer for her, not put her through it.'

'But you said you were the cause of her death?' Was she wrong? Had she put the pieces together all wrong somehow?

'Aye. You do ken how a babby comes about?' He gave a wry smile through the rain on his face, and his tears.

'Is that why you're a monk now?'

'The falling sickness, it came on me after her death and I thought it a sign from the Lord, telling me to atone. So here I am.'

And a desolate place to end up, Linnet thought. But if he wasn't the man in the story – then there was only one other man it could be.

She left Cassian sitting with his thoughts outside the stables, as if he welcomed the rain coming down on him.

The inner courtyard was quieter now, and there was a lull in the storm. She could see Isabelle, picking her way with Pol flying around in a lazy loop around her, letting out odd cries and caws. She needed to ask her more but before she could reach her, the Inspector called the child and spoke briefly to her. Isabelle nodded and followed him up the short stairs into the guest room, Pol now hopping behind her.

She felt a sudden chill that came from inside, not the quickening winds. She started across the courtyard and up the stairs to the guest room, standing undecided by the door, trying to think of what to tell the Inspector, how to explain coming in, unsure of her suspicions even now. Then she heard a scream and a thud, and then a silence.

Chapter Thirty-Three

Without another thought, she tried to push her way into the room but the door was barred. She raised her hand to beat on it when it suddenly opened, and the Inspector's broad frame was blocking the way.

'You just can't stop getting in the way, can you, Linnet? This is why there shouldn't be women in men's holy places. We have nunneries for that, no need to disturb our devotions.'

She was trying to see past him to find Isabelle, but the room was dark and he wouldn't let her past.

'No, no, you're not coming in here. You and I are going for a walk. I'm going to teach you a lesson.'

He clutched her arms and half-dragged, half-carried her down the night stairs into the Priory Church. It was just after Compline and everyone was in their cells or at the inn, or in the Chapter House. There was no one to see or help her. The weather was too wild for anyone to be out and looking.

She opened her mouth to scream but his hand quickly smothered it, the force almost stopping her breathing. She gagged, thinking of those dark wiry hairs on it and he stopped, waiting almost patiently to see if she would vomit. Then he hissed, 'I don't think so,' slapping her hard across the mouth, drawing blood, an iron taste as she licked it off her lips.

Where was he taking her and what had happened to

Isabelle? She could feel herself shaking as she was pushed and pulled through the south aisle.

He'd not brought a candle and it was dark, the gathering storm sucking any remaining light from the stars and the moon, only a little light coming through the big windows. Once or twice he stumbled and she tensed, ready to run for it – but his hand was ever firm on her.

Near the front of the church now, he dragged her up more and more steps. They were climbing the right one of the two front towers by way of a winding staircase, hidden in the thick walls of the towers.

Eventually they stopped. They were in the small room at the top of the tower, with a broken, run-down, open window looking out over the island. Linnet could see the odd flash of a candle, and hear the faint sounds of laughter and some shouts, maybe the masons still. Would they hear her if she called? They might. But by the time they got up here, the Inspector would have killed her.

'You wouldn't stop digging, would you?' He spat the words in her face. She could hardly see him but she could smell him. Unwashed, a faint scent of the incense from the Priory, and something sharp and bitter, fear? Why would he be scared of her?

'What was I doing?'

If she could keep him talking, perhaps she could think of a way to escape.

'Asking questions. Talking about Durham.'

'Were you the killer, then?'

'No, that man is dead. God saw fit to save me and turn me into someone new. He has a purpose for me.'

She could imagine his fanatical, staring eyes. It was working. He was talking now, although there was little sense in what he said.

'That stupid bitch and her stupid brother, they could have ruined my life. It was my right to beat her, everyone knew that. He had no business coming over, sticking his nose in. And she wouldn't stop screaming, so I held her under. It didn't take much. I shouldn't have killed them. I know that now, but God had His reasons. He took me to that knocker at the cathedral and I knew – I knew when I felt it under my hand, this would be a new life for me.'

'So you went to the cathedral?'

She thought she would keep prompting him. Even in her fear, she still needed to know what had happened, why Tom was dead now too.

'Yes and that Prior, he was an arsehole, didn't want anything to do with me. Wanted me gone as quick as he could and didn't care which of his monks he sent off with me.'

He sounded aggrieved, as if he had expected better treatment for his sins. She noticed how the refined voice of the cleric had slipped. He was a common northerner now and not so pretty with his words.

'It weren't a long trip to the coast but those two fools didn't listen to me and we got lost, wandering in a forest for a couple of days. Then we all got sick. It was dark when I woke up and they were quiet. I called out and called out. I thought they were punishing me, keeping silent. You don't know how horrible that was for me, hearing the silence. I hate the silence. When I dragged myself up, I touched one. His face was waxy and cold and I knew. I'd been saved and they'd been struck down.'

He laughed, the incredulity of the moment coming back to him.

'Do you know how hard it is to undress a dead body? They're so heavy, as if something is added in death. I did it though, and got him in my clothes, those robes with the yellow mark on them, the penitent robes, and me in his habit. I told a passing pedlar about the bodies in the wood and to get word to Durham, then I went away, abroad, even learnt some of the tongue over there. They thought I was strange at the monasteries I went to, but since that was what they thought, that's what I became, a strange monk. I never meant to come back to Durham but I thought I'd be safe, no one would remember me anymore as that man who knocked.'

'So who did?'

'Oswyn, of course. I remember him when I came in that day, a skinny novice then but prying about, always looking. And here I tried to avoid him, but he found me after prayers and started insinuating. He was never going to stop.'

Oswyn probably would have kept the secret, Linnet thought. He lived for other people's secrets, their weaknesses, collecting them like Pol collected shiny objects.

'You drowned him?'

'I didn't mean to but God led me to the shore that morning, and when I saw him going to the water, I knew what to do.'

'And Maykin?'

'He kept saying he knew everything Oswyn knew. I had to find out. I sent him that note to meet me but he knew nothing, but by then he'd come to meet me in the night, I couldn't let him go. He stumbled first though, brought the kiln stones down on him. I just added a few on top, couldn't bear the sound of him begging me to take them off.'

She felt a shudder run through her – that poor boy thinking even then that the Inspector would help him.

'So, why Tom?'

'Tom? Was that his name? The fisherman?'

He hadn't even known his name. That made it worse. She went to say something but he was continuing.

'He saw me arguing with Oswyn. When Oswyn was found

dead, he came to see me. Didn't know what I'd done but wanted paying for his silence anyway. I did for a while but he was going to keep coming back.'

So the gaming had done for Tom in the end, his need for coin driving him to blackmail this killer.

'And you hanged him?'

'I hit him over the head first. I had to work hard to get him up on the beam, worth it though – to expose him as the sinner he was. God didn't want him troubling me.'

Again that satisfaction in his voice.

'And Brother Luke? Why did you attack him?'

He didn't answer that, turning his attention back to her.

'And it was all working out and then you and that child and that evil bird started meddling where you had no business. She was in the Chapter House and asking everyone all those questions. And that bird. Looking at me like she knew everything.'

Isabelle. Her heart fell again.

'Well I won't be troubled by them anymore, nor those black staring eyes, watching me, I wrung her neck. I'd have got the other one an' all if you hadn't come knocking.'

And that was when her fear left her and she was consumed with rage. This man who had killed again and again – and now Isabelle, put down like vermin. Linnet was tired of being overlooked and powerless but now that was over. She still had her cloak on from the trip to the island, and beneath was her pouch with her pens – and her knife.

He was still talking, still spinning stories. And in every story he seemed to be the one who was wronged, despite all his murderous violence. But she wasn't listening, she was slowly easing the knife from her pouch.

For a moment the clouds parted, allowing a splash of moonlight into the tower and she saw his face, alight with an entitled madness. She was no longer thinking but suddenly the knife was free and she thrust it hard into his stomach.

He stopped talking and looked at her with incredulity and surprise.

'Why do that? You can't harm me, I told you God has a purpose for me. He saved me from the sickness before. You can't stop God. He made the Bishop favour me when we met in France. I told him I could help him, help him find out the sins the monks had. He had so many places to look at, he was grateful of my help.'

His voice faded. He looked down at the knife and pulled. She shrank back against the wall, not sure what to do. She was still burning with the rage at the thought of Isabelle, but the fear washed back over her.

He had the knife in his hand now but he too seemed undecided what to do. The blood flowed from his stomach, black as ink in what little light there was. Had she done enough to kill him? She knew a knife to the stomach was bad, but how far in had she pushed it?

The stones of the wall were cold and damp against her back. The clouds rushed across the moon's face again and the threatening storm finally broke. It was completely dark now in the tower and the noise of the heavy rain was so loud she couldn't see or hear the Inspector. Could she get away?

Too late. Heat on her face from his breath, and his hand on her arm again, wet with his blood.

'You bitch.' It was said calmly, without venom, almost as if it were nothing but a serviceable fact. Quiet but he was close enough for her to hear above the storm's roaring.

He'd dropped the knife and his other hand was now grasping for her neck. She was sure he'd kill her if he could seize her by the neck.

She struck out blindly and her punch caught him in the

wound. He screamed and let go of her arm and neck. She shoved him hard with both hands and ran.

She groped her way around the wall and found the steps. The stones were rough cut here, not the precise workmanship lower down in the Priory. She inched her way down fast in the pitch black.

He was shouting something she couldn't hear, but she did hear crashing about, a maddened bear.

The steps went on for so long. She moved faster as she grew in confidence but where was she going to go when she got to the bottom?

She was almost there when there was a yell, a roar, and then a sudden rush of movement as the Inspector half-jumped, half-fell down the last steps on top of her, pinning her on the cold floor.

It seemed to be over and she felt like giving up, the weight of him crushing the hope out of her. But he wasn't moving. He wasn't talking. She summoned the last of her strength and shoved him, hard.

He rolled off her but didn't move, and she struggled to get up. Everything in her wanted to run but she was rooted to the spot. She had to know.

She felt along the cold wall until she was touching the rough cloth of his habit. She stooped and listened. His chest was still. He must be dead.

Chapter Thirty-Four

She must have fainted, as she woke some time later. Stiff with cold, curled into a defensive ball but with one hand on his still chest, to prove he was really dead. Awake, she sat up and waited. What was she waiting for? Someone to make this all go away. There was no someone. No Tom, and now no Isabelle.

She knew she was crying but it felt like breathing, no feeling attached and no choice, just water falling down her face. There was a noise behind her, someone trying the door but the Inspector's body lay heavily against it. A muffled exclamation then the door banged hard and opened a hand's breadth. She could see the Prior trying to peer in.

In the light of his candle he looked older, the shadows carving out the lines that had begun to crease his face.

'Linnet? What are you doing? What's stopping the door?'

'The Inspector. He's dead.'

It was as if she'd not answered him. He began to chide her about not going in to the Priory Church, all the while pushing at the door. Finally he was able to squeeze himself in, only to stumble over the Inspector and fall hard on the floor.

'What the…?'

His candle had gone out so they were in the dark, which made it easier for Linnet to start speaking again.

'It's the Inspector's body. He fell down the tower stairs. He was trying to kill me. He's killed the others.'

'What others?'

He didn't seem to hear her when she said the Inspector was dead. She wasn't sure she'd grasped it either.

'Oswyn, Maykin, Tom and—' She choked on the last word. 'Isabelle.'

'Isabelle?' It was a shocked whisper and then, 'No, no, not the child.'

She could hear him gasping and sobbing, before he tried again to speak.

'Why?'

She was about to explain when she thought of something else.

'He wasn't who we thought – he was crazed – but, Father, why are you here now?'

'I was looking for the incense for Nocturn prayers. The novice couldn't find it when he looked.'

'We need to move him.'

Just the sound of his renewed sobbing.

She had to make him understand.

'The Inspector is dead. He fell down the stairs,' she told him again. 'What will the Bishop do if you tell him the Inspector died here and he's been killing people?'

He was breathing heavily but the sobs had stopped. 'What can I do now?'

'We're going to hide his body, and say he's gone.'

'We can't hide a monk, he needs a proper burial.'

'He's a killer! He's not a monk and never was. He was pretending, and he's killed Isabelle.'

'He deserves to burn in hell.' The words were delivered coldly and in them Linnet could hear the Prior's resolve returning.

She helped him to his feet. He began to open the door then stopped.

'We'll have to wait till after Nocturn. I'll lead the prayers and come back when the rest go back to the dormitory.'

'No, don't leave me here, not with him, don't, don't—' She was scrabbling at him, desperate to be out of there.

But he pushed the door shut and went, leaving her again with the body.

There was no peace in the singing for Linnet then, nothing but fear and grief and horror. After the monks fell silent she waited until she thought he was never coming back, but then a quiet knock – and at last she could open the door.

The Prior stood there, helpless in the dark, just outside the Priory Church.

'Now what do we do with him, Linnet?'

Linnet remembered the hole in the floor in the north aisle that she'd seen when looking down on the monks – was that only yesterday? The masons had found a pit and put planks over it rather than fill it in. They were lazy but the poor workmanship was perfect now for what they had to do.

'The pit! In the north aisle, the masons will be laying the floor over it tomorrow.'

'That might be the answer.' The Prior was thinking aloud, clawing himself back to the shrewd man she knew him to be. 'Everyone thinks he's leaving tomorrow. We could send Durham a letter as if from him, with his report, saying he's determined to take a pilgrimage to Ireland. He spoke of going to St Patrick's Purgatory. The Bishop will be furious but unable to do anything. Could you do a letter from him?'

'Yes, I can copy hands.' She had no reason not to admit it now. 'We could change his report too,' she added. She wanted her Scriptorium back. It was the only thing left to her.

They looked back into the bottom of the tower. The

Inspector was lying on his back. His head was twisted awkwardly and she realised he must have hit his head against the stones as he fell. With the faint light from the door, she could see blood around his face and pooling out around his stomach.

They dragged the body up the aisle to the pit. Linnet moved the planks, ready to push the Inspector in, when the Prior stopped her.

'They'll see him if you just put him in like that. We need to dig down so they don't suspect anything.'

She crouched down and scraped at the damp earth with her hands, the cold clumps of mud giving way reluctantly. The Prior wiped the floor behind the body, scuffing and covering any marks that they'd made. At last she'd hollowed out enough earth and they pushed the body into his necessary grave.

Linnet paused to check the Inspector really wasn't breathing, but although he was still warm, she knew he was dead. She reached down and pulled off the small signet ring, with the sign of the fox, a present from the Bishop, Linnet thought, and put it in her pocket. They could use it for the letters she would forge.

They brushed the earth back and relaid the planks. Linnet was panting, hot from the work and sweating through her cloak. She sat down heavily on the planks but the Prior dragged her back up. He had been the practical man of action but his grief overwhelmed him again, and he grasped her shoulders and asked her urgently, 'Tell me again what happened, Linnet. How did he come to kill the child?'

She told him all that the Inspector had confessed – the murders, the Sanctuary Knocker at Durham, his exile, taking the place of the dead monk and then, here on the island, drowning Oswyn because he knew, crushing Maykin because he claimed he knew, and hanging Tom when he was after money to keep quiet. She didn't know why he had beaten Luke but perhaps he was close to the truth too, and, as for poor Isabelle… she had no explanation except his madness. She fell silent and wept at the thought she might have put the child in danger with her questions.

At one point she thought someone else was nearby so she stopped, held up a hand to the Prior and they waited. Linnet thought maybe it was someone outside or on the walkway up above, but there was no more noise.

The Prior was lost in his thoughts. 'God will have no mercy on him,' he said finally. 'But the Bishop must not think we were involved – and we'll need to have more answers for what he might ask. I will not have this man ruin the future I intend for this Priory.'

They were silent again, both looking around as if the walls of the church held an answer.

'It's nearly Lauds,' the Prior said. 'Go to the Inspector's room and gather his things. Throw them into the sea on the far side of the island but put stones in them so they don't wash ashore. Come to my parlour after Lauds.'

'But the Inspector's room… Isabelle's there.' She was trembling. 'What are we…?'

They looked at each other again, numb with the renewed shock. The Prior started to speak but couldn't find words. Then he tried again. 'I know it's hard. We'll have to think about that later. Children have accidents all the time, especially children as lively as Isabelle.'

A sob overcame him again, but he composed his face. Linnet was exhausted but went off to the Inspector's room as she'd been told.

Chapter Thirty-Five

She crept into the Inspector's room, lit only by the embers of the dying fire. She could see a small shape on the floor. She lit a candle from the embers and gathered herself for what she would find.

The child was lying on the ground, still. She went to her and began to smooth her tangled hair. Isabelle stirred and pushed herself up, her eyes swollen from crying.

Linnet gave out a small scream.

'I thought he'd killed you!'

'He killed Pol. Look.' She held out the poor, broken bird, which she'd been cradling and weeping over.

'He tried to beat me an' Pol attacked him, an' he just grabbed him an', and twisted.' The raven's neck was hanging at an odd angle, his bright black eyes dimmed.

'Oh, Isabelle.' Linnet gathered the child and the bird in her arms, and they sat on the floor for some time.

'Where is he?' Isabelle started, looking around suddenly as the bells rang for Prime.

'He's dead.'

'Did you kill him?'

'I don't know, but I know he's dead, so don't be afraid now.'

Linnet remembered she had work to do. The Prior had

given her her orders. The Prior! She had to tell him Isabelle was alive. But he was at prayers, and they had to get rid of the Inspector's things before the Priory got busy.

'You have to help me and you mustn't tell anyone, do you understand?'

'Yes. I'm glad he's dead. I just wish I coulda killed him mysel'.'

Linnet kept his coins but they gathered up his clothes and a cross which he'd have to take on a pilgrimage. The papers, she folded up, they would need them for what they were sending to Durham. Under the blankets they found the whip he'd used on himself. Linnet could barely bring herself to touch it but they put it in a bundle with his clothes.

And there were two books, a simple prayer book and one with sketches of death and damnation. He wouldn't leave them behind but Linnet could never throw a book in the sea. She would take them to the Prior.

It was early and the few people they saw showed no interest in Linnet and Isabelle with their bundles. They left the papers and books in the parlour and walked out to the far side of the island past the rain-washed fields, cutting across with the Heugh and the granite behind them. 'Cockle stone,' Isabelle told Linnet as they passed it. They had walked for a good forty minutes when Linnet felt they'd gone far enough.

It had stopped raining but the clouds were very low, promising more later. They stopped at the coast where the water was deep, even when the tide was out. They tied the clothes into smaller bundles, weighed down with stones, and threw them into the sea, watched only by a small clutch of curious seals.

Pol's body lay on the rocks next to them while they worked, Isabelle refusing to let him out of her sight.

Once they were done, they went back to the parlour and waited for the Prior. Ann came in to start the morning fire.

'What are you doing here? Is the Prior expecting you?'

Isabelle opened her mouth to answer and let out a wail, suddenly looking every inch the child she was. She sobbed and sobbed, holding out Pol's body wordlessly.

'Oh, pet.' Ann looked shocked. She took the child into a big hug. 'There, there, there, there,' she said, patting her back awkwardly.

Isabelle couldn't stop crying and Ann led her out of the parlour, taking her to the kitchen. The noise drew attention and the monks returning from Lauds clustered around. Despite the commotion Pol often caused, it was horrible to see that lively, strutting bird reduced to a limp handful of feathers.

The Prior caught sight of the howling Isabelle and visibly faltered. He sought Linnet's gaze and she nodded, gesturing towards the bird Isabelle was still clutching and comprehension flooded his face, his shoulders dropping in relief.

Linnet saw Guy amongst the crowd. What was he doing here and why was he back? He didn't look at her, he was talking urgently to Godfreyd. Then the Prior called to her and she followed him to his parlour.

Now he knew Isabelle was alive, he was again resolute.

'Why did you think he'd killed Isabelle?' he asked as they spread out the Inspector's papers.

Why had she thought that? She tried to remember his words in the dark tower. 'He was talking about her black eyes following him. I thought he meant Isabelle but he must have been talking about Pol. I think he was going to kill her but the bird was protecting her.'

'Well he was enough of a sinner anyway. Thank God the child is all right. Did you throw away his things?'

'Everything that was there except for the papers – and these prayer books… I didn't want to throw them away so I brought them to you.'

The Prior examined them. 'You were right – I shall keep them here.' He locked them into his book cupboard, it was becoming a tidy collection, she noticed.

They talked about the letter she would scribe. Linnet asked what to say about the Inspector's horse. The Prior thought Cassian could ride it back, or lead it from his horse. They would say the Inspector was doing extreme penance and would be walking all the way. The Prior was still talking but Linnet couldn't hear what he was saying. She was swaying. He stopped.

'You need rest, we can lay the foundations now and finish after you've slept. Come, now.'

Linnet only just had enough strength to get to her room before a welcome blackness overcame her.

Chapter Thirty-Six

She slept through the morning hours and spent the rest of the day with the Prior, working on the Inspector's letter to the Bishop, telling him he was going on a pilgrimage, and on the report.

She quickly grasped his cramped, untidy hand which she found easy to copy. She used the quills he'd cut to make it more his. Now she knew he had never been a monk, that was understandable. No monk would have kept a hand like this, even as a novice. He'd have had it beaten out of him. She'd thought it was to do with his time in France, he must have learnt it there, along with all he needed to pass as a holy man. He was lucky the Bishop needed so many to carry out the inspections and hadn't had time to look into him in more detail. She could imagine the Inspector preaching to the visiting clergy, pushing himself to the front of the crowds, catching Bishop Foxe's eye.

The Prior visited the Inspector's room several times, making sure he was seen, talking loudly and pausing as if someone was replying. He spoke to some of the senior monks about the masons' work, and added that the Inspector had finished his report. He wasn't to be disturbed as he was at his devotions.

After Linnet had finished the letter, they read through the

full report. It was no surprise to find many lines of raving about sin, and about the special purpose God had for him. He must have begun to unravel, the thread of his sanity plucked by Oswyn and then pulled on by the events that followed.

He was sloppy with filling the pages, so it was easy enough for Linnet to add more to temper his sterner conclusions.

'It mustn't appear too favourable or they'll suspect something's amiss,' the Prior said. They kept some mild complaints about the monks' behaviour, about too many women working in the Priory, not enough piety. But they took out the hateful page banning Linnet from the Scriptorium and added a page half-praising the Prior's ideas and concluding that his design for the Scriptorium be allowed, or even encouraged. Linnet made sure she didn't appear in the report at all.

It was when she was reaching for her knife to scrape away a few of the Inspector's words that she remembered where it was. Or where she'd last seen it, in the Inspector's bloody hand at the top of the tower.

She had to get it. It was a good knife. She came into the Priory Church by the south aisle, seeing the masons laying the last of the floor tiles.

'Where are you going then?' Jack gave her a sharp look.

'Prior asked me to get something from the top floor,' she said, acting irritated, as if annoyed by the task. She walked past them to the tower stairs as he went back to tiling.

In the room at the top, she looked over the wooden floor, scuffed and worn, with a patch of dried blood she quickly turned away from. Would it be seen as blood if you weren't looking for it? She didn't think so.

There was no knife and little else – except a dead gull. That put her in mind of Pol and Isabelle. Why had she thought he meant Isabelle? It came back to her then – he'd said 'she', he'd wrung 'her' neck. He'd not known that Pol was a male bird, at least in Isabelle's eyes. She had no doubt he would have killed the child next if he'd not been interrupted.

She came down the stairs slowly, searching every dark corner until finally, a few steps from the bottom, she found her knife. It was dull and smeared and she wiped it on her cloak.

The cloak had more blood on it too, she realised, but at least it was dark and didn't show. Although the thought of walking around with the Inspector's blood on her made her gorge rise, she knew she couldn't wash it now, she had too much to do.

The Prior came down from the Inspector's rooms for a final time, looking grim. He told the stable boy that the Inspector would not need his horse tomorrow and to make sure she was comfortable. He told Ann in the kitchen that the Inspector had no need of food tonight and was tending his own fire. He told the gathered monks after dinner that the Inspector was at his devotions and wouldn't be speaking to them this evening. Several of the younger ones looked disappointed that they wouldn't get their nightly dose of fanatical preaching. Cassian looked as if he had questions but the Prior dismissed everyone to their rest.

Before the Prior and Linnet parted, they discussed the story again. The Prior would find the Inspector gone tomorrow morning. He would find a note saying he was going on a pilgrimage and the Prior was to have his report and letter sent back to Durham with the novice.

The tides would be in their favour, low just before the morning prayers so the Inspector could have left before then, and got to the mainland without trouble.

As Linnet was leaving, Ann knocked on the door and delivered a shivering and hiccupping Isabelle.

'Excuse me, Father Richard, but she won't stop crying. We know it's sad about her bird but I've got my work to do.'

Ann wasn't being unkind but she was clearly at the end of what she could do.

'Now then, Isabelle,' the Prior started, 'you need to stop, child.'

But she just sobbed on, wretched. This was the death that she couldn't absorb, her skinny child's frame was full of grief. She couldn't understand why Pol was dead.

'You can help us, you know.'

That was enough to get her to pause.

'Later tomorrow, we need you to tell people that you saw the Inspector leaving early in the morning, on foot and with all his things. Can you do that for us?'

She nodded, still bleak but determined to help them.

The Prior sat her in his lap and rocked her a little as he talked.

'Once, when the saint was Prior here, long, long ago, he was building a house for visitors. But every time he had the roof laid with fresh straw, a pair of ravens would dance down and pluck, pluck, pluck it out.'

Isabelle let out a reluctant chuckle, but her face remained solemn.

'So eventually, the saint, who loved all the animals and all the birds, he cried out, "In the Name of Jesu our Saviour, be gone from this place!" And the ravens, they heeded him, and off they flew.

'But it wasn't long after that they flew back again, and our saint, he was ready to bid them to leave again, when he noticed they were carrying a lump of pig lard, just for him. And he thanked them and blessed them, and they stay on the isle to this day, and never touch the straw no more.'

Isabelle looked up at this and nodded. A little mollified by the story, although Linnet could see questions forming that she knew the child would come back to.

'Did you want to sleep in with me tonight?' Linnet asked. Another small nod. She wouldn't be parted from Pol, though, and they walked slowly back to Linnet's room with the bird in her arms.

Sir Cyrus stopped them and Isabelle shrank back against Linnet.

'Stupid girl, mourning a bird, it's not Christian.'

'He's more than a bird, he's Pol. And the saint himself loved ravens.' It was enough to get Isabelle back, eyes flashing, and she was on the verge of spitting at the old man.

Linnet hurried her along, they couldn't get caught in more trouble now, and closed the door of her room, relieved but utterly weary.

Finally she persuaded Isabelle to part with Pol, putting him in Tom's wooden box, with a small piece torn from a blanket 'to keep him warm', Isabelle said.

She thought the child would disturb her sleep but they were both dead to the world in minutes.

Chapter Thirty-Seven

The Prior gathered the monks after Prime and announced that the Inspector had left, gone on a pilgrimage to St Patrick's Purgatory in Ireland. Isabelle spoke up to say she'd seen him leaving early that morning.

This was unexpected and the monks' usual quiet muttering rose to excited chattering. They knew of the cave in Ireland but none had seen it. Only the most devout pilgrims would go to such a wretched place, especially as it was only true penance if you walked all the way.

Linnet watched Cassian closely. He looked the most startled by the news.

'But, Father, he would have spoken to me afore going? Did he have words for me?'

The Prior gave the novice a stern glance. 'Was it not your duty to look after your master? I feel you have fallen well short. Still, I see no reason to complain to the Bishop about this, you did try to the best of your abilities.'

Cassian flushed red with shame and a little rage, but shuffled back into the crowd.

Brushing aside the talk, the Prior announced the new bursar, which led to more gossiping but no real surprise as Brother Marcus stammered some thanks. Linnet was to go back in the Scriptorium with Father Thomas and Brother Samuel, and Luke, if he ever got better.

As she pricked out the next illumination for the Gospels book, she felt numb. Could the last few weeks just be buried like that? As if nothing had happened?

Isabelle came in, still carrying Pol's body. A reminder that some things couldn't be scraped away and changed.

'He's going to start to smell soon, Isabelle, you'll need to let him go.'

'I can't.' The words were stark in their simplicity.

Father Thomas came over to help, speaking to her kindly.

'What beautiful feathers he had, your bird, what lovely glossy feathers.'

Linnet had a thought. 'Isabelle, can we use his feathers? Make quills from them? Then it would be like he was still with us.'

The child considered, then gave an uncertain nod and laid him on Linnet's desk. They started plucking and soon had a fine pile of very good quill feathers. Linnet put some in a box for later, gave some to Isabelle who hid them in her skirts and one to each of the monks, keeping a few in her pouch.

'Can you learn me to scribe with that?' Isabelle asked.

'Maybe later,' Linnet said, glancing at the monks, but they had returned to their quires and weren't listening.

'Can we give him a fisherman's burial now, like Tom's, the rest of him?' Isabelle asked, and Linnet was glad to see Isabelle brave again.

The short day had nearly ended, so it was sunset this time as the little raft they'd woven from twigs floated off, burning, into the sea. The flames disappeared into the sun as if it swallowed it up rather than the water dousing it. Isabelle gave one last cry of anguish and then visibly shook herself straight-backed.

One of the fishermen, Peter, was nearby, watching. He nodded in agreement that this was fitting.

'Want me to look out for a raven chick for you, my sweet?' he asked.

'It wouldn't be Pol,' Isabelle said, but she looked like she was considering it.

Guy was in the inner courtyard as Linnet came back from the shore. He greeted the Prior as his equal and strode into his parlour without being asked.

'I have an urgent message from Lady Margaret, she needs you to enlarge the book of hawking for Lord Edmund.'

Linnet had paused outside the parlour listening, and raised an amused smile. This was hardly urgent – Lady Margaret could have sent her servant with a note. But it explained why she'd seen him earlier. The Prior murmured something and she could tell he was writing down the new suggestions, then he opened the door and pretended he'd not caught her listening.

'Come in, Linnet, we need to change the hawking book. Bring your notes.'

In the parlour, she looked at Guy who was even sleeker and more polished than before.

'So are you working as Lord Edmund's secretary now?' the Prior asked.

Guy flushed. 'He's been very busy, he's not been able to see Lady Margaret or myself, so for now I will be helping with her work.'

'She didn't want to send her servant?'

The Prior was goading him, delicately, and Linnet could see he was enjoying it, as was she.

'No, it was important to tell you of the changes she required before you began. Lady Margaret would not want to put you to any more labour than necessary.'

She was plainly toying with him, seeing how far he'd obey her wishes, however fickle. Linnet wondered for how long Guy would be able to hide his annoyance. That would depend on how he was rewarded, in money or any other way. His gamble on joining Lady Margaret's party on the road appeared to be paying off so far.

The Prior told Guy he could have the guest room for the night and he could ride back tomorrow when the tides allowed.

'Has the Inspector left?'

'Yes, this morning. He's going on a pilgrimage to Ireland, to the cave at St Patrick's Purgatory.'

'Which way did he go? I didn't see him.'

'Oh, he left before Lauds and I expect he is walking down the coast.'

'The Bishop won't be pleased.'

'No, I dare say not. But the Inspector has written to the Bishop and I'll be sending the letter and his report to Durham with the novice.'

Guy glanced at Linnet as she left for the kitchen. Could he tell something was amiss? She hoped not. He would pick at a story until it gave up its truth. She wondered if he'd jumped at the chance to come back to the island to torment her further, but she was too tired to let it needle her now.

In the kitchen, the masons were shouting at Ann to bring more potage, singing and swearing and taking up all the space.

'Behaviour more fitting to the inn,' Ann muttered as she filled bowls and avoided their groping hands. Linnet knew she did not like her tidy, well-ordered kitchen overrun by a pack of filthy workmen in their cups.

Jack saw Linnet and waved her over. 'I see Guy's back, must be missing you.'

Ann looked at Linnet sharply. 'Bit soft on the Lady's man, are you?'

Linnet did her best to look indifferent and slightly amused. 'He's a man who thinks more of his clothes than of women.'

Ann smiled thinly. Guy's attention to his clothes had been the subject of much mockery in the kitchen. The masons set up a small jeer. Linnet sat down next to Mees, the large mason from the Low Countries.

'You told me about Father John-the-Lies,' she reminded him.

'Yes, yes.' He didn't look up from his food, shovelling it in fast before they were to go drinking again no doubt.

'What did you say he was doing in Bruges?'

'Working on the old papers, the Church papers, you know? The old *stabooms*, the papers, what do you call them here?'

He waved his hand vaguely then shouted, 'Tree! The trees of your ancestors. He was sorting those for the church faders.'

'And he was newly a monk, a novice?'

Again Mees looked a bit confused.

'Like the one here, Cassian? A learning father?'

'Ah, a greenhorn? Yes? No, Fader John, he tells me he has been a monk many, many years, since he was a boy.'

What could her father be doing with old Dutch Church papers, and why was he saying he had always been a monk? She felt the urge to find out, to solve another mystery. Maybe one day she would travel to the Low Countries and find out more.

Chapter Thirty-Eight

Ann told her to bring some water to Luke who had woken, and Linnet left the kitchen gladly, her head spinning with what she'd been told.

Luke was sitting up, still very pale, and his eyes were struggling to focus. Linnet gave Benedict the water and the cloth and he wiped Luke's face and hands carefully before offering him a prayer.

Luke bent his neck obediently, although it clearly caused him pain, then raised his head, as if searching the dark corners of the room for something.

Godfreyd came in, evidently called away from the table, and annoyed to be interrupted.

'Ah, Luke, that horse gave you some hard kicks, how are you feeling now?' The words were kind but the voice held no warmth.

Luke flinched at the sound, his eyes unable to focus. 'Brother Godfreyd?'

'Yes, yes.'

'I want to go back to my cell. Let me go back to my cell.' His voice was thin, and he was plainly terrified.

'The Inspector's gone, Brother Luke,' Linnet said, hoping to reassure him, but it had no effect.

He sounded like the small boy he once was. 'Please may I go back to my cell, please?'

Godfreyd shrugged. 'If you can see well enough to get there, then why not. You'll be bled again tomorrow.'

Luke pulled himself up and out of the bed, weak but determined. The monk and Linnet stood either side of him to support him, and he limped from the room, wincing but moving as fast as he could. Halfway to the cell, the monk was called away, leaving Linnet to help Luke the rest of the way.

Once he was settled, she turned to go but Luke called her back.

'What do you mean the Inspector's gone? Back to Durham with the report?'

'No, he left a letter saying he was going on a pilgrimage to Ireland.' She shrugged as if she had no explanation for how strange monks could be.

'I wanted to go with him.'

'Why?'

'I wanted to get away from this cursed place.'

'But he beat you, didn't he?' Linnet was too confused to think of a gentle way to say it.

'Who? The Inspector?' He laughed, surprised by the thought.

'Or was it Guy?'

'That strutting one with Lady Margaret?' This time he laughed until he was coughing and then wincing, so she brought him some water.

Once he'd drunk it, he looked seriously at Linnet, his eyes seeing clearly for the first time since he'd woken up. Resolving to trust her.

'It was Godfreyd. He wanted to—' He stopped again and looked away.

She nodded, she knew what Godfreyd had wanted to do.

'Anyway, I told him I was no sinner and I'd be talking to the Inspector.'

She could hear the pious tone, the small boy again, eager to tattle to the teacher.

'Last thing I remember was him saying I wouldn't be talking to anyone and then he started hitting me. And now the Inspector's gone.'

He started weeping, a soft helpless sound.

'You could tell the Prior though, couldn't you?'

'He said everyone knows about him, even the Prior, only the Inspector didn't.'

Linnet thought about that. She supposed everyone did know about Godfreyd. Although she didn't think anyone else had known about him and Tom. But this was surely different.

'Anyway – leave me. I mustn't have a woman in my cell.'

Luke's arrogance was back, he must be feeling slightly better.

She left and went back to the kitchen. Guy came over and sat down with a pleasant smile.

'So when do I get my money, Mary?' he asked.

'It wasn't your money, it was mine.' She had earnt it – she deserved it more than him.

'Trouble is, I think your Prior is going to want to know about your past calling, don't you?'

She laughed then. What could the Prior find out that was worse than the pair of them burying the Inspector like a pauper, with none of the rites for the dying, condemning him to an eternity of damnation? Not to mention telling Lady Margaret that Guy had been in prison. He wouldn't seem quite the fine gentleman servant then, would he?

Guy pinched her leg savagely under cover of the table top.

He thought she was laughing at him and she'd forgotten how much he hated that. He got up and went back to the masons, his smile fading.

Linnet was weary of it all, but what could she do to stop him?

When she went back to her room, Isabelle was already asleep, curled round the cat and clutching the mousie Tom made for her.

Linnet fitted herself into the space left and tried to sleep, but was kept awake for hours by thoughts of Guy, of Warham's men, of what Oswyn had known about her, of poor beaten Luke and his enmity towards her. She hardly slept.

Awake too early, she went to the parlour to see the Prior before Guy had a chance to. She had no idea what she was going to say but she would not give up her new life here. She'd fought hard enough with the Inspector, and Guy could not be allowed to destroy everything again.

She was too late. The two men were by the fire, and the Prior looked grave.

'Linnet, come in. This concerns you.'

So Guy was going to talk after all. She waited. How would he balance what he wanted to say without admitting his own wrongdoing? He adopted a pained expression of piety, but Linnet knew him too well to believe it. And the Prior wasn't likely to be fooled.

'I felt I need to say, Prior, that I am sure Linnet, or Mary, as I knew her, should not be staying here with you. Her past life was not so honest – she is not who she seems.'

The Prior glanced at Linnet and turned back to Guy. 'Truly, my son? Are you sure this is the woman you knew? She is known as Linnet to us.'

'Yes, she must have changed her name to come here.'

'Linnet, what do you have to say?'

She looked at him, the man she'd buried a body with such a short time before.

'I don't know what he's talking about, Prior, I never saw him before he came onto this island.'

Guy looked from one to the other and began to laugh with incredulity until silenced by the Prior's stern look.

'I think you must be confused. The time spent in the service of Lady Margaret has not kept you busy enough, perhaps?'

Guy flushed but outwardly restrained. 'I'm sure Lord Edmund will be requiring me very soon.'

'Well perhaps I can write to him and let him know that we've found you a useful visitor here? Or perhaps we found you surly to his Lady, dishonest with her perhaps? But I am sure you are wrong about Linnet – are you not?'

It was a bribe and a threat. Guy wavered for an instant, but preferment trumped revenge.

'I must have been, forgive me, Father Richard.'

There was something in the way he looked between her and the Prior that gave her a sense of continuing danger.

He left, bowing his head briefly for a blessing on his travels but without saying anything more.

Once he had gone, the Prior looked at her thoughtfully.

'Don't say anything, Linnet, I know you were with him, but I need you as a scribe. I believe the Good Lord means us to employ the tools he gives us as we choose. Now, have you seen Luke since he has recovered?'

She nodded.

'It wasn't the Inspector who harmed him, was it? Enough is enough. I will have my Priory running smoothly.'

She left, the relief leaving her feeling weak with gratitude. She knew now that the Prior would not banish her from the island. She knew too much and he knew too much. And Luke would be avenged.

But Guy was waiting just outside.

'I could find Warham's men and tell them where to find you, Mary. If you don't pay me what you owe me.'

And with a final pinch at her arm, and a shove, he left the courtyard for the stables and the guest room above them.

Chapter Thirty-Nine

She swayed and felt hunger washing over her. She'd not eaten much in the last few days. She was feverishly thinking it all through. No, Warham's men hadn't seen them since Bishop's Lynn. They'd not found them in York. Warham was Master of the Rolls now, safely down in London, and his men with him. This must be an idle threat from Guy, surely.

Ann looked at her and must have seen her exhaustion, sitting her down and coddling her some eggs. She'd just finished them when Isabelle burst into the kitchen, grabbing her by the hand and pulling her out of the room urgently.

'It's that man, the one with the clothes, he's shouting about you and—'

Bewildered, Linnet was trying to make sense of what the child was saying as they came into the courtyard, straight into a mass of monks, and Guy at the centre.

'There she is. Thief!'

Guy pointed at her and the men turned to look at her, suddenly the centre of everyone's gaze.

She looked around trying to glean a sense of what was happening and why. The monks were looking at her curiously, but only Guy had that air of malice about him. Father Thomas looked distressed, twisting his habit in his hands and making little moves to speak but stopping when he realised he had nothing to say.

'What—' she cleared her throat, her voice hoarse, and tried again – 'what do you mean?'

The Prior was standing next to Guy, she saw now, but he looked troubled.

'I'll say it again now that the thief is here, shall I?' Guy was enjoying this moment, she knew. 'I have with me a brooch the Lady entrusted me to take to Lord Edmund. It was in the guest room, with my things. And now, I find it in the Scriptorium, hidden in a piece of paper, on the desk of this, this woman.'

He held up a brooch, and the paper. This was something the Prior couldn't ignore, or make go away, not in front of all the monks, and others who had gathered.

'Who knows what else she has taken? We should search her,' Godfreyd shouted, a sly look of malice at Guy, who looked startled but then nodded.

It was involuntary, but her hand found the signet ring in her pocket, the last thing she'd taken, her fingers tracing the little fox on it as she stared wildly from face to face in the crowd.

Godfreyd took a step towards her and she shrank back, but the Prior stepped forward then.

'Stop. I won't have any of my Brothers tasked with putting their hands on a woman. No matter if it's to uncover a sin, we shan't risk another.'

Brother Samuel spoke up then. 'Should she have the benefit of clergy, Prior? Seeing as she can read?'

'Search her first! See what else she is hiding!'

Guy could tell, he knew by her face, he knew she had something in her skirts.

The Prior looked around reluctantly, then saw Ann who

had come out of the kitchen, drawn by the commotion and Linnet's leaving so suddenly with Isabelle.

'Ann, you can look at her skirts, can you?'

Linnet felt as if everything she was looking at had moved away, a long way away, all the monks, the child, Ann, and Guy, tiny figures in a tiny courtyard, squawking like hens or gulls, their words meaning nothing.

She must have fallen because then she was lying on the stones. She felt her head carefully but someone had caught her and lain her down. The faces were surrounding her, above her now, and Guy was shouting.

She caught the Prior's eye and glanced down quickly at her hand, and hoping no one else would see it, made the sign for a visiting priest, followed by a ring, thanking St Gertrude she'd learnt the monks' secret signs, and thanking her too that Guy never had.

His face changed and she knew he'd understood her. While he couldn't ignore Guy's accusations, if she were found to be carrying the Inspector's seal on her, that would raise a lot of questions that he wouldn't want to answer.

'Step back. Give the woman air or she'll likely faint again.'

Reluctantly, the monks shuffled back a little, allowing Ann forward to help Linnet up. She stood, feeling cornered and wretched, desperately glancing about her in hopes of some way out. A small hand in hers suddenly, Isabelle.

She looked at the Prior again and he nodded very slightly. He must have said something to the child for she was pressing up against her and without anyone seeing, rooting in her skirts. Linnet managed to pass her the seal while the arguments raged around her. Who should search the woman? How should the Prior proceed? Would benefit of clergy be appropriate?

Clearing her throat again, Linnet said clearly, '*Miserere mei, Deus, secundum misericordiam tuam*.' The neck verse, the one a learned cleric might recite to save them from the worst that justice could inflict on them. It may help. She could only try.

'You don't deserve mercy. Prior, get the kitchen woman to search her, enough talking now. I must be away when the tide turns soon and I will not leave without seeing justice done!' Guy wanted to see her shamed, she knew.

Ann shrugged and began patting through her clothes. She found Linnet's knife which she pulled out and showed to the Prior. Linnet stared at it, but she had wiped it clean, of course she had, no trace of blood now.

'Well we can see she has nothing on her but what she needs.' The Prior was reining in the crowd once more, standing with his impassive face, but she could see his mind rushing, like a stream forcing a new way through what seemed like solid rock.

'What made you look in the Scriptorium for Lady Margaret's brooch?'

Guy blustered slightly. 'Well I was going in to see the Brothers there, I saw the paper on the desk and thought I would straighten it.' Gaining confidence, he once again acted for the audience around him. 'Imagine my surprise when the brooch fell out!'

'And Father Thomas and Brother Samuel were in the Scriptorium, but not Linnet?'

'Yes, ask them, they saw me find the brooch.'

Linnet looked at them, they looked uncertain and unhappy but nodded slowly.

The Prior reached forward to take the brooch from Guy, and the paper it was wrapped in, turning both over in his hands and frowning. The monks were silent now, waiting to hear what would happen.

Godfreyd was smiling at her, and also at Guy. She wondered if they had become allies, that would make sense. Both scheming together, prising her out of her place here at the Priory.

'This isn't paper from the Priory.' The Prior was holding up the scrap, a blank piece but with the maker's mark, and Linnet could see, not the ones she'd found in the Scriptorium since she had been here, this was a cross of keys, not the leaping fish.

Briefly she wondered at herself, able to notice this detail in the middle of this danger, but still hoping, hoping that the Prior had a plan.

Guy looked back at the Prior, not offering any explanation but just letting the silence deepen as the monks stole glances at Linnet, some concerned, but most curious and excited.

'It was me did it.'

'No – Isabelle—' She tried to stop the child, fearful of what would happen to her, more fearful than for herself.

The Prior held up a hand. 'Let the child speak.'

Isabelle made sure all the monks were paying her attention. 'I dinna thieve it, I'm a good girl.' Her face pulled into what she must have thought was a pious expression. 'I found it, out by the stables, and coz it was summit wrapped in paper, I though it mun come from the Scriptorium, so I took it there.'

Again, Linnet saw the Prior nod very slightly.

'Did ya drop it? Ann says we're to take good care of things what are precious. Do you need a pocket?' Isabelle was directly addressing Guy now, eyes wide and innocent, but with that touch of sparkle that Linnet had come to know so well.

'Well I think that sounds most likely, don't you, Guy?' the Prior said blandly. 'Let this be an end to the matter.' He gestured to the monks to get back to work, and they drifted away, disappointed to have such a dull result.

'And the tide will be coming in soon, so time to be going. One of the Beale boys is on the isle and can see you safely across.' That last the Prior said with just a touch of menace and Linnet found herself stifling a laugh into a cough.

Guy's glance at her was pure hatred, but he left, thanking the Prior for his help with this matter, and almost sounding sincere.

Linnet fled back into the Scriptorium but found her hands shaking too much to scribe, so just sat, hardly able to believe her narrow escape.

Chapter Forty

The masons were getting ready to leave too, making a lot of noise that could be heard all over the Priory as they packed up their cart. They had more work further down the coast and were no longer needed now that the floor had been laid in the Priory Church.

She lost herself in the book of 'Hawking and Hunting', only to be disturbed once more by shouting outside. Father Thomas and Brother Samuel hurried to the inner courtyard, and she followed, careful to hang back just in case, and found most of the monks crowding round the Prior and a furious Godfreyd.

'You cannot send me there! I will not go.'

'As Prior I can send you where I choose. It is God's will.'

Linnet saw that the Prior was announcing Godfreyd's banishment publicly to serve as a warning to the other monks, and to add to the humiliation.

They were face-to-face, the shorter Prior looking up at Godfreyd but with no appearance of being daunted.

'My place is in the Infirmary. You need me here for my skills.'

'There are other monks who have such skills. Your place for now is on Inner Farne.'

There were gasps from the watching monks. Very few of them were devout enough to emulate St Cuthbert's example and closet themselves away on that remote tiny island. Godfreyd was definitely not one of them.

Godfreyd choked back his fury while the Prior looked steadily back at him.

The monks were silent. Not one spoke up for Godfreyd, not one asked the Prior to reconsider. If he'd been well liked or had friends, someone might have spoken for him, or even offered to take his place. But Linnet understood now that they all knew what he'd been doing, and although no one had been brave enough to challenge him for his sins, he was finally abandoned and exposed. Brother Benedict took a hesitant step forward, but thought again and didn't say anything.

The Prior stood waiting calmly. His authority was not to be questioned, the decision was final. Godfreyd, tall and handsome, could barely contain his rage.

Linnet wondered if a stranger would know which was the Prior and which was the monk being banished. Godfreyd's habit was much better quality and he carried himself with assurance, with the air of nobility he was born to. And where did the Prior come from? She didn't know.

Finally Godfreyd nodded. A single sharp nod seen by everyone. The Prior showed no sign of relief but raised his voice.

'Let it be known that Brother Godfreyd will continue his devotions at Saint Cuthbert's chapel on Inner Farne. Brother Adam will return to the Priory.'

Without returning anyone's gaze, Godfreyd strode back to his cell to collect what he could take to make his exile more tolerable.

One of the novices ran to light the beacon to let the monks on Inner Farne know that someone was coming, and the crowd dispersed slowly, with much gossiping as they did so.

'Are they putting him out?' It was Isabelle, her hand taking Linnet's, as she usually did now.

'They're sending him to Inner Farne.'

The child nodded, looking pleased. 'He were cruel to Pol, serves him right. Lots of birds on Inner Farne too, they'll be shitting on him every day.'

Linnet laughed at the vision the child had conjured.

'And I took the thing,' Isabelle winked carefully, 'to the Prior. Didn't I do well before?'

'Yes, yes you did. Thank you.' Linnet felt tears coming but they dried up as Isabelle nodded, pleased with herself and said, 'Well you taught me to lie, so it were easy,' and skipped off.

The Prior ordered the fishermen to take Godfreyd to Inner Farne at once. If he were given a day or two, he would send to his wealthy family and try and get the decision overruled. He might still try this, but it would be a lot harder from Inner Farne.

Linnet stood on the shore, watching Godfreyd overseeing novices load the boat. He was taking hangings and blankets and bags full of ointments and sweetmeats. It may be an austere cell on Inner Farne, but he had no intention of keeping it that way. The Prior must have decided to turn a blind eye to this luxury.

Brother Benedict came down to see him off. He spoke pleadingly to Godfreyd, his hand on his sleeve, explaining something with many gestures, but the taller man shoved him away. Then, reconsidering, he brought him in close and whispered at length in his ear. Benedict nodded, once, twice, and bustled off, looking relieved.

Godfreyd saw her watching and came over.

'Don't think I don't know about you! Tom told me all about you and your past life. And I had words with your man Guy.' It was a low hiss, too low for anyone else to hear.

She stared back at him, wondering again how much Tom had told him, what new danger she was in now.

'I know more than you think. I know why you think you're safe now but you've more to lose than I have.' He strode back to the boat.

As they cast off, he sat straight, no sign of seasickness yet. Linnet saw him glance over at the spot where Tom had been buried. Had he seen that happen and what did he feel? He turned away and looked out to sea.

'May he rot on that island.'

The voice made her start. Luke was standing behind her, pale and swaying, but looking a lot better.

'Did you tell the Prior?' he asked her.

'No, he knew already. I think almost everyone knew.'

He looked relieved.

'If the Inspector hadn't left, he would have dealt with him, I'm sure of it. Where did he go?'

'To St Patrick's Purgatory in Ireland. He left a note for the Prior.'

'Why would he go without saying something to all of us?' he said, sounding plaintive.

'There often seemed no reason for what he said or did.'

Luke bristled. 'That's because you didn't understand what he was saying. He's a prophet, you'll see one day.'

She tried to divert him.

'Will you be coming back to the Scriptorium?'

'Yes, unless the Prior wants to move me. Anywhere but Inner Farne.'

She caught a brief smile – had the blow to his head finally taught him how to jest?

They walked together back up the slope to the Priory. Luke stumbled and Linnet put out a hand to help him, but he brushed it off, still filled with disgust at the idea of a woman's touch.

The masons and Guy finally left, and the island felt smaller again and quieter. Following behind, sitting on the Inspector's horse, was Cassian. He had the report and the letter from the Inspector in his bag, and the Prior gave him a blessing as he waited to leave.

'Deliver this and we will send good word to the Bishop about you, my son,' he added. Cassian nodded in thanks, but Linnet could tell he was still confused by how things had turned out. As the horse picked its way across the sands, the stable boy leading him from safe stone to safe stone, Linnet saw Cassian look back, thoughtfully, and cross himself.

She slipped into the Priory Church to look at the new floor.

Despite the impression the masons liked to give of being careless at work and play, the floor looked neat and well laid, the stones curving gently in a perfect pattern. She could see it in the light of the candles, which must have been lit in time for the next prayers.

But Linnet knew what was below the floor and looked hard for anything that might reveal its secret. She knew the Inspector was well buried, the grave was at least a yard below the earth, but she felt as if he were close, waiting to burst out shouting and clawing at her. She knew it couldn't be, but the thought was terrifying. She shuddered and fled.

Chapter Forty-One

She awoke in alarm, frozen in fear, sensing the Inspector in the dark. But she knew he couldn't be there and lay still so as not to wake Isabelle who was sleeping peacefully with the cat.

She wondered finally whether she'd been to blame for his death. She didn't know why it had taken her so long to ask herself the question. She'd stabbed him, would that have killed him? Was he already dying as he fell? She ran through those last minutes again in her mind and remembered him screaming as he stumbled and fell on her.

If he'd fallen when she'd stabbed him at the top of the tower, too wounded to move, would she have tried to help? She knew she was a thief, a forger, a sinner, but was she a killer too?

A thin layer of ice settled itself around her heart as she took on the word. After all she'd endured she felt she could live with being a killer.

Almost all the threats were gone. The Inspector was dead and buried, Oswyn too. Guy had left, Jack and the masons had moved on. The Prior knew of her past life and still had her as his scribe. That left Warham's men to hide from and they would be busy with whatever he was doing in London, and the island and the Scriptorium could be her refuge.

There was one question left – what had Oswyn known about her and her father? She'd not found anything in the household book yet, but she needed to look again.

She couldn't sleep so she took a candle and quietly left the room. The Priory was asleep, and the village too.

She lit the candle from the dregs of the Scriptorium fire, and it sent out a small ring of flickering light onto the desk. This time she looked at every page, word by word, starting from a few days before Oswyn's death.

It was tucked away in a line about going to fetch the masons, a few short words but the last one had been scribbled over. He'd probably meant to transfer it to his secret cypher but had been interrupted. It said simply *John-the-Lies and the Duke of Y-* and then the careful hatching of heavy ink, but another few words she could make out, *Flanders*. A few lines later he'd written *Linnet Bastard.*

Her mind was racing. She wished she did know. Mees had given her some information but she needed more. She was going to have to find out what had happened to her father, and what he was doing. It was clear now that it could put her in danger. She didn't know how or where she would start, but it was something to think about in the months to come.

Although she'd told the Prior that her father would be coming to Lindisfarne, she'd not said when. He didn't seem to care. To him she was an accomplished scribe and that was what mattered, and he'd not met John, only heard his name.

She sat and thought about leaving. Would it be best? She had some coins now, taken from the Inspector's room. The Prior would have his scriptorium, although she knew, with pride, that his books would not be as good if she left.

Tom was dead. She didn't know if her father would come. The Prior had probably done enough to allay suspicions about the Inspector… what was keeping her on the island?

'Why are you up now in the middle of the dark?'

Isabelle appeared, giving her one answer.

'Nothing important – let's go back to bed?'

The child nodded sleepily and Linnet put the book back, keeping the candle lit to bring them back to her room.

After a few days, the servant came back from Durham with a letter from the Bishop.

Linnet saw the letter handed to the Prior who beckoned her into the parlour. She was uneasy. She couldn't quite believe the Bishop could be so easily persuaded that the Inspector had gone on a pilgrimage without first returning to Durham.

The Prior read it aloud. The Bishop urged the Prior to carry out the suggestions the Inspector had made and he expressed displeasure at the Inspector's pilgrimage but there was a certain weary note, which made Linnet think he was expecting something of the sort. She wondered how crazed the Inspector had been in Durham before he came to inspect the Priory.

'We may yet need to write a few letters from the Inspector on his travels,' the Prior said. 'Don't forget how to make his hand.'

She didn't think she'd ever forget the Inspector's hand, or the day they buried him.

'And we can use his seal.' He looked at her meaningfully. She'd not thanked him for saving her from Guy's accusations, but she didn't need to. He had also been saving himself.

'Will you stay then, Linnet?'

'I have to finish the Gospels, and the book of hawking.' It was the answer he wanted.

But there was something else that she needed the Prior to understand, or accept, something that lay between them.

'I didn't kill him, he fell.'

The Prior gave her a long look. 'You can't know whether he fell because you stabbed him.'

'I thought he'd killed Isabelle and I was to be next.'

'Yes, I know. Linnet, we will never speak of this again.'

They turned to discussing the plans for the Gospels book. Luke wanted to come back but the Prior said he must fully recover his sight before scribing again.

She wanted to ask about her father but it wasn't the time. If Oswyn had said nothing about him to the Prior, it was best let alone, something to worry about another time.

Isabelle came to the Scriptorium, asking again to be taught how to write and read. Linnet wrote some letters on a scrap, and told her to draw a picture of something that started with each letter. She would tell her what the sound was like to help her.

Father Thomas was delighted and kept breaking off from his own scribing to help her think of things that might match the letters. Luke wasn't in the room or Linnet knew he'd be making a face, and probably keeping a record to show the Inspector in case he ever returned.

Linnet went back to her illumination of Jesus walking on the water at Galilee. She was making the sea violent, a fierce blowing wind for a dangerous day. She added a tiny raven on the shore, watching as Christ strode out, conquering the elements. It was Pol, indifferent to the miracle he was witnessing, waiting for Christ to throw him some food.

Historical Note

I got the inspiration for writing *Consider the Ravens* when I visited Lindisfarne and sat amongst the Priory ruins. **Lindisfarne Priory** was a daughter house of Durham Cathedral and the monks used to be posted amongst the various religious houses, sometimes for a few years, sometimes longer. If a monk was being problematic at one place, he could be sent off to another one, maybe further away. Lindisfarne would have been a great dumping ground for troublesome monks!

The mother house (Durham Priory) would send out Inspectors from time to time to assess how these other religious houses were doing. Letters and reports still survive where the writer complains about their drinking, gambling and unholy habits.

Roll-bearers were like the office greeting card of medieval times. If a holy personage died, the roll-bearer would take a scroll from house to house for abbots and priors and senior monks to write their condolences and prayers. John-the-Lies is the name of an actual roll-bearer from the fourteenth century. (I have relocated him into the fifteenth century as I loved the name.)

Female scribes: partly because of the influence of the Victorians, we are used to thinking that women were not doing much in the way of skilled work before the twentieth century. Women – not just nuns – were often skilled tradespeople, and could be apprenticed into specific roles and so on. They often worked on some of the most prestigious projects. After I started writing about Linnet, this news article about a female skeleton with lapis lazuli in her teeth came out. Archaeologists think the lapis got there because of a lifetime of licking her brush as she illuminated manuscripts.

It would be more unusual for a women scribe not to be a nun, but it's not impossible.

The recent exhibition at the British Library on Medieval Women In Their Own Words explored the women who were writing and reading and scribing at the time.

https://www.bbc.co.uk/news/science-environment-46783610

https://www.bl.uk/press/last-chance-to-see-major-exhibition-that-tells-the-story-of-medieval-women-in-their-own-words/

Ink on the Lindisfarne gospels

It's only recently that it was discovered that the blue ink used on the eighth-century Gospels was not lapis (as had been thought previously) but a form of woad made from local plants on the island.

'One of the most surprising and important findings of the 2004 microscopy report was the absence of lazurite. The brilliant range of blues that are present within the manuscript had long been believed to have been composed of lapis lazuli, suggesting an extensive trade route, but the report discovered that they were organic rather than mineral. They have the chemical compound C16H10N2O2, and are most likely derived from the rather less exotic woad plant.'

(https://www.pure.ed.ac.uk/ws/portalfiles/portal/8401024/Pulliam_BAA_final_proof.pdf)

Scribing

I've done a couple of courses on how to make a pen from a feather, using ink on parchment, illumination and so on, and the ink recipes are based on an actual book that was around at the time. Likewise the *Book of Saint Albans* (the Book of Hawking and Hunting) was one of the first printed books available and was possibly written by Dame Juliana Berners, a prioress in St Albans.

General research

For my research, I looked at books published by the Surtees Society (still in existence) which was formed to preserve ecclesiastical history in the North East. In one of the books about the area written in the mid nineteenth century, the author casually described a body having been found in the ruins of the Priory that was wearing sandals and buried in an unusual way. This is exactly where I was planning on burying the Inspector!

There are still records of inventories from the Priory with fascinating entries such as the fee the coney keeper paid to the Priory for the right to farm rabbits on the land around, and half a porpoise – turns out that was most likely being sent to Durham as a gift. (You can eat porpoise in Lent and on Fridays if you are high enough status.)

Indulgences were sold to raise money for churches and abbeys. Sometimes these were forged to be sold for other profit. The indulgence phrasing in the book is based on a real indulgence.

Bishop Foxe and Warham are both real people who were in positions of power at this time. Any criminal intent on their part is entirely my own invention. I would apologise to their descendants, but as good churchmen, they shouldn't have any…

Acknowledgements

The trouble with taking over six years to write a book is that you have a lot of people to thank along the way, and I am terrified I will forget someone. If I have, come and find me and I will apologise with coffee.

This book would not exist without my family. The idea for the book came about because of my Norwegian brother, Erlend, who is a castle enthusiast, and introduced me to Lindisfarne (his Viking genes showing yet again!), which gave me the germ of a germ of an idea for a book. My father – Malcolm Downing – gave me a further research trip to Lindisfarne as a Christmas present. He has continued to be incredibly helpful and generous, and did the first intense edit of the book, which helped it become a lot better. Meanwhile my mother – Claudia Downing – found a competition, the Lindisfarne Prize, which was for writing the first two chapters of a crime book set in the North East. I used that to force myself to start writing and was delighted to win it! Huge thanks to Louise Ross for generously setting up the prize and for all her support since.

Enormous thanks to all my friends who have been supportive and patient and always asking for updates. And stuck around after those updates were nothing but incoherent swearing…

Thanks to the entire ECG department at Papworth Hospital where I work, for their encouragement and helpful advice on how to kill people where relevant. I will continue to call on them for more research needs in the future. This time I'll tell them it's for a book first though.

Special thanks to Sara Noël, who I run www.readingretreat.co.uk with, and who has been a cheerleader all along; to Charlie Laud, my most enthusiastic reader and who has celebrated every moment of this journey with me; to Guinevere Glasfurd, who is one of the best historical novelists I know and generous to a fault with her thoughts and help; to the women on the ex-school chat who have raised drinks to me all the way through the process; and especially to Claire, Charlotte and Georgie for their many years of love and friendship since we all met aged 13.

A special mention is due to Joe and Elizabeth McWilliams and their garden shed where, during Covid, I escaped to write and edit, along with my coffee machine and their friendly chickens (and occasional atmospheric rats). My first experience of being an 'author in residence'. Also thanks to Joe's monk contacts, very helpful!

My 'virtual' friends who are very far from actually being virtual, always there to cheer me up in an editing crisis – Mags, Miriam, Fenn and Jo.

I'd also like to thank all the coffee shops that have helped along the way when writing this book, including (but absolutely not limited to) Pilgrims' Coffee on Lindisfarne, and Coffee World in Milton. I like to think Linnet would have been a lot more productive if she'd had access to coffee. The British Library has been invaluable for research. Gladstone's Library is a wonderful place for writing and editing. Thanks too, to English Heritage who manage Lindisfarne Priory, and the National Trust who manage Lindisfarne Castle. Patricia Lovett's Calligraphy and Illustration workshops gave an incredible insight into Linnet's work, and her newsletters continue to delight and inform.

Thanks to Luna and Grip from Lavenham Falconry who were lovely to meet, and who helpfully proved that ravens can catch small items from the air (amongst other things), and gave a lot of little personality quirks to Pol's character.

Enormous thanks to another competition – The Debut Over 50s Novel Award run by Jenny Brown Associates. I wasn't over 50 when I started writing this book, but by the time the competition came around, I definitely was! Being shortlisted led me to a great group of women who have held hands as we walk slowly through the writing, editing and publishing process; thank you to Glennis, Julie, Barbara and Gillean.

Thank you so much, Jenny Brown, my lovely agent who took me on and has championed the book from the start. She is always there for questions or advice and sends a lovely book every year for Icelandic Book Flood (everyone gets a book on Christmas Eve – a wonderful tradition!).

You wouldn't be reading this if Carolyn Mays at Bedford Square hadn't offered to publish me, and I am so grateful! There's nothing like reading a query on your text and thinking 'oh I'd not thought about that' and having to come up with something plausible…

Lyra, Kyle and John – you got your thanks in the dedication – but what the hell, here's some more! Here's to many more years of gently mocking my raven obsession (after many years of gently mocking my penguin obsession).

And thank you, reader, for picking up this book. Stick with me, there are more to come…

About the Author

Cressida Downing is a freelance editor, has worked in bookshops and for publishers, and owns a business taking people on reading retreats. She lives near Cambridge and has planned six further novels in the series.

cressidadowning.com